Angelfire

"FIVE STARS—HIGHEST RATING! . . . Linda Lael Miller is a most talented craftsman with the written word. Her characters step out of the pages majestically and the reader is soon on very intimate terms with them."
—Affaire de Coeur

"One of Linda Lael Miller's hottest, most sizzling romances . . . Readers will be captivated by these head-strong, vulnerable lovers, their heartwarming love story and the scorching sensuality that pervades every page."
—Romantic Times

My Darling Melissa

"[An] adorable, sprightly romance. Melissa is a delight —probably the most stubborn heroine of the season. Her determination to succeed, her unbridled sensuality and special brand of humor will capture your imagination."
—Romantic Times

"A fast, entertaining read. Ms. Miller's incorporation of the suffrage movement and the returning Corbin characters gave an added dimension to the story."
—Rendezvous

"Unsinkable fun. The author dishes up her favorite fare: plucky women with the strength to reason and the passion to follow their hearts; powerful men who find an independent woman infuriating yet irresistible; count-less love sequences that leave plenty to the imagination; and a flavorful, 1890s setting."
—Publishers Weekly

Books by Linda Lael Miller

Princess Annie
The Legacy
Taming Charlotte
Yankee Wife
Daniel's Bride
Caroline and the Raider
Emma and the Outlaw
Lily and the Major
My Darling Melissa
Angelfire
Moonfire
Wanton Angel
Lauralee
Memory's Embrace
Corbin's Fancy
Willow
Banner O'Brien
Desire and Destiny
Fletcher's Woman

Published by POCKET BOOKS

Rave Reviews for
"One of the Hottest
Romance Authors Writing
Today" (*Romantic Times*)
LINDA LAEL MILLER

Taming Charlotte

"Miller fills this . . . romance with spirited repartee. . . .
Charlotte is appealing and clever. . . ."

—*Publishers Weekly*

"Another winner from the pen of master storyteller
Linda Lael Miller. In the tradition of *Romancing the
Stone* . . . this sensual story, peppered with earthy hu-
mor, is guaranteed to charm everyone."

—*Affaire de Coeur*

Yankee Wife

"Sweeping and complex . . . *Yankee Wife* is a beautiful
and meaningful romance—one of Ms. Miller's best and
destined for 'bestsellerdom.'"   —*Romantic Times*

"You'll have the time of your life keeping up with this
quartet! . . . Read this highly entertaining tale. . . ."

—*Rendezvous*

Daniel's Bride

"Linda Lael Miller is in top form as she brings readers
into this warm, tender and exciting love story with
touches of humor, poignancy and great compassion.
Daniel's Bride is a delectable tidbit."   —*Romantic Times*

"Linda Lael Miller is the greatest! *Daniel's Bride* sizzles
with humor, danger and romance, encompassing every
emotion and leaving you breathless."   —*Affaire de Coeur*

Caroline and the Raider

"Funny, exciting and heartwarming, *Caroline and the Raider* is a delight—another romance that's as wonderful and hot as you'd expect from Linda Lael Miller!"

—*Romantic Times*

Emma and the Outlaw

"Ms. Miller's unique way of tempering sensuality with tenderness in her characters makes them come alive and walk right off the pages and into your heart. . . . Emma and her outlaw will captivate and enchant you."

—*Rendezvous*

Lily and the Major

"Earthy and sensuous, these two lovers are another wonderful hero and heroine presented to us from Ms. Miller's fertile and very creative imagination. If all the girls' stories are this delicious, have we got a treat in store? Darn tooting!"

—*Rendezvous*

"An absolutely joyous book, it will warm every reader's heart."

—*Romantic Times*

Moonfire

"Linda Lael Miller continues to prove that she is one of the hottest romance authors writing today. This is a novel filled with passion, mystery, drama, humor and powerful emotions. Her love scenes sizzle and smolder with sensuality."

—*Romantic Times*

"Sizzling love scenes and excellent characterization make *Moonfire* a delectable morsel of romantic fiction."

—*Affaire de Coeur*

LINDA LAEL MILLER

PRINCESS ANNIE

POCKET **STAR** BOOKS

New York   London   Toronto   Sydney   Tokyo   Singapore

An *Original* Publication of POCKET BOOKS

A Pocket Star Book published by
POCKET BOOKS, a division of Simon & Schuster Inc.
1230 Avenue of the Americas, New York, NY 10020

Copyright © 1994 by Linda Lael Miller

ISBN 978-1-4516-1115-1

First Pocket Books printing December 1994

10 9 8 7 6 5 4 3 2

POCKET STAR BOOKS and colophon are registered trademarks of Simon & Schuster Inc.

Cover art by Mitzura Salgian

Printed in the U.S.A.

To Kathey Bates,
for blow-drying my wristwatch in Rome,
making sure that nonfat lattes arrive on time,
and best of all,
for the introduction to Francis Crawford of Lymond.
Grazie.

PRINCESS ANNIE

CHAPTER

1

"**W**hat the *deuce* is she doing up there?" Rafael St. James, prince of Bavia, demanded, bending as far out his chamber window as he could without plunging headfirst into the empty moat.

A light and drizzling rain was falling, that gloomy evening in late May, but he could see all too clearly. Annie Trevarren, a lithe, barefooted figure clad in a pair of kidskin breeches and a flowing shirt that might have been pinched from his own wardrobe, was embracing the face of a gargoyle on the crumbling parapet of the south tower.

Rafael felt an inward wrench at the sight of her, a tug born of something other than fear for her safety.

Beside him, his eighteen-year-old sister, Phaedra,

1

fidgeted and wrung her hands. "Annie wanted a clear view of the lake," she said, as if that were reason enough to risk life and limb. "You mustn't be angry, Rafael, she can't help her adventurous nature—boldness runs in the Trevarren family, you know. . . ."

He cursed Miss Annie Trevarren *and* her alleged "adventurous nature" as he whirled away from the window and sprinted across the room toward the yawning doors, which stood a little ajar because of Phaedra's abrupt entrance. The princess scurried along behind him, moving as rapidly as her cumbersome skirts would allow and prattling the whole way. Rafael ran down the hall toward the enclosed staircase in the southern-most corner of the keep.

"Annie occasionally does impulsive things—but she invariably regrets them later and makes up for her errors quite nicely, and she is extremely practical in most instances . . ."

Rafael ignored his sister's breathless blatherings in defense of her friend and schoolmate and ran as fast as he could, directing his thoughts to Annie. *Hold on, you little fool. Just hold on!*

His bodyguard and childhood friend, Edmund Barrett, reached the stairs at the same moment as Rafael. It was plain from the consternation in the other man's normally taciturn face that he had either been advised of Miss Trevarren's predicament or had seen it for himself.

"Let me handle this, Your Highness—" he began. Barrett tended to address Rafael formally in any emergency.

Rafael shook his head and pushed past Barrett to mount the spiral steps. He was still the master of St.

James Keep, however tenuous his hold on the rest of the country might be, and thus responsible for the safety of those within its ancient walls. Not to mention, the young woman's parents, Patrick and Charlotte Trevarren, were among his most valued friends. What would he say to them if Annie fell to her death—that they still had four daughters left and shouldn't trouble themselves over the loss of the eldest? The little minx was a guest in his house—had been for a week—and it was his responsibility to look after her.

The door at the top of the staircase was open, of course, and Rafael stepped cautiously over the threshold. Annie stood several yards away, on the other side of a gap in the parapet, embracing the gargoyle with both arms. Her red-gold hair tumbled down her back and curled in the moist air.

"Don't worry, Annie!" Phaedra called, from just behind the prince's right shoulder. "Rafael will save you!"

"Be quiet and stay back," Rafael hissed, assessing the state of the parapet itself. The rain, smelling of settled dust, cooled his skin. To Annie he said, "Don't move."

Apparently, St. Aspasia's Academy for Young Women of Quality, where both Annie and Phaedra had spent the past few years learning manners and deportment, had served at least some part of its purpose. Even in that dire situation—and it *was* dire, for the girl was standing on loose pebbles and very little else—she smiled bravely and nodded, though she was pale and trembling.

"I won't," she promised, in a stoic tone.

Rafael indulged a perverse desire to look down. The

brick floor of the courtyard seemed to spin in the gathering dusk and a number of spectators had congregated, their torches making spots of fire. He closed his eyes for a moment and offered a silent prayer to a God who had long since abandoned him, then eased out onto the ledge.

Some of the stone fell away beneath his feet, and he leaned back against the moss-slickened wall, arms spread wide, breathing deeply. Should the Trevarren chit be fortunate enough to survive this folly, he reflected, he might well murder her himself.

"Do be careful," Annie counseled, as though *he* were the one who needed rescuing.

Rafael felt color surge up his neck and pulse along his jawline as he moved closer to her, ever so slowly, progressing by inches, and fractions of inches. "I wasn't planning to hang by my feet or do handstands, Miss Trevarren," he replied reasonably. This was no time, or place, after all, to lose his temper. If they were both lucky, he would have that luxury later.

Once Rafael got her inside, he vowed to himself, he'd deliver a lecture this little hellion would never forget. After that, he might just throw her into the dungeon or hang her up by her thumbs.

He reached Annie's side on the strength of these fantasies and slipped one arm around her waist. "All right, Miss Trevarren," he said quietly, with a calmness he didn't feel. "Release your hold on the masonry, if you will, and we'll start back. It's going to be a slow process, though—no sudden moves, or we'll both be splattered on the stones of the courtyard. Understood?"

Remarkably, he felt her bristle, ever so slightly, against his rib cage. "Believe me, Your Highness," she said with stiff dignity, "your instructions were quite clear."

Rafael risked a step, holding his breath, rejoicing inwardly when the parapet held. He muttered something meaningless, even to himself, and they progressed another step. Tiny bits of rock clattered down the tower wall, then tumbled soundlessly through space. The mist had turned to hard rain, soaking Annie's clothes and hair, extinguishing the torches below, and making the stones of the narrow walkway slippery as well as unstable.

Rafael stole a sidelong glance at Annie and saw that she was holding back tears, and that knowledge stung him out of all proportion to good sense. Miss Trevarren might have been foolhardy, but he secretly admired her boldness and courage.

"You'll be all right," Rafael said, in a gentler tone than he'd used before.

Annie snuffled. Like him, she pressed her back to the wall of the tower, one arm out wide for balance. They were a few inches nearer the door. "I was just thinking of my new yellow dress," she told him seriously. "It will be a shame if I never get to wear it. One must take joy in small things, you know."

For one rash moment, Rafael considered pushing her over the edge and being through with the matter. "That would be among my lesser concerns," he said tautly. Out of the corner of his eye, he saw that Barrett was in the doorway, holding a coiled rope.

"Only because you probably don't own a yellow dress," Annie replied, in a tone that somehow made the nonsensical sound rational.

Rafael felt a muscle twitch in his right cheek. The rope snaked out toward him, and he caught the end in

5

his free hand, nearly losing his balance in the endeavor. "Yellow has never been my color," he answered dryly, and at great length. "Here. We'll tie this around your waist. If you fall while stepping across that chasm in the parapet, and you well might, don't panic and start screaming and flailing about. Barrett is more than capable of holding on and hauling you to safety."

Annie's eyes widened in her pale face, and for the first time, Rafael noticed that they were a very dark blue, the color of india ink. "What about you?"

He permitted himself a heartfelt sigh. Perhaps it wouldn't be such a bad thing if he fell; it would save the rebels the trouble of capturing, trying and finally hanging him, not to mention sparing the people of Bavia a long and costly civil war.

Tightening the rope around her middle and testing the knot as best he could, Rafael replied, "Indeed, Miss Trevarren—what *about* me?"

"Ready?" Barrett called, through the thickening twilight.

"Yes," Rafael replied, looking down into Annie's upturned, rain-beaded face. In the next instant, before he could think about it too much, he maneuvered her around him.

She shrieked as a chunk of the parapet gave way and she fell, kicking wildly and clinging to the rope with both hands as she swayed, like a human pendulum, high above the main courtyard.

Rafael's breath burned in his throat and scalded his chest as he watched her. His own purchase was slipping; he could feel the walkway all but dissolving under the soles of his boots. Horrific images flooded his mind—he saw the rope breaking, saw the

6

Trevarren girl plummeting through space, heard her strike the stones below with such vivid clarity that bile surged into the back of his throat.

After that, the pictures became more confused; in an instant, he was back in the palace in Morovia, standing in the receiving line again, with his beloved Georgiana at his side, reliving the events of that night eighteen months before. His father, the last prince of Bavia, had been dead only a few weeks, and Rafael had just returned to the country after some twelve years of exile in England.

The scene unfolded quickly in his mind.

The stranger approached Rafael, the new and untested ruler and, before anyone could stop him, drew a small pistol from the pocket of his evening coat and aimed it at the prince's chest.

Georgiana had apparently seen what was happening, for she stepped between them at exactly the wrong moment, and took the bullet meant for her husband.

Rafael heard the shot echoing in his head and closed his eyes, too dizzy to move, but after a few seconds, he collected himself and looked toward the tower window just in time to see Barrett dragging Annie inside.

Relief swept through Rafael with such force that his knees went weak and again he pondered the attributes of death. If there was an afterlife, he might see Georgiana again, and Barrett's father. More of the parapet crumbled away into space, and he pressed his back hard against the wall, fingers clutching the time-beaten, porous stones.

"She's safe inside now, sir," Barrett said, raising his voice to be heard over the rising wind and the slashing patter of the rain. "Heads up, then. Here comes the rope."

It undulated toward him, that length of woven hemp, and Rafael caught it in both hands and held on with a ferocity that belied his earlier reflections on the advantages of dying. The last of the walkway collapsed while he was knotting the rope around his chest, and he felt its roughness burn into his hands as he slid, the knot giving way, almost to its end.

He slammed hard against the wall of the castle, blinded now by the downpour, focusing all his energy, all the strength of his being, on the simple process of holding on. Barrett pulled him upward, one lurching wrench at a time, while Rafael dangled, his palms raw where he grasped the slick rope.

At last, he felt hands, half a dozen of them, gripping him under the arms, by the wrists, by the back of his coat. They hauled him inside, Barrett, one of his lieutenants, and Lucian, Rafael's young half brother.

He crouched on the landing for several moments, soaked and bruised, his hands bleeding, his heart hammering against his breastbone, his breath grating like coarse sand in his lungs.

Barrett dragged him unceremoniously to his feet. "Are you all right?" he asked, with genuine concern. The affection between them was old, and it was deep.

Rafael managed a bitter, choked laugh, swayed slightly. When he spoke, it was in a furious rasp.

"Where is she?"

Annie had been waiting on the top step of the tower staircase, shivering with cold and residual terror, offering fervent, if silent, prayers that Rafael would be saved. Had she loved him, devotedly if from a distance, all these years, she'd asked herself, only to be the cause of his death?

At the sound of his voice, a low rumbling like summer thunder, however, both she and Phaedra stiffened in alarm.

The princess clutched Annie's hand and pulled. "Quickly!" Phaedra hissed, dragging her friend down the smooth steps toward the hallway. "If Rafael catches up to us now, there's no guessing what he'll do!"

Annie considered a couple of the possibilities and suddenly all the strength came back into her legs. Unencumbered by skirts, she bolted ahead of Phaedra and dashed blindly along the passage, having no earthly idea where to hide. Such was her unbridled agitation, alas, that she tripped on the corner of a rug and went sprawling onto the floor.

Before she could rise again, a pair of hard male hands hoisted her to her feet. She looked into the coldly furious face of the prince himself.

"Rafael—" Phaedra pleaded, grasping her brother's arm.

He pulled free of his sister's hold, his storm gray eyes locked on Annie's face. He spoke to the soldier without looking away. "Take Miss Trevarren to her room and bolt the door. I'll deal with her in the morning. At the moment, I do not trust myself with the task."

Annie was cold and wet and full of remorse for giving in to the more daring side of her nature, but she felt a flush of indignation at his words and took umbrage at the tone in which they were delivered.

"Why don't you just chain me to the dungeon wall and be finished with it?" she asked, with dignity.

"A delightful suggestion," Rafael bit out, still glaring at her. "And don't think I haven't considered it. Have you any others, Miss Trevarren? More drastic ones, I hope?"

She wilted slightly, for bravado will carry one just so far. Then, swallowing, she returned Rafael's icy stare, wondering what she'd ever seen in him and knowing, at the same time, exactly what. He was strong, he was handsome, he was good, and she couldn't so much as think about him without feeling a tug in her heart and a less prosaic response somewhere else.

"No," she conceded. "I haven't."

Only then did the prince unwrap his fingers from around Annie's arm. Mr. Barrett proceeded down the hall, with Lucian following at a reluctant pace and casting backward glances over one shoulder, but Rafael remained, towering there in that chilly passage like some dark specter.

Phaedra, loyal friend that she was, lingered stubbornly.

"Do not delude yourself into thinking that I will forget this incident, Miss Trevarren," Rafael said, bending until his aristocratic nose was almost touching Annie's impertinent, faintly freckled and upturned one. "We shall, as I said, take the matter up again in the morning."

The prince had plainly meant to intimidate Annie, and he'd succeeded, but she was too proud to let him see her trepidation. She squared her shoulders, lifted her chin, and refused to lower her eyes. Annie had learned long since, that one must, in the words of the Bard, assume a virtue if one has it not.

Rafael shook his dark head, murmured something blessedly incomprehensible and walked on with a brisk stride.

Phaedra immediately linked her arm with Annie's and demanded in a whisper, "Are you mad?"

Annie didn't know whether her friend was referring to the ill-advised episode on the parapet of the tower or the more recent exchange with Rafael. She was completely deflated, and now that the prince wasn't there to see, her shoulders sagged and her eyes brimmed with remorseful tears. What had she been thinking, to risk so much for a mere view of the landscape?

The two girls were headed toward their adjoining bedchambers, which were in the west end of the keep, before she replied. "I don't know what gets into me sometimes," she despaired. "I just get ideas—these incredible urges to climb things. The inspiration seemed harmless at the time, I assure you, and the lake was unbearably beautiful, blue as lapis, even with the rain coming on." Annie paused to emit a violent sneeze, and Phaedra muttered something and stepped up her pace, forcing Annie to hurry, too. "Trees, drainpipes, trellises, the rigging of my father's ship—" the errant houseguest went on, "I've scaled them all. There are times when I simply must see the world from a new perspective."

Annie had been nine years old when she'd decided to get a look at her surroundings from the crow's nest of the *Enchantress,* and she'd gotten the one and only spanking of her life after her father brought her down from that lofty perch. Her mother, Charlotte, usually her most ardent supporter, had offered no protest whatsoever, which meant it must have been a very foolish thing to do in the first place. For reasons of pride, Annie did not recount the experience to Phaedra.

The princess, a hoyden of some repute in her own right, was shaking her head in an irritatingly superior way. "What will become of you, Annie Trevarren?" she fussed, with a lofty sniff. "Just look at you— dressed like a boy, climbing out of windows like a monkey! How do you expect to find a man and get married when you behave like a barbarian?"

To Annie's vast relief, they had gained the doorway of her room. She longed for dry clothes, a fire to warm herself by and a nip of sherry, though not necessarily in that order. Her desire to avoid a lecture she'd heard a hundred times before from the nuns at St. Aspasia's, among others, was even greater.

She put her hands on her hips and stared back at Phaedra, who now wore a familiar expression of baffled concern.

"There are other things in life besides finding a man and getting married, you know," Annie said, though, at the moment, she couldn't have named those things with any real exactitude. There weren't many other things to do, after all, if one's sex was female, and besides, she'd thought of little else from the time she'd first laid eyes on Rafael. He'd visited her parents' home on the coast of France when Annie was just twelve, and changed the whole course of her life.

"Like what?" Phaedra challenged. She and Annie had come to Bavia, barely a week before, after leaving

school in Switzerland, to plan a royal wedding—
Phaedra's own—and the celebration was to be a
fairy-tale affair, suitable for a princess. Naturally,
given her current occupation with matrimonial matters, Phaedra was an outspoken proponent of wedded
bliss. Which didn't keep Annie from thinking, on
occasion, that her dearest friend was whistling at
shadows.

Annie sneezed again, with spirit, just in time to
evade the question. "I'm freezing," she said, then fled
into her bedchamber and closed the door behind her.
Fortunately, the fire was still burning on the hearth,
and she hurried toward it.

Once she was certain Phaedra wouldn't follow,
determined to make her point, Annie tore off her wet
clothes and undergarments. Her legs and arms were
badly scraped and bruised where she'd bounced off
the castle walls during the rescue, but remembering
that Rafael's hands had been bleeding, she couldn't
summon up a lot of self-pity.

Trembling with cold, Annie fetched a towel from
the washstand and dried goose-pimpled flesh, then
pulled a nightgown over her head. She had just
finished doing that, in fact, when a soft rap sounded at
the door.

Expecting a maid bearing brandy, which would
have been most welcome, or a repentant Phaedra,
which alas would not, Annie called out, "Come in!"
without a moment's hesitation.

Her heart stopped, missing several beats—she was
to swear to it, forever after—when Rafael stepped
over the threshold. His clothes, the same ones he'd
worn to bring her in off the parapet, were sodden, his

dark hair was beaded with rain and showed evidence that he'd raked his fingers through it a number of times in the few minutes since they'd parted. The undersides of his hands were streaked crimson with dried blood, the backs already swelling visibly.

The firelight cast a sinister, flickering glow over his countenance and, to Annie's fanciful eyes, at least, Rafael St. James looked more like the devil than the reigning prince of a small, doomed country.

She felt his gaze sweep over her, with a certain grand dispatch, leaving a peculiar, achy heat in its wake, and realized that the glow of the fire was probably shining through her nightgown and thus outlining the shape of her body. She stepped away from the hearth, taking refuge behind a high-backed chair.

The silence lengthened.

Finally, Annie could bear the thunderous tension no longer. "If you've truly come to carry me off to the dungeon," she said, in a small and shaky voice, "as you threatened before—I warn you, I shall resist."

St. James stared at her for a long moment, as if confounded, and then, suddenly, he laughed. The sound was purely masculine, deep and rich and intoxicating, and it spawned feelings in Annie that were at once delicious and terrifying.

She looked around for some better shelter than that velvet-upholstered chair and, finding none, stood her ground. "I think you should leave," she said, with polite belligerence.

Rafael's amusement had distilled from a husky laugh, from low in his throat, to a rather demonic smile. He arched one dark eyebrow and studied her at his leisure before responding. "No doubt you're right," he conceded. "I should leave. However, I am the master of St. James Keep, as well as the ruler of this godforsaken country. As such, I go where I please."

Annie swallowed hard to keep herself from pointing out that he was about to be overthrown. It would have been cruel and disrespectful and, anyway, she owed Rafael St. James some degree of civility for saving her life. She felt churning despair, as well as fear, just looking at Rafael, for she had loved him so deeply, and for so long, that it was a part of her nature. If he *was* taken by the rebels and executed, she too would die. Of a broken heart.

"Thank you," she said. "For saving me, I mean."

The prince looked down at his hands, seemed to notice for the first time that his palms had been rubbed raw by the rope, and that they were blood-smeared. When he met her eyes again, his expression was at once weary and wry.

Rafael inclined his head in a courtly way. "You're quite welcome, Miss Trevarren," he allowed. "However, if you ever do such a stupid thing again, while living under my roof at least, I swear by every stone and timber in this keep that I'll personally carry you aboard the first ship that drops anchor off the coast, to be used as fish bait."

Annie blushed. This wasn't exactly the kind of vow she'd dreamed of hearing from Rafael these past six years. "My father would be very angry. I have no doubt, in fact, that he'd horsewhip you for such an offense."

"I'm willing to take that risk, Miss Trevarren." His

15

gaze was steady, unrelenting. He drew a deep breath and forced it out in a noisy sigh. "You're all right, then? You won't need a doctor?"

"No," she said, feeling fathomless guilt for the pain she'd caused Rafael that night, and the danger she'd put him in. Especially now that she realized he'd come to her chamber to make sure she wasn't injured. "But I think you probably need a doctor."

"Yes," he said wearily still looking at his hands. "I'd better have these attended to. Good night, Miss Trevarren." With that, he turned to leave.

"Rafael?"

He stopped and waited, but did not look back at her.

"I'm sorry."

At last, Rafael turned. His gray eyes were snapping with renewed irritation. "Yes," he said. "And you'll be sorrier still tomorrow."

And then he was gone.

Ten minutes after his encounter with Miss Trevarren, in the privacy of his study, Rafael winced and spat a curse as Barrett poured straight whiskey over his wounded palms. The prince was seated in a chair next to the fire while his friend, bodyguard and most trusted advisor stood beside him.

Because they'd practically grown up together— Barrett's father had been the gamekeeper on the Northumberland estate where Rafael had been fostered—the two were closer than most brothers. After the last prince of Bavia had been killed in a duel—William St. James had been a drunken tyrant, justly despised by his family as well as his people—

Rafael had been brought home to take up the reins of government. Barrett, a highly trained and experienced soldier, had made the journey with him.

"That's what you get for rescuing damsels in distress," Barrett remarked, with a half smile, as he dabbed at Rafael's injuries with a clean towel. "But then, you've always been too chivalrous for your own good. One of these days, it's going to mean the end of you."

"What should I have done?" Rafael snapped. "Left a mere schoolgirl, the daughter of cherished friends, out there on the parapet to meet her fate?"

"You could have let me bring Miss Trevarren in," Barrett replied, unruffled. He was winding bandages around Rafael's right hand by then.

"That isn't your duty."

"My duty," Barrett countered smoothly, "is to protect you."

"And you did," Rafael said, "when you threw me the rope and hauled me back inside. Thank you for that, by the way."

Barrett smiled again and began wrapping Rafael's other hand. "She's a spirited little minx, your American Miss."

Rafael felt a flash of irritation, and it only compounded his annoyance to realize that he gave a damn what other men thought of Annie Trevarren, be it good or ill. Even this one, the most loyal of all his companions, would need to tread lightly. "It's an inherited trait," he said evenly. "You would have to know her parents to understand."

Finishing his work, Barrett tied up the bandage neatly, then crossed the room to the liquor cabinet,

17

where he poured brandy into two snifters. He offered the first to Rafael, who lifted it awkwardly to his lips and took a restorative sip.

The bodyguard generally kept his thoughts and opinions to himself, which was the way Rafael preferred matters to be handled, but that night the Englishman seemed unusually talkative. "It's dangerous here," he remarked, raising his own glass to drink. He paused for a few moments after doing so, perhaps savoring the brandy, perhaps sorting his thoughts. Most likely, it was both, for he was an intelligent man, and he appreciated good liquor. "Frankly, I'm surprised you would allow your sister to return to the country, given the current state of political affairs."

Rafael sighed again and closed his eyes. His hands throbbed and so did both his knees and his right shoulder; appendages that had been slammed or abraded against the hallowed walls of St. James Keep while he'd been dangling at the end of Barrett's rope like a wriggling trout on a line. He was in no mood to frame answers to questions he had yet to settle within his own mind.

"No doubt you're also wondering why I allowed Phaedra to bring a guest, as well, when times are so troubled. You've become quite curious in your old age, Barrett."

The bodyguard smiled; like Rafael, he was in his early thirties. Both men had lost their mothers at an early age. John Barrett, Edmund's father, had been kind to the young exile, patiently teaching him to ride and fish and hunt and fight, just as if the boy were his own. Times without number, Rafael had wished that were true.

"Some would call me meddlesome," Barrett confessed, at some length.

"Yes," Rafael agreed. "Still, you've risked your own life to save mine on several occasions, and that entitles you to pry a little." He swallowed a sip of brandy before going on. "For seven hundred years, the women of our family have offered their marriage vows in our own chapel, within the walls of this keep." A memory of his own grand wedding, to his beloved English rose, Georgiana, held in London because of the antipathy between Rafael and his father, filled his mind with color and pain.

He pushed the recollection aside, along with the unprofitable bitterness he held against his own forebears. "I could not deny that tradition to Phaedra, danger or no danger. As for Annie's—Miss Trevarren's—presence here, she's come to assist the princess with the myriad and no doubt tedious details of a royal ceremony. Besides, the young lady springs from very audacious stock, as you saw for yourself, this very night."

Barrett chuckled and shook his head, but something vaguely troubling flickered in his light brown eyes. His gaze, usually so direct, skirted Rafael's. "The bridegroom seems in no particular hurry to put in an appearance."

Rafael frowned and leaned forward in his chair, nearly spilling the brandy onto his late mother's priceless Persian rug. It was one of the few articles of value he had kept after returning to Bavia less than two years before, and in that time, he had given centuries worth of plundered artifacts, treasures and jewels over to the national coffers. Although the fact was not widely known, the St. James family now lived on private money, well-invested.

Rafael never forgot, waking or sleeping, that his efforts had come too late, for him and, very likely, for Bavia.

"What are you looking at?" Barrett asked, in a rather testy fashion, when he realized that Rafael was studying him closely.

"You just made a rather odd remark, it seems to me. What do you care whether the princess's future husband arrives tomorrow or next month or a week after doomsday?"

Barrett's neck turned a dull shade of crimson, a phenomenon Rafael had not witnessed since their shared youth. He started to speak, then tossed back the remains of his brandy, drowning the words before they could pass his lips.

Rafael's nape was taut with tension; he wished he could lie down in a dark room somewhere and sleep until it was all over—Phaedra's wedding, the coming revolution, the utter and final collapse of a family, however self-serving, that had ruled over that small European nation for seven centuries. Rafael yearned for peace and yet he knew full well that he would probably never live to see it.

He settled back in his leather chair and closed his eyes for a moment.

"You've fallen in love with the princess," he said. "When did it happen? Last year, when she was home for summer holidays?"

Barrett was silent for a long time. When he spoke, his voice was gruff and a little defiant. "Yes."

"You know, of course, that it's hopeless. Phaedra's

20

marriage to Chandler Haslett was arranged within days of her christening. He is actually a distant cousin." Rafael opened his eyes, met Barrett's steady gaze, and made an effort to mask the sympathy he felt. "It is a matter of honor, this union. The bargain cannot be undone. Not even for you, my friend."

"She doesn't love him." The certainty with which Barrett spoke worried Rafael.

"That doesn't matter," Rafael replied. "Arranged marriages are seldom, if ever, founded on love. They have more to do with property and political alliance."

Barrett did not argue, for he knew the weight of such customs as well as anyone, and it was tacitly understood that the subject was closed. He nodded and crossed the room to the massive double doors. "I'll post a guard outside your chamber tonight, as usual."

"Fine," Rafael answered, rising from his chair and frowning at the bulky dressings on his hands. How the devil was he supposed to accomplish anything, bound up that way? "Have someone watch Miss Trevarren's room as well. For all I know, she climbs towers and walks on parapets in her sleep."

The bodyguard smiled, though the expression in his eyes was still somber. "As you wish," he said, and went out.

Rafael immediately rose from his chair, pulled off his bandages and tossed them into the fire. He flexed his fingers, grimacing at the pain even as he courted, endured, and finally forced it into a dark corner of his mind. That done, he poured himself more brandy and turned his thoughts to the problem of Annie.

The prince smiled. He couldn't very well have her

thrown into the dungeon—Patrick Trevarren *would* horsewhip him for that, and be justified in doing so. Still, he'd promised that her foolishness would not go unpunished, and he intended to keep his word. He owed himself that much, at least, after such a harrowing night.

CHAPTER
2

Raising the hem of her nightgown a little with one hand, to keep from tripping, Annie climbed the four steps to her high tester bed and slipped beneath the covers. There, watching the firelight flicker and cast dancing shadows across the vaulted ceiling, she reviewed the disasters of the evening.

Her intentions had been innocent, she insisted to herself, however ill-advised. She'd merely wanted an unobstructed view of Crystal Lake, which lay well beyond the keep itself in the heart of a dense green forest, and she had reasoned that the south tower would provide the best vantage point. Upon reaching it, she'd found that there was no window on that side, and her disappointment had spawned an inspiration. She'd climbed out the opening overlooking the courtyard and made her way around the side, taking care, of course, not to look down. Annie had long since learned that that was the cardinal rule of climbing.

It wasn't until she'd started inching her way back around the great stone cylinder that she'd suffered a sudden, heart-stopping attack of fear. She'd latched onto a gargoyle with both arms and clung to it until Rafael had climbed out to save her.

Lying there, safe in her bed, Annie couldn't help feeling a slight thrill at the memory of it. In some ways, being rescued was very romantic—particularly by Rafael St. James.

She turned onto her side with a sigh, her gaze fixed on the place just inside the door where he'd stood earlier that evening, his hands wounded, his hair and clothing torn and wet with rain. She had loved Rafael since girlhood, but that night, when he'd come to her room, she'd felt a strange new mixture of things.

Annie's instincts had urged her to comfort the prince and bind his wounds, but she'd been a little afraid of him, as well as damnably besotted. She had never guessed, until that night, that there were dangerous depths with Rafael, places where dragons breathed fire and dark wings beat and angels of the night held sway.

She closed her eyes, but she could still see the prince clearly behind her lids, looking just as he had earlier, watching her with that expression of bemused fury.

Annie shivered. He'd vowed to punish her for nearly getting the pair of them killed, and she had no doubt he'd meant what he said. The question was, what could he actually do? It wasn't the Middle Ages, after all—he couldn't consign her to the iron maiden, burn her at the stake, sell her to a band of gypsies or banish her to a nunnery somewhere.

Furthermore, she reasoned, much heartened, she was a *guest* at St. James Keep. To treat her with anything less than the utmost courtesy would be unthinkable.

At least, for *most* men, it would be, Annie reflected, as her courage began to wane again. The prince of Bavia, however, was not most men. Annie had little knowledge of the politics of that small country, but she did know that the peasants feared Rafael and considered him a ruthless man, just as they had feared his father and *his* father before that.

Annie tossed restlessly onto her other side, but Rafael's image followed, and haunted her dreams and intermittent minutes of wakefulness for the rest of that night.

The following morning, Rafael was seated in his accustomed place at the head of the table, in the great dining hall, when Annie swept in, wearing a bright yellow dress—the one of fame and fable, no doubt— her coppery blond hair tamed into a neat coronet.

Rafael's anger had been tempered somewhat, and as much as he would have liked to feel differently, he couldn't overlook the fact that Miss Trevarren was by any account an enchanting little baggage.

The prince hid a smile behind the piece of toasted bread he'd just raised to his lips, glad that no one else had come down to breakfast yet. For a few minutes, anyway, this entertaining, infuriating young woman would be his to watch and wonder at. The quicksilver change in his emotions did not escape his notice; Rafael knew himself well, and already he suspected that, given the chance, Annie might make him behave like a fool.

His smile, tentative to begin with, faded entirely. Since Georgiana's death, he'd been numb inside; now, all of the sudden, his emotions were thawing like a mountain stream in spring, and he was having whims and fancies, all of which were painful. He bit into the hard, flavorless bread, chewed and swallowed. By the time Annie had filled a plate at the buffet and turned toward him, he'd summoned up an expression of royal indifference.

She hesitated for just a moment, at the edge of the rug, and then marched resolutely to the table, carrying her plate.

Rafael rose, out of habit more than deference, and remained standing until she'd seated herself, with rather a lot of ceremony, at his left.

"Good morning," she said and, although she wasn't looking at him, her shoulders were squared and her chin was high.

God, but she was a bold little creature, a bright and shining thing. Rafael admired courage above all traits except for honor, and after that came beauty.

"Good morning," he replied, sitting down again.

Annie nibbled at a slice of bacon and pushed her eggs around on her plate with her fork for a time, then forced herself, with visible resolution, to look Rafael directly in the eye.

"Do you plan to send me away?" she asked. There was a slight flush in her cheeks. "In retribution for what happened last night, I mean?"

In truth, Rafael had already forgotten his rash decree. The brandy had done its work the night before; he'd slept well, and his hands, though somewhat sore, were already mending. His worst discomfort, at the moment, was an all-too-ignoble tightening, deep in his groin.

Rafael settled back in his chair and frowned ponderously, but thoughts were rushing through his head. By rights, he should tell Annie the incident was forgotten and let matters go at that, but something in him, something powerful, refused to let her off so easily. He greatly enjoyed watching her displays of spirit, and there were few amusements in his life as it was.

"Yes," he said, at last, in a stern and, he hoped, commanding voice, straightening again and regarding Miss Trevarren through narrowed eyes. "You will stay within my sight all day, lest you climb something, fall off, and break your impetuous little neck."

What, Rafael wondered, the moment the words were out of his mouth, had made him say such a thing? Now the little chit would be underfoot until dinnertime, and he would get little or nothing accomplished.

Not that it mattered, he thought cynically. His father, and the St. Jameses that had ruled before him, had run the country into the ground. There was no saving it now, no stemming the tide of consequence, though Rafael still worked long hours in the attempt, and had been doing so ever since his return from England. Even knowing the cause was hopeless, he could not bring himself to turn from it.

Annie's cheeks grew pinker, and her blue eyes flashed with something that might have been either rebellion or triumph. He couldn't tell which and did not particularly care.

"That ought to be excruciatingly dull for both of

27

us," she remarked, with an impudent little shrug and a sigh. For all her subtle defiance, she still avoided his gaze.

Rafael hoped his amusement wasn't too apparent, for he sensed her great pride, and admired it. "Most of my guests do not climb out onto rotting parapets for a view of the countryside," he replied. Seeing her squirm slightly in her chair, he pressed his advantage, but gently. "If your father had been here to witness last night's episode," he said, "I believe you would have found yourself in considerable trouble."

She looked away quickly, and Rafael wanted to laugh out loud, though of course he didn't. When she met his eyes again, her own were bright with cerulean fire, but before she could utter whatever scathing reply she'd summoned up, his young half brother, Lucian, sauntered into the room.

Lucian resembled Rafael, but he was smaller, slightly built, with fragile, aristocratic features. Being physically agile and quite cunning as well, he made a worthy fencing opponent but, beyond that, he wasn't of much use. The brothers were virtual strangers, since Lucian had been sent to another part of England for fostering, and they had little in common. For the most part, Rafael ignored his sibling, though there were periodic occasions when Lucian got himself into trouble and either Rafael or Edmund Barrett had to extricate him.

Despite his time away from home, which should have served to mature him, the younger St. James son was in many ways as badly spoiled as Phaedra, who had lived in Bavia, fawned and fussed over by a series of nurses, governesses and maids until she was old enough to attend St. Aspasia's.

That morning, as Lucian filled his plate and then approached the table, it seemed to Rafael that there was a faint, predatory gleam in his brother's eyes. He felt a twinge of irritation—nothing new where this dilettante was concerned—watching Lucian smile at Annie, like a young cavalier. He made a mental note to warn him off later, using threats if necessary, for the girl had been safer on the parapet of the south tower than she would be if she succumbed to Lucian's practiced charms.

Ignoring his brother completely, Lucian nodded to Annie as he sat down across the table from her. "I'm glad to see that last night's adventures have left you unmarked, Miss Trevarren. Indeed, you are as beautiful as ever. Perhaps more so, for the joy of surviving."

Rafael's irritation intensified at those words, and redoubled when Annie, the little fool, beamed a smile as warm as sunlight at Lucian. "Thank you," she said.

The prince laid down his napkin and the legs of his chair made a scraping sound on the stone floor when he pushed it back. "Come along, Miss Trevarren," he said briskly. "I don't have all day to sit in this dining room, watching you eat."

To Rafael's delight as well as his chagrin, Annie blushed from the hint of cleavage visible in the lacy V of her bodice to the roots of her hair. She made a great show of pushing her plate away, although in fact she had shown precious little interest in the food, and stood.

"Please excuse me," she said to Lucian, in a crisp and somehow confidential tone, as though excluding Rafael from the conversation. "The prince has decreed that I am not to be out of his sight this whole day."

Lucian's temper flared visibly in his eyes; Rafael watched without emotion as his brother suppressed his anger. "What is this about?" he asked, coldly polite. When Rafael did not reply, he added, "I want an explanation."

Rafael sighed. "Do you? What a pity you aren't going to get one." With that, he took Annie's arm and hustled her toward the doorway, walking so fast that she had to hurry to keep up with him.

Typically, Lucian did not follow, but Rafael could feel his brother's gaze boring into his back. No love lost there, the prince reflected, with only minor regret. The estrangement between himself and Lucian pained him sometimes, but he had learned to accept it.

Annie did not attempt to break away—her dignity was of the regal variety—but she was tight-lipped and silent. He had the impression that, on some level, she was enjoying the drama of the occasion, just a little. She was an enigma, that much was certain, and so were his own reactions to her.

Rafael wished, as he ushered Annie along the passageway toward his study, that he'd eaten a small portion of crow, along with his breakfast, and let her off with a mild scolding. Now, there was no going back.

Two of his cabinet ministers were waiting when they entered the spacious chamber from which Rafael managed an unmanageable government.

Annie slipped out of his grasp and swept grandly over to the fireplace, her dress a flash of sunshine in the otherwise gloomy room. There, with a gentle and graceful billowing of petticoats and skirts, she sat herself down in a high-backed chair and serenely folded her hands.

The elderly gentlemen looked surprised to find a woman in counsel chambers, but neither of them questioned Annie's presence. Instead, they took their places in front of Rafael's massive desk, one of the oldest and most ornate pieces of furniture in the keep, and pretended she wasn't there.

Rafael cleared his throat and ran one stiff, sore hand through his hair. It served him right, he thought, for behaving like an idiotic despot, handing down decrees. He had important matters to deal with and Annie was a distraction to say the least.

"What news do you bring from Morovia?" he asked the visitors, his voice a little louder than normal, and a bit gruffer, as well.

Morovia, the country's capital, overlooked the Mediterranean Sea, as did St. James Keep itself, and was just a short ride down the coastal road. Though the palace was there, and the formal seat of the Bavian government, Rafael rarely visited the walled city; he had too many memories, some agonizing, some poignantly sweet, of that place.

"Things are quiet, for the moment," said Von Freidling, minister of Bavia's northern provence. His gaze, drawn like a plump child to a plate of sweet-meats, strayed to Annie, who sat in prim silence on the other side of the room, then swung back to Rafael's face.

Rafael was not reassured by the news Von Freidling conveyed. Things had been "quiet" just before Georgiana was shot, too. "No incidents of violence, anywhere?" he asked, and his disbelief was plain in his tone.

Von Freidling and Butterfield exchanged glances.

"There was a problem at Miss Covington's residence, Your Highness," Butterfield confided, with the utmost reluctance. He, too, stole a look at Annie.

Rafael leaned forward in his chair, fear spiraling, cold, in the pit of his stomach. Felicia Covington had been his mistress during the year following Georgiana's death and, although their association had settled into a purely innocuous friendship, he still cared for her deeply. If Felicia were hurt or killed, the guilt and regret would be beyond bearing.

"What kind of problem?" he demanded, more breathing the words than speaking them.

Von Freidling shifted uncomfortably in his seat. "Some rebels tried to break in. Mr. Barrett's men were well able to fend them off, however, and Miss Covington is fine."

Rafael was not mollified. If he had taken more precautions to protect Georgiana, she would still be alive. "I want her brought here immediately. Under armed guard, of course."

Neither man opposed him but, out of the corner of his eye, Rafael saw Annie lean forward in her chair. All signs of dignified insurgence were gone from her manner, replaced by a wary and somewhat thoughtful expression.

Rafael had a flash of insight that he found very disquieting.

Annie was stricken by what she saw in Rafael's face and heard in his voice when he and the visitors discussed the mysterious Miss Covington. There could be no avoiding the conclusion that this woman was important to the prince, not after the command he'd issued.

Miss Covington was to be brought to St. James

Keep, straightaway. She was undoubtedly beautiful and sophisticated, and the vehemence with which Rafael had spoken indicated that there was a close and probably intimate bond between the two of them.

Annie wanted to weep at the discovery, even though she knew the news should not have surprised her. It was perfectly natural for a man like Rafael to have at least one mistress, and the practice was common in the upper classes. Several of her father's friends had taken paramours, though Charlotte Trevarren had promised her husband a slow and excruciating death if he ever made the mistake of breaking their marriage vows. Apparently, he'd taken those words to heart, for as far as Annie could tell, the passion her parents felt for each other was as tempestuously joyful as ever.

To hide her crestfallen face, lest Rafael happen to glance in her direction, Annie rose from her chair and turned her back to him, acquainting herself with the room. The walls were bare of the paintings, tapestries and gilt common to most such chambers and though the chamber was vast, there were minimal furnishings. The only things to be found in abundance were books, tattered ones with broken spines, and others that appeared new.

Standing at a leaded window, looking out on a sun-splashed garden, Annie bit her lip and struggled against a sudden and silly urge to cry because Rafael cared for Miss Covington. She'd been a dunce ever to fall in love with him, and naive as well, to think so vital a man would be celibate.

Not that Annie had expected Rafael to notice her as a woman during her visit to Bavia, because she hadn't. To him, she was merely his sister's troublesome schoolmate, the eldest of the Trevarrens' unruly daughters, and there was no redeeming herself, not after last night's escapade on the tower ledge. Upon reflection, the stunt seemed not just foolhardy, but woefully, mortifyingly childish.

Annie thought of Joan of Arc, whom she admired, and tried to be strong. She had known that her love for Rafael would always be unrequited, and she'd long since resigned herself to life as a spinster. All she'd hoped to garner during this brief visit to St. James Keep was a collection of pretty memories to sustain her through the lonely years ahead.

So why did it hurt so much to learn that Rafael loved a certain Miss Covington?

Annie was greatly relieved when the conference ended and the two men left. Perhaps now Rafael would reverse his decision that she must stay within his sight for the whole of the day—she no longer took secret satisfaction from the edict—and dismiss her. At the moment, she wanted nothing so much as some private time, preferably in one of the gardens, to smooth out her ruffled emotions and collect herself.

She felt Rafael's gaze on her and turned, against her will, to look into his eyes.

"Annie—" he began, hoarsely. But then he shoved his fingers through his hair and shook his head, apparently in answer to some inner question of his own. "Lucian and I have plans for a fencing match—"

A surge of spirit lifted Annie on its crest. "Perhaps," she said mildly, after swelling her bosom with an indrawn breath, "I shall have the pleasure of seeing you run through."

Rafael laughed, and some of the tension was dispelled. "Perhaps," he allowed, taking her arm again

34

and escorting her out of the august chamber. "In the meantime, let's just see if you can behave yourself."

She bristled. "You judge me too harshly, Your Highness," she said, hurrying to keep pace with his long strides. "I made one mistake, after all. You make it sound as if I have a whole career of mischief-making behind me!"

Rafael arched one dark eyebrow and spared her a brief, wry smile. "Phaedra wrote me often from St. Aspasia's," he said, without slowing down. "Usually to ask for money, of course, but she did describe you, albeit with affection, as the despair of every nun in that revered institution."

Annie hoped the heat in her face didn't show through her skin. When she saw Phaedra again, she'd have a thing or two to say to her concerning the confidentiality of friendship. After all, in her letters to her own family, Annie had never once been so disloyal and feckless as to pass on a single account of the princess's misadventures. Of which there had been more than a few.

They descended the main staircase and crossed the great hall in silence. Only when they had reached the courtyard where, sure enough, Lucian was waiting with a smile and a pair of rapiers, did Rafael speak.

"Sit down," he told Annie bluntly, "and don't move until I give you my permission."

"Really, Rafael," Lucian protested mildly, before Annie could spring to her own defense. "You are being a bit arbitrary, don't you think? One of these days, the peasants are going to trundle you off to the guillotine for tyranny, like poor Louis of France."

Rafael pulled off his green velvet morning coat and

tossed it aside, revealing a loose-fitting cotton shirt of the sort Annie's father favored. The smile he tossed his brother was a cold one. "It is my privilege to be arbitrary," he replied, at length. "I am, after all, the prince of Bavia. And happily, my fate is none of your concern."

Annie opened her mouth to speak, but Lucian didn't give her a chance.

He flung one of the rapiers to his brother, who caught it deftly by the handle and made it sing with one quick motion of his wrist.

"All hail the prince of a country sliding into its own grave to rot and molder like a corpse," Lucian mocked, with a sweeping bow. "Alas, who will be left to mourn our once-lovely land?"

Rafael did not respond, though Annie saw a muscle pulse in his jaw.

After that, the graceful combatants were in a world of their own, it seemed to Annie, a violent and treacherous place, with laws known only to the two of them. She could probably have sneaked away without being noticed, but grim fascination and a bittersweet ache in the back of her heart held her fast upon the marble bench, her hands clenched together in her lap.

The first ringing clash of the rapiers sent ice water trickling down Annie's spine, and she held her breath as the match grew more and more ferocious with every passing moment. Sparks spilled from the thin blades and the very air seemed charged with tension, and still the battle went on.

First one brother seemed to prevail, then the other. Despite his smaller stature, Lucian fought valiantly, parrying, thrusting, once driving Rafael back until the garden wall blocked any further retreat.

It was obvious that there was something more than a normal rivalry between these two, and it puzzled Annie, as well as frightened her. Her Quade uncles, all lumbermen in faraway Washington State, brawled constantly among themselves—it was a family sport —but the tussles were always good-natured ones, punctuated with colorful insults and much laughter. And Annie's own sisters, Gabriella, Melissande, Elisabeth and Christina, were all much younger than she was. She adored them, though they sometimes made her cross with their pestering, and had no doubt at all that she would die to protect them, should the need arise.

Rafael and Lucian, by contrast, plainly despised one another.

The engagement continued for what seemed like an eternity to Annie, then, finally, Rafael swung his sword arm and sent Lucian's rapier clattering across the stones of the little path that wound through the garden.

The prince was breathing hard, his shirtfront soaked with perspiration, as he watched the crimson-faced Lucian retrieve his lost weapon.

The look in Lucian's eyes was feral as he straightened, the slender hilt in hand, to face his brother. Something passed between the two men, although neither moved or spoke, something intangible and, in its own way, as violent as their fencing match had been.

"Perhaps another time, Lucian," Rafael said, and though his manner was stiff, Annie caught a note of sorrow in his voice.

Lucian lingered briefly, and it seemed that he was on the verge of saying something. In the end, however, he spun about, rapier in hand, and disappeared into the keep without another word.

Annie looked at Rafael, relieved that the encounter was over, amazed that both men would walk away whole.

"I'd like to go now," she announced.

Rafael looked surprised to see that she was still sitting there, on the garden bench. Finally, however, he shook his head. "No," he said, in such a contrary tone that Annie did not offer an argument. "You will stay."

She stood, her knees trembling under the skirts of her new yellow dress. Only the night before, while clinging to the gargoyle on the tower parapet, she'd feared she wouldn't live to wear it. "Your hands," she said. "Look. You've hurt them again."

Annie crossed the short distance between them and took his left hand in hers. He was still holding the rapier in his right.

"You're bleeding," she whispered, examining his injured palm.

When she met his gaze, she saw an angry vulnerability in his eyes. She knew he wanted to withdraw from her, knew also that he could not. It was a surprise to both of them, Annie realized, when he curled a finger under her chin, bent his head and kissed her.

At first, Rafael was tentative, barely touching Annie's mouth with his own. In the next instant, however, he took command, making her part her lips for him, conquering her with his tongue. Sweet fire rushed through her, consuming every awareness but that of his mouth on hers.

Annie was forever changed by that brief and blazing encounter; she knew it even then.

At last, Rafael drew back and muttered a distracted curse. "I'm sorry, Annie," he said, and then he turned and strode away, leaving her to stare after him in wonder.

Her captivity had ended and, at the same time, it had only begun. The effects of Rafael's kiss reverberated through her body while his words echoed in her mind. *I'm sorry, Annie. . . .*

When she could move again, Annie hurried deeper into the garden, one hand over her mouth, crying softly. All around, roses thrived, vibrant red ones, perfuming the air, courting the bees like concubines, but she took no pleasure in their brazen beauty or their scent. Rafael had made everything so much worse by kissing her—he'd awakened her to sensations she hadn't imagined, given her a glimpse of what it would mean to live out a lifetime without him.

Intrepid as she was, she couldn't bear the prospect.

Sinking onto the grass, which was fragrant and somewhat overgrown in that forgotten place, Annie wept in earnest. She was hiccoughing, and utterly spent, when she felt hands grip her shoulders and looked up to see Lucian's face.

He raised her to her feet and drew her gently into his arms, and she didn't resist. She needed, at that moment, to be held.

"Crying over Rafael?" he scolded, in a low and tender voice. "Don't waste your tears, Annie. He's not worth it."

Annie rested her forehead against Lucian's shoulder as she would have done if he'd been a wall or a tree with a sturdy trunk. He'd changed his shirt since the fencing match, but he still smelled faintly of his exertions, and for all her misgivings, Annie found his presence comforting.

She made several false starts before she finally managed to reply. "What makes you think I was crying over him?"

Lucian chuckled and put his hands on her shoulders again. His smile had a hard edge to it and was no longer reassuring. "Women are always shedding tears over my brother. Georgiana, Felicia, and countless others."

Annie swallowed and retreated a step. Georgiana's name had caught in her heart like a fishhook, but not because she was jealous. "He adored Georgiana," she insisted, in a whisper. "Everyone knows that."

"Oh, yes," Lucian retorted, with disgust. "He adored her, all right. I don't believe he mentioned that to any of his mistresses, though."

Annie twisted out of Lucian's grasp. Rafael's love for Georgiana had been legendary, and Annie wouldn't see it tarnished. "You're lying."

"Ask Felicia," Lucian said moderately. "Miss Covington will arrive shortly—she wouldn't dare ignore a summons from Rafael, even now."

Fresh pain speared Annie; it was as though she'd been run through with one of the gleaming rapiers Lucian and Rafael had wielded only a little while before. Still, she straightened her spine, took a deep breath, and released it slowly. Looking Lucian directly in the face, she said, "Of course I won't ask Miss Covington anything of the sort. Her association with the prince is none of my concern."

Although Lucian was smiling, something hateful and hard lingered in his eyes, like splinters of steel. He had the decency, at least, not to remind her that he'd found her on her knees in the grass, weeping as though she would never stop, when she'd been with Rafael just a short time before.

"This is not a fairy tale," he said. "And my brother, prince or not, doesn't ride a white charger. If you allow yourself to love him, Annie, he will destroy you."

Annie had no doubt of the truth in Lucian's words, despite their cruelty, but it was already too late to turn back. She nodded and looked away, and Lucian, after a few moments of hesitation, left the garden.

Annie was crossing the great hall, intent on splashing her face with cold water and hiding out in her room until her eyes were no longer puffy and red-rimmed, when Phaedra came racing down the main staircase, her hair flying behind her like an ebony banner. Her face was alight with an unsettling combination of jubilance and anxiety when she reached Annie.

"He's coming!" she cried, embracing her friend with feverish strength. "His carriage has been sighted from the north tower!"

"Who?" Annie asked, frowning.

"Chandler Haslett, of course," Phaedra chided breathlessly. "My bridegroom. He's come all the way from America to marry me!"

Annie knew all about Mr. Haslett, though she had never actually met the man. Like Rafael, he was well-acquainted with her parents, and his own father had been a Bavian nobleman, his mother, a beautiful young heiress from Boston. He had plenty of money and had hunted tigers in Africa and polar bears in the

Arctic. He looked handsome enough in his photograph, and was perhaps thirty years old—a perfect age for a new husband.

Annie sighed inwardly. It was all so romantic.

Annie and Phaedra had sat up many a night, back at St. Aspasia's, in Switzerland, talking about the marriage that had been arranged when the princess was still an infant, speculating and theorizing. It had been a delicious topic then, a safely distant prospect, but now Annie felt the beginnings of trepidation on her friend's behalf. After all, Phaedra hadn't seen Mr. Haslett since she was a child, and for all anyone knew, he was mean-spirited. Perhaps he gambled, chased unprincipled women or consumed ardent spirits to the point of intoxication.

In a moment, Phaedra's exuberance faded, and Annie saw her own misgivings mirrored in the princess's perfect face.

"What if I don't ever love him?" Phaedra whispered, clutching Annie's hands in a frantic grip.

Annie took charge. After all, one of them had to be strong. "If you find Mr. Haslett unacceptable," she said reasonably, "you have only to tell Rafael that you don't wish to go through with the marriage. I'm sure he'll call it off immediately."

Phaedra was pale, and her brown eyes had gone round. "Oh, Annie, you're so very *American*. I was promised to Mr. Haslett years and years ago. Papers were signed and properties were exchanged. It is a matter of honor—Rafael would never break such a pledge, even though he didn't make it himself."

Annie forced herself to smile for Phaedra's sake. "Never mind that," she said. Her store of confidence was dwindling rapidly, for it had been a trying day, but she drew on what remained. "Mr. Haslett is a wonderful man—he must be, with all he's accomplished. I'm sure you'll fall hopelessly in love with him right away."

"But suppose I don't?" Phaedra fretted, her panic rising in spite of Annie's hasty reassurances.

"We'll worry about that when the time comes," Annie said resolutely. All the same, she was glad *she* hadn't been promised to a stranger like a building or a piece of land, and she was furious at the very suggestion that Rafael would force his own sister into marriage for the sake of his blasted honor.

CHAPTER

3

Chandler Haslett's entourage came through the main gate late that afternoon, with much color and commotion. The party was escorted by hired soldiers mounted upon bay horses and wearing bright blue coats. Mr. Haslett rode in a fancy carriage with brass lamps and a monogram painted on its side. Behind this august vehicle were two smaller, less spectacular coaches.

Annie stood beside Phaedra, while a throng of servants, grooms and others who made their homes within the keep's far-flung walls strained and whispered behind them. Rafael watched the proceedings from the balcony outside his study, Edmund Barrett at his side. Lucian was nowhere to be seen.

Annie held her breath, and knew Phaedra was doing the same, when the liveried driver stepped down from the box of the grand carriage, but he didn't open the door right away. Instead, he walked around to the boot, brought out a set of steps and placed them carefully. Only then did the guest of honor descend.

Relief flooded Annie as she assessed Mr. Haslett. He was of medium height, nicely built but not muscular, with a profusion of glossy brown hair. He wore breeches, riding boots, and a coat and ascot, but it wasn't the simple quality of his clothing that eased Annie's fears. It was the glow in his eyes, and the way his gaze swept the crowd of people and alighted unerringly on Phaedra. He smiled with a warmth that could not have been feigned.

Annie looked up at Rafael just then and saw Mr. Barrett turn abruptly and stride back into the study. The prince lingered and, although she told herself she was imagining it, it did seem to Annie that he was watching her, not his future brother-in-law or anyone else in the small throng.

Quickly, she turned her attention back to Mr. Haslett and was startled to find that he had already crossed the distance between them and was now looking down into Phaedra's pale, upturned face. There was something rapt in his expression, for just a moment, as though he were looking upon an angel instead of the most mischievous princess in Europe.

He took Phaedra's hand, raised it to his lips and brushed a gentle kiss across her knuckles. Standing at her friend's side, Annie felt a shudder of vicarious delight. Phaedra executed a stiff, somewhat awkward half-curtsey and murmured, "Welcome to St. James Keep, sir."

"My pleasure," Mr. Haslett responded. His voice

was melodious, and his maple brown eyes danced with happiness. "I am honored to see you again, Your Highness."

Phaedra's odd pallor was washed from her face by a flood of color. "You must be very weary of the road," she said, after drawing a deep breath and letting it out slowly, "and I am sure you would like some refreshment. Please come inside."

Annie frowned. She'd expected Phaedra to be reassured by the visible proof that Mr. Haslett was a gentleman, and an attractive one at that, but instead the princess' manner was rigidly formal. It took all Annie's forbearance not to nudge her friend in the ribs and tell her to stop looking like a tragic queen, about to be marched onto a scaffold and hanged.

"Thank you," Mr. Haslett replied. If he was disappointed in Phaedra's greeting, he showed no sign of it. "You will excuse me, I hope? I must see to my men and horses." With that, he sketched a slight bow, turned and walked away.

Phaedra fled into the keep, and Annie dashed after her, thinking what a sight they must make, skirts in hand, racing one behind the other across the broad expanse of the great hall.

"Phaedra—" Annie protested breathlessly, when the princess set off at a fast walk through a maze of winding corridors, which were lit only by the occasional stray beam of sunlight sneaking in through some crack or crevice.

The princess kept walking, finally reaching a plain door, rounded at the top, with a crude wooden cross pegged to its center. They had reached the rear pentrance of the chapel, Annie guessed, and when

Phaedra worked the latch and opened the door, she saw that she'd been right.

It was a serene place, large enough to accommodate not only the royal family, but the crofters and tradesmen, servants and grooms of St. James Keep as well. There was an altar, unadorned but hewn from the richest oak, and behind that six enormous stained glass windows loomed, showing several saints in varying poses of suffering or supplication. Even after hundreds of years, the colors were still vivid.

Phaedra took a seat in a front pew, covered her face with both hands and began to sob.

Annie sat next to the princess, putting an arm around her and wishing she'd stuffed a handkerchief into her sleeve or bodice, the way most ladies did. "Phaedra, what is it?" she asked, with gentle impatience. "Mr. Haslett is very handsome, and he did seem kind—"

"If you think he's so wonderful," Phaedra flared, pulling away from Annie and sliding farther down the pew, "then *you* marry him, Annie Trevarren!"

Annie sighed. "If you would only give the poor man a chance, I think—"

"No!" Phaedra cried. "I know now that I could never love him! Never!"

"What did he do to inspire such a violent reaction?" Annie asked, honestly puzzled. "You're acting as though he has horns and cloven hooves."

Phaedra was nearly hysterical by that point and could offer no sensible response. Annie found a cup behind the altar, wiped it clean with the hem of her petticoat and went out into the courtyard seeking water. She found a fountain near the front entrance to the chapel, filled the cup and returned to the princess.

Phaedra took the drink almost desperately, clasping the chalice with both hands, and when she'd emptied it, she was calmer.

Annie sat beside her, waiting in silence.

Finally, after considerable snuffling and a few pathetic whimpers of despair, Phaedra turned to her. "It isn't that he's horrible, or ugly, or bad," she confided, in a small, stricken voice. "It's just . . . well, I've been praying all these years"—she paused and glanced accusingly at the altar—"that I would *feel* something when Mr. Haslett and I finally met. It would have been a sort of sign from heaven that we'd be happy together."

"And you didn't feel anything?" Annie prompted, full of sorrow. Her only experience with love—the star-crossed passion she felt for Rafael—had been rich with sensation.

"That's just it," Phaedra confided earnestly. "I *did*. It was terrible—something dark and crushing. Annie, I think it was a warning."

Annie straightened her spine. "Well, then," she said, resolute. "You'll just have to go to Rafael and tell him the marriage is off. Perhaps he won't welcome the news, but in time he's certain to adjust."

The princess shook her head, the very vision of despondency. "You don't understand. Rafael would rather die than break his word."

"But you said before that someone else made the original agreement. If that's the case, Rafael wouldn't be going back on his word—how could he, when he never gave it in the first place?"

Phaedra looked smaller somehow, as though she were shrinking under the weight of her troubles. "I can't bear it, Annie. I can't bear it."

A feather-brush of fear touched Annie's heart, for there was a note of true desperation in Phaedra's tone, and people did rash and foolish things when they were desperate. . . .

Annie took both the princess's hands in her own and gave them a reassuring squeeze. "If you won't talk to Rafael," she said, "then I will. Somehow, I'll make him understand."

"He'll never listen," Phaedra insisted, but if Annie wasn't mistaken, there was a faint glimmer of hope in her eyes.

"I have to try," Annie said. She knew how brusque and imperious Rafael could be, and the task ahead of her would not be an easy one. Should the effort fail, she and Phaedra could always run away to the Trevarren villa in Nice; Annie's mother and father could be counted on to help.

Phaedra nodded and wiped her ravaged eyes with the heel of one palm. "All right," she said softly.

As it happened, Annie had no opportunity to speak privately with Rafael for the rest of that day, for no sooner had the contents of Mr. Haslett's carriage been unloaded and his men and horses assigned their proper and respective quarters, when another coach arrived. This one, too, Annie saw from an upstairs window, was surrounded by soldiers.

She knew before the elegant, graceful woman stepped down from the carriage that Miss Felicia Covington had arrived, as commanded. Annie's heart twisted in her bosom when she saw Rafael crossing the courtyard, his flashing white smile visible even from the second story, and for some perverse reason she could not look away when he kissed the woman on the mouth.

Involuntarily, Annie raised the fingertips of her right hand to her lips and touched them, feeling Rafael's kiss after the morning's fencing match as if it were happening all over again.

He and that woman, Miss Covington, were laughing together when Annie finally turned away.

Dinner was an excruciating event for Annie. Phaedra, pleading a headache, did not appear at all, and Mr. Haslett accepted the news with admirable grace, murmuring that he hoped the ailment was not of a serious nature. Lucian was in a temper, and his annoyance seemed to be directed at Annie, rather than Rafael. Throughout the meal, he kept flinging sour glances in her direction.

The worst of it, though, was seeing Miss Covington from close up. She sat at Rafael's right, consuming all his attention, and in addition to being as beautiful as an angel, she was an engaging conversationalist as well. Her laughter chimed like fine crystal, struck lightly with a sterling spoon, and her brown eyes were luminous in the light of the candles burning in the center of the table.

Annie forced herself to choke down some of her food, knowing that she'd be prowling in the dark kitchen later on if she didn't, and excused herself, fleeing the dining room, barely able to keep from breaking into a dead run. She saw only a few servants as she crossed the great hall.

Attaining the second floor, she hurried toward her room, stopping first at Phaedra's door. After taking a few moments to catch her breath, she knocked lightly and called the princess's name.

When there was no answer, Annie became concerned and let herself into the chamber. "Phaedra?" she called again, peering into the darkness. The room was lit only by the glow of the fire on the hearth.

She climbed the steps beside the tester bed, but the covers had not been disturbed. Frowning, Annie left Phaedra's room and went into her own.

A maid was there, lighting the lamps. A low fire crackled in the grate, and Annie could see that the blankets had been turned back on her bed.

The woman nodded in shy acknowledgment of Annie's presence.

"Have you seen the princess this evening?" Annie asked, unfastening the broach at the throat of the high-necked brown silk gown she'd worn to dinner. She had wanted to offer a practical and mature image, should the opportunity to speak with Rafael about Phaedra's marriage have presented itself. Regrettably, it hadn't. "I thought she was suffering from a headache, but she's not in her chamber."

The maid shook her head. "No, miss. But it's Sally Jeeves, and not me, who gets the princess's room ready at night. You might ask her about it."

"No," Annie replied thoughtfully, "I'm sure it's nothing." She *wasn't* sure at all, but she didn't want to create an unnecessary stir among the servants. Was it possible that Phaedra had decided not to wait for Annie to talk with Rafael, but to run away instead?

The thought made Annie shiver, despite her own adventuresome spirit. Bavia was a troubled country, on the verge of a bloody revolt, and certainly no place for a young woman to be abroad in the night, alone and helpless. Especially when that young woman was the beloved sister of the prince.

When the maid had gone, Annie dropped her gown to the floor in a rustling heap and rifled through her wardrobe for the breeches and shirt she'd worn the night before when she had climbed out onto the parapet of the south tower. They'd been taken, probably for laundering, and Annie scowled at the discovery. She'd gone to a lot of trouble to acquire those clothes, for riding and other times when she didn't want to be encumbered by skirts and petticoats, and she was going to be annoyed if they weren't returned.

She was wondering what to substitute for them when she heard an odd scrabbling sound from the terrace. She hurried out onto the balcony just in time to see Phaedra climb over the stone railing, wearing Annie's trousers and shirt.

The princess tossed her friend a look of mock chagrin, then bent over the rail to issue a whispered call. "You can take the ladder away now, George. Mind you don't tell anyone!"

Annie took Phaedra by the arm and pulled her into the privacy of her bedchamber. "Are you mad?" she demanded furiously. "You could have been killed, pulling a stunt like that!"

Phaedra gave her friend a wry look. "You're a fine one to talk, Annie Trevarren. Last night—at just about this time, I believe—you were dangling from a tower by a rope!"

Temporarily stumped, Annie didn't say anything, but she continued to glare at her friend in disapproval.

"Sorry for the intrusion," Phaedra said brightly, gesturing toward the terrace. "I wanted my own balcony, of course, but I got yours by accident." With that, she waltzed over to the door that linked their two rooms, opened it and vanished, leaving Annie to bluster and pace.

A few minutes later, Phaedra returned by the same door, wearing a nightgown and wrapper and carrying Annie's breeches and shirt, now neatly folded. "I hope you don't mind my borrowing them," she said. "They're quite handy for mounting ladders."

"Where were you tonight?" Annie demanded, unable to contain the question for another moment.

Phaedra shrugged. "I was out riding, that's all. I needed to think."

"Were you alone?"

The slightest hesitation preceded Phaedra's reply. "No," she said. "Of course not. These are dangerous times, even when one stays within the walls of St. James Keep. I was accompanied by one of Rafael's guards."

Annie was still troubled, although she wasn't sure why. She reached out and snatched her clothes from Phaedra's hands. "You lied to me," she fussed. "You said you had a headache!"

"I did have a headache" Phaedra replied smoothly. "It's marvelous, isn't it, what a little fresh air can do?" She gave a delicate yawn. "Well, good night," she said, walking off again.

"What about Mr. Haslett?" Annie called after her. "Sooner or later, you'll have to face him and tell him you wish to be released from your betrothal."

Phaedra stood very still, and she did not turn to face her friend. "I'm hoping Rafael will do that for me, once you've spoken to him," she said. There was nothing of her former blithe attitude in her tone or manner; instead, her shoulders slumped with despair and her head was bowed.

Annie felt a keen stab of pity. "I'll go to him tomorrow," she assured her friend.

Annie didn't sleep any better that night than she had the one before. She kept rehearsing what she would say to Rafael, and how she would say it, over and over again.

Rising at dawn, she was at once wide-awake and exhausted. She groomed herself and then put on a black riding skirt, a white shirtwaist with ruffles on the bodice, and a dark blue fitted jacket. She forced her unruly hair into a loose knot at her nape and left her room, striding along the passageway with a confidence she didn't feel, rehearsing again as she descended the staircase and crossed the great hall.

After her talk with Rafael, Annie thought, she would reward herself with a horseback ride to Crystal Lake. It was still too cool for a swim, but she might be able to kick off her boots and wade comfortably.

Lost in her varied and jumbled reflections, Annie was taken by surprise when she collided with the prince himself, just at the edge of the courtyard.

He had been fencing again, and the front of his shirt was stained with sweat from the intensity of his exercise. He carried a rapier in his right hand, and behind him was Edmund Barrett, who had obviously been his opponent.

With a circumspect nod, Barrett went on, disappearing into the great hall, but Rafael remained, gazing quizzically at Annie's face, as though she'd come out of a lamp, like a genie.

"Good morning, Your Highness," she finally blurted out, awkward and flushed. Annie clung valiantly to her objective, afraid that if she let it out of her thoughts for a moment, she'd forget it entirely.

The corner of his mouth rose in a slight smile. "I think we've known each other long enough for you to call me by my Christian name, Annie."

The sound of her name on his lips did something dangerous and profound to her, altering her universe in some subtle yet fundamental way, just as his kiss had done the day before.

"All right then," she said, mortified because her voice had suddenly turned hoarse. *"Rafael. I must speak with you on a matter of the gravest importance."

There was a wry light in his gray eyes, or so it seemed to Annie, and in spite of the spell he'd cast over her, she felt her temper rise. "And what matter is that?" he inquired.

She looked around, seeing only a few servants and soldiers moving about in the courtyard. Still, she was uncomfortable, discussing Phaedra's most personal feelings in public.

Rafael must have read her hesitation correctly, for he took her arm and started across the courtyard, handing off his rapier to a passing groom. "We'll talk in the chapel," he explained, belatedly, as he pulled open the door of the tranquil chamber.

They sat together in a pew at the rear of the sanctuary, Annie looking down at her knotted hands, Rafael relaxed beside her, one arm resting on the back of the bench.

"Well?" he urged, when she'd been silent for some time.

Actually, she'd been asking God for help, asking for a persuasive and diplomatic tongue. At last, Annie forced herself to meet Rafael's gaze.

"It's about Phaedra. She's very unhappy."

Annie was heartened by the concern that was immediately visible in his face. "What is it? Is she ill?"

Quickly, Annie shook her head. "No, not exactly. It's just that—well, she's having second thoughts about the marriage contract between the St. James family and Mr. Haslett's."

Rafael's wonderful pewter-colored eyes were narrow now, and Annie wondered what mistake she'd made. She'd taken such care to speak gently and reasonably, but she'd failed somewhere.

"Every bride has doubts. So does every groom, for that matter. It's entirely natural," Rafael said. His tone was clipped, dismissive.

Annie bit her lower lip. She had practiced her speech so carefully, but now the words had scattered and flown out of her brain like a flock of startled birds. There was nothing for it but to brave things through. "This is something different," she countered softly, at long last. "Phaedra wishes to marry for love."

Rafael made a low, contemptuous sound, startling Annie out of her maidenly fascination and into a state of rising anger. "Love," he muttered.

Although the conversation had nothing to do with her, Annie nonetheless felt as though he'd stabbed her, speaking of a sacred sentiment with such disdain. "But you cared for Georgiana," she protested, before she could stop herself. "Everyone knew it."

Rafael had not moved, but a distance had been established between them all the same. His expression was no longer indulgent; a muscle twitched in his cheek, and Annie could plainly see that his right temple was throbbing. She was reminded of Lucian's insinuation, the day before, that his brother had not been a faithful husband.

She wanted desperately for that to be a lie, for infidelity was something she could not forgive.

"Yes," he said, in a ragged voice. "I loved Georgiana and she loved me. But that was merely good fortune. We had been pledged to each other as children—we always knew we would marry one day." Rafael's eyes darkened to the color of charcoal, and he rose abruptly from the pew. "Phaedra *will* marry Chandler Haslett," he said, "and there will be no nonsense in the meantime."

Annie was flabbergasted, even though Phaedra had warned her that Rafael would react in just this way. She simply could not fathom such a rigid custom; her own father would never have forced her to marry against her will.

"Your Highness—"

"Our interview is over, Miss Trevarren," Rafael responded, and then he strode out of the chapel, leaving Annie alone with the stained-glass windows, the altar and the hard pews with their high, curved backs.

She was devastated. She'd been so certain that Rafael would see reason, so sure that his love for his sister would prevail. Now she knew the bitter truth— the prince of Bavia cared most about protocol, about another man's promise, made long ago. Phaedra's welfare was obviously a secondary matter to him.

Annie sat in the chapel for some time, watching colored dust particles dance in the light flowing through the stained glass windows. Then, to put off facing Phaedra with the wretched facts for a little longer, she made the decision to go riding and took herself off to the stables.

The grooms were busy, swapping stories and playing dice with the soldiers, and Annie did not interrupt them. Instead, moving as quietly as she could, she selected a dapple gray mare, slipped a bridle over the animal's head and led her out into the sunlight.

"I'm trusting you to stand here while I go inside and find a saddle," Annie told the horse, one finger upraised to convey sincerity. "We females must depend upon each other, since men are so unreliable."

The mare nickered and tossed her head, as if to agree, and Annie went back inside. Perhaps, she reflected, as she pulled a saddle and blanket off a wooden stand, it had been unfair to say *all* men were unreliable. Her father wasn't, although Annie had to admit it sometimes took rather a lot of hectoring on her mother's part to keep Patrick Trevarren on the straight and narrow. Her grandfather, Brigham Quade, and all her uncles, were trustworthy men, too, insofar as she knew.

Returning to the stable yard, Annie found the mare waiting obediently, reins dangling.

Swiftly and skillfully, for Annie had learned to ride before she could recite the alphabet or button her shoes, she saddled the horse, gathered up the reins, and mounted. She threw her thoughts ahead to Crystal Lake as she rode along the keep's western wall, giving a wide berth to the castle proper.

Phaedra had been regaling her with tales about the magical lake ever since they'd become friends, a few years before, when they'd arrived in Switzerland almost simultaneously. They'd both been lonely and afraid in those first weeks at school, and Annie had grieved at being separated from her parents and younger sisters.

Just remembering brought a lump to her throat as she and the mare trotted along. Patrick and Charlotte Trevarren had feared that their eldest daughter was growing up to be an incorrigible hellion, agreeing that Annie needed refinement and the company of other young girls her age. After much discussion, they had decided that boarding school was the best answer.

They'd been right—Annie could see that in retrospect—but it had been a difficult and painful time for all of them.

In any case, Annie and Phaedra had soon become devoted friends, and they'd managed to carry on their separate traditions of mischief even at St. Aspasia's. To their credit, though, Annie reflected with a smile, the good sisters had smoothed away some of their rough edges and taught them to at least pass themselves off as ladies.

Recalling her own escapade on the parapet, however, and Phaedra's climb up a ladder to the balcony, Annie wondered if all those classes in feminine deportment had not been a waste of time after all.

She passed several crofters' cottages, for the walls of St. James Keep enclosed a small village, as well as the castle itself, and rode into the peach orchard beyond. Since it was early May, there were still blossoms on the trees, and their scent was luscious. Annie's nerves were soothed; it was as though she had entered some enchanted place where there was only gentleness.

She was so absorbed in her fancies that she didn't

hear the other horse and rider approaching until they were right beside her. Rafael, mounted on a huge black gelding, leaned down to grip the mare's bridle and rein her in.

His face was stiff with fury. "What are you doing, riding out here alone?" he demanded. "How did you get away from the stables without an escort? I left strict orders that no one—*no one,* Miss Trevarren— was to go riding unaccompanied."

Annie raised her chin and willed herself not to cry. "No *female* you mean," she pointed out crisply. She couldn't imagine Mr. Barrett following such a silly rule, or Lucian, and certainly not Rafael himself, even though he was probably in the most danger of all. "I am not used to being held prisoner in the houses I visit, sir."

Rafael's horse grew impatient and began to dance and strain at the bit. He controlled the animal easily, and Annie was affected by the sight in a curiously elemental way that caused her to shift in the saddle. "Perhaps," the prince countered coldly, "you do not cause disruption in the other houses you visit. You are free to roam within the keep's walls, Miss Trevarren, but in the future you will do so in the company of a guard."

She opened her mouth, then closed it again. There was no reasoning with this man. Why attempt it? In the course of helping Phaedra escape St. James Keep and a forced marriage, Annie would be free of the place as well. For the time being, however, she could only hold her tongue and try to follow the rules. It wouldn't do to arouse suspicion.

Rafael's manner softened. "Come," he said, and a

tentative smile was his peace offering. "I'll show you the lake."

Annie had been bracing herself for the disappointment of having to turn back, so Rafael's invitation came as a pleasant surprise. "Have you spent a lot of time there?" she inquired, riding behind him through the orchard, with blossoms covering the ground and billowing like clouds over their heads.

The smile Rafael tossed back over one shoulder was almost free of strain. He might have been a carefree young boy, instead of a widower and the prince of a country in the throes of violent change. "There's a cottage on this side of the water. Barrett and I used to fish for trout there, when we came to Bavia for a holiday, and swim when the weather was warm enough."

Rafael's transformation was incredible; the nearer they drew to Crystal Lake, the more relaxed he seemed. He rode beside Annie through a forest of pine and fir trees, smiling as he told of the time Edmund Barrett had climbed too high and one of the grooms had to fetch a ladder to get him down.

Here was a man, Annie reflected, who lived in a castle and reigned over a country. He was undoubtedly very wealthy, and yet the things that made him happy were simple ones. Knowing that gave Annie a bereft feeling; she wished she could show Rafael her beloved Puget Sound, with its dense fringes of blue-green trees and the snow-covered mountains dwarfing it all. She wanted to take him to her parents' island plantation in the South Pacific, too, to walk and run on the pristine white beaches with him, and teach him how to gather coconuts and eat their delicious fruit.

She wanted something more, as well. The thought of it brought a blush to her face and made her heart beat faster, but even then she knew the dream was not just scandalous, it was impossible.

Rafael would stay in Bavia, and he would almost certainly die there.

CHAPTER

4

The cottage was a small stone structure on the rocky shore of the lake. It sported a sturdy gambrel roof of plain shingles, and the leaded glass windows were framed with weathered white shutters. Weeds and wildflowers grew right up to the walls, and it was plain that no one had used the place in a very long time.

The prince dismounted first and held the mare's reins for Annie. Because she was wearing a divided skirt, and she hadn't expected company on the expedition, she'd ridden astride, and being forced to swing one leg over the saddle, with Rafael looking on, embarrassed her mightily.

He must have guessed at her dilemma, for he smiled a slight and secret smile, belonging only to him. Annie would have appreciated a few moments to compose herself, but he did not have the good grace to avert his eyes for even that long.

She turned to look out over the turbulent gray waters of the lake. It *did* seem enchanted, as Phaedra had always claimed it was. Annie wouldn't have been surprised to see a mermaid rise out of the ripples to sun herself on one of the large rocks near the shore.

As far as she could tell, the lake was completely encircled by the dense, fragrant forest. It reminded her of the Puget Sound country, and for a moment she was wildly homesick for Quade's Harbor and the sprawling tangle of family thriving there.

"Sometimes I think this is the only peaceful place in all the world," Rafael said, his voice low and roughened slightly by sorrow.

Annie was anxious to reassure him. "Oh, no," she protested, nearly grabbing hold of his arm in her earnest desire to convince him, but catching herself just in time. "There are so many others—the countryside surrounding the town where my grandparents live, in Washington State, has great, towering trees and meadows where sweetbrier grows. And there's the island—why, it might have been the Garden of Eden, it's so lovely!"

Tenderness flickered in Rafael's eyes as he regarded her, and Annie could not believe he was the same man who fenced with such ruthless determination to win, the very man who would not allow his own sister to choose her husband. "But that's your world, Annie," he said. "This"—he gestured toward the keep, rising against the ominously clouded sky, and the troubled lands beyond—"is mine."

Annie left the mare to nibble sweet grass and made her way toward the lakeshore. Once again, she was trying not to weep, for Rafael's words filled her with sadness and frustration.

"You could leave," she blurted, watching the lake through a sheen of tears.

She felt him standing close behind her. "No. And as the daughter of a sea captain, you should understand the reason."

Annie dried her eyes on the sleeve of her riding jacket, in what she hoped was a subtle motion, then sucked in a deep and somewhat sniffly breath. "Oh, yes," she said tartly, not daring to look back at Rafael. "A captain goes down with his ship. And you mean to perish with Bavia. Well, I think that's insane!"

Rafael crouched beside her, and still she could not look at him. "Americans generally don't understand these things," he said. "It's a matter of tradition, Annie, and of honor. Though I have many enemies, I also have a number of loyal subjects. I cannot simply abandon them to their fate. I must stand with them."

Annie did understand, although she would have preferred it to be otherwise. She looked down at her knotted hands. "I still think you're mad," she insisted.

He chuckled and took her hand. "Come, Annie. I want to show you the inside of the cottage. Besides, in case you've failed to notice, it's about to rain."

The closing of his fingers around hers accelerated her heartbeat and caused a warm spill somewhere deep inside. Even though she knew it wasn't proper, she allowed him to raise her to her feet and lead her toward the little cottage.

They were still some distance away when the sky opened up and a hard, spattering rain began to fall, flattening the tall grass, slapping the surface of the lake, and drenching their clothes. The mare and gelding nickered and fretted.

"Go inside!" Rafael shouted, over the roar of the deluge, flinging Annie in the direction of the little house. "I'll see to the horses."

She obeyed without question and was relieved when the door latch worked on the first try. A flash of lightning filled the room with fiery light, followed by a deafening clap of thunder, and Annie dashed to the window to see Rafael struggling to calm the terrified gelding. The mare had already bolted and was just disappearing into the trees.

Rafael managed to tether the remaining horse to the low branch of a tree, then sprinted toward the cottage.

Not wanting to be caught watching him, Annie turned quickly from the window and scurried over to the stone fireplace, kneeling on the hearth and hastily arranging a few dry twigs on the grate. The first faltering flame was just beginning to lick at the wood when Rafael burst through the door.

He was wet to the skin and, without hesitation, or any apparent consideration for Annie's sensibilities, he hauled his sodden shirt off over his head and tossed it over the back of a chair—one of the few pieces of furniture in the room.

Annie swallowed and tossed a small log onto the fire. "It's a good thing there was some wood on hand," she said, in a voice that was too bright and too brittle.

Rafael had joined her before the fireplace, and she was alarmed to realize that she felt more heat coming from him than from the blaze she'd just kindled. "There's always wood," he replied matter-of-factly. "I come here sometimes to think."

She rose slowly, looking around the cottage for the first time since she'd sprung through the door. Apparently, there was only one room, though there was a loft with a ladder on the side opposite the fireplace. A bed, a wooden table with two chairs, and a cookstove comprised the furnishings.

This was the second time in her life that Annie had been alone in the same room with a man and a bed. She wondered if it was significant that on both occasions that man had been Rafael St. James.

"You'd better take off some of those clothes," he said, in the same practical tone he'd used to announce that there was always wood in the cottage. "Ironic if you survived the incident on the parapet only to catch your death after being caught in a rainstorm."

Annie removed her riding jacket, as a concession, avoiding his gaze the whole time. Pneumonia or no pneumonia, that was the one and only garment she was willing to shed in his presence. It wasn't him she was afraid of, though. It was herself, for where this man was concerned, she had no sense whatever and very few inhibitions.

"I'm sure I'll be quite all right," she told him stiffly.

"Look at me, Annie," the prince commanded.

It was difficult to obey. His chest was bare, after all, and Annie had never seen a man in any degree of nakedness before, let alone stripped to the waist. She knew she was blushing as she raised her eyes to meet his.

"You are safe with me," he said plainly. "I have no intention of ravishing you."

Annie was relieved and, if she were to be entirely honest with herself, somewhat disappointed as well. "You *did* kiss me yesterday."

He smiled, a bit rakishly, Annie thought, at the

memory. "Yes," he said. "I did, didn't I?" He took a step toward her and she stood as if spellbound, unable, or perhaps unwilling, to move.

"I imagine one of Mr. Barrett's men will come looking for us, when the mare returns to the stables without me," Annie said, as a way of reminding the prince, lest he should change his mind about ravishing her, that there was little time.

A curious expression had come over Rafael's face—he looked unscrupulously handsome even with his dripping hair—one of bewilderment. "I will be damned," he whispered, using the reverent tones of one offering a sacred vow and standing very near by then. He reached around to pull the pins from her hair, so that Annie's own sopping tresses tumbled down her back and over her bodice. "I most surely will."

Something had happened, something indefinable had changed, for both of them. Annie was filled with the same ecstatic terror she'd felt while standing on the parapet of the south tower.

She willed herself to step back, out of Rafael's reach, but she couldn't move. Her heart was hammering so hard that she honestly feared it might do irreparable damage to itself, and her breathing was too shallow and too quick.

Rafael laid his hand to the back of her head, spreading his fingers, burying them in her hair. He frowned and said her name and as simply as that, she was lost. She would have let him do almost anything, and the realization shook her to the very core of her being.

"One kiss," he said raggedly, as though making an

oath to himself, not Annie. "Just one kiss—I promise."

She stared up at Rafael, trusting him, baffled and a little shaken to know the extent of his power over her. She raised her face and his mouth came down on hers, not gently or tentatively like before, but with a pleasant ferocity. A hunger.

Annie was transported. Mysterious parts of her, parts she'd never dreamed she possessed, were awakening and making themselves known. She ached, and when Rafael's tongue entered her mouth, she took the thunder and lightning inside herself, into every curve and plain of her body, every secret fold of her soul.

He continued the kiss, and at the same time he caressed her breast with one hand, causing the nipple to ache beneath her shirtwaist and camisole. She willed him to unbutton her bodice and he did, slowly. Ever so slowly.

Annie watched his face as Rafael bared her breasts and looked at them with wonder as well as desire; she sensed his reverence and saw it in his eyes, and she wanted him even more than before.

"You are so incredibly . . ." Rafael's words fell away into silence. Holding the small of her back with both hands, he bent and took one of her nipples into his mouth, and she arched against his palms and cried out because the sensation was so glorious.

He conquered her other breast, drawing on it hard, at the same time bending to lift her into his arms. He suckled her as he crossed the room toward the bed, and Annie couldn't help the soft, eager sounds she made, though she knew they were wanton.

Rafael laid her gently on the mattress and opened

the buttons of her skirt, sliding his hand beneath while he drank hungrily from her breast.

Annie sobbed his name, putting all her wanting, all her needing into the sound. "No, my hellion princess," he rasped, against her well-suckled nipple. "The treasure you would give me is for another man, on another day. But I can teach you pleasure—by God, I will have that much of you!"

Annie felt his hand move beneath the waistband of her wet and clinging riding skirt, beneath her drawers. She raised herself to him, wanting something she didn't fully understand, offering everything.

Rafael reached lower, finding that most sensitive place, and she felt his fingers part the moist folds of her femininity.

She uttered a low, insensible cry and bucked against his palm, but he only murmured, "Soon enough, sweeting. It will happen soon enough."

Annie felt as though she'd been taken with a fever— she was delirious and light-headed, and her body writhed wildly under Rafael's hand. Gently, he pinched the little nubbin of flesh where all her passion seemed to center, and she moaned in desperation and impatience.

"I might have kissed you here," Rafael teased quietly, stroking her now, in a rhythmic circle made of fire, with the pad of his thumb. "I might have taken this into my mouth, the way I did your nipples."

The suggestion, coupled with the spiraling sensation between her legs, made Annie pitch and toss under his patient ministrations like a wild creature. When Rafael bent over her, and took her breast again, she came apart in an explosive riot of heat and satisfaction, shouting hoarsely, raising her hips high off the bed to follow his hand wherever it might lead.

He continued to suckle, more gently now, until she had settled back to the bed, until the sweet, convulsive flexing of hidden muscles had ceased. Then, as she lay dazed, still not truly understanding what had just happened, he stroked her forehead and her hair.

"Shh," he said, consoling her in her inconsolable joy.

After a long time, she turned her head and looked into his gray eyes, seeing sadness there, as well as passion. "I want you to do that to me," she told him. "What you said before—about taking me into your mouth."

He groaned. "Annie, love—have mercy. A man is allotted only so much honor and forbearance."

She didn't know then, perhaps she would never know, what caused her to be so brazen. But she was. She raised her hips off the bed and, at the same time, pushed down her skirt and drawers, revealing herself to him.

Rafael made an elemental, innately masculine sound, somewhere between a moan and a curse. Then he removed her boots and her stockings, as well as her skirt and drawers, and she lay before him, naked except for her gaping shirtwaist and camisole.

"May God forgive me," he murmured. And then, still kneeling on the floor, he turned Annie, so that she lay sideways on the bed, with her legs on either side of him.

A primitive cry of welcome escaped her when he burrowed through the silken tangle and took her hungrily, greedily, into his mouth.

* * *

What in hell had he done? Rafael asked himself, after Annie had been sated not once but several times. What demon had possessed him, that he would teach an innocent young woman the finer points of pleasure?

"Rafael?" She was still naked, but he'd put her legs back on the bed and covered her with a musty blanket brought down from the chest in the loft. The fire was burning low, and if Barrett or his men were out looking for them, they must have run into trouble. . . .

He turned his back on her and went back to the hearth, making a fuss with the fire, wanting to hide the hard arousal pulsing behind the buttons of his trousers. Whatever his other sins, he had not plunged inside her, even though he'd never wanted a woman more than he wanted Annie Trevarren that rainy afternoon.

"Are you angry with me?" she asked, in a small voice, and Rafael cursed, for he did not want her playing the game so many women played, torturing herself for doing and feeling things that were perfectly normal, even instinctive. No, he would have Annie revel in her glorious femininity, not feel shame for it.

"No," Rafael said, but he would not look at her. Indeed, he could not. "There's been no harm done, Annie," he said, testing her clothes, which he'd hung over the backs of chairs close by the fire, for dryness.

"Harm?" he heard the corn husks inside the old mattress rustle as she sat up. "Of course there's been no harm—it was *wonderful,* but—"

Rafael ran one hand down the length of his face, wishing she would be quiet and at the same time feeling her voice brush the strings of his soul like a soft breeze passing through a harp. "But?" he prompted, moving to the window, hoping to convey an air of disinterest. He saw the gelding, still tethered to his branch, ears laid back, hide soaked, flanks quivering, and felt profound pity for the beast.

"But I don't think you enjoyed the experience—" She stumbled in the middle of the sentence, and he knew without looking that she was blushing again. "I don't believe you were as—happy as I was."

Happy. The word struck Rafael funny, and he might have laughed aloud if he hadn't known Annie was serious. She was especially vulnerable now and he didn't want to hurt her.

"It's all right, Annie," he managed to say, turning around at last. She was sitting up in bed but, God be thanked, she pulled the blanket he'd given her up to her throat. "I'll be fine."

Something flashed in her eyes, a sort of wounded fury. "You'll turn to some other woman," she accused. "Miss Covington, perhaps."

Rafael schooled himself to patience. Annie was a woman, and a young one at that, and such things were vitally important to her. He must be gentle, for she might well remember this afternoon for the rest of her life, and he wanted her recollections to be pleasant ones. "I'm a man, Miss Trevarren, not a rutting boar. I can govern my physical desires quite nicely."

He heard the horses then, and knew his interlude of joyful madness was at an end. Now, he would have the rest of his life—a relatively short time, in all probability—to remember that he'd made a fool of himself this day. That he'd wanted a woman badly enough to put aside his values and his better judgment to play her sweet body as if it were a dulcimer or a lute.

He had been a self-centered bastard, and not just

73

because of the things he'd done to Annie, however much she'd enjoyed them. No, his crime lay in the fact that he'd trifled with her feelings. She was young and unsophisticated, a product of the privileged life Patrick and Charlotte had given her, and she might well expect a devotion he simply could not give.

"Get dressed," he said, tossing the still damp garments to her. "Someone is coming."

Annie scrambled out of bed and into her clothes, and Rafael couldn't help watching out of the corner of his eye as she wriggled and tugged in her haste to avoid being caught in a compromising situation.

Little did she know, Rafael reflected, as a thunderous knock sounded at the door, practically shaking it on its hinges, that it was already too late.

"Your Highness," Barrett's voice boomed through the thickening twilight, "Are you there? Let me in!"

Ruefully, Rafael glanced back at Annie and saw that, although she was decently clad again, her red-gold hair tumbled down her back, unconfined, her eyes blazed with a lingering, deep-seated pleasure and, if those things hadn't been revealing enough, there was a telltale glow to her skin. Unless Barrett had gone blind since Rafael had last encountered him, he would know exactly what had been going on.

"Yes," Rafael called back, unable to hide his irritation. Despite the noble things he'd said to Annie about controlling his physical desires, he was vastly uncomfortable, and he would remain so for some time. "I'm here." With that, he wrenched open the door and stood facing his friend and guard.

Barrett wore a cape, splotched with rain, and his expression was uncommonly anxious. "Great Scot, Rafael, I thought you'd been captured, or broken your neck—" He saw Annie then, it was plain that it all registered, in an instant.

Rafael stepped back to admit him. "You took your time starting a search," he remarked, while Barrett studiously avoided Annie's gaze. His neck was a dull crimson. "I might have been hauled halfway to France by now."

Barrett started to speak, cleared his throat and began again. "Lucian said he'd seen you out riding, and that you'd be gone a while," he explained awkwardly. "I know you like to have some time to—to yourself now and then, so I wasn't concerned. It was only when the rain didn't stop, and twilight came on—"

Rafael touched his friend's arm. "It's all right, Barrett," he said quietly. He suspected that the man had been occupied with some pursuit of his own that afternoon; that would account for his embarrassment, as well as his delay. "Have you brought a horse for Miss Trevarren?"

"We didn't know she'd left the keep," Barrett said.

For the first time since Barrett had entered the cottage, Annie spoke. Her voice was clear and strong and ever so slightly defiant. "Didn't my mare return to the stables?" she asked.

Barrett forced himself to look at her. "If it did, miss, I wasn't told."

"Never mind," Rafael interjected. "Miss Trevarren will ride back with me."

Minutes later, they were mounted, with Annie in front of Rafael on the impatient gelding. It was a singular torment, feeling her soft, delectable body against his, breathing the scent of her hair, the faint, musky perfume of her pleasure, and the fresh smell of spring rain. He could endure a great many things, he thought fancifully, as long as he could summon that distinct bouquet and remember Annie as she was at that moment in time.

Annie cherished the sensation of being safe within the circle of Rafael's arms. She knew she would regret her shameless behavior soon enough, but that time had not yet come. In fact, she was still responding to Rafael's lovemaking, feeling delicious little spasms of pleasure deep in her most womanly regions. Her nipples were hard beneath her damp camisole and blouse, wanting the touch of his tongue and the excruciatingly sweet tug of his lips. If she could have lain with him then, in the wet and fragrant grass, and taken him inside her, she would have done just that.

Too soon, they reached the stables, and Rafael swung out of the saddle and reached up to lift Annie down. She allowed it, though she could have dismounted on her own with no difficulty at all, simply because she wanted to feel his hands touching her again.

The rain had turned to a slight drizzle, and the keep and stables were glowing with lantern light. Rafael curved his finger under Annie's chin and raised it, once Barrett and the others had left them, taking the gelding with them.

Annie ached to hear him say he loved her, even though she knew he wouldn't. The events of that afternoon had been a dalliance to Rafael, an hour's amusement, that was the truth of it, and she would forget that at her peril.

"Don't tell me you're sorry!" she pleaded, before Rafael had a chance to say anything at all. She hadn't planned the words, and was wretchedly embarrassed that she'd blurted them out that way. Still, she meant them with every fiber of her being. "Please, Rafael, don't ruin the best afternoon of my life by apologizing."

He pulled her against him, not passionately, but in an effort to lend comfort, burying one hand in her mussed and tangled hair. "All right," he said hoarsely, his breath whispering, warm, across her ear. "I won't. But I want you to keep in mind that there are many such afternoons, and long, wonderful nights as well, in your future. Only the man will be different."

No, Annie mourned inwardly, her face buried in the prince's strong shoulder, shuddering at the prospect of another man—no matter how kind and handsome and honorable he might be—touching her the way Rafael had. She understood Phaedra's trepidation at taking a husband she didn't love as she couldn't possibly have done before.

"Here, now," Rafael protested gruffly, when she began to cry. "None of that. What you need now is a warm bath, something to eat and a good night's sleep." He was already ushering her toward the castle, and she didn't want to go because she knew it meant they would have to part.

The great hall was empty and, at the bottom of the staircase, Rafael swatted Annie lightly on the bottom. "Go on," he ordered, and though his lips were curved into a smile, his eyes expressed some other, darker emotion. "Get to your room. I'll send a maid up immediately."

She lingered for a moment, memorizing his face, terribly afraid that this one interlude was all she would ever have of him, wondering how she could go on with her life, knowing what might have been. God in heaven, she'd been better off with her virginal fantasies, never guessing at the things a man and woman could do to bring ecstasy to each other.

"Good night," she said brokenly. Then she turned and hurried up the stairs and through the dimly lighted passageways to her own chamber.

True to his word, Rafael dispatched a servant right away. Annie was cosseted and fussed over—brandy and hot food were brought to her room and an enormous bathtub was promptly filled with steaming water.

For all those luxuries, Annie was miserable. Like a true gentleman, Rafael had seen that every comfort was provided—she could not doubt that he felt tremendous guilt for the things he'd done to her in that cottage. By now, he was probably in bed with his mistress, appeasing the passions he had not allowed himself to satisfy with Annie.

She had learned a great deal that afternoon; she had seen Rafael's erection, and felt it against her buttocks and lower back as they rode back from the cottage with Barrett and his detail of men. Lying in the warm, scented water of her tub, Annie closed her eyes and imagined what it would be like to have him mount and conquer her. The thought made her breath quicken and her heart race, and inspired an achy throb down below.

She might have died of her unfulfilled wanting, she supposed, if Phaedra hadn't chosen exactly then to burst into her chambers, uninvited, her eyes alight with mischief and some secret she would almost certainly refuse to reveal.

"The keep is overflowing with gossip," Phaedra said, in an eager and delighted whisper. "Everyone says that you and Rafael were alone together in the cottage by the lake. Rumor has it that your hair was loose when they found you, and Rafael wasn't wearing a shirt, and your clothes were mussed and misbuttoned. Tell me precisely what happened—as if I couldn't guess!"

Annie was mortified that a reputation could be ruined so quickly and wondered how she would ever face people, when everyone knew such intimate things about her. "Nothing happened," she lied. "We were caught in the rain, that's all. The cottage was nearby so naturally we took refuge there."

"Very well, then," Phaedra responded petulantly, "don't tell me. Sooner or later, you won't be able to contain the truth any longer, and it will all spill out!"

Annie considered sinking beneath the surface of her bathwater and drowning herself, but the chances of rescue were too great, with Phaedra right there. *"Nothing happened,"* she said again, hoping there were no angels listening in, and putting a mark by her name in some heavenly ledger. As it was, she was probably going to be ushered straight through Purgatory when she died and handed over to the devil's own gatekeeper.

Mercifully, Phaedra was consumed by some news of her own, something besides the secret shining in her eyes. She was bursting with excitement. "Felicia brought a dressmaker with her," she said. "I'm to have the grandest gown in all of Europe!"

Annie was startled out of her own woeful reflections, gaping at Phaedra, openmouthed. Several flustered moments passed before she managed to sputter, "But you said—last night—Phaedra, have you gone mad?"

The princess laughed. "No," she said, fetching a towel and handing it to Annie. "I've simply had a change of heart. It's going to be a marvelous wedding, Annie, like something out of a fairy tale. I'll have a glass coach, and six white horses to pull it—"

"Phaedra," Annie said, using the towel as a curtain while she stood and then wrapping it around herself and stepping out of the tub. She took her wrapper from the bench in front of the vanity table and slipped behind a screen to put it on. A moment later, she was crossing the room again, laying a hand to the princess's forehead.

There was no fever, but Annie's alarm was not assuaged.

Phaedra grasped her hand. "Don't worry, pet," she said earnestly. "I shall be happy, I promise." Her shining eyes lent a certain truth to the declaration.

Still, having just learned how glorious it was to be touched and caressed in the most intimate ways by a man she cared for, Annie was even more of a firm believer in marrying for love. "Have you developed tender sentiments toward Mr. Haslett after all?" she asked hopefully.

"Something like that," Phaedra said cryptically.

Annie was not reassured, but there was nothing she could do to change matters at the moment. She would, of course, give the situation a great deal of hard thought. There was more to this drastic turnabout than Phaedra was telling, that much she knew by instinct.

"You and I are about the same size," Phaedra

observed, taking both of Annie's hands in hers and eyeing her frame critically. "Yes. The dress could just as well be fitted to you."

Again, Annie was flabbergasted, even though she was used to being surprised by her friend. "You want *me* to be fitted for your wedding gown? Phaedra, that is the most incredible suggestion you've ever made!"

Phaedra met her gaze then, and Annie saw such pleading, such desperate hope in those familiar eyes, that she was staggered by it. *"Please,* Annie. Say you'll do this for me. You know I couldn't bear the boredom of it, standing still for hours and hours—I'd swoon for certain, or be taken with one of my sick headaches!"

Annie swallowed a retort concerning the convenience of said sick headaches, having been caught in this same trap many times before. It was madness to consent, but Phaedra St. James was her most cherished friend—all the others were dull by comparison —and something hidden away in her heart told her this favor was important to her friend.

"All right," she said ruefully. "I'll do it."

CHAPTER

5

Annie avoided the dining hall the next morning. Even though she had been ravenously hungry from the instant she opened her eyes, she was afraid to encounter Rafael. Her emotions were in turmoil—one moment, she felt the most profound joy; the next, the most pitiful despair—and the echoes of his lovemaking still thrummed and spilled and caught in the deepest reaches of her womanhood. She was absolutely certain that the prince, with his greater knowledge of the world and its ways, would guess these embarrassing secrets at a glance.

The prospect of that encounter being unbearable, Annie had dressed hastily and allowed Phaedra to lead her through endless passages to the other side of the castle.

"This is the solarium," Phaedra announced, when

they stepped into the large, round, sunny room, with its towering windows, flourishing plants, and bare stone walls. "In the old days, the ladies of the keep used to come here to chat and work their embroidery, and sometimes musicians played for their entertainment. Papa had glass put into the windows—they were open before—and there were the most beautiful tapestries for decoration, until Rafael inherited the crown." The princess paused, a slight frown crinkling her otherwise flawless face. "He said the air was ruining them and gave the lot to the public museum in Morovia."

Annie turned slowly, admiring the vast, chilly chamber. It was circular, with a high, dome-shaped ceiling and a balcony that stretched all the way around. Imagining the place as it must have been in medieval times, she could almost see the St. James women in their kirtles, smiling and sewing, and hear them chatting and humming under their breaths with the soft notes of a lyre for accompaniment. "What a wonderful room," she whispered.

Phaedra pointed to the balcony, which loomed at least twenty feet off the cold stone floor. "A long time ago, a princess leaped to her death from up there. The servants claim that her ghost haunts St. James Keep to this day."

A delicious tremor coursed down Annie's spine. She would like to make the acquaintance of such a creature, she decided, provided it was well-behaved and not too ugly.

"Now remember, you promised to be fitted in my place," Phaedra added, in a whisper, as a clatter sounded near the open arch that served as the main doorway. A short, plump woman with gray hair and an unfortunate mole just to the left of her nose bustled in, with two servant girls bumbling at her heels.

The first young woman carried an enormous bolt of shimmering white moire, the second a sewing basket overflowing with lace and ribbon and measuring tape. Both looked harried and anxious.

The woman in the lead placed her hands on her ample hips and assessed both Annie and Phaedra with bright, beadlike eyes. "Which one of you is the princess?" she demanded, and from her tone a person might have concluded that there was a beheading scheduled for that sunny, rain-washed morning, instead of a fitting for the most magnificent wedding dress in all of Europe.

"I am," Phaedra responded coolly, drawing herself up. While there was nothing of the snob in her nature, she did not like to be addressed in too casual a fashion. "This is my friend, Miss Annie Trevarren. She'll be standing in for me during the fitting. Annie, Miss Augusta Rendennon."

The new arrival, obviously the seamstress Miss Covington had retained, and a personage of some renown in addition to that, reddened slightly and pursed her lips. She had used none of her purported skill in the making of her own garments, for hers was a plain gray gown, unremarkable in every way. Her high-button shoes were scuffed and the small lace cap perched on the crown of her head had seen better decades. Her eyes were narrow as she studied Annie.

"Hmmm," she said, her tone and expression ripe with censure.

Annie blushed, both embarrassed and indignant, and would have elbowed Phaedra in the ribs if the princess hadn't been judicious enough to step out of reach. "I don't think—" she began lamely.

"Hush!" hissed the dressmaker, walking around Annie in a slow circle now. "Madame is not called upon to think. Yes . . . yes, I believe you will do, though I dare say I'll need to make adjustments at the waist." She reached out and gave Annie's side a hard pinch. "A bit fleshy, but to tell the truth, men like a woman to be soft in the appropriate places."

Annie cast a scathing look in Phaedra's direction, though the heat in her face rose not from this current humiliation, but from memories of the day before, when Rafael had touched and stroked and kissed every inch of said flesh. "Surely if it is to be the princess's dress, then she should be the one to—"

Phaedra was already flitting toward the door, nimble as some forest nymph vanishing into the trees. Eyes narrowed in warning, she nonetheless blew Annie a farewell kiss. "Miss Rendennon will take care of everything," she chimed, before vanishing as quickly as any ghost could have done.

Annie's stomach gave a loud and unmistakable rumble, and Miss Rendennon sighed in a martyrly fashion.

"Barbarians," she muttered to herself. "Nothing but barbarians."

One of the maids, having set her bundle of fabric down on a nearby couch, curtseyed to Annie and said, "I could find you something to eat, miss."

"Eat?" bellowed Miss Rendennon, horrified. "There will be no food within a hundred fathoms of these exquisite goods! Besides, I won't have the seams bursting."

Annie's cheeks burned anew. Perhaps she *was* a bit

more voluptuous than Phaedra, but Miss Rendennon made it sound as though she were an oddity, fated to spend the rest of her days touring with circuses. "My dear woman, I hardly think—"

The dressmaker did not allow her to finish, but clapped her hands loudly and ordered one of the maids to fetch sheets to cover the floor, so that the precious moire would be protected, and began taking Annie's measurements, clucking and muttering and fussing all the while.

Once a large part of the floor had been covered, and Annie had been stripped to her chemise, the length of fabric was unfolded and the process of draping began. Annie stood like St. Joan at the stake, her stomach grumbling, watching dust motes floating in the spears of sunlight stabbing through the windows, and passed the time by plotting revenge against Phaedra.

A tingling sensation on her nape was the first indication that she was being observed, and when Annie raised her eyes, she was startled to see Rafael standing on the balcony, arms braced against the ornate masonry railing, watching her. Although she could not make out his expression, because of distance and shadows, she felt oddly vulnerable, as though she'd been bared for him, like a harem favorite for the sultan.

When Miss Rendennon looked up and saw the prince, her insolent manner changed in an instant. She nodded and beamed. "Good morning, Your Highness," she said.

Rafael, wearing a white shirt and dark breeches, nodded an acknowledgment but did not speak. Annie willed herself to look away, but she found that she could only stand there, aching with passion and with pride, remembering that she'd made a fool of herself for this man only the day before. And wanting with all her heart to do the same thing over again.

The prince remained where he was, without speaking, and Annie couldn't guess who was more undone by his presence—herself or Miss Augusta Rendennon. Alternately murmuring and twittering, the formidable dressmaker bungled her way through the rest of the fitting. She finally undraped the glimmering fabric and left Annie standing in the middle of the floor in her chemise.

One of the maids had the presence of mind to hand Annie her gown, and she fairly leaped into it, being careful not to raise her eyes to the place Rafael had occupied on the balcony, telling herself that he would certainly have gone by now. As prince of Bavia, he surely could not waste his time standing about on balconies, watching dress fittings.

Annie had no more reached this comforting conclusion when she heard the sound of boot heels clicking on a stone staircase. In a sidelong glance, she saw Rafael crossing the chamber floor, his expression pensive.

Still only half-dressed, Annie clutched the bodice of her gown closed and stared stupidly as he approached. He came to a graceful stop a few feet in front of her.

"What are you doing?" he demanded, in a distracted undertone.

Annie felt accused somehow, as if she'd been caught pilfering in the counting house, and her irritation was profound. Did Rafael think she'd *enjoyed* standing still as a statue, for upward of an hour, while Miss Augusta Rendennon pricked her with pins and muttered comments?

She executed a brief and slightly mocking curtsey, her eyes flashing with indignation. "It seems that Phaedra had better things to do this morning than being fitted for her wedding gown," she said. She swallowed as some of her bravado deserted her.

The sudden flash of his smile startled Annie, and she blinked, as dazzled as if she'd glimpsed the center of the sun. By the time she could see clearly again, Rafael's face had turned solemn.

"There is to be a ball this Saturday evening," he said, as though the upcoming event were a funeral instead of a celebration. "At the palace in Morovia. Both you and Phaedra will be wanting proper gowns, I suppose."

Annie was buttoning her dress, a spring green garment of soft, whispery cotton. She couldn't help smiling at the prospect of a visit to the royal palace and a gala in the bargain. "Phaedra's engagement ball—how wonderful!"

Rafael sighed. "Yes. Wonderful," he said glumly.

She tilted her head to one side, watching him with curiosity. "You don't want to go?"

"It isn't that," he replied, his gaze leaving Annie's face to scan the balconies and the shadowy heights of the ceiling. "Morovia is a dangerous place, for members of the St. James family, at any rate. And to the people of Bavia, the palace symbolizes seven hundred years of excess and abuse." When Rafael met her eyes again, he seemed to regret what he'd confided. "Don't worry, Annie. We'll all be perfectly safe—Barrett and his men will see to that."

Before Annie could assure him that she wasn't at all fearful, for herself at least, he raised one hand and brushed the backs of his fingers lightly over her cheek.

His mouth curved into a brief and somehow sorrowful smile, and then, in a low voice, he spoke again.

"I'm sorry about yesterday, love."

Annie averted her eyes. She trembled with the effort of keeping herself from shouting that she didn't want him to be sorry, that she had always loved him and always would, and her heart was pounding so hard that she was certain he would hear it. She said nothing, not daring to speak.

Rafael cupped his hand under her chin and made her look at him. "Somewhere on this weary earth," he said quietly, his pewter eyes full of mirth and mourning, "there walks a man so fortunate that even the angels must envy him. One day soon, he will put a golden band on your finger, Annie Trevarren, and take you to his bed with all the blessings of heaven. When you give yourself up to his love, my sweet, nothing in the past will matter any longer."

Annie was about to blurt out that her time alone with him, in the cottage by the lake, would always matter, that there would be no other man for her, ever, when she heard slow, mocking applause from the balcony.

Both Annie and Rafael looked up at the same moment and saw Lucian standing high above their heads, clapping.

He smiled and let his hands fall to his sides.

"An excellent performance, Brother," he said. "Very poetic, with just the right touch of drama."

Annie shifted her gaze back to Rafael's face, just in time to see him clench his jaw.

"Enough," Rafael said simply and quietly. Still, the word carried to the balcony and struck Lucian with visible impact, like a stone from a slingshot.

Lucian recovered in an instant. His smile returned, at once chilling and cordial, and he leaned against the balcony railing with the same easy grace Rafael had shown earlier. "So the rumors are true," he said, with acidic cheer. "You've had your way with yet another lovely wayfarer. And now you're telling her the tragic truth—that nothing can come of the episode, however pleasurable it was, because you are fated to die a grand and noble death. Brilliant, Rafael. Nothing less than brilliant."

"Lucian," Rafael said hoarsely. "I'm warning you. Stop this, now."

Undaunted, the younger brother descended the same stairway Rafael had used and entered the great chamber. "Did you believe him, beautiful Annie?" he asked in a soft, sly voice. "If so, you mustn't berate yourself. You certainly aren't the first."

Rafael did not immediately respond, and yet the room seemed to pulse with tension and fury. Looking on, Annie felt genuine fear, as well as outrage toward Lucian, for she recognized violence in the prince and knew that he could barely restrain it.

Lucian went recklessly on, ignoring his brother, concentrating on Annie. "You must be more discreet in the future, Miss Trevarren," he said, "or at least give up the pretense of being a lady."

It was then that Rafael sprung, his hands closing around Lucian's throat.

Annie screamed, certain that there would be a murder, and Lucian freed himself, temporarily, by flinging his arms upward and breaking Rafael's hold. Only an instant later, however, Rafael landed a punch in the middle of Lucian's stomach, driving the breath from his lungs in an audible rush.

Rafael hurled Lucian down and straddled him, once again pressing his thumbs deep into his brother's windpipe. Lucian, his eyes bright with angry disbelief and humiliation, was turning purple for lack of air. Nevertheless, his hatred was palpable.

Annie made an effort to pull Rafael off, only to be pushed away with such force that she nearly fell. God only knew what would have happened if Edmund Barrett hadn't dashed into the room just then, followed by two of his men. Breaking Rafael's hold on Lucian, Barrett dragged him back off of his brother.

Rafael struggled, strong as a panther, but Barrett, gripping the prince's arms from behind, had gained the advantage. Barrett's men hoisted Lucian to his feet and, at a nod from their captain, one of them led him, stumbling, from the chamber. Rafael freed himself with a violent shrug, but did not pursue his retreating brother.

"Good God, Rafael," Barrett growled, having apparently forgotten, as the prince had, that Annie was there, "isn't it enough that you insist on staying in Bavia until the rebels run you to the ground and kill you? Are you so bent on sacrificing yourself that you'll do murder under your own roof, just so you can hang for it?"

Rafael muttered something, and his gaze skimmed over Annie and then came back to her face. In that instant, she saw in his eyes the depths of his suffering, and the sight nearly brought her to her knees.

He was in agony.

"Annie," he whispered. The name sounded ragged, broken.

She took a step toward him and stopped. Rafael was determined to die. She covered her mouth with one

91

hand, to stifle a sob, and fled. In the doorway, she nearly collided with none other than Miss Felicia Covington.

Miss Covington's pretty forehead was crumpled into a concerned frown, and her dark eyes were full of kindly concern. Up close, she was as beautiful as a Botticelli angel and apparently as compassionate. She gripped Annie's shoulders for a moment, in a distracted effort to steady her, before proceeding into the chamber.

Annie lingered in the shadows just beyond the threshold, wanting to be elsewhere and yet too stricken to move.

"Rafael," Miss Covington cried, hurrying over to the prince and taking his upper arms into her hands. "What did you do to Lucian?"

Rafael moved to twist free of her, but she held on in a way only an intimate friend would dare to do. "It's nothing," he spat. "Leave me alone, Felicia. Please."

She smoothed his hair and, oddly, the gentle gesture tore at Annie's heart, causing her to shrink deeper into the shadows and hold her breath while she struggled for self-control.

Felicia nodded to Barrett, who reluctantly left the room, passing Annie without seeing her. "Why, Rafael?" Miss Covington whispered, slipping her arm around his lean waist. "Why do you hate Lucian so much? He is your half brother."

Rafael sighed and shoved a hand through his hair. Although some of his fury had dissipated, Annie could see that there was still tension coiled within him. "I don't hate Lucian," he responded. "He hates me. And sometimes I share his opinion."

Felicia smiled up at Rafael, smoothed his tousled hair and stood on tiptoe to kiss his cheek. Annie, still looking on, wanted to despise the woman, but she found it impossible.

"Was it your poor brother you wanted to kill," Felicia asked gently, "or was it yourself?"

Rafael sighed again, and slipped his arm around Felicia's slender waist. Miss Rendennon would never call *her* fleshy, Annie thought, in despair, slipping behind a suit of armor as the two of them passed by.

"I'm ten kinds of a bastard," Rafael confided.

Annie watched through tears of envy and despair as Felicia linked her arm with Rafael's and smiled up at him.

"And why is that, Your Highness?" she teased.

Even though they were retreating rapidly along the passageway, Annie heard Rafael's reply with brutal clarity. "Lucian accused me of using someone," he said. "And he was right."

The admission struck Annie with all the force of a battle-ax. She sagged against the wall, unseen, feeling the cold stone at her back, and breathed deeply until the worst of the pain had passed. When she'd recovered a little, and was certain Rafael and Felicia were in another part of the keep, she made her way back to her room.

There, she splashed her face with tepid water, took her hair down from its pins, brushed it fiercely, and then put it up again. After that, she got her writing box and set out for the gardens. She meant to draft a letter to her mother and father in Nice and tell them to expect her soon. She could not stay in Bavia; she realized that now. It would be unbearable to remain, even for something as important as Phaedra's wedding, knowing that Rafael pitied her, that he had indeed used her.

She was striding resolutely through the great hall when it struck her that she was hungry, in spite of all that had happened that awful morning. She would start trembling soon, and develop a headache as well, if she didn't take the trouble to feed herself.

Annie headed for the kitchen, only to find Lucian there, having his aristocratic forehead bathed in cool water by a very sympathetic maid. He spotted Annie before she could retreat, and then it was too late to flee for her pride was not going to allow her to be driven off.

She passed him, with a cool nod, and swept into the pantry, where she helped herself to some brown bread, an apple and a portion of cheese. When she came out, balancing these items along with her writing box, Lucian had dismissed the maid and stood waiting, blocking her way to the door.

Looking closely at his fine-boned, elegant face, Annie had a flash of insight. Lucian would never be anything but a caricature of his older brother, she realized, and she felt a stab of pity for him.

"Let me pass," she said, raising her chin. "I have nothing to say to you."

"But I have something to say to you," Lucian responded smoothly, folding his arms. In spite of the thrashing he'd taken from Rafael, he was actually smiling. "I didn't mean to insult you this morning. I was attempting, in fact, to protect your virtue."

The objects Annie was holding shifted, and she struggled, for a few moments, to keep from dropping them. Then she met Lucian's gaze directly. "I can do

94

without your particular sort of chivalry, Mr. St. James," she said, in even tones. "Furthermore, I am quite capable of taking care of myself."

He arched one eyebrow. "The way you did in the cottage the other day?" he countered.

Annie felt heat surge into her face, and in that instant she hated Lucian, truly hated him. She'd had quite enough humiliation since arriving in Bavia without his reminders that everyone in the keep knew about her afternoon of indiscretion.

"You are a gossip, Lucian," she said. "Among other things. You need something constructive to keep yourself occupied."

He grinned, but there was a tightness to his mouth that frightened her just a little. "It is so refreshing," he said, ignoring her question, "that you don't bother to deny what happened between you and Rafael. I warned you about him, Annie. Why didn't you listen?"

She lifted her chin. "I will not discuss this with you. Let me pass."

He stepped aside, but his reply made her stop after only a few steps. "Rafael will seduce you again. Despite his pretty apologies, his talk of his own doom and his noble predictions of another lover awaiting you beyond some future sunrise, he will make you his mistress, Annie. He'll set you up in a grand house in Paris or London or Rome or Madrid, and shower you with jewels and gowns and gifts, none of which will shine half so brightly as the things he'll say to you, late at night, after he's made love to you. And once you've given him what he wants—a sturdy, strapping son with fresh, bold American blood in his veins—he'll take your child to raise as he wishes and kick you aside like some piece of filth he's stumbled across in the street."

Annie turned slowly and met Lucian's eyes. "You are wrong," she said. "If Rafael wanted an heir—and I don't believe he expects to live long enough to sire one—he would not take a mistress. He would marry, so that the child would be legitimate."

Lucian chuckled, and the sound trickled down Annie's spine like a spill of icy water. "Perhaps in other countries, other families, that would be true. In ours . . . ?" he paused, shrugging. "Things are a little different. Rafael himself is a bastard, sprung from the womb of my father's gypsy mistress—she was only one of many, of course—and there was never any doubt that he would inherit the crown. It broke her heart, you know—Papa's first wife, the woman who was supposed to be Rafael's mother. She went into seclusion and eventually died of grief."

Annie retreated a step, and the apple fell to the floor and rolled beneath the cookstove. "None of that is Rafael's fault," she said shakily. Nothing in her past had prepared her for such intrigue and ugliness; her own family was a loving and joyous one, and the passion between her parents was something beautiful and pure. "Why do you hate him so much, Lucian? What did he do to you?"

"Take care that you don't meet the same end as the prince's 'mother,'" Lucian said, before answering her questions. "What did Rafael do to me? He was born first. He stole my birthright and tossed it to the dogs!"

"You're mad," Annie said.

Lucian went into the pantry and returned with another apple, polishing it on his shirt as he approached. Reaching Annie, he held the fruit out to her, an insolent offering. "Here you are, my lovely. Mind you don't take a bite and find yourself sleeping for a hundred years."

Annie accepted the apple and stood silently in the kitchen while Lucian traced her lips with the tip of his index finger and then walked out of the room, whistling.

Felicia's gentle, reasonable words could not comfort Rafael. There were only two remedies for the wildness that had seized him—a violent fencing match or an afternoon in a whore's bed. Since there were no whores present—and he knew even then that only Annie Trevarren would appease his desires—Rafael decided on swordplay. He sent for Barrett.

"Poor Edmund," Felicia commented, watching as Rafael took the rapiers he'd inherited from his wastrel of a father down from the study wall. "He's too proper and too conscious of his place to let himself win, which means he'll get the worst of it, and all the time it's Lucian you really want to skewer."

Rafael scowled at his friend over one shoulder. She understood him as virtually no one else did, and her directness was often unsettling. "If I were to encounter my brother just now, I would probably run him through. Barrett is definitely the lesser of two evils."

Felicia shook her head. "No, Rafael. Barrett is an innocent bystander, and it's his misfortune to be loyal enough to obey your insane demands."

Although the rapiers were a matched set, Rafael had a favorite and he could always recognize it. He grasped the handle and turned the blade to a silvery blur with a few twists of his wrist. "You should be so obedient," he told Felicia, without meeting her eyes. "If you were, you would have left this cursed country long ago. You're a beautiful woman, Felicia, and you are wasted on this wretched place."

She sighed and plopped into a chair with a great flurry of skirts and blond curls. Felicia was more fragile than he'd ever seen her; thinner, with dark shadows under her eyes, and he was worried. "I've told you before, Rafael. When you leave Bavia, so will I."

"Have a care," Rafael replied lightly, hiding his frustration as well as his concern, "that you don't wind up making the journey in a box, the way I probably will."

Tears filled Felicia's eyes, and she leaped out of her chair. "Damn you, Rafael!" she cried. "How can you speak of your own death as though it were some sort of joke!"

He lowered the rapier and watched her as she paced back and forth in a second burst of agitation. "That's the only way I can talk about it at all," he said. "For God's sake, Felicia, you don't have to stay. Get out of Bavia, as soon as the wedding's over, if you won't go sooner, and give up the idea that you can save me from my fate. No one can do that."

"No one but you!" Felicia sobbed. "And you're too stubborn and too stupid to make the effort!" With that, she fled the room, nearly colliding with Barrett in the process.

"That's the second time today you've made a woman flee a room in tears," the bodyguard remarked. "Or were there others I don't know about?"

"Shut up and fight," Rafael replied, taking the second rapier down from the wall and tossing it to Barrett, who caught it deftly.

Barrett shrugged, and they took an outside stairway down to the courtyard, where there was space enough for a battle.

"According to Miss Covington," Rafael said, while Barrett was warming up his sword arm, "you've been letting me win all these years, out of some misguided sense of duty. Is that true?"

The bodyguard smiled. "You are one of the finest swordsmen I've ever run across," he said. "But, yes, there were a few times when I could have bested you."

Rafael was pleased by the honesty of the response, though in truth it stung a little. "Perhaps this is one of those times," he said, raising his rapier. The sunlight sent sparks tumbling along the length of the blade.

"Perhaps," Barrett replied easily, turning to face his opponent.

The rapiers collided with the melodious clang of steel.

"Come now," Rafael scolded. "Is that the best you can do?"

Barrett laughed and, with a hard swing, nearly sent Rafael's rapier flying from his hand. "You wouldn't want the match to end too soon, would you, Your Highness?" he asked. Their blades tangled fiercely, relentlessly, for several minutes. "I didn't think so," Barrett replied, his question answered.

The battle progressed, and the more difficult it became, the better Rafael felt. He fought until he lost all sensation in his arm, until his breath ached in his lungs and his shirt clung to his back and chest, soaked with sweat. He went beyond pain, beyond weariness, and Barrett kept pace, though it was plain that he too had already gone well past his own limits.

Finally, after Rafael had lost track of time, he caught Barrett in a weak moment and disarmed him. The bodyguard's rapier clattered over the stones of the courtyard, and Rafael turned and walked away, strangely disappointed in the victory.

CHAPTER

6

Annie took refuge in a quiet part of the garden near a moss-splotched and crumbling statue of Pan, and seated herself on an equally ancient bench. After sitting still for a few moments, recovering from her confrontation with Lucian in the castle kitchen, trembling with rage and other emotions she couldn't so easily put a name to, she looked down at the wooden writing box on her lap. The food she had purloined from the pantry had vanished, no doubt having been dropped in her wretched hurry to be alone. Despite her agitated state, Annie was hungry.

She sighed, stroking the gleaming cherry wood box with an unsteady hand. The hinged lid slanted, making a desklike surface, and there was a small inkwell at the top, along with a place for pens and pencils to rest. Inside were an assortment of writing implements, a few Swiss postage stamps, which would be useless in Bavia, and a good supply of vellum stationery.

Annie smiled. The lap-desk had been a Christmas gift from her younger sisters—they'd found it together, the four of them, in a little shop in Paris with, so they claimed, no help at all from their mother and current governess. This last assertion was surely an embroidery on the truth, since Gabriella, Melissande, Elisabeth and Christina would not have been permitted to go on such an errand unaccompanied. Patrick and Charlotte Trevarren were not strict parents in the conventional sense, but they cherished their children and made every effort to keep them safe and well.

Feeling better just for thinking about her family, Annie took out a bottle of india ink, her favorite pen, a small felt pen-wipe and several sheets of paper. She had inscribed the date and the words "St. James Keep, Bavia" in the upper right-hand corner, following that with, "Dearest Mama and Papa and Beloved Sisters," when all inspiration abandoned her.

A rustling in the overgrown shrubbery made her stiffen and nearly drop the letter—desk, ink, pen and all. She was in no frame of mind for another encounter with Lucian, nor did she wish to see Phaedra or even Rafael.

It was with considerable relief that Annie recognized Chandler Haslett. His expression was warm and cheerful; there was a refreshing lack of tragedy about this man, and he seemed a straightforward and even-tempered person.

Annie wondered, as she returned his smile of greeting with one of her own, what inherent character flaw had caused her to fall hopelessly in love with a complicated man like Rafael. How much simpler it would have been if she could have given her heart to someone who would cherish her affections and return them in kind.

"I hope I'm not disturbing you," Haslett said, hesitating at the edge of the shrubbery. Annie noticed that he was carrying a small bundle, something wrapped in a checked table napkin, in one hand. He heaved a great, beleaguered sigh, though his eyes were still smiling. "Rafael needs to speak with his gardeners. This part of the grounds puts me in mind of a jungle I once explored. Wouldn't have been at all surprised to meet up with a white tiger or perhaps a band of screeching monkeys."

Annie laughed and slid over a little way on the bench in tacit invitation. Gratefully, Mr. Haslett sat down beside her. His gaze rested on her with kindness, and he held out the bundle.

Annie accepted the offering, only too aware that her eyes were puffy and her nose was red. "What—?"

Before she could complete the question, Mr. Haslett graciously explained. "I confess, Miss Trevarren, that I saw you dashing through the keep a little while ago, dropping bits of food as you went. It was plain that you were upset, and I gambled that you might be hungry as well."

The gentleman's kindness undid Annie as nothing else could have. She sniffled, and her fingers trembled slightly as she untied the corners of the bundle. "You are very thoughtful, Mr. Haslett," she said softly.

"Please," he reprimanded, "call me Chandler. We are friends now, are we not?" His tone was gentle and gruff, and it made Annie want to fling herself into his arms and soak his shoulder with her tears—just what she would have done with her father, if he'd been nearby.

With laudable effort, she held onto her dignity. "Thank you," she said. The words had barely any strength behind them, but she was certain that Chandler had heard them.

Setting aside the lap-desk, she took a large bite of cheese. Her companion waited politely until she'd devoured an apple, a generous slice of bread and every last crumb of the cheese.

"Now," he said, taking her hand, "would you like to talk? I assure you that I am trustworthy, and you'll probably find me sympathetic as well."

Annie felt stronger already, even though the hastily consumed food had barely had time to settle in her stomach. Still, she had not reached her decision to leave St. James Keep lightly, and the prospect of unburdening her heart—just a little—was appealing indeed.

"I'm afraid I won't be able to stay in Bavia for the wedding, Mr. Hasl— Chandler," she confided quietly, brushing bits of cheese and bread from her lap. She'd tossed her apple core into the tall grass, where some small and diligent creature was already laboring to salvage it.

Chandler looked genuinely concerned. "I'm sure the princess will be gravely disappointed, as am I," he replied. "Has there been some offense committed—?"

An offense. Annie took the time to consider the question, making a project of shaking out the checked table napkin in which her food had been wrapped, folding the bit of cloth meticulously, and finally handing it back to her companion.

"Not exactly," she answered. It wouldn't be fair to describe the lovely interlude with Rafael as an offense, however ill-advised it might have been, for she'd enjoyed the experience too well to describe it so. And she wasn't prepared to recount the things Lucian had said to her in the kitchen, either, for she knew that families were like the wild blackberry bushes that grew around Puget Sound—the roots went deep, even in hard ground, and the thorny vines were always entangled with each other.

"Something happened," Chandler insisted, taking her hand. "Did it have to do with Rafael?"

Annie's philosophical mood vanished, as quickly as that, and hot color surged into her cheeks. She'd forgotten, at her peril, that practically everyone in St. James Keep knew about her fall from grace the day before, out by the lake. She would probably have bolted from the bench and gone plunging into the underbrush if Chandler hadn't caught her chin in one hand and made her look at him.

"I love Rafael," she blurted out, without intending to at all. "I *love him.*"

Chandler slowly lowered his hand. "I see," he replied. "And how long have you felt this way?"

Annie battled a fresh spate of tears. Good Heavens, she hadn't cried so much since her first lonely nights at St. Aspasia's, when she'd believed with all her heart that her mother and father had decided to wash their hands of her forever.

"Since I was twelve," she said, and though she managed to make her voice sound brave, for the most part, it did tremble just a bit. "Papa and Mama have been Rafael's friends for a long time, though I daresay they weren't nearly so fond of his father, and with good reason, it would seem. He came to our villa in France quite often, sometimes with his father, and sometimes alone. I had always adored him, but the feelings deepened that particular year, into something I knew would never change."

"You were on the threshold of womanhood," Chandler said. Coming from another man, the statement might have been improper, but Annie knew he'd meant no harm or insult. And he was right.

"Yes."

He smiled fondly. "It must have been wonderful, falling in love that way."

Annie bit her lower lip for a moment, then shook her head. "No, it wasn't wonderful," she said sadly. "It was dreadful. Rafael had brought Lady Georgiana with him on that visit, and he proposed marriage to her on a bench under a pepper tree in our courtyard. They'd been promised to each other as children, and the proposal was only a formality, but it came as a terrible shock to me all the same."

Chandler took her hand and squeezed it lightly, but his expression was one of benevolent amusement. "Poor Annie. You eavesdropped?"

Annie laughed suddenly, surprising herself as much as Chandler, even as the tears she'd been battling stung her eyes. "Quite literally," she replied. "I was in the tree, as it happens, and I fell out, before Georgiana could say yea or nay. I landed at their feet in a heap of crinolines and self-pity."

Chandler chuckled at this recounting, but he also

handed back the napkin Annie had folded so carefully only a few minutes before. "Were you hurt?"

She dabbed at her eyes with the cloth, drew a deep breath and turned to face her new friend, smiling. "Oh, yes. My pride was fractured, and my heart was crushed."

He arched an eyebrow, regarding her with that inherent warmth and humor she had seen in him from the first. "But all your bones were intact?"

"Every last one."

"Did Rafael have any idea that he'd broken your heart?"

Annie shook her head. "I don't think so. But Georgiana knew. And I'll never forget how kind she was, and how gentle. Mama and Papa were away that afternoon, you see, so it was Lady Georgiana who saw to my scrapes and bruises and told me I would find a love of my own someday."

Chandler sighed. "Ah, Georgiana. She was a remarkable woman, and fine—too fine for this earth, I think. It was inspiring, though, to see a love match in our circle."

It was the perfect opportunity to broach a certain concern of hers, and Annie wasn't about to let it pass. "Are they uncommon? Marriages of love, I mean?"

The look in Chandler's light brown eyes told Annie, even before he spoke, that she hadn't been subtle enough. He smiled again, but the expression was sorrowful somehow. "Are you asking me, Annie Trevarren, if I'm in love with the Princess Phaedra?"

She squared her shoulders, trying to ignore the fresh blush burning in her face. "Yes, I guess I am. Are you?"

He rubbed his eyes with one hand and sighed again. "And what gives you the right to ask so personal a question?" he inquired, with curiosity but no evident rancor.

"Phaedra is my best friend. We share everything." *Not everything,* corrected a voice in the back of Annie's mind. *You haven't told Phaedra what really happened between you and Rafael, and she's keeping a secret from you, too. You saw it shining in her eyes just last night, remember?*

"I see. Well, I guess it is only fair, after your account of tumbling out of the pepper tree in the middle of Rafael's marriage proposal, that I speak frankly. No, Miss Trevarren, I do not love Phaedra in the way you mean. I have had neither the time nor the opportunity to develop such a sentiment."

Annie was disappointed. "But the way you looked at her, when you got out of your carriage—the way you kissed her hand—"

Chandler chuckled and shoved splayed fingers through his hair. "Oh, Annie, what a fanciful spirit you are! Yes, my expression was probably fond when I first looked upon Phaedra—she is, after all, a breathtakingly beautiful woman. And our families have been connected for centuries—"

"That was all?" Annie cried, leaping to her feet.

Chandler rose, too, and stood facing her, his gaze earnest and pained. "No," he said. "When I saw Phaedra, all grown up, I realized that one day, with thought and effort on both our parts, we might love each other very much. And that knowledge made me happy indeed."

Annie opened her mouth to speak, realized she had nothing sensible to say and closed it again.

Chandler laid his hands lightly on her shoulders, as a brother might have done. "It's no wonder, really, that you have such whimsical ideas about love," he said hoarsely. "You are a young girl, after all, and you've been sheltered—how could you know that such glorious passion is rare? And what a wretch I am for disillusioning you with the sad truth." He drew in a deep breath, let it out again in a heavy sigh. "Annie, my lovely one, most of us *never* find that kind of love. We have to content ourselves with lesser sentiments that might eventually blossom into happiness."

When he was through, Annie lifted her chin. "How glad I am," she said, "that I am not you."

He allowed his hands to fall to his sides. "God help us all," he murmured. "You're telling me that you feel this sort of love for Rafael, aren't you?"

Annie's chin went up yet another notch. "I believe I said that in the first place. And if you don't feel the same for Phaedra, and she for you, then there shouldn't be a wedding. Not yet."

Chandler turned from her, in apparent frustration, plowing a hand through his hair in an agitated gesture before facing her again. "Forget about Phaedra and me, for the moment," he said. "Annie, you *must not* allow yourself to care so deeply for Rafael St. James." He raised both hands when she started to protest. "No, no, I'm not saying he isn't a good man—he's one of the finest I have ever known. But Rafael is doomed, Annie, just like this crumbling old keep and this damnable country. If you give him your heart, he will probably take it to the grave with him."

Annie retreated a step and closed her eyes, just for a moment, against the painful impact of Chandler's words. "So be it," she said.

109

"Dear God," Chandler murmured, pale. "You can't mean that, Annie. You're so young, so beautiful—you were born to marry, to drive some fortunate fool crazy with exasperation and the wanting of you, to mother children and to spin dreams . . ." He fell silent, regarding her with quiet despair. "Run away, Annie. Leave this place and take your sweet, foolish heart with you."

Annie herself had made almost exactly that decision, not an hour before. As she stood there in that lush, untended garden, however, she knew she would never willingly leave St. James Keep, before or after Phaedra's wedding, unless Rafael was at her side. Slowly, she shook her head.

"I'm staying," she said, and knew she'd just made the most sacred vow of her life.

Chandler sighed and, with a muttered farewell, left her alone in the garden. Annie watched him go—she didn't blame him for doubting the wisdom of her decision, since all his assertions about Rafael had been rational ones. Yet Annie knew from watching the lifelong romance between her parents continuously unfold that love was not necessarily a rational thing.

Rafael had been watching the garden encounter between Annie and Chandler from a high window and he was not pleased. What the devil had they found to talk about, in that out-of-the-way place? What did Haslett think he was doing, touching Annie the way he had, ministering to her so tenderly, as though she, not Phaedra, were his intended bride? And then there was the most troubling question of all—what had ended their meeting so abruptly?

He'd found that more disturbing, somehow, than the earnest conversation and the touching.

Irritated with Chandler, with Annie and, most of all, with himself, Rafael turned from the window and proceeded along the passageway toward one of the rear stairways. He'd been a fool to go after Annie when she'd ridden away from the castle the day before, and an even greater one to kiss her, to teach her the first poignant lessons of pleasure. Now, because he'd so nobly turned from her before taking the satisfaction she would willingly, even eagerly, have given, he was obsessed with the little chit. He had come close to strangling his own brother, and now he was watching people from windows, like some gossiping old woman, and imagining intrigues and betrayals in the bargain.

Cursing, Rafael sprinted down the ancient, foot-worn stairs and strode out into the forgotten garden. Annie was gone, and only Pan remained, with his weather-pitted pipe and impish, insolent smile.

Rafael scowled at the statue and went back inside the castle, fully intending to get a grip on his emotions and press on with the business of preparing for Bavia's inevitable apocalypse. By an ironic coincidence, he almost collided with Chandler, who was standing in the same hallway Rafael chose to pass through, his back and one foot resting against the wall, his head lowered in grave thought.

"You," Chandler scowled, as though faced with the devil himself, and privileged to demand an accounting.

Rafael merely nodded. He was grimly amused but, at the same time, he wanted to pummel his old friend to a pulp for daring to touch Annie Trevarren.

Chandler straightened, tugging at his sleeves—he'd always been insufferably neat—and then turned to face Rafael squarely. "You must send the Trevarren girl away," he said. "Immediately."

A venomous sensation surged through Rafael's system, an ugly one that he had never felt before. "Oh?" he asked calmly. "Why do you ask such a thing? Does the lady present a temptation?"

Blood surged up Chandler's neck and throbbed along his jawline, which had gone taut with fury. His hands were knotted at his sides, and his eyes flashed with what Rafael would have sworn was righteous indignation. "A 'temptation,' Rafael?" he countered. "Are you implying that I would betray your sister's trust? That, indeed, I would betray you, my cousin as well as one of my oldest friends?"

Rafael tasted bile in the back of his throat. He ached to fight with this valued ally and despaired, in the same moment, of his own reason. He tried to speak, but nothing came out.

Chandler relaxed slightly, and laid a hand to the prince's shoulder. "This is no time for us to have differences, Rafael," he said. "You must know by now that I am a man of my word, even if your burdens press you to pretend you believe otherwise."

Now it was Rafael who leaned against the wall, bracing himself with one shoulder and struggling for control. "What were you saying to Annie, out there in the garden?" he asked raggedly, and at great length. "Why were you touching her?"

Chandler laughed, but the sound was bitter and hollow. "So that's why you were suspicious of my intentions. You saw me with Annie."

Rafael nodded. All his earlier tension returned; it took all the restraint he could muster not to grasp Chandler by the throat and choke an explanation from him.

"Annie told me that she's in love with you," Chandler said mercilessly.

"No," Rafael said. It would have hurt less if Chandler had run him through with a broadsword or bludgeoned him with one of the archaic spiked clubs gathering dust in the dungeon. "Dear Jesus, *no*. Annie is a girl, barely out of the schoolroom. She only *thinks* she feels—"

Chandler shook his head. "No, Rafael," he said gravely. "You're wrong on all counts. Annie Trevarren knows precisely what she feels, I'm convinced of that. Furthermore, if the rumors that have been rattling the walls of this old pile of rocks since yesterday are true, you've given the young lady reason, damn your eyes, to think you might care for her in return.

"Damn it, Rafael, you can't just leave that lovely creature twisting in the wind. Either treat her honorably, or send her from this place while there's still time to spare her reputation and her life!"

Rafael did not answer, indeed, he could not. The things Chandler had said were too true, and they'd struck too deeply.

And he, Rafael, should have known what Annie thought and felt, after the way she'd surrendered the day before, after the way she'd bucked and strained under his tongue and his hands and his silken urgings. Yes, he should have known, but he hadn't—he truly hadn't. He'd been loved purely and thoroughly by Georgiana, his cherished, lost Georgiana, and no mortal man could be so blessed twice in one lifetime. Surely not him, Rafael St. James, the gypsy's whelp, the imposter prince.

"Send her away," Chandler pressed, when the silence lengthened.

Rafael moved past his friend, dazed, stumbling a little, blinded to his surroundings by visions of a soft, sweet, yearning body, writhing and arching in unabashed pleasure on the cottage bed. What had he done? What in the name of God had he done?

Annie found Rafael in the chapel an hour after nightfall, sprawled facedown on the front pew, still as death. He might have been a penitent saint, had it not been for the fact that he reeked of whiskey.

Annie glanced nervously toward the altar. "He's been under a lot of pressure," she whispered, to Whoever might be listening. "And it wouldn't hurt You to help him out a little, either."

The prince stirred on the pew, then groaned. Annie hoped he wouldn't retch right there in the chapel, because of his sinful indulgence in ardent spirits. Rafael had trouble enough, it seemed to her, without throwing up on God's sandals.

Tentatively, she touched his shoulder.

"Go away," he moaned.

Annie drew a deep breath, strengthening her resolve. "I'm not going anywhere, Rafael St. James, unless you go with me." She wasn't just refusing to leave the chapel; she was refusing to leave the keep, and Bavia, but she didn't elaborate for he obviously wasn't ready to hear her declaration.

"Rafael," she insisted, in an anxious whisper. "Sit

up. I think you're committing blasphemy or something."

He laughed, a low, rumbling and utterly despondent sound, and turned over onto his back, nearly rolling off the pew onto the cold stone floor in the process. "Ah," he said, with a crooked grin. "An angel. I must be dead."

"You're very much alive," Annie said, grasping his upper arms and hauling him upright, "and it's a good thing, too, for it's certain you're out of grace just at this moment."

"Out of grace," Rafael echoed stupidly, slurring the words and sagging against the back of the pew.

Annie had seen her share of drunks alongside the docks while sailing on her father's ship, though her parents had done their best to shelter her, and she knew an accomplished rum-sucker when she met one. Rafael St. James was definitely an amateur.

"Get up," she ordered, laboring in a largely fruitless effort to hoist the prince to his feet, "before you're struck by lightning or something. Though, of course, you probably deserve it."

"Hasn't anyone ever told you," Rafael inquired, staggering verbally, "that it's foolish to coddle a drunk? Only makes them worse, you know."

"I quite agree," Annie said, breathing hard as she managed, at long last, to get Rafael up off the pew, "and once we're out of this chapel, you're on your own!"

He threw back his head and laughed. "You really think I might be smited by the hand of God," he accused.

Annie headed for the door with very little help from

Rafael, who was leaning heavily on her shoulder. "Smote," she corrected. "Not 'smited.' And I'm taking no chances."

They traveled the length of the center aisle and passed through the doorway into the courtyard, which was now lit only by moonlight and the glow of a few torches on the castle walls.

"I have a confession to make," Rafael said.

"You might have thought of that in there," Annie replied, indicating the chapel with a toss of her head. They were approaching a stone bench, next to the fountain, and Annie's strength was flagging. *Just a few more steps,* she told herself.

Rafael drew in a great gulp of fresh air and promptly hiccoughed. "About my confession," he persisted.

They were getting nearer and nearer their destination. Annie concentrated on the goal and said nothing.

"I used you, Annie."

"I know," Annie replied. Then, with a great and final expenditure of effort, she pushed Rafael St. James, prince of Bavia, into the small pool beneath the courtyard fountain.

He went in with a satisfying splash, and came up tossing his head and swearing. He was furious, but he was on his way to sobriety.

"You were right before," Annie said sweetly. "One should never coddle a drunkard." She started toward the castle doorway at a quick pace then, but Rafael caught up to her in only a few paces and wrenched her around to face him.

Annie might have been frightened of another man in a similar state of annoyance, but this was Rafael, and he was a prince, in his heart as well as his country.

116

For the longest time, he just glared down into her face, breathing hard, his hair drenched and his pewter eyes smoldering with fury. When he spoke, however, his voice was not a shout or a snarl, but a near sob.

"Don't love me," he pleaded. "I'm the wrong man."

She touched his pale, dripping face. "You don't get to decide what I feel, Rafael," she replied. "And believe me, if I'd had any choice in the matter, I certainly wouldn't have lost my heart to you, of all people."

Rafael removed her hand from his cheek, but only after planting a light, defiant kiss on her palm. "Who would you have chosen?" he demanded.

Annie raised her chin. "Not you." She started to walk away, but he still held her wrist, and he drew her back so that she collided with him and felt the wetness of his clothes seeping through her dress.

"Who then?"

Annie thought quickly. "Someone honorable and brave—like Chandler Haslett, or Edmund Barrett. If one of them seduced a lady, they'd do right by her."

Rafael's face tightened, then relaxed again. It was an interesting spectacle and Annie enjoyed it. "Are you saying that I seduced you?" he asked.

"What would you call it?" Annie countered. "You might not have actually . . . well . . . *deflowered* me, but you most certainly took liberties. And now, of course, my reputation is ruined."

He opened his mouth, clamped it shut again, then pushed his hair back from his face with an angry, abrupt motion of one hand. That freed Annie to walk away, and although Rafael didn't try to stop her, he kept pace.

They were midway across the great hall which,

fortunately, was empty, before he found his voice. "What do you want me to do?" he rasped.

Annie assessed her prince out of the corner of one eye. "I want you to marry me," she said, calling upon all the boldness she'd ever possessed.

"What?"

Annie sighed. "To tell you the absolute truth," she confided, as they proceeded toward the stairway, "I enjoyed the things we did. I want to do them all again—as your wife."

"Annie!" Rafael sounded so shocked, so scandalized, that she had to smile.

"If you won't marry me," she said, pressing her advantage, "I shall have no other choice but to seduce you. Your virtue is not safe with me, sir."

At that, Rafael stepped in front of Annie, blocking her way, glowering down into her earnest and upturned face. "Good God, woman, do you have any idea what you're saying?"

"Of course I do," Annie said. "You're the only man I've ever loved, and most likely the only one I ever *will* love. Therefore, if you insist on staying in Bavia and getting yourself killed, I'll just have to make the most of the time in between, won't I?" With that, she moved around Rafael and left him standing, flabbergasted and sopping wet, in the middle of the great hall.

CHAPTER
7

Annie had already climbed the stairs and vanished into the upper regions of the castle before Rafael regained sufficient wit to move at all.

His flesh was clammy beneath his wet clothing and his stomach, unaccustomed to the vast quantities of liquor he'd consumed that evening, was doing a slow, ominous roll. Despite all that, his manhood had risen to embarrassing prominence and taken on the consistency of English oak, pressing painfully against the buttons of his breeches.

Rafael credited *that* to the scandalous things Annie had said to him in the courtyard—after pushing him into the fountain pool, no less. She wanted him, she'd told him so straight out, looking him in the eye the whole time.

These Americans. Even Georgiana had never been so bold, and she'd been a responsive woman.

Hoping he wouldn't meet anyone, Rafael chose a circuitous route to his chambers, navigating the rear passageways and hidden staircases he knew so well. As little as a week before, he could have eased at least one of his maladies by sending for a woman, but now that was impossible. In a peculiar way, although he had no intention of marrying the little chit, he belonged to Annie Trevarren, as surely as he'd once belonged to Georgiana.

Passing Annie's chamber—the room was some distance from his own and he had to go out of his way to do so—Rafael actually considered knocking on the door, going inside, and burying himself in the lush, supple warmth that was Annie.

Honor stopped him, combined with the fact that he was on the verge of losing the contents of his stomach.

In his own quarters, a fire had been lit and the covers of the massive, lonely bed had been turned back. Rafael peeled off his wet clothes and stood naked on the hearth for several minutes, warming himself. His stomach had calmed down by that time, but his erection was as insistent as ever.

He was miserable, needing Annie so desperately, knowing he could not take her and still meet his own gaze in the mirror afterward.

Presently, he blew out the lamps and got into bed, staring up at the darkened ceiling. He would think of Georgiana, he decided, but when he tried, he couldn't bring her image into clear focus. For several terrible moments, Rafael could not recall what his wife had looked like, and the realization filled him with panic and shame. And when the delicate features finally took shape in his mind, they were quickly gone, shifting and blurring and, in the end, fading away.

In the next instant, Annie's face was before him.

Tears burned in Rafael's eyes. "Georgiana," he whispered, trying to bring her back, begging her not to leave his memory and his dreams and his heart.

All the while he knew the effort was futile; Georgiana was gone forever, and so was the child she'd been carrying at the time of her death. Rafael was no longer numb, thanks to Annie Trevarren, and it was impossible to go on pretending that his wife was only away for a little while, visiting friends or shopping in Paris or London.

She was never coming back.

For the first time since the nights immediately following his wife's death, when all the brandy in Europe would not have dulled his sorrow, Rafael wept freely for Georgiana and for the part of himself that had turned to dust with her. It was a new and deeper phase of his mourning, a grief he had not known he felt. His suffering was keen-edged and raw; it loomed over him, took the shape of a dark angel, and he wrestled it the whole night through. He was broken over and over again, utterly defeated a hundred times. His soul was crushed, and there were times when he thought his mind would shatter with the pain, but for all his exquisite anguish, he was somehow purified by the experience. Somehow tempered to a new strength and resilience, like steel put to fire.

Come the light of morning, he was a different man than before; he'd met the dragons lurking in his own spirit, and done battle with them. Though sorely wounded, and tried to the very limits of his endurance, he'd prevailed.

In essence, Rafael had dragged himself out of Georgiana's grave and clawed his way back to the surface. Out of incredible agony had come a new and fierce desire to live.

At dawn, Rafael rose, bathed his sweat-soaked, aching body in tepid water, and put on fresh clothes. Then, after breakfasting in the kitchen, to the consternation of the cook and her giggling minions, he went out to the stables and saddled his favorite horse.

Georgiana's grave was on a high knoll, among many other St. James tombs, shaded by an oak tree and guarded by a circle of elaborately sculpted marble angels. From that sacred place, Rafael could see well beyond the walls of the keep to the glistening sea.

He crouched beside the alabaster headstone and rested a hand against it, but he didn't speak. He'd already said his farewells to Georgiana, and he'd accepted her death. His visit that bright morning was a tribute to all they'd shared, and a promise to be strong, for she would have wanted that more than anything else. There was still much to be faced and endured before the penance of all the St. Jameses was served.

Perhaps an hour passed before Rafael returned to the keep, surrendered his horse to a groom, and made his way to his study.

Barrett appeared within minutes, looking unusually rumpled and not a little sheepish, and while Rafael was troubled by his friend's disquiet, he quickly forgot it. He had other, more pressing matters, to deal with.

"I want you to put together a small detachment of men," Rafael announced. "I'm going out into the countryside to get a firsthand look at the situation. I should have done it long ago."

Barrett went white, and he set down the cup of coffee he'd brought with him on the corner of Rafael's desk, nearly spilling the stuff in the process. His gaze sliced to Rafael's face. "Have you lost your mind entirely?" he demanded. "There are people out there who want to kill you, *Your Highness*, and not in a quick and merciful way!"

Rafael settled back in his chair, one eyebrow raised. "Bavia is still my country," he pointed out quietly, "and I am still its ruler."

The other man leaned against Rafael's desk, bracing himself with both hands, his eyes blazing with weary fire, his right temple pulsing visibly. "I will not stand by and see you commit suicide!" he rasped.

Rafael sighed, took up the pen he'd laid down when Barrett came in, and resumed work on one of the documents his personal messenger had brought from the capital during the night. "Your commitment to my safety is commendable," he said, "but unless you mean to resign your post as head of the royal guard, you will obey any order I give you—regardless of whether or not you think said order is wise. Is that understood?"

Barrett did not back off. "No, damn you, it is not 'understood'! You can take your bloody commands, and your royal guard, and—"

Rafael met Barrett's furious gaze. "What would you have me do?" he asked. "Run away, whimpering and slavering like a kicked dog? Desert my people? You should know me better, after all this time."

A spasm of pain moved in Barrett's usually placid features. He thrust himself away from the desk with an abrupt motion and turned his back on Rafael for a few moments, while struggling with some inner turmoil. When he met Rafael's gaze again, he had recovered somewhat.

"I know you well, my friend," Barrett said. "But being cautious is not the same as running away, or abandoning those subjects who have remained loyal to you. I am merely asking you to—"

"You are asking me to stay within these walls until the rebels scale them. I might as well lie down in my coffin and await their arrival as do that, Barrett, can't you see? I want to look upon my people with my own eyes, hear their words with my own ears, instead of trusting Von Friedling and the others to relay everything."

"Rafael—"

"Arrange for the journey," Rafael broke in coldly, "or step down from your position. The choice is no more complicated than that."

Barrett picked up his coffee cup and hurled it toward the fireplace. It shattered on the hearth, and tiny shards of china exploded into the air. The door of the study, made of ancient wood several inches thick, shuddered on its hinges when he slammed it behind him.

Calmly, Rafael picked up his pen and continued writing. He'd been hard at work for several minutes when a second visitor stormed the citadel.

It was Lucian, the intractable, still visibly ruffled from their confrontation the day before, but smiling with his usual insolence. "I hear Barrett's in a foul mood," he remarked, after some cheerful reflection. "I take it he's against your grand plan to bestow your royal presence upon the adoring rabble?"

Rafael frowned. "Eavesdropping again? That's getting to be a bad habit with you, Lucian."

"It can be a vital skill, for a second son." Despite the early hour, Lucian went to the liquor cabinet and poured himself a stiff drink. Rafael's still-sensitive stomach turned. "Barrett's right, you know," Lucian continued. "Leaving the keep at this point is a genuinely stupid thing to do. Almost certainly suicidal."

Rafael gave up all pretense of working and folded his arms. "I'm sure you'd be crushed to see me go on to my reward," he said, giving the words a wry and bitter twist.

Lucian laughed, spreading the fingers of his right hand and pressing it to his chest. "I would be devastated," he said.

Something tightened within Rafael, but he'd almost throttled his brother the day before and he did not wish to give in to those primitive instincts again. He drew a deep breath, closed his eyes for a moment and spoke in a moderate tone. "I don't have time for this, Lucian," he said. "Make your point, if you have one, and get out."

Raising his brandy in a mocking salute, Lucian smiled savagely. "Congratulations are in order, Your Highness. I've decided to marry."

Despite the enmity between the two of them, Rafael was relieved. He knew Lucian did not share his devotion to the people of Bavia, and once the little rogue was assured of an adequate income, he would surely agree to settle elsewhere with his bride. For his part, Rafael would sleep better, once Lucian and Phaedra were both safely out of the country.

He lowered his gaze to the document on his desk,

not wanting Lucian to see that he was pleased. "You must introduce me to your bride," Rafael said, as if distracted. "In the meantime—"

"Oh, but you know her already," Lucian replied, with wicked relish. "I'm going to marry Annie Trevarren."

Rafael had guessed what Lucian would say, a moment before the name fell from his brother's lips, but knowing hadn't prevented an ugly gorge of fury from rising within him. "Forgive me for pointing up the obvious," he said, after only the briefest hesitation, "but Miss Trevarren has already made it plain that she despises you."

"I can change her mind," Lucian answered confidently. "I'll start by apologizing for all the *terrible* things I've said and done of late. Then I'll show her how noble I am, demonstrate that even though my brother trifled with her virtue and then spurned her affections, *I*, Lucian St. James, am willing to uphold the family honor by taking her to wife." At a low, contemptuous sound from Rafael, he smiled broadly and leaned against the edge of the desk, much as Barrett had done earlier. "You don't think it can happen, do you? Well, consider this, Your Highness: After you've perished at the hands of the rebels, lovely Annie will need consoling. She'll be grateful for my tender sympathies, and we both know, don't we, Rafael, how easily gratitude can be mistaken for love?"

Terrible images whirled through Rafael's mind—he saw his own grave, not on the hillside next to Georgiana's, but at the edge of some blood-washed battlefield. He saw the fiery Annie, weeping for him, envisioned Lucian hovering at her side, waiting like a scavenging bird, catching her when she was most vulnerable. And he knew that to warn Lucian off now would only feed his determination to make his plan succeed.

Rafael was silent.

Lucian crossed the room, filled a second snifter, brought it back and set it down in front of Rafael. "Will you not drink to my happiness, Brother?"

By some miracle, Rafael kept himself from knocking the snifter to the floor in a fit of rage or flinging its contents into Lucian's smug face. Instead, he spoke calmly, coldly. "Report to Barrett within the hour," he said. "He'll assign you a horse and a bedroll for the journey."

Lucian's smile evaporated. "What are you talking about?"

"You've just been conscripted," Rafael replied. "You are now a soldier in the Bavian army."

"You bastard," Lucian breathed. He'd gone white to his hairline and probably his knees as well. "You bloody gypsy *bastard!* You can't do this to me!"

"I can do it," Rafael said, "and I have. Now, report to your commanding officer or I swear by all that's holy, Lucian, I will have you locked up."

"You know I'm not a soldier! I'll be killed—"

Rafael leaned to one side. "Guard!" he called, and instantly the door opened and one of Barrett's burliest men stepped over the threshold, bowed and awaited the prince's command. "Well?" Rafael inquired, his gaze fixed on his brother's face. "Will you show yourself to be a brave man, or a coward?"

Lucian had turned a disturbing shade of gray and broken out in a cold sweat in the bargain. Rafael might have taken pity on him, if it hadn't been for

Lucian's earlier boasts about the plans he'd made for Annie Trevarren.

"Rafael, in the name of heaven—"

"Choose."

Lucian closed his eyes briefly, and when he opened them again they glittered with a new and much deeper hatred than ever before. "I'll serve in your damnable army," he muttered. "But watch your back, Your Highness, because I'm going to make you suffer for this."

Rafael spoke to the guard. "My brother wishes to help defend his country," he said dispassionately, never taking his eyes from Lucian's face. "See that he's outfitted as a soldier."

The moment Lucian and the guard were gone, Rafael fell back in his chair, staring at the glowing amber liquid in the crystal snifter Lucian had set before him so triumphantly. And even though he wondered if he hadn't gone too far this time, he had to smile when he thought of his spoiled younger brother wearing rough clothes and sleeping on the ground.

Annie endured a second seemingly interminable fitting of Phaedra's wedding gown that morning in the solarium. The third time she looked for Rafael on the balcony, he was there, standing in the same spot as before.

Annie's heart quickened at the sight of him, like a bird taking wing. Her first instinct was to lower her eyes demurely, but her native stubbornness prevailed and she held his gaze. She had meant everything she'd said the previous evening, after pushing Rafael into the fountain pool, and it would be foolish to pretend that nothing had happened.

Rafael waited, in silence and shadows, while Miss Rendennon, unaware of his presence this time, completed her endless rituals of pinning and snipping, tugging and twisting. Even when the dressmaker had gone, he didn't speak or move.

Wearing only her chemise and a pair of cotton stockings, Annie was painfully conscious of Rafael's gaze, yet she felt triumph, for even from that distance she sensed his desire. Slowly, resisting the maidenly urge to cover herself in haste, Annie put on the pink shirtwaist and black sateen skirt she'd worn to the fitting.

When Rafael made no move to come down the stairs, Annie climbed them herself, her heart pounding, her cheeks aching with heat, and stood facing him.

His gaze remained fixed on the floor below, and his powerful body exuded both tension and restraint. A pulse leaped along the edge of his jaw.

Annie hesitated, then took a step nearer, laying a hand on his arm. Even through the fabric of his shirt, she could feel the sudden hardening of his muscles and the heat of his flesh. He started to wrench away, then stopped, turning his head toward Annie at last.

She saw anger in his eyes, and the profoundest of sorrows. Their need for each other shimmered between them, like a heat mirage.

"I came to say good-bye," he said, after a long, charged silence.

Annie had expected recriminations, arguments, even fury from Rafael, anything except that quiet, unemotional farewell. She let her hand slip from his arm, too stricken to speak.

Rafael reached out and touched her hair, but the

gesture was an unwilling one, and he quickly withdrew. "I'll be gone a week or ten days," he said. "In the meantime, soldiers will escort you and Phaedra and Felicia to the palace in Morovia to prepare for the wedding ball. During that time, I want you to put aside all your foolish fancies about me."

By biting her lip, raising her chin and thinking defiant thoughts, Annie managed to prevent herself from bursting into tears. "Are you in love with Miss Covington?" she asked. That was the one thing that would have turned her from her course; she would not interfere if Rafael had given his heart to another woman.

He hesitated, just long enough, and when he averted his wondrous silver eyes for a fraction of a moment, Annie knew the truth.

"Suppose I am?" he stalled.

Annie folded her arms and smiled, waiting.

"All right," Rafael snapped, in a harsh undertone. "I love her! Are you happy?"

"Ecstatic," Annie replied. "You're lying."

He swore, grasped her chin in his right hand—another grudging gesture—and bent his head to touch her lips with his own. The contact was featherlight at first, but in the space of an instant, it became a deep, ferocious, soul-jarring kiss.

Annie was transported, conquered, thrilled and terrified, and when Rafael finally tore his mouth from hers, she sagged against him, unable, for the moment, to stand on her own.

He murmured an oath as he held her, but hold her he did, and Annie smiled into the hard warmth of his shoulder. Rafael did not belong to Felicia or to any other woman; she'd seen it in his eyes when he'd tried to lie, and felt it in his kiss. He wanted her, Annie, and as stubborn as he was, he would not be able to resist his own nature for long.

As if he'd somehow managed to divine her thoughts, Rafael gripped Annie's shoulders and held her a little distance away so that he could glare at her. He gave her a slight shake, but she knew somehow that he was more exasperated with himself than with her.

"Damn it," he hissed, "it would serve you right if I took you to my bed this minute and showed you what it means to surrender to a man!"

Annie felt her eyes widen. "I think I know," she said loftily. But she didn't, of course, not really, even though she'd seen the act of love once, in a book of erotic drawings one of her classmates had smuggled into St. Aspasia's.

Rafael laughed, but there was no joy in the sound. It was a low, harsh bark of fury and frustration. "You think you know?" he taunted. He took her hand in his and pressed it to the long and frightfully hard bulge at the front of his breeches. "Feel the reality, Annie," he commanded. "Imagine taking me inside you—*deep* inside you—"

Heat suffused Annie, body and soul, and she nearly swooned, she was so overwhelmed, but she made no effort to pull away. Even though touching Rafael that way terrified her, it also made her want him more.

Quietly, boldly, she turned the tables. "Imagine *being* deep inside me," she told him. "Think how it would be, Rafael."

He released Annie with a furious motion and turned his back on her, and she watched, fascinated, full of joy and power, while he struggled with emotions she could only guess at. Tentatively, she laid her hands on his shoulders, felt him flinch beneath her touch as if her fingers had burned his flesh.

"I'm not afraid," she said softly.

Rafael tilted his head back, but he did not turn to face Annie. "Well, I am," he replied hoarsely, and then he strode away, leaving her there on the balcony to stare after him.

Annie stood still for a few moments, breathless and flushed, then hurried off in the opposite direction. She did not regret anything she'd said or felt or done, but the sensations were new to her, and powerful, and they raged inside her like a sweet storm. She hurried down the stairs and out of the solarium, stopping only when she'd reached the privacy of her bedchamber.

There, she tore off the confining dress and the petticoat beneath, replacing them with her beloved breeches and shirt. After adding boots to the ensemble, Annie left the keep, by way of the kitchen, heading in the opposite direction of the stables, where there was a great deal of activity. If she didn't keep moving, if she didn't find a way to dispel the frightening energy that had gathered in her middle when Rafael kissed her, and then pressed her hand to him, she was certain she would explode.

The important thing was to *do something,* to avoid standing still and thinking at all cost.

Beyond the kitchen was a vegetable garden and beyond that, a chicken yard and a variety of small, ramshackle sheds. Annie made her way past them, toward the high outer wall, with its crenelated top. No trees were allowed to grow near the structure, for obvious reasons, and a close examination proved that there were no handholds in the ancient stone.

She'd gone less than a mile when she found a gate hidden behind a cascade of thick ivy.

The iron latch was rusted, and Annie struggled with it until she was breathless, until her hair was tumbling down and her shirt was damp with perspiration. Finally, however, her persistence paid off, and she was able to slide the long bar to one side.

The gate's hinges were almost as recalcitrant as the latch had been, but she managed to haul it back far enough to peer through the opening.

At first, Annie was disappointed, because she'd expected to see open countryside, and the distant ocean, on the other side. Instead, she found a dark, cavelike room, full of dust and cobwebs and spiders. After making sure that the gate wasn't going to close behind her, entombing her in that cool and spooky place, she took a few steps inside.

At first, there was only gloom, but as Annie's curiosity drew her farther, she saw that thin splashes of sunlight were spilling through in places. The cave had not been used in decades, perhaps even in centuries, but here and there she glimpsed indications of human habitation.

There were crude cooking pots in one corner, and a rotted saddle in another. At the far end, swathed in spiderwebs, was another gate, but this time, even using all her strength, Annie could not get it open.

When a rat the size of a house cat brushed against Annie's ankle, her fascination give way to fright. She dashed back to the entrance and floundered through the ivy and out into the sunshine. There, Annie stood gazing upon her discovery and wondering if Rafael, or anyone in St. James Keep, knew of its existence.

She hoped not.

After carefully closing the gate and making sure the dusty vines and leaves of the ivy hid the passage completely, Annie started back, by a different way, toward the castle.

There were at least fifty horses and riders in the outer courtyard, and the main gate stood open. Annie, hiding behind a mossy statue at the edge of the garden, caught her breath when she saw Rafael, mounted on the ·magnificent black gelding. Beside him, as usual, rode Edmund Barrett.

Although Rafael had told Annie he was leaving the keep, she was devastated by the reality of seeing him go. She watched, in silent despair, as Rafael and Mr. Barrett led the troops through the great gate.

The hooves of all those horses, striking the hard wood of the drawbridge, raised a deafening clatter. Annie watched until the last rider had passed through the archway and winced when the portcullis crashed into place.

Closing her eyes, Annie offered a quick, silent prayer that Rafael would return, safely and soon. When she turned to go inside the castle, she nearly collided with Chandler Haslett.

She would have preferred to encounter no one at all, but at least she didn't have to pretend with Chandler. He knew how she felt about Rafael because she'd confided in him the day before, in the garden.

Taking in her tumble-down hair, her smudged shirt and breeches, Chandler smiled and shook his head. "What a delightful little hoyden you are, Annie Trevarren," he said, with gentle humor. "I almost envy Rafael the reckless passion you feel for him."

For one wretched moment, Annie thought he'd witnessed the interlude between her and Rafael on the solarium balcony, and she went crimson with mortification. Just as quickly, she realized that she'd jumped to conclusions, and she smiled shakily as she ran damp palms down the sides of her dusty trousers. "Was that a compliment or an insult?"

Chandler laughed and took her arm, pulling her gently toward the castle. "The former, of course," he said. He looked at her disreputable clothing again. "Good heavens, what have you been doing? Climbing trees? Crawling through gopher holes?"

Annie didn't want to tell anyone except Rafael about the hidden gate she'd found, or the stranger chamber beyond it, though she couldn't have explained her reasons. She changed the subject. "Where were Rafael and Mr. Barrett going with all those soldiers?"

He sighed. Annie saw concern in the pleasant, aristocratic face and liked Mr. Haslett all the more for knowing that he cared about Rafael's safety. "It would seem that my future brother-in-law has decided to meet with the common people."

Annie stopped in her tracks, as chilled as if someone had flung a bucket of icy well water all over her. "But that's dangerous—Rafael has so many enemies!"

Chandler nodded and tugged Annie gently into motion again. "Yes," he agreed solemnly. "Even a day ago, I would have feared that Rafael was deliberately riding out to meet his own death. I spoke with him before he left, however, and I saw an interesting change in him."

They entered the great hall, but not before Annie cast one last, longing glance toward the main gate, which was just visible through the portcullis.

"What sort of change?" she asked, as hope pooled like sun-warmed honey in her heart.

Chandler gave her a wry, sidelong glance. "I wouldn't presume to guess," he said. "Now, I'd suggest you take yourself to your room, put on some proper clothes and pack your bags." He laughed at her startled expression and hastened to go on. "No, my sweet, you're not being banished from the castle, if that's what you're thinking. There is to be an engagement ball in Morovia at week's end, remember? You and Phaedra and I are traveling to the palace—Miss Covington will accompany us, as a chaperon—to make ready."

Annie recalled then that Rafael had mentioned the journey earlier, and her heart sank. Without a certain prince in attendance, it wouldn't be much of a ball.

CHAPTER

8

Annie stood on the terrace outside her bedchamber, still clad in her mannish garb of breeches, boots and shirt, watching Rafael's party moving away along the seacoast road. Her throat was tight and her eyes burned, and several minutes passed before she heard the soft, wretched sobbing coming from the room next to hers. Frowning, Annie turned and saw that the French doors leading onto Phaedra's terrace were slightly open, their gauzy curtains blowing in the breeze.

"Phaedra?" she called.

The weeping ceased, and the princess came out onto her balcony, her dark hair tangled and trailing down her back, her eyes huge, her skin pale as lilies on a moonlit night. She was wearing a long, flowing white nightgown, even though it was midafternoon, and the garment added appreciably to her air of tragedy.

Annie crossed to the railing and leaned forward, shocked by the state of her friend's emotions. "Good heavens, Phaedra," she whispered, "what's happened?"

Phaedra was following the progress of the departing troops, her arms folded across her bosom. "Suppose he's killed?" she murmured.

Although Annie had fears of her own, she felt duty-bound to encourage the princess and help her see the situation from a positive prospective. "Rafael is an excellent swordsman, and I'll wager there isn't a better rider in the whole of Bavia. We must depend on his strength and skills, and our own prayers, of course, to see him through—"

Phaedra's eyes were haunted when she turned, in slow surprise, to look at Annie. "Rafael?" she murmured, as though she'd never heard the name before. Recognition stirred, followed by impatience. "I wasn't thinking about him."

Annie was confused and not a little annoyed. "Then who?" she demanded.

Another change came over Phaedra just then; she straightened her back and raised her chin, and when she looked toward the rapidly disappearing soldiers again, Annie saw color rise in her face. She met Annie's gaze once more, and this time her eyes were bright with some fiery emotion—resolve, perhaps. "Lucian," she said, in a brittle tone. "Didn't you hear? Rafael forced him into the army. He's a soldier, now."

Annie did not believe for a moment that Phaedra had been weeping so aggrievedly over Lucian; the two had never been close. She knew, however, that it wouldn't help to press for the truth while the princess was upset, so she forced a cheerful note into her voice and asked, "Have you started packing for the trip to Morovia, yet?"

Phaedra shook her head, cast one last forlorn look toward the coast road, then turned and retreated into her room.

That afternoon, when they set out for the capital, there were three passengers in Chandler Haslett's spacious and well-appointed coach besides himself—Annie, Miss Felicia Covington and a silent, distracted Phaedra. Another carriage would travel behind theirs, loaded down with trunks and boxes, and a contingent of two dozen soldiers had been reserved for the purpose of escorting the little group safely to the front entrance of the palace.

Although she missed Rafael dreadfully and feared for his well-being, Annie was cheered by the prospect of adventure. It would have been excruciating to be left behind at St. James Keep for upward of a week, with nothing to look forward to except the prince's return. And if she wasn't particularly thrilled by the idea of attending the ball, there was still the pleasure of exploring Morovia in general, and the palace in particular.

Phaedra stared wanly off into space, while Chandler and Miss Covington engaged in benign gossip about a mutual acquaintance in England. Annie listened for a while, grew bored, and turned her attention to the sparkling blue-green sea. She caught its salty scent through the open carriage window, felt the mist on her face, and knew a poignant longing for the peace and relative safety of the family island in the South Pacific.

The trip from St. James Keep to the walled city of Morovia was short, and they arrived at the great outer gate after only about two hours of travel. Phaedra remained listless and inattentive, even after they had been granted entrance and the carriage was rolling over stone streets so old that knights and wandering troubadours had trod upon them. Annie saw that Chandler had noticed his future bride's pensive mood, and that he was troubled by it. Felicia, too, had turned thoughtful since their arrival, though a vague smile played at the corners of her mouth.

Annie had concluded that Rafael and Miss Covington were not lovers, but she knew the bond between them was a close one nonetheless. It would be a grave mistake to think the other woman wasn't a rival for the prince's affections. As Annie had already learned, marriages among the European aristocracy were seldom based on love and passion.

Evidently sensing Annie's perusal, Miss Covington turned from the window and smiled. Her brown eyes shone with good-natured amusement and some private and vaguely frenetic excitement.

Caught staring, Annie blushed and looked away. Mentally scolding herself, she fixed her attention on the narrow streets of Morovia, the little stone houses with their ornate balconies and tiled roofs, the fountains and statues in the squares they passed. Housewives and merchants and tradesmen, children and old women, gathered in doorways and shop windows to watch the procession, their expressions sullen and sorrowful. Even with Mr. Barrett's guards on all sides, Annie didn't feel safe.

When the streets grew wider and the houses were larger and farther apart, Annie concluded that they were nearing the palace. Before they could reach it, however, a stone or brick struck the side of the carriage, and there was a great commotion among the soldiers. There were shouts, fearful cries from the horses, and then a shower of stones.

Annie's fear was exceeded only by her curiosity, and she tried to lean out the window to get a look at their attackers, only to be wrenched unceremoniously back onto the seat by Chandler Haslett. He'd already pushed Phaedra to the floor of the carriage, where she crouched, trembling, along with Felicia.

"For God's sake, Annie," he rasped, as gunfire was heard outside, along with angry bellows, "get down!"

When she didn't immediately obey—she was stunned, not stubborn—Chandler swore and virtually flung her onto her face on the carriage seat opposite his own. Having done that, he attempted to shield the women with his own person, an act that won him Annie's eternal admiration.

There was a great clanging sound, and the terrible din outside subsided a little. Annie looked up, through the crook of Chandler's elbow, and saw one of the soldiers peering in through the carriage window.

"You're safe now," the guard said.

Chandler rose and climbed nimbly out of the coach. Annie scrambled out after him, while Phaedra and Felicia untangled themselves and got up from the floor to follow.

They were inside the palace courtyard, Annie quickly deduced, and soldiers and horses milled all around them, in a sort of organized uproar. The gates, twelve feet high and made of what appeared to be woven iron, were closed and secured, and the brick walls on either side were being patrolled by sentries. The mob could be heard grumbling and shouting in the street beyond.

Felicia came to Annie's side and took her arm, ushering her toward the entrance of the palace, a massive building constructed of quartz-speckled white stone. Annie glanced back over one shoulder just in time to see Phaedra slip into a swoon. Fortunately, Chandler was standing close by, and he caught the princess deftly and lifted her limp form into his arms.

"Hurry," Felicia said, pulling Annie between the towering pillars, up the marble steps and into the vast entryway beyond. "Some of those people out there might have guns."

Phaedra was already coming around as Chandler carried her inside, but her skin was the color of milk, and her eyes seemed twice their normal size. Jawline tight, Chandler called for a servant and proceeded up the curved stairway to the second floor.

Annie started to follow, then stopped, gripping the gilded newel post. "Do you think Phaedra will be all right?" she asked.

Felicia spoke matter-of-factly. "Yes, the St. Jameses are a hardy lot—it takes more than a mere revolution to finish them."

When Annie turned, she saw that the other woman was adjusting the hairpins that held her masses of silver-blond curls in place. She had already shed her cloak and tugged her gloves off.

Even inside the palace, with the doors closed and servants bustling up the stairs in response to Chandler's brusque summons, Annie heard shouting between the soldiers and the people outside the gates. For the first time, she truly understood the seriousness of the situation that Rafael faced and she was shaken to the heart.

At that moment, she would have given everything she had to be at Rafael's side, wherever he was. Even if she couldn't protect him, and she was wise enough to know that she couldn't, she would at least have known what was happening to him.

One of the maids stood ready to show Annie and Miss Covington to their rooms. The girl was understandably agitated, and Annie wondered if there was a riot every time someone left or entered the palace grounds. She decided to ask the question later, along with a few others.

Her chamber was a charming, airy place, with a balcony overlooking a small rose garden. Within the tangle of budding flowers was a fountain encircled by a stone bench. An enormous yellow tabby cat slept there, sprawled on its back, paws akimbo, abandoning itself to the afternoon sunshine. Obviously, the incident in the street hadn't disturbed the puss unduly.

With a tentative smile, Annie left the terrace for the interior of the room. A second maid had arrived, carrying a plain wooden tray. She set a crockery teapot on a small table next to the windows, along with a plate of scones and the appropriate condiments, and scurried out. Only then did Annie glance at the walls and floors and realize that, like those in St. James Keep, they were bare of decoration.

The first serving girl lingered, unpacking Annie's trunk and laying out her gowns, one by one, on the spacious bed.

Annie sat down at the table, poured tea, and added butter and jam to a scone. She was feeling melancholy and quite hopeless at the moment, but she knew a little sustenance would do wonders for her state of mind.

"What's your name?" she asked the maid, who looked up at the question, and flushed crimson.

"It's Kathleen, ma'am," she said, with a quick curtsey.

Annie felt a touch of exasperation. "You needn't call me 'ma'am' or bend your knees like that when I speak to you, Kathleen. I'm not a member of the aristocracy, after all."

Kathleen glanced at her and smoothed the skirts of Annie's new yellow gown with stubby-fingered, work reddened hands. "Very well, ma'am," she said, bobbing her head. "Whatever you say."

With a sigh, Annie reached for her teacup, which was chipped at the rim. "What's it like to live here?" she asked, once she'd swallowed a few sips of the hot, bracing brew. "I mean, are there riots whenever you try to go out to the shops or the market?"

The servant unpacked another garment and laid it out carefully. There was something almost reverent in the way Kathleen touched the rich fabric. "No, miss," she said. "We don't have no problems of that sort unless someone from the royal family comes to stay." She risked a look in Annie's direction and blushed again. "Begging your pardon, miss."

Annie finished her tea and nibbled at the scone with an unusual lack of enthusiasm. "It's Rafael—the prince—they hate, isn't it?" she asked sadly.

Kathleen had progressed to hanging Annie's gowns in the ornate antique armoire. "Yes, miss," she answered, with a note of resignation in her voice. Plainly, she would have preferred silence to conversation.

Pushing her chair back, Annie left the table and

stood at the window, her back to the room, and gazed on the tops of roofs and trees rising beyond the palace walls. "No one who really knew the prince could ever hate him," she said.

"No, miss," Kathleen agreed readily.

Annie sighed, *Rafael*, she pleaded silently, *be careful.*

The village was a small one, nothing more than a few huts huddled together at one end of a long meadow, really. There were a handful of sheep wandering about, bleating mournfully, and most of the residents kept chickens, which scattered, squawking, when Rafael, Barrett and the band of soldiers arrived.

Rafael didn't see one woman or child. He supposed they'd been ordered into hiding when the party of horsemen was first sighted, but the men of the village had gathered to greet them. They were armed with primitive weapons, stones and bits of firewood, and Rafael felt genuine grief as he looked upon them.

They had reason to fear, he thought bitterly, after the raids his father and grandfather—and countless other St. Jameses before them—had carried out in village after village. Women had been raped, children terrified and trampled, precious sheep and cattle killed and roasted over the raiders' campfires.

"Tell them we don't mean them any harm," Rafael said to the man who rode at his left. Barrett, as usual, had stationed himself to the prince's right.

The soldier nodded and climbed down from his horse to approach the villagers. While all Bavians spoke English, and had done so for centuries, because of an early alliance with Great Britain, Rafael dared not approach the common people without an emissary to open the way. To speak to them without proper introduction would have been a violation of custom.

While Barrett's man addressed the villagers, they muttered among themselves, and cast suspicious glances at Rafael.

Barrett shifted uneasily in his saddle. He hadn't wanted to make this journey in the first place; he'd made that plain enough, and he'd been sulking ever since they'd left the keep. Without looking at Rafael, he muttered, "Here they are, Your Highness. Your loyal subjects."

Rafael's only reply was a rueful smile. The soldiers behind them stayed in ranks, but he could feel their restlessness and impatience; they were boys, really, used to being billeted at the keep in relative comfort, where they played at cards and dice in their free time, and stood guard or practiced with swords and rifles while on duty. In actual warfare, they would probably be virtually useless, Barrett's leadership skills notwithstanding.

The conference between Barrett's lieutenant and the men of the village continued in fiery undertones. Finally, the young soldier turned from them, addressing his words to Barrett, not Rafael himself.

"They're afraid of us, sir. And they're hungry."

Rafael spoke before Barrett had a chance to reply. "Tell them we'll share our rations," he said.

This announcement roused an angry murmur in the ranks; Rafael quelled it by standing in his stirrups and taking in the entire company in one scathing glance. His gaze caught on Lucian's pale, furious face and he tendered a mocking salute before shifting his attention back to Barrett.

To Rafael's relief, he saw a certain amused approval in his old friend's eyes. Barrett inclined his head, then reined his horse around and rode to the rear. The supply wagon was just catching up to the troops.

Dried beans, potatoes, flour and turnips were hauled to the front and given to the villagers, who quickly divided the booty and carried it off to their huts. In the meantime, Barrett ordered his men to set up camp in the next meadow and, as the sun crumbled into dancing crimson pieces on the dark sea, bedrolls were unfurled on the soft grass and campfires were kindled.

"Just what do you hope to accomplish by this?" Barrett asked of Rafael, once the soldiers had settled down to eat and talk and play dice near the fires. They were seated on the ground, consuming their dinners of boiled turnips and hard bread from metal plates. "Giving these poor wretches a few staples won't make them forgive seven hundred years of oppression, you know."

Rafael set his plate aside. "I had only one aim in mind," he replied grimly. "To fill their bellies for a day or two."

Barrett consumed a second piece of bread, the reflection of the fire flickering over his face. "You're a few centuries too late, I think." He sighed and turned to face his old friend in the gathering darkness. "All your efforts have been too long in coming. You can't change anything by staying in Bavia. Or by dying here."

The image of Annie Trevarren filled Rafael's mind; he felt a corresponding wrench in his heart and a heavy thickening deep in his loins. She hadn't been far from his thoughts since that morning on the balcony

147

of the solarium, when she'd touched him so intimately, and flung his own challenge back in his face. *Imagine being inside me, Rafael,* she'd said.

Rafael had been suffering exquisitely ever since.

"I don't want to die," he told Barrett, at length, "though I know that's what you think."

"Of course it's what I think," Barrett scoffed, taking up a stick and idly stirring the fire from where he sat. "Some part of you wants to atone for the sins of the St. James family, like a sacrificial lamb. If that wasn't so, you'd have closed the palace and the keep long ago and left Bavia forever. God knows, you've got private money—enough to start a new life anywhere in the world. Or have you given that away, too?"

Rafael's smile was bitter. Yes, he had a small fortune—the remains of his grandmother's dowry, wisely invested—but Bavia was the only home he'd ever known. For all the sins of his forefathers, and they were many, he loved that small, beautiful country, tucked between France and Spain, the Mediterranean Sea sparkling at its white, sandy throat like a living jewel. He cherished the fishing villages, the medieval churches, the broken remnants of roads built by the Romans, the castles and the cottages. Most of all, he loved the people, the simple, hardworking, spirited souls who were the essence of the country.

And they despised him in return.

"This is my home," he said, after a long silence.

Barrett settled back against his saddle. "Home isn't necessarily a country or a castle, Rafael," he replied. "Sometimes, it's a person."

Rafael was vaguely troubled by Barrett's words,

poetic as they were. He almost asked his friend if he'd gotten over his silly infatuation with Phaedra, but in the end he kept silent. Barrett was no fool; he knew the preparations for the princess' wedding were well underway, and of course, he'd met Chandler Haslett. By now, he had surely come to his senses and taken up with some maid or tradesman's daughter.

"Someone like Annie Trevarren, for instance," Barrett said, reaching for the metal cup that held the grainy, foul-tasting coffee.

The remark took Rafael by surprise, though he supposed it shouldn't have. Rumors had spread quickly after he and Annie had been found together in the fishing cottage and Barrett had arrived in plenty of time to assess the situation for himself.

"Exactly what do you mean by that?" Rafael asked evenly, reaching for his own mug of coffee, and staring blindly into the fire. He took a mouthful of the swill and spat it out before Barrett had a chance to reply.

The bodyguard laughed, but there was sadness in the sound, a sorrow that resonated in Rafael's own spirit. "We are old friends," Barrett said, after a few moments of reflection. "Still, I suppose there are some things we cannot speak of."

"Oh, yes," Rafael agreed grimly. "There are, indeed."

"But the lovely Miss Trevarren is another matter." Barrett took the liberty of presuming. "Sometimes I think she is not a mortal woman at all, but an angel come to lure you out of this godforsaken place."

Rafael made a low, contemptuous sound. "Annie? An angel? Have you forgotten already, Barrett, that she nearly got herself killed through mischief, only a few nights ago?" The more he thought about the idea, the more preposterous it seemed. "An angel," he muttered, recalling how she'd deliberately tempted him, on more than one occasion, how she'd pretended to come to his aid and then pushed him into the courtyard fountain at St. James Keep. "More like a devil," he finished.

Barrett chuckled and, once again, despondency echoed in the sound. "Or a perfect combination of the two," he speculated, rubbing his chin thoughtfully. His face was in shadow when he turned to look at his companion. "Don't be a fool," he urged, and by his voice, Rafael knew he was utterly serious. "Annie is beautiful and spirited, and she loves you. Take her to France, or to America—good God, Rafael, take her *anywhere* away from here! Marry her, and sire a houseful of children—"

"Never," Rafael vowed, looking up at the dark sky, scattered with silvery stars, but the dream had been roused, and it would not be laid to rest so easily.

With an exasperated curse, Barrett thrust himself to his feet. "I'll see to the men, Your Highness," he said, with biting politeness. "Rest well, and in the morning, we'll proceed on our foolish and useless quest."

Rafael would not have tolerated such insolence from any other man on earth, but because Barrett was his closest friend, and because he understood the man's frustration, he said nothing. After laying out his bedroll Rafael went to the edge of camp to check on his horse. Along with all the others, the gelding was confined within an improvised corral of rope strung between several trees.

Nodding to the guards, Rafael summoned the animal with a low whistle, and it came to him eagerly, nickering, ready to take wing and fly if that was what its master wanted.

Rafael stroked the gelding's coal black nose and gave him one of the lumps of sugar he'd brought along in his saddlebags for just this purpose.

"He obeys you," commented a familiar voice, from just behind Rafael's right shoulder.

He didn't turn to face Lucian, but continued to stroke the horse. "Yes. You might learn from him."

Lucian would not be ignored; he moved to stand beside Rafael. He looked different in his plain soldier's clothes, a blue coat and breeches, boots and a gray shirt. "You win, Rafael," he said hoarsely. "I've had enough of taking orders from men who wouldn't have presumed to look me straight in the eye just yesterday."

Rafael sighed. He meant to release his brother from the Bavian army before the revolution came, of course, but in the meantime, he thought a little discipline might do Lucian good. Perhaps it would even strengthen him, render him fit for some kind of useful life after he'd left the country. "Not yet, Lucian," he said.

Lucian started to grab Rafael's arm in a burst of temper, but when one of the guards started toward him almost within the same instant, he let his hand fall to his side. "What do you mean, 'not yet'?" he demanded, in a harsh whisper. "Do you want me to grovel, is that it? Do you expect me to beg?"

"No," Rafael said, reluctantly turning away from the faithful gelding and starting back toward the main part of camp. "That would be a pointless humiliation, considering that no amount of pleading would ever change my mind. You're a soldier in the Bavian army, Lucian. Accept it."

Lucian scrambled along at his side, barely controlling his desperation. "Rafael," he gasped, "I'm afraid."

At that, Rafael stopped and faced his half brother, laying his hands on Lucian's shoulders. When he spoke, it was with genuine affection for the boy Lucian had once been, and for the man Rafael knew he could become if only he made the proper choices.

"I'm afraid, too," Rafael said. "We all are."

Tears of anger and frustration rose in Lucian's eyes, but he offered no further arguments. He simply twisted free of Rafael's grasp and strode away toward the main part of the camp.

Rafael hesitated briefly, then returned to his own fire, pulled off his boots and crawled into his bedroll. He held off sleep as long as he could, fearing the terrible nightmares of blood and fire and death that had been troubling him of late.

Still, he was exhausted and was soon overtaken by slumber. Instead of destruction, he dreamed of Annie Trevarren, smiling up at him as he stood on the balcony of the solarium at St. James Keep, swathed in the glimmering white silk of a wedding dress.

After the drama of their arrival at the Royal Palace of Morovia, the quiet days that followed were something of a disappointment to Annie. Everyone else in the house, however, seemed vastly relieved to enjoy some peace and quiet.

Phaedra soon recovered from whatever had ailed

her on the journey from the keep to the capital, though Annie often found her standing at one of the windows, watching the gate and the street behind it.

Miss Agusta Rendennon followed them into the city, unmolested by rebels or malcontents, and brought Phaedra's burgeoning, unwieldy wedding dress with her. The tiresome fittings continued, and the princess always managed to be in some other part of the palace—no one seemed to know exactly where —whenever Miss Rendennon decided to work.

It was after one such session, when the dressmaker had gotten into her carriage and gone back to her shop, that Annie managed to run Phaedra to ground in the library, and confront her.

"I'm tired of being fitted for a dress I'll never wear," Annie blurted out, without offering so much as a nod of greeting first. Having gotten up steam, she continued with conviction. "Why, it's downright silly, Phaedra St. James! What do you mean to do if, on your wedding day, you go to put the gown on and it doesn't fit? Answer me that, if you please. What will you do?"

Phaedra laughed. "You're letting your imagination run away with you, Annie," she scolded, taking a leatherbound book from a shelf and tracing its edge with the tip of her index finger. "Of course the gown will fit, goose—we're almost exactly the same size. How many times have we worn each other's frocks?"

Some of Annie's steam evaporated, but her irritation did not abate. "It's still odd," she insisted. "Any other bride would be excited—"

That dreamy, somewhat tragic expression shadowed Phaedra's eyes again, but only for a flicker of time. "Oh, Annie, do stop behaving like such a curmudgeon. I am excited—Mr. Haslett is a dear and kind man—it's just that standing still for those fittings would bore me to the very edge of madness!"

Annie sighed. "I can testify from personal experience that it would," she agreed ruefully, but a smile was already tugging at one corner of her mouth because this was the Phaedra she knew and loved. The one she'd almost given up for lost.

"And speaking of excitement," Phaedra began, lowering her voice and glancing toward the library doors to make sure they weren't overheard, "I believe it's high time we had some."

A rush of expectancy and sweet terror went through Annie's system. She, too, glanced toward the doors. "Tell me!"

Phaedra came to stand within confiding distance, her forehead practically touching Annie's. "We're going to explore the shops," she whispered.

Annie loved an adventure as much as the next young woman, perhaps more, in fact, but the memory of the angry, stone-throwing mob that had greeted them on their arrival at the palace had not faded from her mind. "You can't be suggesting that we leave the grounds—"

Already, Phaedra was nodding. "It's not a suggestion, Annie Trevarren," she teased. "It's a royal decree."

"But the rebels—"

The princess folded her arms and tapped one daintily slippered foot in annoyance. "For mercy's sake, Annie, I'm not saying we should have the palace carriage brought around! We'll dress as maids, in plain dresses, with scarves on our heads and baskets to carry."

The idea was rash, but it was also intriguing. It would be an expedition like none they had ever undertaken, even in their heyday at St. Aspasia's. It would be a spectacular exploit they could both smile over in later years.

Provided, of course, that nothing went wrong.

Annie recalled the young maid, Kathleen, telling her that the servants traveled in and out of the palace without difficulty. "But we couldn't actually go into the shops, could we? Not dressed as servants?"

Phaedra was already heading purposefully out of the library. "We'll look through the windows," she told Annie in an impatient whisper, "and if we see something we want, we'll send for it later. Besides, we'll have the run of the marketplace."

Within half an hour, Phaedra and Annie had climbed, via a rear stairway, to the uppermost floor of the grand palace, where the female servants were quartered. The long, narrow chamber was vacant, since all the maids were working at various tasks in other parts of the house.

Annie hesitated in the doorway, touched by the row of Spartan, neatly made cots lining the wall, by the plain washstand and pitcher that stood next to each bed. On one pillow rested a bedraggled cloth doll, with a stitched-on mouth and single black button for an eye. The servants' spare dresses—it seemed each possessed only one—were hung carefully from pegs arranged beneath the high windows. "Phaedra," she said, "these things are all they have."

Phaedra grasped Annie's hand and tugged. "Don't be a coward," she said. "It's not like we're stealing the things we need—we're only borrowing." The princess took a gray frock down from its peg and held it against her chest. "If it'll make you feel better, we'll leave a few coins behind." She preened as if she were holding up a jeweled gown of the finest silk instead of a rag that had been pressed and mended with pride. "What do you think?"

It seemed more diplomatic not to answer at all.

CHAPTER
9

Barely fifteen minutes later, Annie and Phaedra were wearing the ill-fitting frocks they'd "borrowed" from the servants' quarters. Scarves covered their hair and shadowed their faces, and they were careful to keep their eyes down when they approached the tradesman's gate behind the carriage house.

The guard on duty was a young man, with spots on his skin and a sullen set to his mouth, as though he'd been made to do better things than oversee the comings and goings of servants, messengers and errand boys. He allowed the disguised princess and her companion to pass with a desultory air.

Annie was naturally pleased that the venture would not be thwarted at this early stage, but it also troubled her to know how easy it was to leave the palace grounds. No doubt a clever person could contrive to *enter* the compound with equal facility.

Phaedra hooked her arm through Annie's and hurried her along the narrow alley that ran parallel to the street fronting the royal residence. "Don't dawdle!" she hissed. "We might have deceived that idiot of a guard, but if Chandler or Felicia happened to see us from a window, the jig would be up, my friend. And believe me, we'd sooner be caught by rebels than have word of this outing reach Rafael!"

Annie glanced anxiously back over one shoulder, her eyes rising to the narrow windows of the servants' quarters. She wanted an afternoon of anonymity and escape as much as Phaedra did, and she wasn't the least bit afraid of Rafael St. James. In fact, she'd welcome an encounter with the prince, however tempestuous, just so she could see him, touch him, and know for certain that he was alive.

All the same, when she thought of that room on the uppermost floor, and the occupants' few but clearly cherished possessions, her conscience was pricked. Annie had never wanted for anything, but she had been taught to have compassion and respect for those who were not so fortunate.

Still, as Phaedra had already assured her, they would return the dresses and scarves, and offer a few coins in payment. No real harm would be done.

She hoped.

They reached the marketplace by a circuitous, winding route, carefully avoiding the wide, fashionable streets where servants did not walk.

Annie's heart swelled with excitement when she saw the market, for it was teeming with noises and smells, colors and textures. She smiled, recalling her mother's story about a similar place, a *souk* in the kingdom of Riz, and what had happened to her there.

Phaedra nudged her. "Keep your eyes down," she said quietly. "Servants don't gawk."

Reluctantly, Annie lowered her gaze, but she took in her surroundings all the same, in furtive, side-to-side glances. Moving among the stalls, she admired everything from imported fruit to lengths of colorful grosgrain ribbon. At one booth, over Phaedra's whispered protest, she purchased a small, pretty doll with a china face and a pink dress and bonnet. The merchant was happy to make the sale, it seemed to Annie, and not at all suspicious. Still, to assuage the princess, she tucked the toy into a corner of her basket and covered it with a cloth napkin.

Phaedra purchased half a dozen huge, succulent oranges and didn't bother to hide them. After all, servants bought food of all sorts for their employers' kitchens.

A few streets over from the marketplace was a square lined with elegant shops. Phaedra and Annie lingered in front of each window, admiring gowns and bonnets, shoes and parasols, books and paintings. Despite the uncertain political climate in Bavia, the merchants seemed to be doing a brisk business.

The two adventuresses were on their way back to the palace, by way of the marketplace, when a young man standing on a box in front of a fountain caught their attention. He was speaking with heated eloquence to a sparse but attentive audience, shouting about crimes against the people. The gist of his message chilled Annie's heart.

This man wanted to see Rafael not only deposed, but hanged. Publicly.

Forgetting she was supposed to be a servant, Annie started toward him, fully intending to set him and all

of the listeners straight where the prince's true character was concerned, but Phaedra stopped her by grabbing her arm and hauling her back. Before Annie
could pull free, or even protest, there was a great
clatter at the end of the street and suddenly the square
was filled with men on horseback.

They were soldiers, led by a fair-haired man with
striking brown eyes. Even in the midst of chaos, Annie
noted that there was something familiar about him as,
brandishing swords, he and the other soldiers sent the
small crowd fleeing in terror. The merchants in the
market cowered in their stalls and those few shops
that were nearby were immediately closed and locked.

The young man who had been speaking scrambled
onto the fountain's edge and yelled above the furor.
"These are your prince's own men! These louts who
would trample you beneath their horses' hooves and
run you through with their swords serve Prince Rafael
St. James of Bavia!"

"No," Annie whispered, but even as Phaedra tried
to pull her away, she knew by their uniforms that these
soldiers were indeed allied with the crown. Even as
she watched, a member of the militia leveled a gun at
the dissenter and shot him in the center of the chest.

He toppled into the pool surrounding the fountain,
his blood staining the water, and Annie screamed in
horror.

"Stop!" she yelled, flinging herself at the nearest
horseman, the blond man who had been giving orders
from the beginning. She clawed at his saddle, trying to
climb his leg, shrieking in furious, hysterical protest.

The soldier laughed, centered his boot in the middle
of her chest, and pushed hard, sending her tumbling
onto the cobblestones. Phaedra fell to her knees

beside Annie, trying to shelter her and at the same time using all her strength to keep her from bolting back to her feet and flying at the man like a scalded cat.

"No, Annie," Phaedra pleaded, in a sobbing whisper, "he'll kill you."

Frenzied, the riders began knocking down the merchants' booths, upsetting carts and letting their horses trod upon precious fruit and vegetables. Vendors knelt on the ground, weeping over their lost goods, and Annie heard screams of fear all around her.

She and Phaedra clung to each other, in the middle of it all, their faces wet with tears. At some point, Annie came to her senses and crawled under a stone bench, pulling the princess after her.

There they stayed until Rafael's soldiers had grown weary of their game and ridden away. Not an hour had passed, according to the clock in a nearby tower, yet for Annie Trevarren, the whole world had been forever altered. She loved Rafael St. James as much as ever, but her loyalties had shifted to the side of the Bavian people.

Slowly, silently, still clasping the handles of their baskets, Annie and Phaedra made their way back to the palace. Once, along the way, the princess stopped to retch into the ditch.

When they reached the same gate they'd passed through before, the guard hesitated to admit them, peering at them through the bars.

Before Annie had a glimmer of what Phaedra planned to do, the princess pushed back her scarf and raised her head. "Admit us at once," she commanded.

Recognizing her instantly, the guard reddened to the roots of his hair and fumbled to work the lock and open the gate. "Yes, Your Highness," he babbled. "I didn't know it was you, honest, I didn't—"

Pale and shaken though she was, Phaedra swept through the opening in a grand and regal fashion. Annie followed, images of the murdered man bleeding in the fountain next to the market filling her mind. Her innocent, romantic illusions were gone and her heart was broken.

Rafael was not a storybook prince, as she had always believed. He was, instead, a despot, the head of an army of fiends. But that wasn't the worst of it, oh, no—the most terrible thing was that Annie knew the truth about Rafael and loved him in spite of it. Which meant that she was either a madwoman or a monster in her own right.

Phaedra and Annie had almost reached one of the rear entrances to the palace when Chandler Haslett appeared, looking harried and furious. "Where have you been?" he demanded.

To Annie's surprise, and apparently, to Chandler's as well, Phaedra dropped her basket of oranges and went sobbing, into his arms. "It was terrible!" she wailed. "We were nearly killed!"

Chandler hesitated, obviously not sure where to put his hands, his gaze linked with Annie's, and then embraced the princess in a gingerly manner. "What happened?" he asked again.

Annie bent to gather Phaedra's oranges and put them back in the basket. After the chaos she'd just witnessed, she needed to have some semblance of order, however small. "There was a riot," she said simply. "At the marketplace."

Chandler gripped Phaedra's shoulders and held her

away from him. "Are you all right?" he rasped, and Annie knew the question was meant for both of them.

"I suppose we will be, eventually," Annie answered sadly. Then, carrying Phaedra's basket as well as her own, she proceeded into the palace, leaving the princess to weep against her future husband's shoulder.

Once inside, Annie immediately sought out the rear stairway that led to the attics and the servants' quarters. The room was empty, as before.

Annie took the china doll she'd bought at the market from her basket—miraculously, it had survived the episode intact—and laid it beside the rag doll resting on one of the cots. That done, she put one of Phaedra's oranges on each of the beds and hurried out.

In her room, she took off the borrowed clothes, folded them carefully, and set them on the chest at the foot of her bed. Then, wearing only her chemise, Annie crawled between the covers, pulled them over her head, and wept until there were no tears left to shed.

Annie didn't go down to dinner that night, nor did she eat the breakfast Kathleen brought to her room the following morning.

The maid gathered up the little stack of clothes Annie had worn to the marketplace the day before and hugged the garments to her chest. "It was kind of you to leave the doll, miss," she said. "Little Nancy, she's sure the angels brought it. She lost her mama to a fever last year and thinks a lot about such things."

Annie, who was sitting in bed with her knees drawn up and her back to the headboard, closed her eyes for a moment and swallowed. "Did you ever wish you could be someone else—just stop being yourself and step into another person's life?"

Kathleen looked puzzled, bless her. "No, miss. It would be foolish to think of such things, when there's no way of doing them—wouldn't it?" She paused and glanced toward the table, where she'd left a tray. "Won't you please eat something, miss? It isn't good to go hungry."

Just the thought of food made Annie's stomach do a somersault. The memories of the incident at the marketplace were still too fresh in her mind, and her heart was in pieces, jagged pieces that speared her insides like splintered glass.

She shook her head and Kathleen reluctantly left the room, taking the purloined garments with her.

The next morning, a formal announcement was made: The princess's engagement ball had been postponed for a week. Annie wondered, somewhat cynically perhaps, how important that news would be to the merchants in the marketplace. Or to the friends and family of that slender, earnest young dissenter, who had died so ingloriously in the fountain pool.

For the first time since they'd met at St. Aspasia's, Annie and Phaedra found that they had little to say to each other. Phaedra kept to her room during the days to come, playing endless games of solitaire, by Kathleen's accounting, and refusing visitors. Annie spent most of her time in the garden beneath her terrace, trying to sort through her thoughts and emotions and making friends with the yellow cat.

She was there, in fact, when the clamor of many horses and men at the front gates indicated that the prince had returned from his travels.

Annie stood, then sat back down on the bench, then leaped to her feet. She wanted to see Rafael immediately, and never again, as long as she lived. She yearned to fling her arms around his neck and, conversely, to do him lasting and painful injury.

She heard the gates creaking on their iron hinges, heard the hooves of many horses on the cobbled driveway. She paced, damning Rafael with one breath, adoring him with the next.

Annie had been suffering in this state for about a quarter of an hour when the prince himself appeared at the edge of the little garden, his plain clothes dirty and rumpled, his hair shaggy, his jaw scruffy with the start of a beard. His gray eyes glittered with restrained passion, weariness and a benevolent malice.

She started toward him, her pulse leaping, then stopped herself, locking her fingers together. Like so many dark angels, Rafael was beautiful to look upon.

"How did you know where to find me?" she asked, though that was the least of her concerns.

Rafael arched one eyebrow and scratched his chin. Although the beard lent him a certain roguish charm, Annie reflected, somewhat fitfully, she liked him better clean-shaven. "The head of the palace guard told me," he said. His tone was quiet, controlled, and there was something ominous in the way he folded his arms. Plainly, other things had been said as well. "Is it true, Annie, that you and Phaedra dressed as servants and went to the marketplace on your own?"

Annie squared her shoulders, raised her chin, and took one step backward. Her emotions were a confusing tangle—joy, because Rafael was home safe, trepidation, because she knew she and Phaedra had done a dangerous and stupid thing, for which he would

165

certainly call them both to account, and lastly, a deep-seated, indignant wanting that could not be denied. Rafael was either a cruel leader or a heedless leader, or both, and innocent people were suffering because of him. And still Annie loved him.

"Yes," she answered evenly. "That is true."

Rafael's right temple pulsed, and Annie sensed the burgeoning anger in him, but the prince did not move from where he stood. "What in the name of heaven would induce you—*even you*—to do something so outrageously, recklessly foolish?"

Annie's stomach wobbled as she recalled the terror of that afternoon; she saw blood unfurling in gossamer folds in the fountain pool, turning the water to pink and then to scarlet. "Rest assured, Your Highness—I most certainly do regret the impulse that took me to that dreadful place." She backed up to the bench, where the yellow cat usually sunned itself, and sank onto the cool stone surface. Despite the weakness that came from remembering all she had seen in that horrid place, Annie met his gaze directly, and continued with conviction. "Your people are justified in rising up against you. You are a tyrant, Rafael St. James, with no apparent compassion for the citizens of your own country."

He whitened, beneath all that road dust and beard stubble, and Annie knew her words had struck him deeply. His right hand clenched at his side, and he started to speak, then stopped himself. Finally, he came and sat down on the bench next to her, though not too close. "Tell me what happened that day," he said, in a quiet voice. "Tell me what you saw."

Annie looked away for a moment, struggling to keep back tears of disillusionment, pain and the awful, lingering fear. Her throat constricted, and it took some effort to finally answer. "We were children, Phaedra and I, when we went off to the marketplace," she said sadly. "Children, wearing disguises and looking for mischief. We bought a few small things and walked over to the square to peek in the shop windows. As we were passing through the market again, on our way home, we saw a man—he was very young, a student, probably—making a speech by the fountain." She paused, her cheeks coloring, and would not let herself look away from Rafael's face. "He was opposed to your government. While he was talking, soldiers suddenly converged on the square on horseback—it seemed they came from every direction—and they behaved as though they'd gone mad." At this accounting, Rafael closed his eyes for an instant, and he braced himself visibly when Annie went on. "One of them shot the student, and he fell into the fountain, bleeding." She stopped again, to swallow the bile that had surged into the back of her throat. Her hands were knotted in her lap, white-knuckled. "They tore the marketplace completely apart, your soldiers, trampling goods and terrifying the people. I'm sure others must have been killed or injured, besides the first man."

They were both silent for a short, terrible interval. Finally, Rafael spoke, his voice gruff and stricken. "And you believe I commanded that such a thing be done?"

Annie studied his gaunt face and felt a crushing relief, followed just as quickly by sorrowful resignation. "No," she said gently. "I don't believe that. But those were *your men*, Rafael. They were wearing your uniforms, riding your horses, carrying your swords and guns. You must bear a grave responsibility in this matter, there can be no denying that."

He rose swiftly from the bench, turning his back on her, and Annie saw defeat in the set of his strong shoulders. She ached to comfort him, and yet she could not—would not—align herself with his government. "I'm not trying to deny anything," he said, after a very long time, facing her again at last. "There is, of course, nothing I can do to change what has already taken place. But I can promise you one thing: The men involved in this will be relieved of their duties and brought to trial."

She merely nodded.

Rafael's expression remained grave, and he pointed a damning finger at her. "You'll give an accounting for your own actions as well, Annie Trevarren. God knows, I'd like to shake you for putting yourself and my sister in such peril, but I shall resist the temptation and write a long letter to your parents instead. I believe Patrick will be interested to know what his eldest daughter has been up to since her arrival in Bavia."

Annie swallowed and did not raise the valid argument that Phaedra had actually planned their adventure.

She couldn't help thinking of the loud and lengthy lecture she would be subjected to if her parents got wind of the risks she'd taken for the sake of curiosity. No doubt her allowance would be cut off for a while, and she might even be hauled home and confined to the house in Nice. Although Charlotte and Patrick were both quite intrepid in their own right, and while they had always been tolerant of minor acts of derring-do, such as climbing trees and walking along the tops of stone fences, they had never cultivated outright recklessness in their daughters.

What Annie had done would surely try their patience.

Rafael gazed at her for a few moments longer, his expression utterly unreadable, and then left the garden. "Barrett!" Annie heard him shout.

It had been one hell of a homecoming, Rafael thought glumly, an hour later, settling back in the copper bathtub that had been brought to his chamber, set close to the fire, and filled with steaming water. His country, his entire *life*, for God's sake, was crumbling about his ears. He'd spent upward of a week either in the saddle or sleeping on the hard ground, and all he'd thought about, practically every moment of that time, was Annie Trevarren.

He reached for the shaving mug and brush that rested, along with a straight razor and a snifter of brandy, on a small table close by, and began to lather his face. The fascinating Miss Trevarren had had a rude awakening in the marketplace, it was true, and the experience had obviously changed her thinking in a number of ways.

Take her opinion of one Rafael St. James, prince of Bavia, for instance, he reflected ruefully, gripping a small mirror in one hand now, taking the razor in the other, and carefully shaving his throat and the underside of his chin. Annie had certainly revised her romantic ideas where he was concerned, and doubtless there would be no more scandalous talk of wanting him to bed her.

Rafael shook off the razor and attacked his beard from another direction. He should have been relieved to have Annie out of his hair, but instead he was disappointed. Being separated from Annie had only heightened her charms and, accordingly, his resolve to resist her had lessened considerably during their time apart. It did him injury to know that she thought of him as a tyrant who deserved to be overthrown, but learning of the travesty his own soldiers had committed in the marketplace had been agonizing.

Annie was quite right; even though he hadn't known about the incident, let alone given the order for it, the army was his to command, and he bore an undeniable culpability for its actions. It made him sick to his soul to imagine what other brutalities his men might have engaged in, without his knowledge, on other days, in other cities and villages.

No wonder the people did not trust the gestures he'd made since he'd come to power.

Rafael finished shaving, set aside the razor and mirror and reached for the snifter of brandy. There were some two hundred troops garrisoned within Morovia's walls, and he had Barrett's word that they would be assembled at sunrise, in front of the palace, for review. At that time, Rafael would give the men who had raided the marketplace a chance to come forward and admit their guilt, though he doubted that anyone would do so. In the meantime, Annie and Phaedra would be standing on one of the palace balconies, well-protected, of course, pointing out as many of the offenders as they could recognize.

He downed the brandy in one searing gulp, set the crystal snifter on the table, and went about finishing his bath. *One crisis at a time, St. James,* he told himself. *One crisis at a time.*

An hour after his bath, when Rafael descended the

170

main staircase, impeccably groomed, except for want of barbering, and wearing formal clothes, he found only Chandler Haslett and Felicia awaiting him at the dinner table. He was surprisingly disheartened to discover Miss Trevarren absent. Phaedra wasn't there, either, but common sense told Rafael that his temper needed a little more time to cool before he dealt with his sister.

Chandler seemed preoccupied, though he was pleasant enough, but Felicia was clearly fretful.

"Barrett tells me you intend to assemble the entire Morovian garrison in the morning," she said to Rafael, after the soup had been served. "Do you think that's wise? It seems to me that there might well be reprisals . . ."

Rafael regarded the other man in thoughtful silence for a lengthy interval before remarking, "Barrett is very free with sensitive information. I shall have to speak to him about that."

Felicia was pale, and an odd, disturbing light gleamed in her brown eyes. Her hand trembled as she gave up the pretense of eating and laid down her soup spoon. "Don't you dare reprimand Edmund," she whispered, as if by lowering her voice she could keep Chandler from hearing her. Naturally, her effort only caused him to perk up his ears. "He knows he can trust me, and you should know it, too!"

Because he had been living on army rations and rabbit meat for over a week, Rafael had a special appreciation for palace fare, and he continued to eat. Between sips of wine, he asked moderately, "Is it your brother you're worried about?"

Felicia's only sibling, Jeremy Covington, was a lieutenant in the Bavian army, garrisoned in Morovia.

She and Jeremy were close, but Jeremy was Lucian's contemporary, and Rafael had probably never exchanged more than a few words with young Covington.

"Yes," Felicia said, with unusual bitterness. "I don't want Jeremy shot by a rebel, just because you insist on lining up every soldier in Morovia for a scolding."

Out of the corner of his eye, Rafael saw Chandler lean forward in his chair, making no effort to hide his interest.

"A scolding?" Rafael echoed, just as bitterly. "Do you know what those men did, Felicia?"

She flushed. "Yes, of course, I do. But why should *all* the troops be put in danger because of the actions of a few?"

Rafael reached for his wineglass and took another sip, though now the fine sangria flowed untasted over his tongue. "I believe the men are quite capable of protecting themselves," he said quietly. "Jeremy more than most, since he has risen rather rapidly through the ranks."

"You could make an exception—"

Rafael cut her off with a shake of his head, and Felicia flung down her napkin, pushed back her chair and dashed from the room. Chandler rose halfway out of his chair either out of deference or habit and frowned at the prince.

"You might have summoned Lieutenant Covington to the palace for a private interview, Rafael," he suggested quietly.

"No," Rafael replied. "Every man will be treated in exactly the same way, including my half brother, Lucian." The subject was closed, and Rafael could see by the resignation in Chandler's face that he'd made that clear. "Now, tell me—how is Phaedra?"

At dawn, by Rafael's orders, Annie joined Phaedra, Mr. Barrett and the prince himself on a high balcony, partially hidden by tree branches but affording a clear view of the courtyard and the street in front of the palace. For all of that, Annie did not recognize any of the men she had seen in the marketplace that terrible day. There were several soldiers with hair the same startlingly fair shade as that of the leader, the one who had kicked Annie to the cobblestones from his horse, but to sort them out she would have had to look directly into their faces.

"Perhaps if I saw them up close," Annie said, gripping the wrought iron railing enclosing the small balcony. "From this distance . . ."

Rafael hesitated a moment, then turned to his sister. "Phaedra?"

The princess shook her head, and it seemed to Annie that she was leaning toward Mr. Barrett, just a little. Phaedra was trembling visibly, and she was frighteningly pale. "No, Rafael . . . they look so much alike . . ."

Rafael and Mr. Barrett exchanged a look.

"Don't worry," Mr. Barrett said to the prince. "I'll find the guilty ones by other means."

Rafael was watching the soldiers again, his expression pensive. "See that you do. In the meantime, I would like to address the men personally."

Annie saw Barrett set his jaw and knew he was exercising considerable restraint to keep from issuing a protest. Annie, however, had no such compunction.

173

"That could be dangerous, Your Highness," she said. "And foolish in the bargain."

He turned his head and pinioned her with his pewter gray gaze. "And you are an acknowledged expert on both, aren't you?"

Annie blushed.

Rafael executed a slight, impudent bow. "Please allow me to run my army as I see fit, Miss Trevarren," he said. "In the meantime, you and my sister may occupy yourselves with the preparations for tonight's ball."

His remark was politely framed, but it stung, as it had surely been intended to do. Annie suppressed an urge to kick His Royal Highness in the shin and instead, performed an absurdly elaborate curtsey. "As you command, sir," she said, with a pointed emphasis on the final word. "I would not think of disobeying you."

The prince muttered a curse as Annie rose from the pool of her skirts and swept into the palace. Phaedra followed soon after.

The royal residence was in an uproar, and not only because there were several hundred soldiers rallied just beyond the main gates. The kitchen was buzzing, and there were florists and musicians and maids in the grand ballroom on the first floor, preparing for the great event.

Both Phaedra and Annie were distracted and fretful, but there was much to do and they went their separate ways—Annie to yet another wedding dress fitting with Miss Rendennon, Phaedra to try on an array of gowns sent over from that lady's fashionable shop. When Annie had finished the interminable session, and escaped to her chamber, she was pleased

174

to find that a selection of elegant frocks awaited her, as well.

She chose a glittering yellow silk, trimmed with golden lace, and it needed only a few simple alterations, performed by one of Miss Rendennon's assistants, to fit perfectly.

Hours later, when the clatter of horses' hooves and carriage wheels had been heard in the courtyard for some time, Annie descended the stairs. She had made up her mind to enjoy the ball, although her heart was broken and her illusions were gone. She saw Rafael conversing with a man in the foyer, near the foot of the stairs, and prepared to be cordial as she passed.

When Rafael raised his eyes to her, however, his blond companion turned as well, and Annie found herself staring straight into the face of the man who had led the raid on the marketplace.

CHAPTER
10

The blond man held Annie's gaze, a slight smile curving his perfectly formed mouth, almost daring her to confront him. Fear slammed against her heart, then pervaded every part of her, like vile and acrid smoke. Her fingers tightened convulsively on the banister and she stood still as a mouse facing a cobra, unable to move forward or turn and flee back up the stairs.

"Annie?" It was Rafael's voice, echoing through the pounding haze of terror and shock; she saw him as if through water, mounting the stairs toward her. "In the name of God, what is it?" He put an arm around her waist just when her knees would have given way, and held her upright. "Are you ill?"

Annie looked into his face for a moment, and then past his shoulder. The man was still standing there, his gaze holding a warning now, as well as impudence, one arm curved gracefully around the ornate newel post. Annie felt the bruising force of his boot on her chest again, and heard the screams, the shot, all of it.

And her fear gave way to cold fury.

She pointed one hand. "He was there, at the marketplace," she said clearly. "He gave the orders."

Rafael was still supporting her, and she was grateful, because despite the upswell of anger inside her, she doubted she could have stood on her own. "Covington? Are you sure?"

Covington's face had taken on a gray cast now, though whether from fury or fear Annie could not tell. "Now see here, Rafael," he protested. "The girl's lying—"

"He kicked me," Annie said. "I screamed at him to do something, to stop what was happening, and he pushed me to the ground with his boot. Don't you believe me?"

"Of course I believe you," Rafael muttered, annoyed, but the real weight of his anger was directed toward the fair-haired, aristocratic man at the base of the stairs. "Get Mr. Barrett, immediately," the prince said, to a servant passing through the foyer bearing a tray of crystal glasses.

Covington was sweating, and a muscle ticked convulsively in his right cheek. He shoved one perfectly formed hand through his glimmering hair, and Annie had the odd thought that this man did not seem suited for soldiering. Like Lucian, he resembled a poet or a musician more than a fighting man. And that only went to prove that appearances really were deceiving, for there could be no music and certainly no poetry in a soul as cruel as this one.

"I won't endure this, Rafael," he sputtered, loosening the starched collar of his elegant shirt with a hooked finger. "It's an outrage . . ."

Rafael left Annie's side and descended the stairs. "Do not speak to me of outrages, Lieutenant Covington," he warned, in a low, lethal voice. "I will not countenance that, especially from you."

Covington's brown eyes flashed with hatred as he looked past Rafael to Annie. "Have I been pronounced guilty, then, with no trial, by word of this woman?"

The prince did not reply to the question, for Mr. Barrett came striding into the foyer just then, looking unusually grand in his evening clothes. He glanced at Covington and then at Annie, but then all his attention was focused on Rafael.

"What has happened?" he asked.

Rafael, standing at the base of the stairs, gestured toward the lieutenant. "Place this man under military arrest, immediately. Annie—Miss Trevarren has identified him as one of the raiders from the marketplace."

Barrett blanched and muttered a curse, but then he reached for Covington's arm. The prisoner wrenched free, straightening his coat and fastening his collar. Although his manner was controlled, it was plain to Annie that he was seething. She thought he would truly have murdered her, with his bare hands, if they'd been alone.

"Don't touch me," he said, addressing Barrett, his superior officer, as though he were the lowliest of servants. His gaze sliced upward again, to Annie's face, before he was led away for questioning. "You will

178

pay for this lie, miss," he said, "and your alliance with the prince will not save you."

"Enough!" Rafael rasped. Then, to Barrett, he said, "See that he's held. I'll deal with the matter in the morning."

Barrett nodded and squired Lieutenant Covington out of the palace by way of the front door. Only when they had gone did Annie notice that a crowd had gathered—servants were clustered in the back of the hall, and some of the dancers had left the ballroom to gather on the edge of the foyer.

Rafael made a gesture of polite dismissal and, as if by magic, they were alone again. He held up one hand, and Annie descended the stairs, moving slowly and carefully, to take it.

"I will not let the travesty you witnessed go unpunished," he promised quietly, when Annie was facing him, her hand enfolded in his. "Justice will be done, Annie."

Annie believed him, and she had never loved him more, but of course a few words could not undo what had happened to that poor student, or to the merchants whose stalls had been destroyed. Annie's innocent view of the world was spoiled for all time, and she mourned it. She said nothing, though she suspected the expression in her eyes told Rafael a great deal.

"Come," he said, pulling her gently in the direction of the ballroom. "After all you've put me through, Annie Trevarren, the least you can do is favor me with a dance."

Annie's heartbeat accelerated slightly at the prospect. She did not want to love Rafael St. James, but the decision had been made in some other, higher realm where she had no influence whatsoever. The encounter with Lieutenant Covington had left her sorely shaken, too, and she was still afraid.

"You believed me," she said, as they crossed the salon, moving through crowds of beautifully dressed French, Spanish and Bavian aristocrats, gathered in the eye of the political storm to celebrate the impending marriage of one of their own.

Rafael raised one eyebrow, just slightly. "You are far too honorable to lie about something so important," he said. "Covington and the others—and I have no doubt that he'll name his companions—will suffer for what they've done, Annie. Whoever fired the shot that killed the student will be brought up on charges of murder."

Annie swallowed and nodded. It was only right that Covington and the brutes who'd ridden with him should be made to account for their actions, but knowing that didn't make the reality any less ugly or tragic. "Is the lieutenant related to Felicia?" she asked, just as they stepped into the ballroom.

It shimmered with candlelight and color, and the mirrors on the walls redoubled those things, splashing them back upon the happy dancers. The scene was magical, and Annie would have been transported by it, at least for a few hours, except for the encounter just past. As it was, when Rafael drew her into his arms, her breath caught and the flesh tingled where he touched her.

Rafael stiffened, almost imperceptibly. "Yes," he replied ruefully, scanning the crowd with a troubled gaze. "Lieutenant Covington is her brother."

Annie could feel word of the episode spreading

through the ballroom; it was a buzzing vibration, flowing beneath the sounds of music, ordinary conversation, and the tinkle of crystal glasses touching each other in private toasts. Before she could react to Rafael's words, however, there was a flurry in the far corner of the room, followed by shocked gasps and murmured protests as Felicia Covington pushed her way through the gathering to reach Rafael.

Felicia was frighteningly pale when she stood before the prince, putting an end to their dancing, and her brown eyes were glazed with panic, confusion and rage. She did not so much as glance at Annie, who remained at Rafael's side, her arm linked with his.

"Is it true, Rafael?" Felicia demanded, as Chandler Haslett came to stand behind her. "Did you have Jeremy arrested like some common sneak thief?"

Rafael sighed. "Not here, Felicia," he said softly. "Not now."

Felicia seemed unsteady, though Annie had no way of knowing whether it was her agitated state or too many flutes of champagne that had made her so. She felt sorry for Felicia and wanted to offer comfort, but she knew no such gesture would be welcomed, especially from Jeremy Covington's accuser.

"You've always hated him," she accused, her voice rising, becoming more and more shrill. "Just the way you've hated Lucian!"

Rafael closed his eyes for a moment. His manner was one of compassion, and no little personal misery, for there was nothing he could say that would soothe his friend's rising hysteria. "Chandler," he said, making a request of that one word, and Mr. Haslett nodded, took a gentle hold on Felicia's arm and started to lead her away.

181

She resisted him, though, just long enough to glare at Annie in the same way her brother had done. "You," she breathed. "It was *you* who concocted this terrible lie about my brother!"

Annie stood there in silence and ached, for she had liked Felicia, and hoped that she and the other woman might someday be friends of a sort. Now, of course, there was no chance of that. Doors were closing, lives were changing, countries were falling apart.

"Come with me, dear," Chandler said quietly to the overwrought Felicia, and lead her away with a firm gentility that made Annie like him more than she ever had. She valued his friendship and his opinion, and hoped he wouldn't dislike her after that fateful night. She'd had quite enough acrimony as it was, first from Jeremy Covington, then from his sister.

Rafael gazed after them for a long moment, then patted Annie's hand. "I'd better make certain Felicia is all right. Will you save a space for my name on your dance card, Miss Trevarren?"

Annie could not have refused him and, although she felt a pang of envy over his attentiveness toward Felicia, his chivalrous streak was one of the things she loved most about Rafael. She nodded, and they parted, Rafael following Chandler and Miss Covington out of the ballroom, Annie turning to assess the crowd of strangers.

She found Phaedra, looking like the princess she was in a gauzy blue dress exactly the color of an April sky, standing on the other side of the room. She was drinking champagne from a flower shaped flute, and her dark hair glowed like jet reflecting firelight.

Phaedra seemed, to Annie, remarkably unconcerned with the events of the evening. It was possible that she hadn't heard about Lieutenant Covington's arrest, though quite unlikely, given the charged atmosphere of the room. Under no circumstances, however, could the princess have missed witnessing Felicia's outburst—even the music of the small orchestra on the platform had faded to silence during that.

Annie made her way to her friend's side and gripped her elbow. "I want to speak with you in private, please," she said, with cheerful ferocity.

Phaedra opened her mouth in protest then thought better of the idea and excused herself from the circle of admirers that had gathered around her. There was an irritated expression on her face when she and Annie reached the spacious garden and courtyard just off the ballroom.

"What is so important," she demanded, "that it couldn't wait until tomorrow?"

Annie folded her arms. "Lieutenant Covington was arrested just a few minutes ago," she said, trying to moderate her tone of voice and finding it difficult to do.

Phaedra shrugged. "This is about *that* tiresome little lizard?" she asked, with airy indifference rather than venom. "Whatever he gets, he's earned."

Annie felt a flush of frustration surge up her bosom to throb in her face. "I quite agree, Phaedra, but that isn't my point. You obviously know Jeremy Covington, so you must have recognized him that day at the marketplace. And yet you stood on that balcony with Rafael and Mr. Barrett and me, just this morning, and said you didn't see anyone who had participated." Annie paused for a few moments, endeavoring to control her rising temper. "Phaedra, why didn't you say something? Were you protecting Lieutenant Covington?"

"Protecting him? Annie, what's gotten into you, that you'd ask a question like that? I was frightened that day—I was *terrified,* in fact, just like you were! I didn't mention Jeremy Covington because I didn't see him!"

Annie bit her lip, buying time to calm herself, to think. The experience had been horrid, like wandering in a nightmare, and Phaedra had no reason to lie about the events of that day. If Annie had remembered the lieutenant, and she'd been scared half-blind herself, it was probably because she'd looked directly into his face, and because he'd kicked her.

She put a hand to her forehead and sighed, and Phaedra took a step nearer.

"It's a terrible time for all of us," the princess said gently, touching Annie's shoulder, "and everyone is overwrought. But we dare not dwell on the sorrows, Annie. We must dance while we can, and look ahead to better days."

Annie caught the start of a tear with the tip of one gloved finger and braced herself up by an act of will. "You're right, of course. This is your engagement ball, and we've still got the wedding to look forward to, as well."

"Yes," Phaedra agreed, but her tone was distracted, her expression sad. She gazed off into the starry distance as she spoke, as though she were wishing herself far, far away. "There is still the wedding."

When Annie returned to the ball, there was still no sign of Rafael, but she had no shortage of dance partners. By the time the prince entered the grand chamber, with its gleaming marble floors, exquisite chandeliers and mirrored walls, Annie's feet had been trampled by military officers, cabinet members and aristocrats of every size, shape and description.

The guests at Phaedra's engagement ball had much to say to Rafael, and he was waylaid so many times as he made his way across the room that Annie feared he would never reach her. At long last, however, he took her hand and inclined his head slightly in greeting. Although he was smiling slightly, she saw the despair in his eyes.

"I trust you've saved a dance for me," he said.

Annie was overcome by emotion as she looked at him, and she could only nod. Too soon, she reflected as he drew her into his arms and they began to waltz, the wedding would be over and she would have to leave Bavia forever. And of course that meant leaving Rafael.

She let her forehead rest against his shoulder for a moment, while she struggled to regain her equilibrium, and Rafael curved a finger under her chin and lifted it, making her look at him.

"Would you like to leave, Annie?" he asked. "You've had a very difficult evening."

His concern was her undoing; she began to cry, and no amount of sniffling and wiping of eyes would stem the tide.

"Perhaps . . . I should say . . . good-night . . ." she babbled.

Deftly, Rafael maneuvered her through the French doors that led out into the courtyard and garden where she and Phaedra had talked before. He did not stop to converse, however, but simply pulled her along behind him as he strode through shadows and patches of moonlight, past shrubs and statues and marble benches and kissing lovers. Finally, at what seemed like the center of a maze of hedges and rosebushes, they were alone, and Rafael stopped and drew Annie into his arms. He looked down into her watery eyes and she saw wrenching emotions in his face. "I've tried to put you out of my mind, Annie, and I've failed. I have no right to ask anything of you, and yet I must. I need your comfort, if you're still willing to give it."

Annie didn't ask what he would give her in return, because she knew the answer. If Rafael made love to her, and then sent her away after Phaedra's wedding, as she was sure he would do, Annie would have the memories and the magic of their time together. She knew she would never give herself to another man after Rafael.

She raised her chin and spoke in a firm voice, although her heartbeat was thrumming in her ears and she felt dizzy, as if she might crumple to a heap at his feet like a silly schoolgirl. "Yes," she said. "I want to give myself to you."

Rafael made a despondent, hungry sound as he pulled her closer still and crushed her mouth beneath his own, urging her lips apart, ravaging her with his tongue.

Annie gave herself up to him willingly, joyously. She had been raised to be independent, and the decision was hers and hers alone—no one else could be blamed or credited for it. She would know the ecstasy of lying with Rafael and, one day soon no doubt, she would know the consequences as well.

It was Rafael who ended the fevered kiss, gasping as he put his hands to Annie's waist and set her slightly away from him. "Dear God," he murmured, and it sounded almost as though he were asking for help, for guidance, for restraint. And most of all, for solace.

Annie moved to touch him, but he kept her at that small distance.

"No, Annie," he said raggedly, "don't touch me just now or I swear I'll have you right here, this moment. And that isn't the way I want it to be."

For one wild instant, Annie thought he was going to suggest marriage. Then she realized he would never offer that, no matter what happened between them. For him, time was grinding to a stop and the world was ending. Rafael St. James had no tomorrows to give.

"How is it to be, then?" Annie managed to ask. She wouldn't have cared if Rafael had taken her there, in the moonlight, in the fragrant grass, just so long as he did. Where he was concerned, she was frightfully wanton, and she felt no shame for it.

Rafael released her waist and raised one hand to caress her upturned face. He smoothed her lips with the pad of his thumb, which was surprisingly rough, and bent his head to touch his mouth ever-so-lightly to hers before he replied. "After the ball is over," he said, "I will bring you to my chamber and I will make proper love to you there, by the fire."

"Not *too* proper, I hope," Annie said quickly.

Rafael chuckled with genuine pleasure and shook his head. "What an enigma you are," he marveled. "I would bet my life that you are a virgin, and yet you have the spirit of a concubine." The sparkle faded from his eyes. "And dear God, how I will despise myself for this night."

Annie took a step toward him and touched her

fingers to his mouth. "Don't, Rafael," she whispered. "Don't spoil it. Please. This may be all I ever have, and I want it to be wonderful."

He frowned, closing his hand around hers, pausing to kiss her palm before lowering it to his chest, where she felt his heartbeat. "All you will ever have? Annie, you're so young, and so beautiful—legions of men will want you. You'll have your choice of them."

She concentrated on the pounding of his heart, on the merging, through her skin, of their two pulses, and shook her head. "No, Rafael. For me there can only be one lover, ever, and that is you."

He still held her hand, and he raised it to his mouth again, and distractedly brushed his lips across the knuckles. His breath was warm, and it made Annie shiver in some deep and hidden part of herself.

"Go back to the ball, Annie," he said, his tone as rough as the pebbles that made up the path beneath their feet.

She was terrified that he'd changed his mind, that he would withhold what he'd promised. "Rafael—"

He bent and kissed her, lightly this time, but with passion. "Go back," he said again, when it was over.

Annie returned to the ballroom and danced, and drank champagne, and watched Rafael surreptitiously throughout the remainder of the evening. She knew it was madness to want seduction so much, especially in light of all that had gone before and all that still lay ahead, but her desire only grew as the evening passed.

At midnight, the celebrants made a great circle, and Phaedra and Chandler, the guests of honor, waltzed in its center. Phaedra was smiling and her flawless skin was flushed with excitement and wine. Her future bridegroom, on the other hand, seemed starkly sober, and he couldn't seem to help casting the occasional glance toward the door.

The guests applauded when the waltz ended, but as she sought Rafael in the crowd, her gaze caught on Edmund Barrett. The captain of the guard was leaning against one of the mirrored walls, his strong arms folded and, like most everyone else, he was watching Phaedra. The look on his face was grim and sorrowful, however, and as Annie watched, he thrust himself away from the wall and strode out of the ballroom.

Annie said good-night to the princess, as convention required on such formal occasions, fended off a series of hopeful dancing partners as she crossed the ballroom, and kicked off her slippers when she reached the foyer. Then, carrying the delicate velvet shoes in one hand, she started up the stairs.

She wondered, as she had been ever since their conversation in the garden, whether or not Rafael had changed his mind about taking her to his room that night. If he didn't come to claim her as he'd promised, she decided, she would go to him.

In her own chamber, with the help of Kathleen, Annie got out of her ballgown and then her corset. Wearing only her petticoats and a camisole, she sat wiggling her toes in front of the fire while Kathleen poured hot chocolate into one of the chipped cups.

"You must have near danced your feet off, miss," Kathleen commented, with amusement.

Annie nodded, frowning at the cup. "What a queer mixture of luxury and poverty this place is," she mused, meaning the palace itself. "Here's this china, cracked and chipped, and there's no art on the walls. The floors are bare and I haven't seen a single ornament of any kind. And yet we drank from crystal champagne flutes at the ball—they might have been sculpted from giant diamonds, the way they shone in the candlelight—"

"They've always kept the ballroom nice, the St. Jameses have," Kathleen interrupted, in a fond tone of voice. "It's the only place they ever entertain anymore, you see. We get dukes and duchesses visiting from England, and even kings and queens from lesser places sometimes. We've got to put them someplace, now don't we?"

Annie smiled. "Yes," she said. "I suppose you do."

Kathleen sighed and moved to the other side of the room to turn down Annie's bed. "Cook says we've seen the last great ball, this very night," she said. "It's crumbling into dust, this way of life."

"That's for the best, I suppose," Annie agreed, setting aside her cup. "No one could doubt that after what happened in the marketplace, and yet it makes me sad. Without princes and princesses, kings and queens, without palaces and castles, how can there be fairy tales?"

Kathleen stared at her, pausing in the midst of fluffing Annie's feather pillow. "Why, miss," she said, "there aren't any fairy tales now, are there, except in storybooks?"

Annie felt a strong desire to break down and weep again, but she didn't give in to her tears. She'd done enough sniveling for one night and besides, she still had high hopes of spending a wonderful evening with Rafael.

"I like to think there's still a little magic in the world," she said.

Kathleen looked upon her with a moment's pitying affection, then excused herself and left the room.

Annie sat by the fire for a long time, reviewing the evening in her mind. It had begun so badly, with Lieutenant Covington's arrest and Felicia's outburst, but the dancing had been wonderful and Rafael had kissed her in the garden. . . .

She settled back in her chair, sighed and closed her eyes, reliving the interlude, tucking it away with the other memories like a delicate flower pressed between the pages of a book. She dozed and dreamed pleasant dreams full of music and champagne and candlelight. When Annie awakened, however, it was with a start.

The fire had gone out, and the room was dark, except for a wash of moonlight flowing in through the terrace doors. Rafael had not come for her—or, if he had, there had been no answer when he knocked.

Annie rose from her chair, her muscles cramped, her motions awkward. Earlier, she'd boasted to herself that she'd go to Rafael if he did not come to collect her, but now it seemed that her courage was faltering. On the other hand, she'd seen the state of the country for herself, not only in the marketplace but on the day they'd arrived at the palace in a storm of curses and stones. The situation was grave, and Rafael was the target of much hatred. Perhaps that night was the only one they would ever have to share.

She climbed resolutely into bed, stretched out, and wrenched the covers into place, then bolted right out again. She was afraid Rafael would knock at the door, and even more terrified that he would not. Where that man was concerned, Annie had to admit, her behavior was downright irrational.

The majority of young women from good families guarded their virtue assiduously, surrendering what the nuns at St. Aspasia's had called their "Precious

Purity" only when the man in question was or would soon be their husband. Annie had no doubt whatsoever that she was a fine person, kind and fair-minded and energetic, but when it came to Rafael, she seemed to have no sense.

While she was pondering the unfortunate ramifications of this conclusion, a gentle knock sounded at the door of her chamber.

Annie stopped moving, stopped thinking, stopped breathing.

There was another rap, this one even softer than the first, and then, incredibly, the door opened and Rafael was there. He had shed his coat and tie, but still wore the fitted trousers and pleated white shirt he'd had on at the ball. The shirt was unbuttoned to the middle of his chest, and Annie was mesmerized by the swirls of dark hair she saw there.

The prince had the good grace—or perhaps it was just the opposite—to step over the threshold and close the door behind him.

He watched her for a long moment, his eyes glittering like fine sterling, one corner of his mouth turned upward in the merest suggestion of a smile. "Have you changed your mind, Annie Trevarren?" he asked quietly. "Or will you share my bed tonight, as you promised?"

CHAPTER
11

Have you changed your mind, Annie Trevarren? Or will you share my bed tonight, as you promised?

Annie could only stare at Rafael in joyous shock. The room was dark, except for the muted glow of a small lamp on the bedside table and the soft and silvery shimmer of the moon, and she was profoundly aware of the warm and rumpled bed looming behind her.

Rafael merely folded his arms and waited; the decision, Annie knew, was hers to make. Rash as it seemed, given the far-reaching effects a night of illicit passion might have upon both their lives, she knew this singular communion with Rafael was as much a part of her destiny as her next heartbeat. And for all that, there was nothing involuntary about the choice.

"I haven't changed my mind," she said, once she'd found her voice.

Rafael held out one hand to Annie then, and she went to him, her fingers interlocking with his, her face upturned and trusting.

Rafael lifted Annie's hand to his lips and kissed it gently. He closed his eyes and said her name.

Annie rested her forehead against his shoulder, drinking in the scent and feel of him, filled with an overwhelming sweetness, a profound awareness that every moment was precious. "My dearest love," she murmured, her soft voice muffled further by the cloth of his shirt and the solid warmth of the flesh beneath.

Rafael traced her lips with the tip of his index finger, and even that simple touch sent fire surging through her veins. He bent his head and lightly kissed her, then lifted her into his arms, his eyes smiling into hers.

"What a delectable creature you are," he marveled. "It grieves me to know that you'll come to despise me for what is about to happen between us."

Annie stiffened in his embrace, about to say that she could never despise him, but he silenced her with another light, soul-searing kiss.

"Yes, love," he insisted, afterward. "One day— perhaps as soon as tomorrow—you'll curse my name. And you'll be right to do so."

Tears brimmed in Annie's eyes. "Never," she vowed.

Rafael sighed and touched his lips to her forehead. Then he carried her to the bed and laid her gently upon the linen sheet. He stood over her in silence for a few moments, admiring her as though she were the work of some master painter, come to life, then crossed the room to lock the door. That done, he returned to Annie's bedside and turned down the lamp wick, extinguishing the light.

His features were in shadow—she could not see his eyes—and yet Annie felt her flesh turning molten under his gaze. She raised her arms to him in silent invitation.

Rafael muttered something, caught her wrists in his hands and gently pressed them back to her sides. "Not yet," he said, his voice a tattered whisper. He released her and began unbuttoning his shirt.

Annie barely kept herself from reaching for him again, and she was too stricken by the beauty of this man cloaked in darkness and moonlight to speak.

He pulled the tails of his shirt from the waistband of his trousers, shrugged out of the garment and tossed it aside. Then, with the utmost grace and tenderness, he grasped the hem of Annie's nightgown and smoothed it upward, over her knees and thighs.

She gasped softly as the gown reached her waist and her femininity was revealed. "Hurry, Rafael," she whispered.

The prince chuckled, and the sound itself was a caress. "Oh, no," he said, pausing to stroke the thatch of moist, silky curls he'd uncovered, "there will be no hurrying tonight. Lovemaking is a very slow process, when it's done properly. It might well be morning before I have you."

Annie moaned and moved her legs a little farther apart as Rafael brushed the sensitive skin on her inner thighs with the tips of his fingers. "M-morning?" she whimpered. "What if someone—hears us?"

Rafael bent, slowly, and kissed the bare, quivering skin of her belly. "You'll make plenty of noise before the night's over," he said, before making a wet, fiery circle around her navel with the tip of his tongue. "But rest assured, my darling, the walls of this old palace are thick. No one will hear."

He tormented her a little longer, with feather-light kisses that made Annie arch her back and groan in frustration, before pushing the nightgown up far enough to reveal her full breasts. Her nipples felt hard, and they ached to be taken, teased and suckled.

Rafael gave a long, sensual sigh as he admired her bounty and curved his skilled fingers around one breast, weighing it in his hand, stroking the peak with the pad of his thumb. "Annie, Annie. What a beautiful creature you are."

As he fondled her, Annie raised both arms above her head in an unconscious gesture of surrender. Rafael immediately caught her wrists together and held them.

A delicious tremor moved through Annie's supple body like an intangible wave. "Rafael," she said, and the name was at once a vow and a plea.

"Like fruit," Rafael murmured, his breath warm on the breast he'd chosen, and soft as a tropical breeze, making the already-taut nipple ache with readiness and wanting. "Sweet and warm and ready—so ready."

Annie *was* ready; in fact, she was frantic. "Oh, God, Rafael—please—*please!*"

He deigned to appease her, at least a little, by taking her straining nipple into his mouth, lashing it lightly with the tip of his tongue while beginning a slow suckling motion.

The pleasure seemed to consume Annie like fire. She writhed, her wrists still pleasantly manacled by

Rafael's fingers, and a sheen of perspiration broke out on her stomach and her upper lip, between her shoulder blades and behind her knees.

Rafael drew greedily on one breast, and then the other. "Only the beginning, Annie my love," he warned, before returning to the first nipple and starting the whole process all over again.

Annie began to sob, ever so softly, but her weeping was from joy, and not sorrow. Nothing existed beyond Rafael, and the lovely things he was doing to her.

"Please," she said again, while he feasted at her breast.

Still holding her a willing prisoner, still suckling with a ferocious hunger that inflamed Annie's soul, Rafael slid one hand down over her abdomen and burrowed through the silken curls to find, with two fingers, the small swell of flesh hidden there. Slowly, and so lightly that it seemed he was barely touching her, Rafael began to roll the nubbin back and forth, up and down—gently. So gently.

Annie's plea for satisfaction was answered with the creation of a need so deep, so violent and primitive, that she feared her very being would dissolve in its heat. She remembered what Rafael had done to appease her that day in the cottage behind St. James Keep and wanted that again.

Rafael pushed her further and further, plunging his fingers deep inside her while continuing to stroke her with his thumb. Each time she neared the peak of ecstasy, however, he somehow sensed that she was approaching the summit, and slowed his pace, easing a sweat-soaked, whimpering Annie back down into a hellish heaven of wanting.

She hardly noticed when he finally removed her

nightgown and tossed it aside, and she was like a wild creature when he stripped off the rest of his clothes and stretched out on the bed beside her.

Now, she thought, in glorious despair, *now at last—at last.*

But once again, Annie was made to wait. Rafael took her into his arms, holding her close against his hardness and his heat, and his lips brushed her ear as he whispered to her.

"Be patient, little one," he said. "It takes time."

She was hardly coherent, and being held that way only increased her desire and heightened her desperation. "You want to make me suffer," she accused.

Rafael smiled against her temple. "No," he told her. "I want to please you, my love—please you so thoroughly that you'll forgive me, someday."

Annie remembered the most scandalous of the pictures in the book of erotic drawings she and her schoolmates had exclaimed over back at St. Aspasia's. Boldly, she reached down and took Rafael's manhood in a firm grasp.

A delicious sense of power swelled her pounding heart and quickened her breath when he cried out in surprised pleasure, and she felt him burgeoning against her palm. She moved her thumb in a leisurely circle around the tip of his masculinity, and it seemed he grew even larger and harder.

"Annie," he gasped.

She leaned over Rafael, kissing his chest, finding the flat male nipples hidden in whorls of dark hair and sampling them, one by one, with the tip of her tongue.

He said her name again, this time in warning, but he didn't try to push her away.

Annie grew more and more brazen with her kisses,

198

moving lower and lower, until she'd reached his abdomen, and felt his member against her cheek. Just when she would have turned her head, and taken him as boldly as he had once taken her, he grasped her by the shoulders and thrust her onto her back in a motion so quick and forceful that it took her breath away.

Rafael held her wrists, pressing them into the pillow on either side of her head, and gazed into her eyes. His breathing, like Annie's, was quick and shallow, and although she saw the muscle leaping in his jaw, she was no more afraid of him than a tigress would be of its mate.

"I want you," she said.

"You'll do considerably more wanting," Rafael immediately replied, "before you're satisfied."

He was as good as his word; the deflowering of Annie Trevarren was a long, thorough and exacting process. Rafael teased her for what seemed like hours, kissing her, stroking and suckling, whispering the glorious details of what he meant to do into her ear. At last, he poised himself over her, and interlocked his fingers with hers, again pressing her hands into the pillow, while she felt him between her legs and strained to take him inside her.

By then, Annie was drenched in perspiration and half out of her mind with need, and whether it brought pleasure or pain, she wanted only one thing— utter union, of form and of spirit, with Rafael.

He mounted her and gave her just enough of himself to make her want more, and that stripped away the last vestige of her control. Annie went wild beneath Rafael, freeing her hands, clawing at him, urging him, finally clasping his muscled buttocks and driving him into her.

There was an explosion of pain when her maidenhead was breached, but before Annie had fully registered that, the sensation changed to a pleasure beyond anything she'd ever imagined. The rapture was intensified by the knowledge that Rafael had finally lost control as well.

At first, he moved slowly, deliberately. But when Annie raised her hips high, and forced him back into her depths with her hands, he gave a hoarse cry and began to flex and delve with a powerful, frantic rhythm.

Finally, when Annie knew for certain that she could bear no more waiting, there was a blinding shattering of all that held her within herself. Their souls, as well as their bodies, seemed to collide and then merge into one fiery entity.

Annie was lost, transported, her body convulsing in response long after Rafael's fierce thrusts had ceased, long after he had collapsed against her, his face buried in her neck. He made no move to pull away, and she was grateful, for being held was as pleasant as the lovemaking had been.

She could not have said whether an hour or a year had passed when Rafael finally raised his head to look into her face. Although the room was dark, she saw bewilderment etched in his features, and something deeper that she couldn't recognize. He didn't speak, and neither did she, for there was no need. Their communion had been complete.

Presently, when the first pinkish gold hint of dawn glowed at the windows, Rafael left Annie's bed. He pulled on his clothes, not bothering to button his shirt, and carried his boots in one hand. He bent to kiss her on the mouth, but the contact was brief, and somehow final.

He started to speak, but Annie touched her fingers to his lips.

"Don't," she pleaded softly. "Don't say you're sorry, Rafael. It would hurt too much to bear."

Rafael's eyes seemed to shimmer for a moment. He reached out to caress Annie's cheek, and his reply was gruff. "By all rights, I should be sorry, but I'm not."

Annie could hardly breathe, and though her body was still humming with the euphoria she'd known in Rafael's arms, her heart was breaking. "And now?"

He sighed. "And now we must forget; I because there can be nothing else between us, and you because there will be another, better man to claim you, one day soon."

She didn't bother to deny that she would ever love another, although she knew she wouldn't. She closed her eyes and nodded, for it had been the bargain from the first, that they would part. She had sold her soul for one night with the man she loved, and she didn't regret it.

Rafael went out, closing the door gently behind him, and Annie lay alone in the darkness, weeping even as she savored and cherished the memory of an almost inconceivable joy.

She awakened late the next morning to find Kathleen in her room, humming and rattling dishes.

"Good morning, miss," she said, when Annie sat up in bed. Her eyes felt swollen and itchy, her heart was in pieces and, conversely, her traitorous body was jubilant, fairly pulsing with well-being.

"Good morning," Annie grumbled. She had been

201

forever changed by the events of the previous night, and felt certain that such profound differences must show, but Kathleen didn't seem to notice anything.

In fact, she simply crossed the room and set a tray across Annie's lap.

"Cook says you'll be going back to St. James Keep today," the maid commented. "Now that the ball is over, there's no reason to stay, is there? And besides, it's so dangerous here."

Annie lifted the lid off a plate and found eggs and sausage and toasted bread beneath. She immediately discovered that, while her heart might be broken, her appetite was still intact. She picked up her fork and tried to speak casually.

"Have you seen the prince this morning?"

Kathleen moved to the vanity table and straightened Annie's comb, brush and hand mirror. "Yes, miss—he left the palace early, with Mr. Barrett. They went to the Parliament building to see about Miss Covington's brother."

Annie's hunger vanished, and she put down her fork. She watched in silence as Kathleen opened the door of the armoire and gazed thoughtfully at the array of dresses inside.

"Would you like to wear blue today, miss? It looks so nice with your eyes."

Annie felt a surge of impatience and quelled it. "I'll choose my own dress, Kathleen," she said moderately. "Will you please take this tray away and have hot water sent up for a bath? And find out, if you would, if Miss Covington is all right."

Kathleen nodded and collected the tray. "Yes, miss," she said, and went out.

Soon, warm water was brought to Annie's room,

along with a small copper tub. She ached from last night's lovemaking, and the bath soothed her body, if not her troubled soul. Annie knew she would never regret giving herself to Rafael. Still, having visited paradise, it was doubly difficult to know she was barred from its gates. She thought she knew how Eve must have felt, being driven from the Garden.

Presently, Annie dried herself and dressed, putting on the cornflower blue dress Kathleen had suggested earlier. She had tamed her wild hair and wound it into a single thick braid when the maid returned, with two helpers, who immediately removed the tub. Kathleen lingered to strip the sheets from Annie's bed and replace them with clean ones.

Annie said nothing, but her cheeks were hot as she swept out of the chamber and went in search of Phaedra. Kathleen would know exactly what had happened to her charge the night before, if she hadn't guessed already, when she got a good look at those linens.

There was no sign of the princess in her chambers, the dining room, the main parlor or the gardens.

Annie's wanderings eventually brought her to the other side of the palace where six different sets of French doors, all standing open to the morning air, offered admittance to the ballroom.

The grand chamber was still bustling with activity, although the servants had long since cleared away champagne glasses, punch bowls, flowers and paper decorations left from the ball. By that time, they were polishing the marble floors and the mirrors that lined three walls.

Annie lingered a few moments, remembering how it had been to whirl round and round in Rafael's arms, her heart soaring in a waltz of its own. When she turned from the doorway, she was restless, and wanted to spend what was left of the morning exploring the palace grounds and her own hopelessly confused thoughts.

Felicia was standing directly behind Annie. She was pale and subdued, and the shadows under her eyes were like bruises. Tears welled along her dark lashes and she started to speak, then stopped herself.

Annie's heart went out to Felicia, but she didn't know what to say. While she regretted the woman's pain, she felt no remorse for identifying Jeremy Covington as the leader of the men who had raided the marketplace and murdered the young dissenter.

"You're—you're certain it was Jeremy you saw?" Felicia whispered brokenly.

"Yes," Annie said.

Felicia gnawed at her lower lip, absorbing Annie's response as though it had been a physical blow, and finally gave a distracted nod. "Jeremy was always getting into trouble as a boy," she said. "Papa thought the army would make a man of him." Felicia paused and uttered a hysterical sound that was part laughter, part strangled sob. "Instead, it will be the end of his life."

Annie held her tongue, knowing it would serve no purpose to say what she was thinking, that the army had not destroyed Jeremy Covington. He had done that to himself.

Felicia seemed to be speaking not to Annie, but to some unseen person standing next to her. Her beautiful brown eyes were unfocussed, her brow furrowed, her skin almost transparent, with tiny blue veins showing through. "Rafael will make an example of Jeremy, a sacrifice. He'll throw him to the wolves."

Putting a firm arm around Felicia's waist, Annie guided the other woman to the nearest bench and sat her down. "You're overwrought," Annie said. "Let me bring you some water . . ."

"No." Felicia shook her head, caught Annie's hand in a frantic grasp and tugged hard. Annie took a seat beside her.

"You could change Rafael's mind," she said. "He cares for you, Annie. If you asked him, he might exile Jeremy from Bavia, instead of putting him on trial."

Annie closed her eyes, hearing the shrill whinnies of the horses, the clattering of their hooves on the cobblestones of the marketplace, the soldiers' shouts and the terrified screams of the merchants and their patrons. And she heard the shot that had taken the life of the student.

She made herself look at Felicia's wan face. "I have no influence over the prince," she said, as kindly as she could.

Felicia started to protest, but she was silenced by a masculine voice from behind them.

"Miss Trevarren is right, Felicia," Rafael said.

Miss Trevarren? Annie thought, injured, even in light of their agreement that they must forget last night's interlude, that he could refer to her with such cold formality.

His gray eyes were like frosted steel as he looked at her. "While I admit to a certain fondness for our American guest," he said, "I do not consult her on matters of state."

Annie lowered her gaze. His words were perfectly

true, and undeniably reasonable, but they still made her feel as though she'd been slapped. Only last night, after all, Rafael had moaned in her arms, and cried out hoarsely when she pleasured him. Now, he might have been a stranger.

Felicia was agitated, jumping to her feet, clutching the lapels of Rafael's dark morning coat in both hands. "Please," she begged. "Let Jeremy leave Bavia —send him to England or France—punishing him will change nothing—"

Rafael gripped Felicia's wrists and held them, and Annie saw a shadow of pain move in his eyes. "Lieutenant Covington has identified the other men who were with him that day," he said quietly. "They have all been relieved of their duties and put into prison, pending trial."

Felicia began to sob. "Rafael, no—oh, God—don't do this, I beg of you—"

The prince drew Felicia into his arms then, murmuring words of comfort and compassion but gazing at Annie over her head the whole time. His self-control was remarkable.

Annie rose from the bench without a word and hurried into the palace, nearly colliding with one of the maids as she traversed the ballroom's slippery floor.

That afternoon, by Rafael's order, Phaedra and Annie were sent back to St. James Keep, with a large contingent of armed soldiers to escort them. Mr. Haslett remained in Morovia, as did Felicia, who was clearly in no state to travel.

Phaedra sat silently in the carriage seat opposite Annie's, absorbed in a slim volume of poetry, apparently untroubled by this sudden separation from her intended husband. Every so often, the princess closed her book and stared out at the passing countryside with a pensive expression.

Annie was anxious, and she needed her friend's attention and the sound of another voice, however mundane the conversation might be. "The ball was beautiful," she said, hoping for a lengthy response.

Phaedra turned from the window and looked at Annie as though surprised to see her there. "Yes," she replied. "You spent a great deal of time with Rafael. There was quite a lot of comment on that, you know."

After pressing her lips together for a moment, and averting her eyes, Annie gave a straightforward reply. "I've never made a secret of my feelings for him," she said. "Especially not with you."

The princess sighed, removed her black traveling bonnet, with its pleated brim and wide ribbon ties, and set it beside her on the cushioned seat. "You seem different today, Annie," she observed, studying her friend frankly. "You're subdued, but there's something defiant about your manner, too. I hope you have not been so foolish as to surrender to my brother's formidable charms."

Fire throbbed in Annie's cheeks; her emotions were so close to the surface that she could hardly hide them from strangers, let alone from her closest friend. "It is my own affair what I do, Phaedra St. James, and none of yours."

Phaedra looked genuinely sorrowful. "Oh, Annie," she murmured. "Rafael will never marry you. He couldn't, with Bavia collapsing around him."

Rafael had told Annie the same thing, in so many words, and she'd believed him. Phaedra's words certainly came as no surprise, and yet for Annie the pain of hearing them and accepting them all over again was devastating.

She swallowed hard to keep from wailing in grief.

Never particularly tactful, Phaedra went on. "Even if there wasn't a war coming on—one Rafael cannot and will not run away from—he would have to marry someone with a title." She straightened her kid gloves. "He might make you his mistress, though, provided he lives long enough to set you up in a proper house."

Annie had sacrificed a great deal to share that one night with Rafael St. James, but she didn't regard herself as his inferior, title or no title. Furthermore, her love was an eternal one, with no beginning and no end, and she had no intention whatsoever of living out the remainder of her life in a gilded cage.

"Phaedra," she began, when she could trust herself to speak in a moderate tone, "there are times when I'd like to push you out the nearest second-story window. I love Rafael—in fact, I adore him—but I won't be a paramour to him or any other man."

Phaedra flushed a little, and subsided. "What will you do, then?" she asked, after a long and awkward silence, her voice small.

Again, tears threatened. "I don't know, precisely," Annie said, when she'd braced herself up. "On the one hand, I wish I'd never heard of Rafael, or of Bavia. On the other, I wouldn't trade what happened last night for a month in heaven."

The princess didn't answer. Instead, she turned her attention back to the book of poetry again.

They reached St. James Keep in good time, and the wheels of the carriage and the hooves of the team and the soldiers' mounts clattered loudly over the ancient wooden drawbridge. Metal squealed against stone as the portcullis was raised, then lowered behind the band of travelers with a rib-shaking crash.

Annie kept to herself for the rest of the day, walking in the gardens, reading in her room, taking her meals in the kitchen with the servants.

After sunset, she was standing on one of the parapets, gazing toward Morovia, when she saw a vague crimson glow shimmering in the night sky. Others must have spotted it, too, for an alarm was raised and there was much running, shouting and maneuvering within the vast keep.

Annie managed to stop one of the soldiers dashing by, catching him by the sleeve of his tunic. "What is it?" she demanded. "What's happening?"

The young man bobbed his head once, in hasty deference, and said, "It appears that the capital is under attack, miss," before racing off to be about his duties.

Morovia—the palace—*Rafael.* Annie sagged against the wall, breathless with shock and horror and near to swooning. It was happening at last, the war Rafael had been expecting for so long was finally beginning! She closed her eyes tightly against the terrible, bloody images that rose before her, but there was no blocking them out.

Bavia was at war, the loyalist army was in chaos, and Rafael himself was the enemy's prime target.

Annie managed to keep herself from fainting, but her stomach was threatening violence of its own and she was trembling so hard that she had to keep one hand on the wall as she made her way along the walkway toward the nearest staircase. She wished frantically that she'd stayed in Morovia, though she knew she would have been more a hindrance to Rafael than a help. She imagined saddling a horse and racing back to the capital on her own, although she was well aware, all the while she was formulating the fantasy, that it would be impossible to do. As well as foolish.

At the bottom of the stone staircase, in the torchlit courtyard, she watched as more soldiers rushed about, carrying rifles and even crossbows, preparing to defend the keep. Annie stood still for a few minutes, caught up in the maelstrom, but then she hurried across the courtyard and into the castle. She raced up the main stairs and along the hallway to her chamber.

There, she ransacked her trunks and the clothes the maids had already unpacked, tossing petticoats and camisoles, stockings and nightgowns in every direction. Finally, she found what she was searching for—her breeches and shirt. She put them on, after fairly tearing off her dress and underthings, and was hopping about trying to pull one riding boot onto her foot when Phaedra burst into the room, her gray eyes enormous.

"It's the end!" the princess cried. "We'll all be killed!"

CHAPTER

12

Orange and crimson flames leaped in the darkness, consuming filth and splendor, dreams and nightmares, loyalties and defiances. Chaos was the order of the night, and as Rafael gazed out over the blazing city from one of the high windows in the Parliament building, his emotions reflected what he saw.

He despaired because the world he knew and—for all its myriad flaws—devoutly loved, was in the throes of violent death. At the same time, he rejoiced in the certainty that Annie was reasonably safe behind the ancient walls of St. James Keep. Grief for the people of Bavia, both rebels and patriots, tore at his spirit. Yet Rafael was exultant because Annie Trevarren had received him into her bed, and her body, and he had found in the abjectness of that intimacy a solace unlike anything he'd ever known before. Annie had depleted him, exhausted every secret reserve of passion, demanded everything he was and everything he had. And by taking him to the edge of utter destruction, she had resurrected him.

For a moment, Rafael closed his eyes and allowed himself to savor echoes of the excruciating joys and glories he had found in Annie's arms, but the present loomed fierce and fiery before him, and would not be denied for long.

Nor would Barrett, who stood at Rafael's side and laid a hand on his arm. "The army awaits your command to either defend Morovia or to flee," his friend said solemnly. "Have you made a decision?"

Rafael bid a silent farewell to the homeland he had known—one that had, perhaps, never truly existed outside his own thoughts—that pastoral principality overlooking the sea, that green and rocky place where tinkers wandered in brightly painted wagons and sheep grazed upon the hillsides. Letting go was as painful as a lance wound.

"Yes," he answered at last, turning to look into Barrett's wan and worried face. "I want you to dispatch troops into the countryside to defend the villagers and crofters against marauding rebels. I will return to St. James Keep to see Phaedra married, and then you, Barrett, will escort my sister and her new husband safely over the French border."

A shadow appeared over Barrett's eyes, a shade of frustration or anger or pain—Rafael could not discern which. "And then?"

"And then you will keep going. You will dismiss your men and start over somewhere else—America, perhaps, or Australia. There's a fund on deposit for you at the Carver Bank in London, enough to ensure that you won't want for anything while you're reestablishing yourself."

Barrett was silent for a few moments, looking not at Rafael but at the burning city beyond the window glass. Finally, still without meeting Rafael's eyes, he asked, "And what about you?"

Rafael gave a sigh that was almost explosive in its force. "We've discussed this before. I'll be staying in Bavia."

"Until the keep is overrun and you are led into the main courtyard with your hands bound, and hanged?" Barrett asked, and although he spoke quietly his words carried a sting.

Rafael set his jaw and then relaxed it again, forcibly. "A very melodramatic image, Barrett," he said. "Perhaps you should consider writing bad plays for a living."

"Listen to me, damn you!" Barrett rasped. "I'm not leaving this blasted country without you. If I have to knock you unconscious and carry you out of here in a barley sack, I'll do it." He paused to draw in a ragged breath and released it again. "My God, Rafael," he went on, "do you think I could live out the rest of my life knowing I'd abandoned the best friend I ever had?"

Turning from the window and, however momentarily, from the hellish flames reflected in the glass, Rafael spoke gently. "Your responsibility to protect me will end, Barrett, the moment you ride over the drawbridge at St. James Keep for the last time. Perhaps it would be better—and kinder—if I relieved you of your duties now."

Barrett's face contorted as he struggled to rise above his emotions. "We've been friends for more than twenty years," he pointed out, and his voice was taut with fury. "What about the responsibilities that come with *that*, Rafael? Will riding over a drawbridge or surrendering my commission put an end to them as well?"

Rafael's patience was wearing thin; he dreaded the parting from Barrett with his whole soul—only saying good-bye to Annie would be worse. The last thing he needed, considering all he had yet to face and deal with, was to be reminded of a bond that spanned much of his life. For that reason, he spoke harshly as he strode across the chamber to the doorway.

"For God's sake, Barrett, you sound like a woman who's just been cast off by a lover. Stiffen your backbone and keep your feelings to yourself or resign —one or the other. I have neither the time nor the inclination to listen to your sentimental ramblings."

Barrett was seething, Rafael could feel fury emanating from the man like heat from a stove, but he said nothing more until they had descended the broad staircase that led to the building's huge, marble-floored foyer. There, in his military stance with hands clasped behind his back, Barrett addressed the prince with the cool formality of a stranger.

"I would recommend that you leave Morovia as soon as possible, sir," he said, his gaze impassive and focussed on a point just beyond Rafael's left ear. "I can have an escort ready within fifteen minutes. In the meantime, what do you want done with the prisoners —Covington and the others, I mean?"

The muscles in Rafael's neck clenched, producing an instant headache. He could not abandon the men to the rebels, but to set them free, even in the midst of a revolution, would be a travesty of justice.

"I want them brought to the keep for trial," he said at last.

Barrett offered no comment, but simply inclined his head in a brisk, cold expression of obedience and walked away to speak to his lieutenants, who stood a little apart, awaiting their orders.

Within a quarter of an hour, just as Barrett had said, a sizable detachment was assembled in the street behind the darkened Parliament building. There were at least fifty men, by Rafael's estimate, and his own horse was saddled and waiting. Covington and his band of outlaws were marched out of the stockade where they'd been held since the night before, their hands manacled behind them, and put into two large prison wagons.

Rafael watched them impassively, but he was thinking of Felicia's terrible grief, hearing her frantic pleas, feeling her trembling in his arms when he'd tried, without success, to comfort her. Refusing her entreaties had been among the hardest things he'd ever had to do, but a young man had been killed and several merchants had been injured, while many others had lost their livelihood. To release Covington and the others would have been wrong.

He had mounted the gelding when Lucian rode up beside him and executed a mocking salute. "A moment of your time, *sir*, if you please," Lucian said. His horse, a nervous bay, sidestepped fitfully, its hooves making a clatter on the cobblestones.

Rafael ignored the sarcasm in Lucian's tone and manner and treated him as he would any soldier. "What is it?" he asked, somewhat curtly.

Lucian drew nearer and spoke in an urgent whisper. "It would serve you right, you arrogant tinker's bastard, if I kept what I know to myself and let you ride straight into the trap that awaits you. For Phaedra's sake, and for Annie's, however, I will resist the temptation!"

Swiftly, Rafael swung his arm, backhanding his brother so hard that Lucian nearly toppled from the saddle. The boy recovered with surprising promptness, wiping blood from the corner of his mouth and glaring at Rafael with a pure and elegant hatred.

"I, too, have been tempted, more times than I can count," Rafael told him furiously, "to do what I just did. Do not push me any further, Lucian, for I swear by all I hold dear that if you do, I'll drag you off that horse and beat you senseless, right here and now."

Lucian neither flinched nor fled, but there was a grudging civility in his voice when he spoke again. "The rebels want Covington and his band of merry men," he said, nodding toward the prison wagons. "You'll save a lot of lives, including your own probably, if you surrender them now."

Rafael leaned forward, resting one arm on the pommel of his saddle, his eyes narrowed thoughtfully as he regarded his young half brother. "How do you know what the rebels want?"

The dilettante-soldier stiffened slightly, but smiled. "I hear a great many things, now that I've been banished from the royal hearth."

Rafael straightened as Barrett rode toward them. "Tell your contacts, whoever they are, that these men will stand trial at St. James Keep, and their fate will be decided by a jury of ordinary people, drawn from the villages and farms—not by a mob."

Lucian gave a second insolent salute, indulged in

another fleeting and bitter grin, and reined his horse away.

Barrett's attitude was still distant, and while Rafael knew that it was probably for the best, his old friend's disapproval made him ache inside.

"Ready, Your Highness?"

Rafael swallowed a surly response and said simply, "Yes."

The party left Morovia through the western gate and, to Rafael's surprise, they were neither challenged nor pursued. The rebels, he reflected ruefully, were probably too busy razing the city to give chase.

There were dozens of men, women and children fleeing Morovia by the coastal road, however. The track was choked with them, and they pleaded for protection, crying out in the darkness like disembodied spirits. Against Barrett's advice, Rafael issued the command that twenty men accompany the refugees to the keep, where they might have sanctuary.

It seemed that luck was with the prince that night, for even with a diminished escort and two lumbering prison wagons to slow them down, the company reached the drawbridge of St. James Keep without incident. A long delay ensued, during which a guard came out to make certain that it really was the master of the house asking admittance, and not a party of crafty rebels. At last, after much ado, the massive gates were thrown open and the portcullis was raised.

Rafael rode wearily into the main courtyard, swung down from the saddle, and surrendered his horse to a waiting groom. All around him, pandemonium reigned, while men who had gone traveling exchanged tales with those who had stayed behind. The prison wagons roused a great deal of curiosity, of course, and when it was learned that the men inside were to be confined to dungeons that had not been used for the better part of fifty years, there was a considerable stir of interest.

Pulling off his gloves, emotionally exhausted, Rafael started across the courtyard, thinking of the store of fine liquor in his study and the clean comfort of the feather bed in his private quarters. He was caught off guard when a slim but shapely form slipped out of the shadows to bar his way, and he had already clasped the handle of his sword before he realized that it was Annie.

He hid a smile as he assessed her boy's clothes. He wanted her as much as ever—nay, more, now that he knew what pleasures she could offer—but to indulge would be a breach of honor. "It's late, Miss Trevarren," he said. "You should be in bed."

Light from the moon and the torches inside the great hall glimmered in her hair, which was doing its best to escape the thick plait that trailed over her right shoulder like a rope woven of fire and shadow. She stiffened and raised her impertinent little chin. "I'm well past the age where I need someone to remind me of my bedtime," she pointed out coolly. Then, in the next instant, she flew at him, hurling her arms around his neck, clinging to him and burying her face in his shoulder. Her tempting body trembled with the force of her sobs and although Rafael knew every angel in heaven was bidding him to put her away from him, he could not obey. He held her close against his chest.

"Annie," was all he could say, and it was a murmured sound, barely more than a breath.

"I thought they'd killed you for certain!" she

wailed, dampening his shirt with her tears. "I was sure I'd never see you again!"

It was then that Barrett walked up alongside them. His gaze linked with Rafael's for a moment, over Annie's head, but he proceeded into the great hall without speaking.

"Hush, now," Rafael said, loosening his embrace and cupping Annie's face in his hands so that she had to look at him. "I'm here, safe and sound. I need you to be strong, love. Nothing weakens me like your tears."

She nodded and snuffled with an endearing lack of grace, and Rafael put his arm around her shoulders. Together, they entered the castle, and they got as far as the main staircase before Annie made another of her outrageous announcements.

"I want a sword," she said.

Rafael, who wanted to take Annie to his bed and knew he could not, had been silently consoling himself with the prospect of brandy, a hot bath, food and sleep. He stared at her, certain he must have misunderstood.

"What?" he asked, stupidly perhaps.

"I said I'll need a sword." Annie indicated his own blade with a nod. "I'm not very good with guns, you see, and—"

Rafael held up one hand to silence her. The thought of Annie armed, be it with pistol, bow and arrow, cannon or sword, chilled his blood. "Miss Trevarren," he said evenly, "in this keep, the men still do the fighting. If you truly want to help, then just stay out of trouble until we can return you to France and the safety of your family."

Annie looked stunned, as though he'd slapped her.

Rafael suppressed an urge to pull her back into his arms, knowing that if he did so, he would certainly be lost, honor or no honor. He knew his own limits only too well, and when it came to Annie Trevarren, they were severely strained. He could not allow his need to prevail over his good intentions.

She sniffed once, disdainfully. "I see," she said.

"Good," Rafael sighed. God in heaven but he was weary, to the very marrow of his bones and the center of his soul. Despite his better judgment, and his integrity, he longed to seek sanctuary in Annie's embrace, to lose himself in the sweet fury of her passion and spill his seed into her warm depths. Oh, to sire a child with her, that very night, to make a son or daughter who would live on after he'd perished. The wanting was so keen-edged, and so hopeless, that he wanted to weep for the sorrow of it. "Leave me," he murmured. "Please."

Annie regarded him for a long moment, and he read a parade of emotions in her blue eyes—frustration, and then tenderness, followed by resignation. Standing on the first step, so that her face was almost level with Rafael's, she leaned forward and kissed his forehead. "I know you mean well," she said gently, while the kiss still burned upon his flesh, like the thumbprint of an avenging angel, "but you need me, Rafael. You need my love and my help. Let me stand beside you, as I was born to do."

He closed his eyes, remembering his beautiful, brave wife. Georgiana had been his helpmate and his lover. She'd taken her place at his side, and believed with her whole heart that she'd been created to share his life. She'd been standing beside him, in fact, when an assassin's bullet had pierced her chest and exploded in her heart.

"No," he said aloud, speaking to Annie as well as to the memory. Desperation swelled within Rafael; it was too easy to imagine Annie dying in the same way Georgiana had. "Jesus, *no.*"

Annie laid a cool, soft hand to his face. "I love you," she said.

She had spoken those words to him before, but now Rafael knew that she meant them, and he was terrified for her. He had to avert disaster somehow, to make Annie stop caring before it was too late.

Rafael spoke with cold dispatch, though the truth of what he felt for Annie Trevarren was something very different, something he wasn't ready to face or put a name to just yet. "You are not the first young woman to make that mistake," he said. "But the fact is that I don't return your tender sentiments. I wanted a woman last night. You were there, willing and untried, and I used you."

The color drained from Annie's face, and Rafael gritted his teeth to keep from taking back the lie. To her credit, she raised a hand and slapped him so hard that he felt the blow all the way to the soles of his feet. Tears brimmed in her eyes as she watched him touch his fingers to his jaw, but he soon concluded that these weren't tears of remorse. No, they were made of pure fury.

"You can lie about your feelings all you want, Rafael St. James," Annie hissed, "but it's already too late, because last night your body told me the truth!"

Rafael closed his eyes for a moment, summoning all his inner resources. "No, Annie," he said. "You're wrong. Last night, you believed what you wanted to believe, because you were too naive to *accept* the truth."

She stared at him, her eyes shimmering, and her cheeks, pale as death a moment before, were suddenly mottled with crimson and pink. "You're pretending," she said, with unnerving conviction. "You want to protect me, to stop me from loving you so I won't be hurt. Again, Rafael, it's too late. God knows you don't deserve it, but I've long since pledged my heart to you, and there's no going back!"

Having said that, Annie turned and fled up the stairway, leaving Rafael to stare after her and wonder exactly when he had lost control of the situation.

If, he thought ruefully, he had ever *had* control in the first place.

What, Annie asked herself, had she expected? An avowal of undying devotion? A proposal of marriage? She paced her room, pounding her palm once with her fist. Rafael was cornered; he was fighting for his life. He had been honest with her before coming to her bed, explaining that he could offer her nothing beyond the pleasures of that one encounter. What had made her think things had changed?

Annie brushed away her tears with a wild motion of one arm. She'd been overcome with relief when she'd seen Rafael crossing the courtyard earlier, fearing until that moment that he was dead or dying. She'd lost her head, plain and simple, and now she owed him an apology.

She went to the washstand and splashed her burning face with tepid water. Then she stood in front of the looking glass for nearly a minute, trying to decide whether to exchange her breeches and shirt for a dress. In the end, she went as she was, leaving her chambers and hurrying toward Rafael's study on the other side of the keep.

Annie made the trip for nothing, as it happened; the room was dark and there was no sign of the prince, within or without.

That meant Rafael was in one of two places—his bedchamber, or the kitchen. It was conceivable that he might be hungry after his journey, and had not wanted to rouse the servants from their much-needed slumber. It was also possible that he'd gone to bed, and was already sleeping, Annie admitted to herself. In that case, he probably wouldn't welcome an intrusion, no matter how high-minded the intentions of the intruder might be.

Annie went downstairs to the kitchen and found that chamber empty, too, except for a gray cat sleeping on the hearth.

Reasoning that she could just as well extend her apologies to Rafael in the morning, Annie was disappointed nonetheless. She knew her conscience would keep her awake the rest of the night and, besides, Rafael would probably be leaving the keep on some mission or closeted away with his advisors before she even went down to breakfast.

It might be days, in fact, before she could tell him she was sorry for her lapse. Frankly, Annie couldn't bear the prospect of that.

She made her way resolutely through the dark passageways, carrying a single candle purloined from a wall sconce to light her path. After traveling a considerable distance, she arrived at the threshold of Rafael's bedchamber.

There was a golden strip of light under the door. Annie hesitated only a moment, then rapped on the heavy wood.

A muffled response came from within—Annie decided it was a summons and turned the heavy brass latch.

Rafael was standing in front of his fireplace, naked except for a towel wrapped around his middle, his hair wet and his flesh glistening from a recent washing. In one hand, he held a snifter with a splash of amber liquid in it.

Seeing Annie, he nearly dropped the glass.

"I thought you asked me to come in," she said, closing the door for the sake of privacy but staying near it.

Rafael's expression was ominous. "The devil himself had better be chasing you, Annie Trevarren," he warned. "I won't accept any other excuse."

She flushed at the implication that she might have come to Rafael's quarters for an improper reason. She wasn't above doing that very thing, of course, but since it really hadn't been her intention, she felt justified in being insulted. "I'm not here to seduce you," she replied briskly. "I came to apologize, though now, to be quite frank, I'm wondering if the exercise wouldn't be utterly wasted."

He rolled his magnificent silver eyes and muttered something that might have been a plea for patience. "And what, pray tell, has inspired this noble effort?"

Annie kept her temper, though just barely. "Perhaps you should have passed a term at St. Aspasia's yourself, instead of sending Phaedra. The nuns might have taught you to be charitable when someone is trying to make amends."

Rafael put down the snifter and stepped behind a folding screen. When he came out again, he was tying the belt of a dark green robe. Only then did he respond to Annie's remarks. "Did they ever mention, these illustrious nuns, that it is worse than improper for a young lady to venture into a man's bedchamber, Miss Trevarren?"

She swallowed hard. "No," she replied, at length. "They didn't."

"That would account, then," Rafael observed, taking up his brandy again and regarding Annie solemnly over the rim of the glass, "for your unfortunate oversight."

Annie had endured all she could or would. "Do you want me to apologize or not?" she snapped.

It seemed that Rafael's eyes twinkled, but it might have been reflected candlelight she saw in them, instead of amusement. "Oh, by all means, Miss Trevarren. Pour out your many sins."

"If you want to be ungracious, go ahead," Annie retorted. "I came to tell you that I'm sorry for throwing myself at you when you returned from Morovia tonight. It was only that I was glad you weren't dead."

Rafael took a leisurely sip of brandy while considering her words. After a long and awkward silence, he finally answered. "Thank you for that. Being glad I'm not dead, I mean."

Annie raised her chin a notch. "If you persist in this attitude, sir, I may have to revise my opinion."

He laughed and saluted her with the snifter, but then his expression turned serious again. "I still don't quite understand why you felt you needed to ask my pardon." he said.

Her lips were dry, all of a sudden, and she moistened them with the tip of her tongue. "I forgot our bargain," she said.

Rafael arched one eyebrow. "Our bargain?"

She nodded, still leaning heavily against the door, hands at her sides, fingers outspread. "You told me, before we made love, that we would have to forget afterward and go on as if nothing had happened. I accepted your terms, and yet tonight . . ." Annie paused miserably, averting her eyes briefly before meeting his gaze again. "Tonight I asked you to let me love you, and I said I was born to be at your side, and I shouldn't have spoken of those things. Even though I know they're true."

Rafael was silent for the longest time, but then he uttered a hoarse sound, like a groan of pain or despair. "Oh, God, Annie, you have no conception of what you're doing to me and to yourself. You can't have, or you wouldn't be so foolish, or so cruel!"

Annie's eyes widened at his words, but she didn't move or speak. Not even when he set his glass on the mantel and crossed the room to stand so near that she could see the torment etched plainly in his face.

"What I told you last night was true, Annie," he said, in a fierce whisper, taking a firm grip on her chin. "I can't give you anything—*anything* but grief!"

She knew it wasn't wise, but Annie couldn't stop herself from raising her hands to his shoulders and resting them there. "That's not true," she said gently. "You've already shown me so much joy." He released her chin, and she stood on tiptoe to press a light kiss against his mouth. "You're so worried about what you can't give me, Rafael. But what about the things *I* can give *you?*"

He closed his eyes and let his forehead rest against hers. "Oh, Annie," he rasped, "don't. Please don't. For both our sakes—"

" 'For both our sakes'?" Annie mocked tenderly, holding his face in her hands now, caressing his cheekbones with her thumbs, memorizing the feel of them. "For all we know, we might both die tomorrow, or next week. And then all this nobility, all this self-denial, will have been for nothing. Rafael, happiness can be like a wisp of smoke or a firefly on a summer night, there one moment, and gone the next. If we've found joy, however fleeting it might be, shouldn't we embrace it? Shouldn't we hold it in our hands and in our hearts, as long as we can?"

"Annie," he said again, in anguish.

She kissed him once more. "Good night, my love," she whispered, just before she turned to go.

Rafael's hand closed over hers when she grasped the door handle. "Stay," he said.

CHAPTER

13

Stay.

Annie turned to look into Rafael's eyes, which had darkened from their normal silvery shade to a deep, smoky gray. "Is that what you truly want?" she asked.

Rafael's throat was dry. He was standing so close to Annie now that she could feel the heat, the hardness and the restrained power of his body. "God help me," he answered, his voice as rough as dry, porous stone, "but it is."

"What about your honor—"

"Damn my bloody honor!" he rasped. "I've gone beyond that now, don't you see? My need for you is greater than anything else."

"But you don't love me," she said.

"To win my love is to be cursed," Rafael muttered, frowning, his mouth so close to Annie's then that her lips tingled in anticipation of his kiss. He braced his hands against the door, on either side of her head. "Far better—and safer—to be counted as my enemy . . ."

Annie sagged against the ancient wood with a deep sigh as he took her mouth in that preliminary conquest. She had not come to Rafael's bedchamber to seduce him, and yet she was shamelessly glad to know she'd broken through his resolve.

The kiss lasted a long time, during which Annie's very bones seemed to melt. Her breasts swelled, their tips straining against her cotton shirt, and something coiled, tight and sweet and warm, deep in her abdomen.

At last, Rafael raised his head and looked into her eyes. She was still trapped between his strong arms, and she had no desire to be rescued.

"Leave now, if you're feeling timid, for if you stay, I shall ravish you. And I'll take my time at it, like before."

A tremor went through Annie, for the things she'd felt in Rafael's arms before had been ferociously, sometimes frighteningly, pleasurable. Time and again, the passion had been so great that it seemed to part soul from body, and even in her ecstasy, Annie had feared she would not find her way back to herself. Rafael would arouse terrible needs in her and she knew he'd meant what he said moments before; she'd suffer sweet agonies of wanting before he appeased her.

She began unbuttoning her shirt. "When have I ever been timid?" she asked.

Rafael made a low, strangled sound, and then, while

Annie still leaned against the door of his bedchamber, he finished undressing her. When her boots and breeches and shirt had all been tossed aside—she'd worn nothing beneath them—he spent a long time just looking at her.

Finally, fumbling just a little, he unbraided her hair and combed it with his fingers. Although Annie was naked and completely at Rafael's mercy, both physically and emotionally, she felt like a goddess. She knew that even at the height of her yearning, when she would plead for the release only Rafael could give, when his power over her would seem absolute, he would worship her with his body.

He kissed her again, falling to her with a groan the way a starving man might fall to food, and she opened his robe and embraced him, spreading her fingers against the muscles girding his back. She felt hard sinew flex beneath her palms, and Rafael groaned again, thrusting his tongue deep into her mouth, where it met and battled her own.

Presently, Rafael scooped Annie into his arms and carried her across the floor to his bed. It stood on a dais, but he mounted the steps with ease and flung her onto the mattress.

Annie knew that a part of Rafael was furious because she'd made him want her so desperately, and that there was an element of punishment in making her wait for her deliverance. She didn't care as long as she could hold Rafael, caress him, and finally woo him deep inside her.

She raised her arms to him and he shed his robe and stretched out beside her on the vast bed.

Once again, they kissed, deeply, their tongues and limbs entangled. There were interludes of tenderness,

of almost unbearable beauty, followed by fierce, fevered battles that set them rolling from side to side.

Annie heard a clock strike in the distance, and then
heard it again later through a pounding delirium of
desire, but Rafael was still stoking the flames within
her, even then. Much more time would pass, she
knew, before he allowed her the fulfillment she
craved; he meant to make her fight, and finally plead,
for that.

The small rituals he put her through, over and over,
nearly drove her mad. First, he kissed and caressed
the arches of her feet, then the insteps, progressing
with exquisite slowness to her calves, the backs of her
knees, her inner thighs, her belly and breasts, the
insides of her elbows, her neck and earlobes. Then,
because she was whimpering, he would make his way
back down her body until he'd reached the moist,
aching delta between her legs.

He toyed with her, not once but many times, and
finally burrowed through to kiss her there, tease her
with his tongue, and finally suckle. Always, always, he
knew when she was about to explode with gratifica-
tion, however. He invariably withdrew just short of
that moment, and left Annie trembling and frantic.

They had been engaged in this methodical battle for
more than two hours, by the chimes of the clock, when
Rafael finally mounted Annie. Her entire body was
slick with perspiration, tendrils of her hair clinging to
her cheeks and her temples and her nape, but at least
she had the comfort of knowing that he was no better
off.

She felt Rafael's damp flesh quiver against her own
as he struggled to control his desire. "Annie," he
whispered. With this final word, he entered her but,

although the thrust was powerful, and made Annie's nerves scream with expectation, he stopped just half-way and held himself there.

Annie was about to lose her mind; she clutched at Rafael, planning to force him into her to the hilt, as she had done the night before. But he was ready for her, muscles clenched, and she could not move him.

She arched slightly, raising glistening breasts to him, silently begging him to reach into her depths and assuage her primitive, violent need.

Rafael remained where he was, and incredibly his member seemed to grow even larger and harder, pressing against the walls of her femininity as if to burst them. Promising ecstasy and giving only torment.

Annie made an incoherent sound, and without plunging deeper or withdrawing, Rafael bent his head and took suckle at one of her reaching nipples. Presently, the muscles in his arms and chest visibly corded as he struggled to retain control, he treated her other breast to the same delicious plundering.

Annie's mind reeled and her body buckled and writhed, but still Rafael did not take her.

Finally, in desperation, she began to gasp out words, senseless ones at first. She painted a mental picture in which their positions were reversed, and Rafael was at her mercy, and told him all the scandalous things she wanted to do to him.

At long last, his control snapped. He delved into her, with a raspy warrior's cry, and she rose to meet and receive him. Annie matched every sleek, powerful surge of Rafael's body with a graceful arch of her own and their pace increased until that final moment when all the walls came down and they met as one soul. The result was an endless, shattering, cataclysmic fire-storm, unchaining emotions and sensations that had never been named.

When it was over, they clung to each other, and finally slept.

At dawn, Rafael awakened to find Annie curled in his arms. As always, with this woman, his emotions were mixed. He would be damned for the worst kind of liar if he pretended, even for a moment, that he hadn't reveled in taking her. He knew, too, that to speak of honor again would make him a hypocrite—he could no more resist Annie than his next breath. For all of that, however, Rafael wished, for her sake, that she had never heard or uttered his name, let alone come to Bavia and offered up both her heart and her body as a sacrifice.

It was hopeless, and such a damnable waste.

She awakened as he was thinking these thoughts, and raised herself on one elbow to look into his face. She touched his lower lip with the tip of her index finger and as easily as that set his blood blazing.

He was hard and heavy in an instant, and with a muffled groan, he poised himself above her. She made a crooning sound, and shifted beneath him, opening her legs to receive him.

Rafael set his teeth and thrust himself inside her—just far enough to entice them both in the direction of madness. A long time later, when Annie's nails had raked his back, when she'd cursed and threatened and finally begged, he took her completely. In that one frantic motion of his hips, Rafael became both con-queror and captive.

Appeased again, Annie slept when it was over, but

Rafael could not afford the luxury. He rose, used a copious amount of tepid water, and donned his clothes. When he came out of the small dressing room reserved for that purpose, he was startled and then furious to find Lucian standing just inside the door, watching Annie sleep.

Lucian met Rafael's gaze and smiled. "As much as you'd like to kill me right now," he said, in a quiet voice, "you won't lay a hand on me. You won't even raise your voice, will you, because that might frighten your luscious little bedmate."

"Get out," Rafael said, very softly.

Lucian uttered a long-suffering sigh, and Annie made a murmuring sound and shifted in her sleep. "I suppose I should be grateful to you for teaching Annie the pleasures of the flesh," he confided. "She'll want a lover when you're gone. Still, just thinking of her thrashing in your bed makes me feel as though I've just been gutted."

Rafael maintained his temper; Lucian could have had only one purpose in entering the chamber uninvited—to goad his elder brother into some rash and foolish action. "You have stepped over the line," the prince said, folding his arms, "and I will not play your games. Do not delude yourself, Lucian: while it is true that I am reluctant to box your ears in Annie's presence, I can be pushed only so far. And while you are relatively safe, here in this room, at this moment, there are many other rooms in St. James Keep and there will be many more moments when I might have my revenge."

Lucian cast a sorrowful look in the direction of the bed, where Annie still slept, and spoke with less bravado than before. "I must speak with you, Rafael. It has nothing to do with Annie or my aversion to soldiering."

Rafael saw something in Lucian's bearing that wasn't typical of him. Sincerity. He gestured toward the door, and when Lucian went out, Rafael followed him into the empty passageway.

"What is it?" Rafael demanded, keeping his voice low.

Lucian looked in both directions. "There is a plot underway," he replied. "The rebels plan to infiltrate the castle and take Covington and his men back to Morovia. They mean to execute them, one by one, in the courtyard, next to the market." He paused and sighed. "Do not ask me how I know this, Rafael, for I won't tell you."

Rafael frowned, his arms folded. He couldn't help feeling skeptical—Lucian had few scruples and he thrived on trickery—but he was certainly intrigued. "And how do these rebels intend to get past our gates?" he asked.

The look in Lucian's eyes was earnest, which was no indication of guilelessness or truth-telling. "The answer is as old as time, Rafael: You have enemies within these walls. People you trust are contriving, even now, to deceive and destroy you."

"Which people?"

Lucian smiled ruefully. "Ah," he said. "Therein, as the Bard said, lies the rub."

Rafael already knew he had foes within the keep's walls; it would have been naive to believe everyone wished him well. That didn't worry him.

What did trouble Rafael was the approaching wedding. All sorts of people would be passing in and out of the gates over a period of at least a week. The rebels would have no need of a Trojan horse—they could enter in merchants' wagons and guests' carriages. Some of them probably even had bona fide invitations.

"I see I've set you thinking," Lucian said, resting his hand briefly upon Rafael's shoulder. "There is one more thing I would bid you to consider."

Rafael said nothing, but simply waited.

"If you find this information helpful," Lucian went on, "perhaps you will be moved to release me from your damnable army."

Rafael wasn't really listening; he would speak to Chandler and Phaedra about eloping, he decided. If they agreed, he could call off the formal wedding, send Annie out of Bavia once and for all, and concentrate on the tasks at hand.

". . . sleeping with Barrett."

The tail end of Lucian's sentence snagged Rafael's attention on a sharp hook. "What?"

"I said, Phaedra has been sneaking off to the lake cottage, among other places, and meeting Barrett." He cast a meaningful glance at the closed door of Rafael's bedchamber. "Seems to be the season for deflowering virgins."

Rafael clasped his brother's shirt in both hands and thrust him against the opposite wall. "Barrett and Phaedra?" he demanded, giving Lucian a hard shake. "Think twice before you lie to me, Brother."

"I'm telling the truth," Lucian spat, struggling to free himself and failing. "Ask your good friend, if you don't believe me!"

Rafael freed Lucian with a contemptuous motion, but he had an uneasy feeling in the pit of his stomach. Barrett had told him, after all, that he cared for Phaedra. Rafael had warned the other man off and, having no reason to believe that his sister returned Barrett's affections, he'd put the matter out of his mind.

"Damn!" he whispered, shoving a hand through his hair. Barrett had been moody as hell of late, but Rafael had attributed that to the stress inherent in the man's work. Now he wondered.

Lucian moved a few strides down the passageway before speaking again. "Well?" he asked, spreading his arms. "Am I out of the army? May I sleep in my quarters again and wear my own clothes?"

"Yes," Rafael answered distractedly, gesturing in dismissal. "But don't burn your uniform. After the wedding, I'll decide whether your discharge is permanent or not."

The erstwhile soldier did not wait, but vanished around a corner, beyond which lay his old room.

Before Rafael could return to his chambers, awaken Annie and send her back where she belonged, a maid appeared with an armload of linens and a generous smile.

"Good morning, Your Highness," she said, with a quick, polished curtsey.

Rafael nodded. "Good morning, Evelyn." He maneuvered her away from his door and pointed her in the direction from which she'd come. "Save that for later, if you would," he said, indicating the sheets and towels.

Evelyn blushed, for it wasn't the first time she'd

politely steered away from the prince's door early in the day. "Yes, sir," she said. "I'll just make up another room. Lots of company coming, with the wedding."

Yes, Rafael thought, in silent agreement. And if he didn't keep his mind on the business at hand, it wouldn't be old friends occupying the castle's many beds, but conquering rebels. He imagined Annie as part of the victor's spoils and felt a renewed sense of desperation.

He moved through the passageways between his chambers and his study by memory, blinded by his thoughts. By God, if Barrett truly had bedded Phaedra, he reflected, he would kill the bastard with his bare hands.

The hypocrisy of that wasn't lost on Rafael—even then Annie was curled up, naked and warm, in his bed. Still, Annie wasn't pledged to another man, and she sure as hell wasn't his sister.

Rafael had been in his study less than five minutes —he'd just taken his rapier down from the wall, in fact—when Barrett appeared. Rafael pressed the tip of the blade to his friend's throat, then lowered the weapon to his side.

"I expected better of you," he said.

Barrett's eyes revealed the truth even before the confession passed his lips. "I cherish Phaedra. In point of fact, I would die for her. If you must uphold that fool's code of yours, then run me through and get it over with." He paused thoughtfully, a comical, pained expression taking shape on his face. "I'm not sure it wouldn't be a mercy, given the agonies of loving that particular woman."

Rafael could have told his friend something about agony, but he didn't. In the first place, he did not wish to discuss his ill-advised attachment to Annie Trevarren, and, in the second, that wasn't the issue in question. "How the devil did this happen? Phaedra is committed to another man, as you well know, and *by God* she will still marry him if he'll have her!"

Barrett brought an apple from the pocket of his tunic and started to peel it with a small, pearl-handled knife. Rafael skewered the piece of fruit with the point of his rapier, took it off the blade, and polished it against the front of his shirt while he awaited a reply.

"Don't worry," Barrett said, with a weariness of spirit to match Rafael's. "Phaedra plans to go through with the wedding. I'm a commoner, remember? Fine for dalliances, but not quite suitable as a husband."

Rafael felt relief, but not because he didn't think Barrett was worthy to take Phaedra to wife—his sister would have to do a great deal of growing up before she could appreciate, or deserve, a man of that caliber. He put up the rapier and bit into the appropriated apple.

"Did she actually *say* that?" he asked, chewing.

Barrett collapsed into a chair, gazing through the window behind Rafael's desk. It was still quite dark out, though it was well past dawn—the sky was overcast, promising rain. "She didn't have to," he replied, rubbing his temples with his thumb and forefinger and sighing in a melancholy fashion. "Just kill me now," he finished. "Put me out of my misery."

Rafael paused in his apple-chewing, long enough to mutter disgustedly, "God, Barrett, you are such a horse's ass. The capitol is in ruins, we're probably going to be up to our balls in rebels before a fortnight's gone by, and *you're* sniveling because some benevolent angel has seen fit to spare you from spending the rest of your life with my sister!"

Barrett did not retreat. In fact, there was an openly mutinous glint in his eye as he pondered the remains of the apple Rafael was eating. "Do you want to know the worst of it?" he demanded.

"No," Rafael replied. "But I fear you're determined to tell me."

"I told Haslett exactly what's been going on, in rather unchivalrous detail."

Rafael dropped the apple core and did not bother to retrieve it. *"What?"*

Barrett laughed hoarsely, but the sound was devoid of humor. "I thought he'd set Phaedra free or challenge me to a duel or something. Instead, he just patted my shoulder and said these things happen, that in the long run, they don't mean much."

"Good God," Rafael marveled.

"Ironic, isn't it?" Barrett asked. "The idea of Phaedra marrying another man makes me want to jump from a tower window, and here's Haslett, telling me it *doesn't matter* that his future wife and I have been ripping off each other's clothes every time we got the opportunity!"

Rafael closed his eyes against the inevitable images. "Great Zeus, Barrett, this is my *sister* we're talking about! If you don't exercise a little tact here, you won't have to jump from a tower window because I'll throw you out of one myself."

"I'm sorry," Barrett said, with an utter lack of conviction. "Well? What is the royal decree, Your Highness?" When they were boys, Rafael recalled with a shadow of a smile, Barrett had often addressed him as "Your High-Ass." "Shall I resign and leave the castle, or join Covington's band in the dungeons?"

Rafael sighed, still smiling a little. "Neither," he said. "I've never needed your help and advice the way I do now. Just tell me one thing—would it do any good at all to tell you to keep away from my sister?"

"Would it do any good to tell you to keep away from Annie Trevarren?" Barrett countered, rising at last from his chair.

"No," Rafael admitted.

"There you have it," Barrett replied.

"Perhaps I can still reason with my sister."

"Perhaps you can reason with Miss Trevarren. Or with the courtyard gate."

Rafael conceded the battle, if not the war. "You have a point," he said. "Now, about our prisoners. We have a fortnight until the wedding, and I want them tried and dealt with before then."

It was divine punishment, Annie decided, when Miss Rendennon arrived at midmorning. Morovia had still been in flames when the seamstress left it, and she'd had words with a rebel guard at the city's main gate, too. On the way to St. James Keep, the woman reported, she'd encountered refugees of less than sterling character, glimpsed a soldier who was up to no good, by the look of him, and lent moral support while her carriage driver contended with a broken wheel. She reasoned that if she could do all those things before luncheon, Annie could stand still for a simple fitting.

"But it isn't even my gown," Annie pointed out, somewhat pitifully. She wouldn't have minded, she thought sadly, if the splendid dress were her own. As it was, she would probably never be a bride.

With that gloomy thought, thunder crashed through the keep like a pronouncement from God, and lightning glowed against the inner walls. Annie shivered.

"Sounds like cannon fire," Miss Rendennon remarked, around the row of pins between her lips. "We'll be fortunate, I'll tell you that, to see the princess married before the whole country falls to those anarchists!"

For a time, Annie had believed Rafael was indeed the tyrant the rebels painted him to be, but she knew better now. Still, being an American, she wasn't without a certain sympathy for the revolutionaries. They had been oppressed by Rafael's father and grandfather, and countless other St. Jameses before them, and now they wanted freedom and justice. They could not know that they were fixing their hatred on the wrong man, and it was too late to turn the tide.

Annie's eyes filled with tears, and Miss Rendennon gave her a good slap on the wrist.

"Stop that. You'll get water spots on the dress!"

Annie had suffered all she would at this woman's hands. "Do you know what you can do with your dratted dress, Miss Rendennon, and with every last one of your pins?"

The sound of applause made Annie look up, while Miss Rendennon struggled not to swallow said pins. Lucian was standing a few feet away, clapping his hands.

The seamstress recovered enough to sputter, *"Well!"* take up her skirts and trundle out of the room. As she disappeared through the solarium's arched doorway, a clap of thunder exploded again and Annie felt the floor vibrate under her feet.

She put her hands on her hips and narrowed her eyes at Lucian. "What are you doing here?"

He looked genuinely contrite, but Annie hadn't forgotten that he'd behaved like a scoundrel on other occasions. "I've come to apologize," he said. "I guess my brief time in the army helped me grow up at last."

Annie remained skeptical. "Wonderful," she said, taking in his well-made civilian clothes, a dove gray waistcoat, white shirt and impeccably tailored black breeches. "What happened, Lucian? Did Mr. Barrett throw you out of the military?"

Lucian smiled, caught his hands together behind him, and raised himself onto the balls of his feet, then rolled back onto his heels. He was clearly very pleased with himself. "As a matter of fact, I wasn't a bad soldier. It's just that Rafael, in his infinite mercy, has absolved me of my sins and returned me to the family fold. I'm a new man, Annie, and I'd like a chance to prove I can be a loyal and valuable friend."

"By doing what?"

He laughed. "I could start by showing you through the castle. Normally, the tour would include the dungeons, but since they're occupied at the moment, we'll save those for another time."

While Annie had her reservations about being alone with Lucian, especially in isolated parts of the keep, she was feeling bored, restless and very confused. It was raining, and Rafael was busy with his blasted war, and she wasn't sure she could have faced him anyway, after the way she'd howled in his arms like a she-wolf the night before. She blushed and averted her eyes, fiddling with the billowing skirts of the dress.

"If you're worried that I won't mind my manners,"

Lucian said, with a smile in his voice, "don't be. I've just returned from Purgatory, and I know that Rafael is fiercely protective of you. There's still no love lost between my brother and me, and I'm neither rash enough, nor stupid enough, to cross him. I have no desire to end up in the dungeon playing cards with Jeremy Covington."

Lucian had mentioned that the dungeons were occupied, but Annie hadn't taken the remark seriously. Now, however, she realized with a lurching shock that he had not been joking.

"He's here? At St. James Keep?" she asked.

Lucian frowned. "Yes," he answered, beckoning to a maid, who was just passing the doorway. "Come and help Miss Trevarren out of this enormous dress," he called. He lowered his voice as the servant came toward them. "Didn't Rafael tell you? Covington and the other are to be tried here, as soon as a jury can be assembled."

Annie felt sick, remembering the brutality she'd witnessed in the marketplace, and the stunned hatred that had shone in Lieutenant Covington's gaze the night of Phaedra's ball when she'd told Rafael what he'd done. And even though she knew her enemy was locked away in the dungeons, she was afraid.

"Annie?" Lucian took her arm, steadying her, while the maid hovered nearby, not knowing what to do. "Are you all right?"

She bit her lip, nodded, and managed a smile.

He frowned, not entirely convinced, and gave her elbow a gentle squeeze. "I'll meet you in the great hall in ten minutes," he said, and left her.

With the maid's help, Annie got out of Phaedra's wedding gown and into the purple one she'd put on that morning after waking up in Rafael's bed and sneaking back to her own chambers. Trembling, she straightened her hair and then set out purposefully for the heart of the castle.

Lucian was there, flirting harmlessly with a maid. When he saw Annie, he smiled and offered his arm, for all the world like a gentleman.

"Come with me, sweet Annie," he said, when she curved her fingers around the inside of his elbow, "and see for yourself the wondrous, musty secrets of St. James Keep."

CHAPTER
14

Lucian behaved himself, as he'd promised, showing Annie through one of the oldest parts of the keep, a rabbit warren of impossibly small rooms with low ceilings and dank, dripping walls that predated even the great hall and the solarium. It reminded Annie a little of places in America, where vast houses had sometimes been built around log cabins.

"People were much smaller back then," Lucian said, ducking his head to keep from cracking it on a beam. He held his lantern high, though, and it spilled golden light into the dusty, cobweb-draped passageway ahead.

Annie wished she'd exchanged her morning dress for her trusty shirt and breeches before coming on this adventure. Given the possibility that the keep might soon be commandeered by rebel forces, she wanted to learn every possible escape route. She thought of the hidden gate she'd found in the keep's outer wall that day before they'd traveled to Morovia, and wondered if Lucian knew about it.

She almost asked him, but some vague instinct stopped her.

"Are you scared?" she inquired instead.

"Of these passages and pitiful cells?" he countered cheerfully, without looking back at her, proceeding deeper into the heart of the castle.

"No," Annie replied abruptly. The awareness that Jeremy Covington and the other rogue soldiers were being held somewhere nearby nagged at her. She would have preferred to share the place with ghosts. "Of what's happening to Bavia, to your family."

Lucian sighed philosophically. "It's plain that the St. Jameses have outlived their time." With his free hand, he struck one of the walls. "Don't you think it's symbolic, the way the castle is crumbling to rubble around us? It parallels what's happening to the country, to a whole way of life."

Annie felt an infinite sadness, even though she knew, of course, that many of the old ways were terribly wrong. A number of quaint and courtly graces would almost certainly fall by the wayside as well. Even if Rafael survived the revolution, which he seemed determined not to do, he would be without a country. His entire history would have vanished into a void, and that was a thing of magnitude and consequence, not to be blithely dismissed.

When Annie didn't speak, Lucian glanced back at her over his shoulder. He seemed to have read her mind.

"Don't be sad, little one," he said quietly, stopping and turning in the narrow hall to face her. "It's all for the best. Even Rafael would tell you that."

Annie retreated a step, somewhat dazzled by the light of the lantern and more than a little wary of Lucian's intentions. "You're right," she said, after swallowing once, "but there are still things that must be mourned."

"You're afraid of me," Lucian observed sadly. "Please don't be, Annie. I would never do anything to hurt you."

A brief silence fell between them, then Annie broke it. "Aren't there any secret passages in this place?"

Lucian gave a rueful chuckle. "Follow me, my dear, and I'll show you a thousand ways out of St. James Keep, ways even Rafael doesn't know about."

Annie bit her lower lip. She'd asked to see secret passages and now she was about to get her wish. Still, she couldn't help drawing the obvious conclusion: If there were a thousand ways out of the castle, there were just as many ways *in.* Furthermore, if Rafael truly didn't know about them, as Lucian claimed, she would personally point out every one.

Despite cobwebs, mildew, the vague sounds of scurrying rats and her own misgivings concerning the future, Annie enjoyed that excursion into the bowels of St. James Keep. There were, besides numerous niches and cells in which to hide, several tunnels leading outside the castle. Some passed under the gardens, according to Lucian, while others would end beneath the floorboards of various outbuildings.

"Provided," Lucian reminded a thoughtful Annie, "that parts of the tunnels haven't caved in over the last few centuries. And that the wooden floors—

which would naturally have rotted by now—haven't been replaced with brick or fieldstones."

Annie peered into the tunnel her companion had revealed by moving aside an old wine cupboard. It was dark, of course, and probably full of rats and spiders. Worse, it was hardly large enough for a full-grown person to crawl through.

Still, such things could be accomplished, if the need arose and one was determined enough. Annie's own mother, Charlotte Trevarren, had once escaped a sultan's dungeon in precisely that way.

"It's probably strewn with moldering bones," Lucian remarked, startling Annie and causing a shiver to run through her.

She turned to face him, hugging herself, but Annie was more afraid of rebels, and men like Jeremy Covington, than skulls and skeletons. "I think I've seen enough," she said, looking down at her dress, which had been spoiled by dust and the dampness clinging to the walls.

Still holding the lantern in one hand, Lucian brought out his pocket watch with the other and frowned at it, as though displeased. "Half past twelve. I hope we haven't missed lunch."

Annie's stomach grumbled, rivaling the thunder they'd heard earlier. "So do I," she said.

Lucian escorted her back to the great hall, where their odyssey had begun, and they went their separate ways—Annie mounting the stairs, Lucian venturing out into the rainy courtyard.

Fifteen minutes later, when she had washed, brushed the dust and cobwebs from her hair and replaited it, and then put on a fresh dress, Annie entered the dining hall. There was no sign of Lucian, despite his protestations of hunger shortly before, but Rafael was seated at the head of the table.

He appeared to be ignoring the plate of food in front of him; his elbows rested on the surface and his fingers were interlaced. When he realized Annie was there, he stood, nearly overturning his chair in the process, then sat down again.

Annie found the prince's lack of grace disturbing, for he was, due to years of fencing and horsemanship, one of the most agile men she had ever encountered. On the other hand, he had a great deal on his mind, what with his political problems, Phaedra's impending marriage, an event that couldn't help but complicate matters, and the volatile situation between himself and Annie.

She took a plate, helped herself to a few items from the offerings aligned on the sideboard, and joined Rafael at the table, taking care not to sit too close. Every nerve in her body had come alive as soon as she saw him, surely a lingering effect of last night's lovemaking, and she feared that if his hand so much as brushed against hers, she would fall apart.

Annie's voice trembled only a little when she finally spoke. "Lucian tells me you've brought Jeremy Covington here to be tried."

Rafael gave up all pretense of eating and pushed his plate away. He took up his wineglass and settled back in his chair, one eyebrow slightly raised, seeming to regard Annie through the jewel-like liquid. "Since when have you become my brother's confidante?" he asked, and Annie was able to read nothing of his mood in the tone of his voice.

She opened a small sandwich and studiously sprinkled pepper over the unrecognizable contents. "Lucian and I have buried the hatchet," she said, watching Rafael through her lashes. "He showed me several escape routes this morning. Do you think the tunnels in the cellars would be passable, after so many years of neglect?"

His fist slammed down onto the tabletop, making the crystal, the silver and Annie jump, in concert with each other. "Blast it, Annie, do you pass your nights working out ways to drive me insane?"

Annie blushed and made a ceremony of smoothing the napkin in her lap. "I guess that depends. I think I did a pretty good job of it *last* night."

Given his previous display of temper, Rafael made a creditable effort at speaking calmly. "I want you to stay away from Lucian," he said evenly. "My brother is not a trustworthy man, and his intentions toward you are not honorable."

"Oh?" Annie pretended the possibility had never crossed her mind. *Men.* "Exactly what are Lucian's intentions toward me, may I ask?"

Rafael drained his wineglass before replying. "He plans to marry you," he said.

Annie was surprised by that, but she didn't let it show. It was still raining, Phaedra was nowhere around, and she'd already explored the catacombs beneath the castle. Baiting Rafael was likely to be the only fun she'd have for the rest of the day.

"Excuse me," she began, with acid sweetness, dabbing at her mouth with her napkin, "but you seem to have things turned around, Your Highness. Offering marriage to a woman is *quite* honorable. Especially if you've"—she paused, coughed delicately and lowered her voice a notch or two—"enjoyed her favors."

Rafael turned crimson. "Go ahead and marry the

little rotter," he hissed. "Then maybe I could get something done around this place!"

Realizing she had pushed Rafael slightly too far, Annie subsided a little. "No hope of that, Your Highness," she said cheerfully. "I've told you before —if I can't have you, then I shall be a spinster." She followed these words with a dreamy sigh. "I can imagine myself living in an old mansion on a cliff, at the edge of a windswept moor. I'll write poetry and walk the night in billowing white dresses, and all the people for miles around will believe I have mysterious powers—"

"Poppycock," Rafael broke in rudely. "You'll go home to America and marry someone solid and respectable—a lawyer or a banker, perhaps. Your good father will see to that. In a decade, you'll have six children who are forever climbing things. You'll take up slightly more room on a carriage seat, but you'll still be a beautiful, voluptuous woman. Furthermore, once you get over these silly, romantic notions about traipsing across the moors in your night rail, you'll make a very good wife." He refilled his wineglass and raised it in a diabolical toast. "How I envy that future husband of yours, whoever he is, Annie-my-love, for having the incredible good fortune to lie beside you every night for the rest of a long and fruitful life!"

Annie did not know how to respond. Rafael had said outrageous things, but he hadn't insulted her— had he? She sat, hands knotted in her lap, cheeks flaring.

"In the meantime," Rafael finished, in a quiet, grave voice, "do as I tell you and keep away from Lucian. He's nothing but a vulture."

"Charming," commented a third voice, from the

doorway. Annie did not need to look to know that the newcomer was Lucian. He went on affably. "I'm crushed, Rafael. I thought we were making some headway, you and I—learning to be brothers, and all that sentimental stuff."

Rafael made a low, contemptuous sound in his throat. In the length of a heartbeat, he was out of his chair and clasping Lucian by the lapel of his coat. Looking for all the world like a man gone mad, Rafael thrust his brother toward Annie.

"Do you want him?" the prince demanded irrationally. "Then here he is!"

With that, Rafael stormed out of the dining hall, and thunder roared behind him, as if to accentuate his fury.

Lucian straightened his coat and gazed after his brother. "I guess I expected too much, too soon," he murmured.

Annie wasn't thinking about Rafael's outburst, however, or the tempestuous truce he had apparently entered into with Lucian. She was pondering the fact that the dungeons of St. James Keep were filled with renegade soldiers and wondering what Rafael planned to do about them.

She finished her meal, listening with half an ear as Lucian chatted about his experiences as a soldier—one would have thought he'd crossed the Alps with Hannibal, instead of spending a little over a week as a member of the royal guard—then excused herself and hurried out.

She asked the first servant she passed—a young maid carrying a pot of fresh coffee toward the dining hall—where to find the Princess Phaedra.

The girl averted her eyes and bobbed her head

respectfully. "I saw her earlier, miss. She needed a hot bath prepared for her, since she'd been out riding and gotten caught in the rain. I told her she'd catch her death if she wasn't careful."

Annie was immediately concerned, but she could see that the pot was heavy and she didn't want to keep the girl from her duties. "Thank you," she said, and walked away.

She found Phaedra tucked up in her enormous bed, sipping tea and looking wan. Her dark hair was still damp, and she was wearing a bright blue bed jacket.

"Don't you dare give me a lecture for going out riding in the rain," Phaedra said, as soon as Annie started to open her mouth. "You'd have done it yourself if you'd thought of it."

Annie sighed. "I didn't come here to scold," she said. "I simply wanted to make sure you were all right."

Phaedra looked away for a moment. "Only two weeks until my marriage," she said, meeting Annie's gaze. "That is, if Rafael can hold the country together that long. Did you know that people are coming to the wedding, Annie—even with rebels and highwaymen on the roads and Morovia in shambles? Messages have been arriving for days."

The situation in Bavia was frightening, but Annie had noticed that people were more likely to attend such celebrations during bad times than good ones.

"Your dress is coming along well," Annie said, with a wry note in her voice. "You'll make a beautiful bride, if neither of us gains or loses any weight in the next two weeks."

Phaedra tried to smile, but the effort faltered. "Poor Annie. I've put you through so much, just by bringing you to Bavia. It's bad enough that you've had to put up with my impossible brothers, but those dreadful people threw stones at our carriage, and after that there was the incident in the marketplace—"

"Shhh," Annie said, squeezing Phaedra's hand because she could see that the princess was about to cry.

It was too late; Phaedra's tears brimmed along her lower lashes and spilled down her cheeks. "I was so mean to you in the carriage—the things I said about what's happened between you and Rafael—"

Annie embraced her friend briefly. "You're about to be married, and the world seems to be falling apart around you. It isn't any wonder that you're a bit temperamental these days."

Phaedra wiped her cheeks with the back of one hand and sniffled. "Would you like some tea? I could ring for another cup and saucer."

Annie shook her head and glanced nervously toward the terrace doors. Rain pounded at the glass, making a sound like gunfire. She imagined how the bricks in the courtyard would look, shimmering bright orange in the wet and listened with her heart to hear the trees in the orchard whispering to each other. She pictured the statues in the fountains, sleek and shiny figures with bits of dancing water at their feet.

"Did you know that Jeremy Covington is here, in the dungeons?" A shiver wound its way up Annie's spine as she recalled the look in Covington's eyes the night of Phaedra's ball, when she'd told Rafael what she'd seen the lieutenant do.

Phaedra shifted, plainly bored with the topic, and nearly spilled her tea on the immaculate Irish linen bed sheets. "I don't suppose Rafael felt he could leave them behind, with the city falling and everything. You can just imagine what the rebels would have done to them."

Annie shuddered. She hadn't thought the situation through that far. No matter what crimes they had committed, they were entitled to a fair trial—at least where Annie came from.

"Do you know where Felicia is?" she asked quietly. "If Rafael wouldn't leave the prisoners in Morovia, then surely he didn't abandon Miss Covington to the rebels."

Phaedra had apparently grown weary of lying in bed, waiting to be sick. She set aside her tea, reached for her wrapper and got up. "She's in France," she replied reluctantly, well aware of the part Annie herself had played in the situation. "Felicia suffered a nervous collapse of some sort, and Rafael had her taken out of the country, to a sanatorium. You mustn't blame yourself—you did the right thing, after all."

Annie rubbed her right temple, but it didn't ease the headache that had suddenly overtaken her. "I had to do what I did," she said. "But that doesn't mean I'm not sorry for hurting Felicia so badly. She didn't deserve it, Phaedra—she was always so kind to me."

"I guess that university student and those merchants weren't the only innocent people who were hurt that day." Phaedra selected a dress from her wardrobe and stepped behind a screen to put it on. "Now, no more talk of gloomy matters," she called. "I want to think about happy things. We've got to decide what we'll serve for the wedding supper, and where each of the guests should be placed . . ."

Annie smiled. It was good to know Phaedra was feeling better.

* * *

That night, Rafael did not put in an appearance at dinner. According to Lucian, the prince was locked away with Mr. Barrett, planning the defense of St. James Keep. It was generally agreed that the task represented a special challenge, since there was to be a wedding in the castle.

At the mention of the impending nuptials, Mr. Haslett cleared his throat and reached for his wineglass, and it seemed to Annie that Phaedra took pains to ignore his presence entirely.

And the rain continued.

After dinner, Annie went to her room to read and, if she was to be honest, to wait for Rafael. He did not come to her, and when the fire burned low and the lamp guttered, Annie dropped off to sleep.

She awakened early the next morning, feeling a strange sense of urgency, of excitement. Something was going to happen, and soon, though she couldn't guess what.

The rain had stopped, and the world was washed clean. For Annie, for the moment, it was enough.

She washed and dressed quickly, in a riding skirt, boots and a cotton shirtwaist, and was only a little disappointed when she found the dining hall empty. It was better, given the circumstances, if she and Rafael didn't encounter each other too often.

Annie took an apple from the bowl of fruit on the sideboard, bypassing the eggs, toasted bread, sausages and other foods, and hurried out into the courtyard. The air was fresh and moist, the sunlight bright.

For all the beauty of the morning, there were reminders of war everywhere she looked. Armed sentinels walked the parapets, and the deafening clatter of steel striking steel meant that soldiers were preparing for a siege. Wagons and carts loaded with food were rolling through the gates, and people from the villages and farms surrounding the keep sought and were given refuge within its walls.

Annie paused for a few moments, listening while two of Mr. Barrett's lieutenants questioned the frightened peasants. There was, of course, no way to tell whether they were loyal to the prince, or simply rebels in disguise. From what she'd heard the soldiers say, Rafael had given the order that no one who would swear allegiance should be turned away.

It didn't seem right to stand idly by and watch, so Annie made her way through the courtyard and the gardens toward the village where most of the refugees were heading. When she arrived, she found two more of Rafael's men, making a pitiful and disorganized attempt to dispense food and blankets to the new arrivals. There weren't enough cottages, and the grass was still wet from the recent rain.

Annie moved through the crowd until she reached the beleaguered lieutenants. Climbing into the back of the supply wagon, she clapped her hands to get the crowd's attention and told them to form a line. After much gesturing, some order was established. She sent the soldiers back to the keep for more food and blankets, along with whatever tents they could find.

The sun was high before the new people stopped arriving. The blankets were gone, according to the soldiers, and a number of the villagers had been taken with a mild fever. By Annie's order, the worst cases were taken to the chapel, where pews served for beds.

Annie soothed fitful babies and frightened grandmothers and gave water and comfort to the patients resting in the church. Some of the servants from the keep came to help, but most of the work was done by the women of the village. By the end of the day, Annie's hair was straggling and her riding skirt, trimmed in mud at the hem, was ruined. She was starved, tired to the bone, and heartsick because she was beginning to understand what a war might mean to these people and others like them, all across the country.

She was standing outside the chapel door, holding a feverish baby against her shoulder and watching the sunset, when Rafael passed, saw her out of the corner of his eye and stopped. His face was grim as he took in her disheveled appearance.

"What are you doing?" he demanded, in a quiet, ominous voice.

"I'm trying to help."

His face was in shadow, and she could not make out his expression. "I don't want your help."

"Perhaps you don't," Annie said softly, as the infant in her arms began a pitiful mewling, "but these people do."

Rafael's sigh was a harsh, impatient sound. "They've been given food and sanctuary."

"They're terrified," Annie responded, "and some of them are sick. They've been hungry a long time, Rafael."

He was silent; it was a stricken silence and Annie's heart went out to him because she knew he had done everything he could for the people of Bavia and it hadn't been enough. Annie wanted to touch Rafael, to lend him some simple comfort, but she sensed that too much tenderness would only weaken him now.

At last, Rafael spoke. "You'll be of no use to anyone if you don't eat and get your rest," he said. "And Annie?"

A woman came out of the chapel and shyly claimed her baby.

"Yes?" Annie asked, when she and Rafael were alone again.

"Thank you," he said. Then he turned and walked away.

Annie watched until he disappeared into the shadows. Then, her vision blurred by tears, she entered the castle through the great hall. It was well-lighted, and there were soldiers sitting and lying everywhere.

As she hurried through the hall, toward the stairway, Annie wondered which of these newly arrived men were traitors, for some of them surely were.

She was startled to find Kathleen, the maid she'd gotten to know at the palace in Morovia, building up the fire on Annie's hearth.

"Hello, miss!" Kathleen cried, beaming. "Just look at you, all dirty, and your hair trailing. I'll just bet you haven't had any supper, either, for you're white as the underside of an angel's wing. . . ."

Mr. Haslett had assured Annie that the palace servants would be safe, since the royal family had always been the rebels' main target, so she hadn't worried too much about Kathleen and the others. Still, she was very glad to see the other young woman.

Annie sagged into a chair by the fire, too weary even to wash her face and hands, and Kathleen gave her a cup of hot, bracing tea.

"How did you get here?"

Kathleen seemed invigorated by her experiences,

rather than worn down. "The rebels put us out when they took the palace, miss," she said. "There were loyalist soldiers along the road, and they knew us from when they served in Morovia. They let us ride with them, the other girls and me, on their horses—except for old Cook, of course. She traveled in a supply cart."

Fatigue, relief and gratitude brought fresh tears to Annie's eyes. She reached out, with her free hand, and squeezed the maid's fingers. "I'm so glad you're here. I need help, Kathleen, and not the sort you're probably thinking of."

"I've got some water heating down in the kitchen," Kathleen said. "Just let me get that, so you can wash up a little before I fetch your supper, and then you can tell me what sort of help you're wanting."

An hour later, Annie had given herself a sponge bath and eaten as much of her dinner as she could. She was barely able to keep her eyes open as she sat near the fire, cosseted in a warm wrapper, while Kathleen brushed her hair. Annie told her about the refugees choking the village, all of them frightened and confused, many of them ill.

"Well, miss," Kathleen said, when Annie had finished her tale of woe, "of *course* I'll help you. All the same, I plan to look after you proper, so you don't wind up lying in a sickbed yourself. You're the sort, if you'll pardon my saying so, who tends to bite off more than she can chew."

Annie smiled. There could be no denying *that* accusation. "Have they given you a bed in the servants' quarters?"

"Oh, yes, miss," Kathleen replied, putting aside the hairbrush. "I've got a nice cot and a chest for my belongings. Don't be worrying your head about me, if you please, because I'm like you. I can take care of myself."

Annie imagined what it must have been like to see the palace taken over by rebels, to leave with only those things one could carry, to brave streets full of overturned carriages and plunder dragged from houses, and walk roads that must have been knee-deep in mud from the long rainstorm. "Oh, yes, Kathleen," she agreed. "You can most definitely take care of yourself."

A little later, Annie climbed up the steps to her tester bed and collapsed onto the mattress, so tired that she couldn't think. And that, she would reflect later, was a mercy.

The next morning, exhausted as she'd been the night before, Annie was wide-awake at dawn. Kathleen, having already lighted a lamp, was stirring the embers of the fire back to life, and a tray of hot, fragrant food waited on the bedside table.

"Don't rush through that, now," Kathleen ordered briskly. "Even angels of mercy need their breakfast— the flesh-and-blood ones, anyway."

"It's fitting that you should mention angels," Annie said, reaching for the tray and setting it carefully on her lap. "This coffee smells like heaven."

CHAPTER

15

He loved her.

Rafael had been holding the knowledge at bay ever since the night he'd climbed out onto the parapet of the south tower to save Annie from toppling two hundred feet into the courtyard. Earlier in the evening, however, when he'd seen her standing outside the chapel door, face smudged, hair a-tumble, holding a baby in her arms, the realization had broken through his defenses and struck him with all the force of a spiked cudgel.

Seated on the wide stone sill of one of the windows in the gate tower, gazing out over a moon washed sea, Rafael knew absolute despair. Recognizing his true feelings had only made things worse; he was still doomed, along with his country, but before Annie he'd been numb, body and spirit, and he could have died without a moment's regret. Now things had changed—dying would mean leaving Annie to God-knew-what fate or, worse, watching her perish before his eyes, the way Georgiana had. Bitter fluid rushed into the back of Rafael's throat and for the first time in his life, he was mortally afraid.

Barrett's voice startled Rafael, for he'd thought himself alone.

"It's late, Your Highness," he said. "You need your rest."

Rafael folded his arms and smiled bitterly into the darkness, where the sea whispered and beckoned and made its elemental promises. "Now you are not only the head of my army, but my nursemaid as well. How versatile you are, old friend."

Barrett ignored the jibe, as usual. He was, despite the occasional lapse, an even-tempered and reasonable man. In fact, his counsel had kept Rafael from making any number of impulsive mistakes over the years. "Your Annie Trevarren is quite a lady," he said. "Did you know she spent the afternoon in the village, ordering everyone around and passing out generous portions of food and advice?"

"Yes," Rafael replied. "I knew. It's dangerous, what Annie's been up to, but nothing short of tossing her into one of the dungeon cells could keep her from what she undoubtedly sees as her moral duty. God's truth, Barrett, I wish the woman were a coward and a twit, afraid to dirty her hands or sully her skirts in the mud. At least that way she'd be safe."

"None of us is safe, Rafael. And perhaps it's better that she's occupied."

"Perhaps," Rafael agreed wearily. He scanned the sea and the countryside once more before stepping down from the windowsill. "What do you hear from Morovia?"

"It's quieter—the burning and looting seem to have stopped, for the time being anyway."

"That's some consolation, at least," Rafael said. "Tomorrow we'll select the jurors and begin the process of trying Covington and his raiders."

"It'll be a nasty business, what with everything else that's happening just now," Barrett remarked. "Who will serve as magistrate and hand down a sentence, if the men are convicted?"

Rafael paused in the tower doorway. "The villagers will choose a judge from among themselves." He started down the inside stairway, with Barrett a few steps behind.

"This is a delicate situation," the soldier pointed out. "While I deplore Covington and the others for what they did, I wonder if letting the peasants try these men is any more just than turning them over to the rebels. Obviously, they could wind up bearing the brunt of the people's anger and paying not only for their own crimes, but those of other soldiers, in other years and even other centuries."

"It is an imperfect solution," Rafael answered. "If you have something better to suggest, I'd like to hear it."

"The prisoners could be removed to France or Spain," Barrett said, "and tried there."

"No," Rafael said flatly, as they entered the passageway at the base of the stairs. It was unlit, except for the light of the moon, and both men walked in intermittent shadow. "This crime occurred in our own country. It is the right and the duty of the Bavian people to dispense justice."

"I agree," Barrett conceded. "But there will be trouble, Rafael, if the penalty is too harsh. There is already grumbling in the ranks—some of the soldiers believe you're throwing Covington and the others to the wolves in an effort to get the ordinary people on your side."

"Even if that was my aim, it's far too late to clear the St. James name. You know that."

Barrett only nodded.

When Annie and Kathleen reached the great hall on their way to the chapel, they found the place jammed with villagers, soldiers and servants. Craftsmen and shepherds, farmers and fishermen stood in line to speak with Rafael and Mr. Barrett, who sat at a table, asking questions and making notes.

Although relations between Rafael and Annie were strained, her curiosity would not permit her to pass the scene without finding out what was happening. She went to the back of the line, tugged at a man's sleeve and asked him why he was there.

"There's going to be a trial," the man sputtered. "Right here in the great hall. We're here to apply to be members of the jury."

Annie nodded and felt a nervous shiver in the pit of her stomach. She would have to testify, of course, and while she would not have shirked her responsibility, she was frightened. Jeremy Covington hated her, and she knew only too well what a cruel and violent man he could be.

There was much to do in the chapel, for although many of the patients had recovered from the malaise, others had fallen ill during the night. Annie and

Kathleen brought broth from the kitchen and, with help from the village women and some of the other servants, began spooning the thin soup into waiting mouths.

Annie was bathing a feverish toddler late that morning when Phaedra came into the chapel. At first, Annie thought the princess had come to help, for even with a dozen women working, there was a lot to do. The terrified expression on her friend's face soon disabused her of the notion; the princess might want to lend a hand, but she was plainly squeamish.

"Phew! It smells in here," she said, not unkindly.

Annie controlled her irritation, reminding herself, once again, that Phaedra had never been called upon to serve in any sort of emergency. "Of course it smells," she replied quietly. "These people are desperately ill."

Phaedra's gaze swept the room, disconsolate and genuinely confused. "Why can't they be in the barracks, or even the stables?" she whispered. "I'm supposed to be *married* here in just two weeks. What if we can't get the smell out?" She paused to glance at the little boy Annie was bathing. "Have you ever seen such a pitiful child? Just look at him—his ribs are showing."

Annie closed her eyes for a moment. *Patience,* she thought. "Phaedra, think about what you're saying. You sound like Marie Antoinette."

The princess pulled a snow-white handkerchief from the sleeve of her pale rose gown and pressed it to her mouth, looking downright ill. "I'm so sorry," she said, in a sorrowful wail. "You know I don't mean to be unkind, but—"

Annie's heart softened slightly. "Do leave, Phaedra, before you add to the mess. If you truly want to help, go to the kitchen and ask for more broth."

The princess nodded in a brief and frantic way and fled.

Throughout the morning, wedding guests could be heard arriving in their carriages and carts, but Annie was not thinking about the coming ceremony. She and Kathleen had their hands full.

When, on occasion, Phaedra crossed her mind, she reminded herself that people have different strengths and talents. Not having the fortitude or temperament to be a nurse was not a failing of character. Her own grandmother, Lydia McQuire Quade, had taken care of Union soldiers during the War Between the States. Perhaps Annie had picked up the knack from her.

At one o'clock, Kathleen convinced Annie to take a meal.

In the kitchen, Annie scrubbed her hands carefully before touching her food, for her grandmother Lydia had often stressed the importance of cleanliness when dealing with the sick. The topic of conversation among the servants was not the revolution or even the royal wedding, but the trial of the men who had ransacked the marketplace in Morovia and murdered a young student.

Annie was uneasy with the topic, but it was interesting and, besides, it was always more prudent to listen than to bury one's head in the sand.

"Does anyone know which of the soldiers shot the lad from the university?" Kathleen inquired, between bites of stew.

At that point, everyone at the long trestle table turned to look questioningly at Annie. Obviously, it was no secret that she'd witnessed the dreadful event. But while she had seen the student fall, bleeding, into the fountain pool—indeed, it was an image she would never forget—she had not seen who had fired the fatal shot.

She bit her lower lip and shook her head. She was almost glad she hadn't seen the killer; the look of unbridled hatred in Jeremy Covington's eyes had been terrifying, and the memory of it would be burden enough as she went through her life. Cook, a sturdy woman with square corners like a box, took another helping of bread from the platter in the center of the table. "He's had more than his share of grief, our Prince Rafael," she said, using the bread to sop up the last of her stew. Her mouth was full when she went on. "His Highness deserves to be happy, like he was before the Princess Georgiana died."

Annie found it comforting to know that Cook, at least, knew Rafael was a good man. There must be others, too, who saw him as he was and did not blame him for the things his forbearers had done.

She blushed at the belated realization that, at Cook's reference to the prince, everyone had turned to look at her again. An awkward silence descended.

Blessedly, Kathleen put an end to it. "Well, I guess Miss Trevarren and I should be getting back to our sick ones, or they'll be wondering where we took ourselves off to." She turned to the two old tyrants— one had reigned over the palace kitchen in Morovia and one had been making meals at St. James Keep since Rafael's father was a little boy—with a bright and guileless smile. "We need still more soup, and as much weak tea as you can make." Before either woman had time to refuse, she finished with, "The Lord will bless you for your kindness."

Annie carried her empty stew bowl to the sink without speaking, watching with amusement as the two women scrambled to put themselves in the way of the Lord's blessing. The soup and tea Kathleen had requested were certainly forthcoming.

Annie and Kathleen went back to the village, this time taking an outdoor route through a series of gardens instead of passing through the great hall. They worked in the chapel and the cottages for the rest of the day and, by the time twilight fell, Annie was twice as tired as she had been the night before.

She didn't have the luxury of bathing and tumbling into bed, however, for more of Phaedra's wedding guests, distant cousins who had traveled for days, through axle-deep mud and the obvious dangers of the road, had indeed arrived that afternoon. Good manners prompted Annie to attend the formal dinner, so she washed, put on an emerald green gown, had Kathleen dress her hair, and went down to the dining hall.

Rafael occupied his usual place at the head of the table, and although he looked harried, he was an attentive and engaging host. Annie might have been invisible, for all the notice he paid her, but she was too tired to be insulted. In fact, she nodded off twice before the main course had been served, and was saved from disgrace only by the subtle application of Phaedra's royal elbow to her rib cage.

At that point, Annie excused herself, for the first

time garnering Rafael's attention, and left the dining hall. She was back in her chamber, sitting at the vanity table while Kathleen brushed her hair, when a knock sounded at the door.

Annie's heart did a little flip under her throat. She knew, even before Kathleen went to answer the summons, that her visitor was the prince.

If Kathleen had any views on the propriety of the matter, she kept them to herself. "Good evening, Your Highness," she said, with a deep curtsey. Instead of immediately dashing out, however, she threw Annie a questioning glance.

Rafael, always perceptive, read the look accurately. "Please stay," he said to the maid.

Annie did not turn around, but watched Rafael's approach in the vanity table mirror. She could feel the pulse at the base of her throat throbbing like a drumbeat.

Finally, Rafael stood beside her. He laid a hand on her shoulder. "I appreciate the way you've been helping out in the village," he said gently, "but I fear you've taken on too much. Annie, you were so exhausted at dinner tonight that you could barely sit upright."

Annie's primary instinct was to lay her hand over Rafael's, but she resisted. Too much physical contact with this man was dangerous, and he was already touching her, searing her skin, heating the muscles beneath, igniting that mysterious, familiar ache deep inside her.

"I don't know how you could have made that determination, since you didn't look at me once during the entire evening."

Rafael laughed, and his fingers tightened, just briefly, on her shoulder. "You are quite wrong, my Yankee Princess. I hardly took my eyes off you."

Annie turned to gaze up at him, searching his face. She saw so many things in those pewter eyes—humor, worry, compassion, frustration and, yes, if not love, a significant degree of affection.

"I understand now," she said awkwardly, "why you insist on staying in Bavia, no matter what. And it's the same for me, Rafael—I can't abandon those people, not as long as there is something I can do to help."

Rafael released Annie's shoulder to brush her cheek lightly with the backs of his fingers. She could see that he was moved by some deep emotion, and several moments passed before he spoke again. "I'm glad you understand—I'm not sure anyone else does. But our two situations are not the same—I owe the people my loyalty, but you are only a guest here. It is not your responsibility to tend the sick."

"No, it isn't my responsibility," Annie agreed, and it took an effort to speak firmly because she was melting under Rafael's touch. "I know I can't save the world and, yes, my conscience would bother me if I didn't do something, but I'm helping because that's what I *choose* to do."

"But, Annie, the risks—"

She sighed. "What would you have me do?" she asked patiently. "Sit in the solarium and play the harp all day? Rafael, I have to be *doing* things—it's not in my nature to be idle."

A muscle twitched in Rafael's jaw; Annie knew she had made her point, and that he did not like conceding it. "At least be careful," he said, lowering his voice, "I have enough on my conscience where you're concerned, and if anything happened to you, I would never forgive myself."

Annie clasped his hand. "I want to help you, Rafael, not add to your worries. I promise I won't take any unnecessary chances."

Rafael squeezed her fingers and made an attempt at a smile. "I guess I will have to be satisfied with that," he said. He bent and placed a gentle kiss on the top of her head. "I'd better go back to my guests. Good night, Annie."

She nodded, and he went out.

Kathleen asked no questions, but kept busy turning back the covers on Annie's bed, fluffing the pillows, banking the fire. Annie was grateful for her silence. Her encounter with Rafael was a momentous one for her, and she needed a few minutes to quiet herself.

Over the next several days, more wedding guests arrived, their mud-splattered carriages clattering merrily over the drawbridge, while the process of choosing jurors continued in the great hall. Annie stayed busy in the village and the chapel, and tried not to think too much about the immediate future, when she would be called upon to testify against Lieutenant Covington and the other soldiers. No sooner would that ordeal be over when it would be time for Phaedra's wedding, and once the princess was married, Annie would be sent home to her family.

Most likely, she would never see Rafael again.

In the meantime, Annie was determined not to add to the prince's worries. She took regular meals, although she never tasted the food and could not have said what she'd eaten five minutes after leaving the table, and made a point of sitting quietly in her room for an hour every afternoon. Each night, after eating supper by the fire, she tumbled into bed at precisely eight o'clock and was immersed in slumber within moments.

After four days, the trial began, and Annie was forced to leave her tasks to Kathleen and the few other women who weren't crowded into the great hall to view the spectacle. Lieutenant Covington and fourteen other men were brought up from the dungeons in shackles and seated on a row of benches that had been set end to end. The jurors sat opposite them, while spectators occupied the space in between. The villagers had selected a magistrate from among themselves, and he sat at a small table on an improvised dais, overlooking everyone else. Rafael and Mr. Barrett stood watching from a distance, their arms folded, faces impassive.

Annie forced herself to look directly at Lieutenant Covington, since she knew she would have to face him sooner or later. He looked pale, and his clothes were rumpled, but it was plain that neither he nor any of the others had been starved or abused. As if he'd felt Annie's gaze, he turned to meet it, and she saw such coldness in his eyes, and such fury, that she shivered.

She was the first witness called to testify, and it was with both relief and trepidation that she made her way forward to stand next to the magistrate's desk. Because she'd been working, she was wearing a simple brown dress Kathleen had found in a storage closet. Her hair was pulled back into a loose braid. She wasn't an aristocrat, and felt a sincere kinship with the villagers.

Lieutenant Covington's stare held a silent threat, and Annie felt it like a slap, but she was also aware of

Rafael's nearness, and his support. She drew a deep breath, clasped her hands together and waited.

Mr. Barrett came forward, holding a Bible, and asked Annie to swear an oath of truth. She did so, in a tremulous but clear voice, then sank into the chair provided, hoping no one had noticed that her knees had failed her.

Mr. Barrett's voice was even and deep, and Annie clung to it, like a ribbon strung through a dark wood. All she had to do, she told herself, was hang on tightly and tell the truth.

He asked her to give an account of the events in the marketplace and she did so, unflinchingly, though she felt sick at her stomach all the while. The jury, the spectators and the prisoners all became part of a pulsing blur. She wished she could see Rafael.

After she'd given her testimony Mr. Barrett asked her a few brief questions for the sake of clarification and then dismissed her. Annie rose, holding her head high, and shook her head when Lucian stepped out of the void to offer his arm. The experience had been a difficult one, but Annie was determined to see it through without leaning on anyone else.

She walked slowly and steadily out of the great hall, having no wish to stay and hear Phaedra's testimony. In the courtyard, she sat on the bench next to the fountain and raised her face to the dazzling sunlight.

Only a few minutes had passed when Kathleen arrived, carrying a cup of cold water. Annie accepted it with gratitude and drank deeply. The drink restored her, settling her stomach and easing her trembling.

"You'd best go in and lie down for a while, miss," Kathleen said gently. "It's taken a lot out of you, speaking up like that, and having to recollect those horrible things." When she saw that Annie was about to refuse, she hurried to make her case. "Remember, now, you promised His Highness that you wouldn't add to his troubles by pushing yourself too hard."

A breeze blew a tendril of hair across Annie's forehead, and she pushed it aside. "All right," she agreed reluctantly. "But it isn't as if I'm sick or anything."

Kathleen smiled, somewhat mysteriously. "I know, miss," she said. "An hour's rest and you'll be back at your post, all the stronger for taking time to collect yourself."

They entered the castle by a roundabout way, avoiding the great hall. Since going to her room in the middle of the day and lying down would have made her feel like an invalid, Annie went to the solarium instead. There was an old rocking chair near one of the windows, and she curled up in that.

"Would you like some tea, miss, or something to eat?" Kathleen asked, in the kind of quiet, indulgent voice one might use with a child.

Annie shook her head. The chair was large and its velvet cushions, though worn smooth with age, were comfortable. "No, thank you, Kathleen," she said, with a yawn. "And don't you dare go back to the village or the chapel without me. You work twice as hard as I do and you need to rest, too."

Kathleen smiled. "I'll be fine, miss," she said, and then she turned and walked away, and Annie was alone in the vast, ancient solarium with all its sweet-tempered ghosts.

She closed her eyes and settled deeper into the chair, dozing but not really sleeping. She thought she heard faint, poignant notes, played on a harp or a lyre, and the soft murmur of feminine voices exchanging confidences.

After both Annie and Phaedra had given their versions of the story, the defendants were offered an opportunity to address the court, one at a time. Rafael stayed to listen, but what he really wanted to do was find Annie, hold her in his arms, tell her how proud he was of her, and how much he loved her.

The testimony seemed to go on forever. One after another, the accused men stood and spoke up for themselves. Most seemed genuinely remorseful, but a few were sullen, casting defiant glances at the crowd in general and Rafael in particular. The worst of these was Jeremy Covington, who evidently believed that coming from a good family gave him the right to run roughshod over anyone who got in his way. He made it clear that he saw the proceedings as a travesty of justice and considered himself the true victim of the case.

It was hot in the great hall, and the smell of too many sweaty bodies confined to too small an area was almost overpowering. Underlying it all was Rafael's primal urge to shoulder his way through the crowd and throttle Covington with his bare hands.

The lieutenant finished his oration by spitting at the feet of the magistrate, a man all the villagers admired, according to what Rafael had been able to learn, for fairness and wisdom. How ironic it seemed that, after all that had been done to them and to their loved ones in the name of arrogance and power, these people had still tried to elect a judge who would serve the cause of justice.

Barrett signaled two of his men to remove Covington from the great hall, and even though the lieutenant's hands were manacled, it still took both of them to drag the prisoner away. Privately, Rafael thought Jeremy ought to be grateful that he'd ended up in the dungeons of St. James Keep during a fairly enlightened time. Many of those who had gone before him had not been quite so comfortable.

After a conference with the magistrate, Barrett announced that the trial was over for the day, and the jurors and spectators alike were dismissed. Other soldiers escorted the remaining prisoners back to their cells.

"I need a drink," Barrett said, as he and Rafael crossed the great hall in the direction of a passageway that led to a small, private stairway.

Out of the corner of his eye, Rafael caught a fleeting glimpse of a woman in peasant's clothes. She was familiar in some way, although he didn't see her face. When he turned his head, she had already gone.

Rafael felt a flicker of uneasiness, but the incident was minor, after all, and he pushed it to the back of his mind. "We still don't know who killed that university student," he reminded Barrett, leading the way up the rear stairs.

Barrett sighed behind him. "No," he agreed ruefully. "We don't."

CHAPTER

16

Annie stood at the back of the great hall all through the following morning, listening as more droning testimony was given. For practical reasons, she wore the same plain dress she'd donned the day before, and her hair was pinned into a loose bun at the back of her head. She felt somewhat listless but, like Kathleen, she seemed impervious to the fever raging among the villagers. The malaise had felled a number of peasant women and some of the servants who had been helping when they could, but so far no one had died.

That was a blessing, and not just for the obvious reasons. The village's sewage system had been primitive in the first place, but now, between the influx of new people and the nature of the fever itself, sanitation was becoming a real problem. There could be an outbreak of typhoid or cholera at any time.

Being preoccupied with these dilemmas, Annie was startled when Jeremy Covington, still manacled, bolted to his feet, shouting incoherently and struggling within his bonds. His eyes were glazed, like those of a wild beast in a snare; his shirt was soaked with sweat, and his face and neck glistened with it.

The young soldier who had been stating his case, as was his right, stared at his commander, open-mouthed.

Reluctantly, two of Barrett's guards moved to restrain Covington, but he was powerful in his rage and fear. He fought so hard that it took four more men to finally subdue him.

He was sobbing wretchedly by then, and Annie felt pity for him. Plainly, Lieutenant Covington's imprisonment and trial had broken him.

The men would have dragged him back to the dungeons if Rafael hadn't stepped forward.

"Let him speak," the prince commanded in a quiet, even voice that carried, nonetheless, to every part of the great hall.

Covington stood trembling. "I don't want to die," he said. "I won't hang for what someone else"—he turned his head and fixed his gaze on one of the other soldiers—"for what *he* did."

The soldier went crimson, and then white. He shot to his feet and would have lunged at Covington, manacles and hobbles not withstanding, if Mr. Barrett and one of the villagers hadn't restrained him.

"Damn you to hell, Covington!" the accused shrieked.

Rafael turned calmly to face the man. "What is your name, Soldier?"

Even from a distance, Annie saw the man's throat

work as he swallowed. "Peter Maitland, Your Highness."

"Did you shoot that student, Peter Maitland?"

A visible shudder moved through Maitland's small frame. He looked wildly from Covington to the other men lining the prisoners' bench and finally met Rafael's gaze again. "Yes, sir," he said.

"Why?" Rafael asked reasonably.

The great hall was silent for a few moments while everyone, peasant and visiting aristocrat alike, awaited the answer. When it came, it caused a furor.

"I was defending you, sir. He was speaking treason!"

Rafael looked sick, as well as exasperated and weary, and Annie barely restrained herself from rushing forward to stand at his side. Instead, she sent a silent message from her heart and he seemed to feel the contact, because his gaze sought and found her in the crowd. For a moment, they were linked, alone in the great hall.

When at last Rafael spoke, it was with disgust and utter despair. "Take him away," he said. "Take them all away."

There followed such an uproar that the very walls of the hall seemed to tremble with the force of it. The man appointed to serve as judge hammered at the table before him with the gavel provided for the purpose. "Silence!" he bellowed, and everyone obeyed him, from the lowliest peasant to the visiting nobles who had come to St. James Keep for Phaedra's wedding.

Annie lingered while the crowd reluctantly dispersed. Finally, only the magistrate, the jurors, Rafael and Mr. Barrett remained. While Annie did not think it would be appropriate to approach the prince just then, she couldn't bring herself to leave his range of vision, either. It might have been nothing more than romantic whimsy on her part, but she felt that somehow her presence encouraged Rafael, and even lent him strength.

Seeing that her mistress wouldn't be moved, Kathleen found chairs for them both. They sat in silence while the judge and jurors conferred among themselves. Rafael and Mr. Barrett stood a little apart, listening but offering no comment.

Within the hour, a decision was reached and, though Annie and Kathleen were too far away to hear what it was, Rafael's expression was grim as he took it in. He nodded and then the small group separated and dispersed.

As Rafael approached, Annie rose from her chair.

Kathleen squeezed Annie's hand and said, "I'll be in the chapel, miss." With that, she hurried out.

Annie swallowed, searching Rafael's face as he drew nearer. Most probably, there would have been no trial if she and Phaedra hadn't defied the rules and gone to the marketplace that afternoon. Annie felt a certain remorse for that, although the raid would surely have taken place anyway. In that event, of course, Covington and the others would most likely have escaped punishment.

Finally, Rafael stood in front of her. She wanted to touch him, but resisted the urge and simply waited for him to speak.

"Covington and most of the other men will be held in the dungeons for six months or until the keep is taken over by the rebels, whichever comes first," he said, in a grave, hollow tone. "Maitland will be sentenced to hang for the murder of the student."

Annie squeezed her eyes shut for an instant against the images her imagination readily provided, but it didn't help. She could envision Maitland swinging from a gallows too easily, and knowing that Rafael half-expected to meet the same fate at some point made the thought still worse.

She and Rafael had not discussed his views on the subject of capital punishment, but she sensed that he had serious reservations. "Will you permit the sentence to be carried out?"

Rafael shoved a hand through his already rumpled and somewhat shaggy hair. Annie had the peculiar thought that the prince would need barbering, if he wanted to present a proper appearance at his sister's wedding. "I have no choice," he said. "The decision was the peoples' to make, and they've done so."

Annie was again prompted to touch Rafael, and this time she did, laying her fingers lightly to his cheek. "I'm so sorry that all this is happening," she said, in a broken whisper. "It must be like wandering in a nightmare."

He smiled solemnly and turned his head just far enough to kiss her palm, and she felt the now-familiar shock of pleasure race through her bloodstream. "It will pass, Annie," he replied. And then he stepped back a little way, a wry expression sparkling in his eyes as he took in her servants' garb. "I do believe you are a peasant at heart, for all the money and prestige that accompany the name of Trevarren."

The sound Annie made was part laugh and part sob; she wanted to fling herself into Rafael's arms and beg him to forget Bavia and go away with her. She knew he couldn't grant her wish, though, so she refrained. "Yes," she said instead. "I guess we Americans are all peasants, at our roots, whether or not we have money."

Rafael took her arm, and they walked together into the sunlight that splashed over the courtyard and made a spray of diamonds of the water spewing from the fountain. They sat down on the familiar bench, both oblivious to the soldiers, crofters and wedding guests moving busily around them.

"I've been wanting to ask you about the fever," Rafael began, and when Annie started to protest that she was in no danger, he stopped her with a raised hand. "I know better than to tell you to stay away from the village," he said, with good-natured resignation. "What I want is your assessment of the situation."

Annie felt a rush of pride, for in her experience, men seldom asked for a woman's "assessment" of anything. She considered the facts carefully before answering. "The fever doesn't appear to be fatal. People come down with it quickly, but they also recover in good time. What worries me is the lack of sanitation facilities in the village—there are open pits of sewage, and that could result in another and much more serious epidemic."

Rafael listened intently, as he would to Mr. Barrett or to his advisors, and Annie was deeply moved. She believed that he loved her, though he might not have realized that yet, and he had treated her with respect for the most part. This was something more than courtesy, however, and Annie cherished it.

"The men can shovel lye into the pits and build

temporary latrines farther from the village," he said. He smiled, looking up at the towering keep and narrowing his splendid eyes against the bright sunlight. "In times of old," he confided, "the facilities were suspended over the moat."

Annie shuddered, but his smile was still infectious, if a bit wan, so she returned it. "So there were no alligators guarding the castle, like in fairy tales?"

Rafael gave a comical shudder. "In that water? Even sea monsters couldn't have lived in that stuff, Princess."

There was a sweetness in simply sitting in the sun with Rafael, and talking of silly things, that made Annie's heart ache. The memory of that interlude would be, Annie knew, as precious to her as those of their lovemaking.

Her eyes brimmed with tears, though she refused to let her smile falter. "Being here, in this keep—it's like traveling back in time or slipping into the tale of some medieval troubadour. What's happening to us now couldn't occur anywhere else on earth."

Rafael took her hand, almost shyly, as though he had never touched her intimately with those same fingers, never driven her into a delirium of pleasure with his caresses. "Therein lies the problem," he said, in a sad voice. "The days of castles and kings are over. The world is changing, Annie, in ways you and I can't begin to guess. And Bavia has no place in modern society."

Annie felt another swell of emotion. Rafael was right—progress was inevitable. Still, Annie didn't like to think of a world with no castles and kings—and no princes. "It doesn't seem fair," she said at last, in a soft and tremulous voice. "There are still dragons, after all. And evil knights. They simply come in different guises now."

Rafael smiled and kissed the tip of her nose, and the gesture, innocent as it was, sent a soft, unruly passion spinning through Annie's being. "That's true of princesses, too," he said. "Some of them dress like servants and insist on looking after ailing peasants, but they have royal hearts all the same."

Too soon, the enchantment was broken.

A clamor of excitement exploded within the keep, overshadowing and then drowning out the normal din of creaking wagon wheels, horses' hooves on the cobblestones, swords clashing as soldiers practiced for war. Even before Edmund Barrett bounded into the courtyard, Rafael was on his feet.

"What is it?" he demanded.

"There's a rebel battalion on its way, Your Highness, riding bold as brass along the coast road!"

Rafael turned to Annie and she braced herself, expecting him to order her into hiding and therefore ruin the effect of having asked her opinion, just minutes earlier, about the fever raging in the village. He took her elbow and spoke in a low, earnest voice.

"This will probably be nothing more than a minor skirmish, if there's any fighting at all," he said, "but if things go wrong, will you look after Phaedra? I don't have to tell you that she isn't strong or particularly courageous, despite all the mischief."

Annie felt a spilling sensation in the region of her heart. She nodded and, though she wanted to touch Rafael's face or only his arm, she refrained. She was afraid such a contact might weaken him, and for the same reason, she refused to cry.

With that, Rafael turned and strode away with Mr.

Barrett, toward one of several sets of stone stairs that led to the battlements. Annie watched their progress, shading her eyes with one hand. Soon, they disappeared into one of the towers.

Annie watched soldiers scurrying back and forth along the parapets for a few moments, wishing with her whole heart that she could see what they saw from their high vantage point. She bit her lip, hands resting on her hips, as she pondered the situation.

Following Rafael and Mr. Barrett up the stairs was out of the question; she would only be underfoot on the battlements, where everyone had a task to perform. Still, she wanted to see the approaching rebels and gauge the danger in her own mind.

Her gaze strayed to the abandoned tower she'd climbed once before, with its crumbling ledge and long, narrow windows. Since the coastal road and the lake lay in opposite directions, there would be no need to venture out onto the parapet this time; she'd be able to see plainly without endangering herself.

Determined, Annie set off for the oldest part of the keep, going unnoticed in all the excitement and confusion, and within five minutes she was hurrying along the passageway toward the tower steps. Breathless with haste, she burst into the round, shadowy chamber, pausing just over the threshold to collect herself. As her eyes adjusted to the change of light, she made out the shapes of objects, which was odd, since she was certain the room had been empty before.

"Hello?" she inquired.

No one answered, but the shapes Annie had seen before solidified into recognizable articles—a pile of blankets, a basket, a water jug and a crude wooden basin. She took a step nearer, crouched and raised the cloth that covered the contents of the basket to see brown bread, cheese and several apples beneath.

For a few moments, Annie's curiosity was such that she forgot the rebels riding toward the keep. Someone was obviously living in that room, but why would anyone want such Spartan accommodations, when the castle had more bedchambers than most grand hotels?

Annie rose to her feet, frowning, the answer only too clear in her mind. Whoever was using that chamber was doing so because they did not want to be seen.

She glanced uneasily toward the doorway, but it was empty. Though Annie strained her ears, all she heard was the distant shouts of Rafael's soldiers and the heavy thudding of her own heartbeat. She went to the window and peered out. For an instant, the dazzling dance of sunlight on the blue-green sea practically blinded her. She blinked and then shivered, certain that the unknown occupant of the tower chamber would return while she had her back to the door.

Annie drew a deep breath and let it out slowly in an effort to calm herself. Then, after only one furtive glance back over her shoulder, she turned her attention to the rebels riding along the ancient track that wound beside the sea. There were over a hundred of them, by her estimate, and while they were plainly a ragtag bunch, most were mounted. Even from that distance, Annie could see that they were armed with rifles and sabers, and several cannon-bearing caissons rolled behind the troops, drawn by mules.

Bitterness burned the back of Annie's throat, and she swallowed. The walls of St. James Keep were ancient, and there were surely weak places, easily found if one simply walked or rode along the outer perimeter. Her imagination was vivid, and she could picture the cannons aligned on a hillside, hammering away at the old stones until they gave way.

She thought of the secret gate and the cave that lay beyond it. If she, on an afternoon's lark, had uncovered the passage with such ease, surely a clever rebel could do the same from the outside.

Annie knew, with the clarity of hindsight, that she should have told Rafael about her discovery, so that guards might have been posted, or the gate sealed. In all the excitement, however, she'd never gotten around to mentioning what she'd found.

She went to another window and tried to see the gate, but her view was obscured by the trees in the orchard. As far as she could tell, there were no rebels advancing on the keep from that direction, but they might have been creeping along the outer wall instead of riding boldly down the road like their counterparts.

Gnawing at her lower lip, Annie tilted her head back to gaze up at the conical ceiling, wondering if she'd be able to see farther from the roof of the tower. There were plenty of cracks and crevices in the stone walls, she recalled, that would serve well enough as handholds. If she could just scramble up the roof and get a good grip on the spire . . .

Annie shook her head, dismissing her own thoughts. The last time she'd made an attempt like that, she'd been fine one moment and frozen with fear in the next, and Rafael had risked his life to save her. There was no rescuer at hand, should her courage fail again—indeed, her folly would probably go undiscovered until after she'd fallen and splattered herself all over the courtyard like an overripe tomato.

The thought of it made Annie wince. She turned

away from the window and caught a fleeting glimpse of a small, robed figure standing in the doorway.

"Wait!" she cried, and dashed across the dusty floor. From the stairs, she heard someone running lightly along the passage, but by the time Annie reached the opening, the visitor had vanished. He or she could be behind any of the dozen doors lining that particular hall, and Annie knew all the chambers were abandoned. She had no wish to pursue the tower resident through curtains of cobwebs and the nests of rats.

She put the experience on a mental list of things to mention to Rafael and soon forgot it. By the time Annie gained the main courtyard, it was jammed with those residents of the keep who had not been felled by the fever or pressed to man the battlements. According to Kathleen, who soon materialized at Annie's side, the rebels had ridden right up to the base of the drawbridge, which hadn't been raised or lowered in two hundred years. Even now the rebel soldiers were training their cannons on the entrance of St. James Keep.

Annie squinted, searching the battlements for Rafael. She soon spotted him looking down upon the walkway above the great wooden gates, and even at that distance, with his back turned to her, she read controlled fury in the angle of his head and every line and sinew of his body. He shouted something to the would-be invaders which Annie found unintelligible and the rebel leader replied in kind, his voice ringing with defiance.

With a reluctance Annie knew went soul deep, Rafael raised a hand to signal his men, and they trained their rifles on the rebels and began to shoot.

The men on the drawbridge never even got off one round of cannon fire before they were driven into retreat.

Annie felt sick, thinking of the bodies that were surely lying at the castle gates, and her knees buckled. Kathleen, ever-ready to lend a hand, took her arm and ushered her away toward the chapel.

"Come along, miss," she commanded, in a brisk whisper. "We're only in the way out here, and there are still those who need us inside."

It was true. The chapel was packed with moaning, dehydrated villagers, and the few servants who were willing or able to help with the nursing were skittish with fear. Everyone was well aware that there would be other onslaughts, and even the sick clutched at Annie's skirts and wrists and begged to be hidden from the invaders.

She crouched beside one old man, who lay fretting on a pallet in the corner, to bathe his gaunt and grizzled face with cool water. "Hush," Annie admonished gently. "No one is going to hurt you. The walls of St. James Keep are thick." She remembered the secret gate and pushed the thought out of her mind again as the elderly peasant fretted. "You're safe here," she insisted.

"No," he said, shaking his head. "They're inside—the rebels are—they're in the walls and under the floors—"

Delirium, Annie thought. She offered up a silent prayer that the fever wasn't taking on new dimensions. "Please rest," she replied, stroking the man's burning forehead.

He subsided into a fitful sleep, finally, but there were others who were afraid. Annie thought their whimpers and muffled sobs would haunt her forever, and she was practically stumbling with weariness when Kathleen finally dragged her out of the chapel at moonrise.

The great hall was bright with the lights of many candles and lamps, and when Annie saw the line of wounded men lying on the floor, she gave a small gasp and put one hand to her mouth. They were rebels, judging by their hodgepodge clothes, which had probably been scavenged from houses in Morovia. It was plain that they were all dying, with only awkward young soldiers to tend them.

Annie started in their direction, but Kathleen tightened her grasp on her mistress's arm and stopped her.

"No, miss," she whispered sharply. "There's no saving any of these, and I won't let you waste yourself trying."

Too exhausted and dispirited to argue, Annie swallowed hard, nodded, and allowed Kathleen to lead her toward the stairs.

Annie had every intention of asking to see Rafael, so that she could make sure he knew about the secret gate, but her weariness was consuming, and she was asleep before she'd finished the light supper Kathleen brought up from the kitchen. Somehow, Annie got into her bed and collapsed onto the mattress with her arms spread wide and her mouth open.

Several hours must have passed before she stirred from dark dreams and tried to raise her eyelids.

At first, Annie thought she was imagining the cold, sharp edge of the blade pressed against her throat. She stiffened in reaction, and a broad masculine hand covered her mouth, stifling the scream that had risen automatically from her diaphragm. She was awake now, but all she could see was a looming shadow and a thatch of fair hair.

Her heart clenched painfully, like a fist, as she realized what was happening.

"You're right to be afraid," Jeremy Covington said, in a hoarse, moist whisper. She felt the blade shift against the delicate flesh of her neck, and her whole body broke out in a cold sweat.

Covington sighed and, with his free hand, stroked her hair back from her face with an eerie tenderness, as if they'd been lovers. "It's not going to be easy to kill you, though," he lamented. "You're such a beautiful creature, tawny and wild like a lioness—"

Annie fought a primitive urge to squirm and flail— her shock had abated a little, and she knew her only chance lay in keeping calm.

The lieutenant suddenly knotted his fingers in her hair and pulled and Annie closed her eyes against the pain. Sourness burned at the back of her throat, and her heart was racing so that she thought it would finally outdistance itself and burst.

"Damnable little bitch," Covington hissed, bending so that his face was close to hers. She smelled madness on his breath and in his sweat, and she felt a new surge of terror when he forced one knee between her legs. "If only you'd kept that sweet mouth closed . . ." He lifted the blade from her throat and traced both her eyebrows and the length of her nose with its tip. "But, no. You couldn't do that, could you? And now, thanks to you, I'll have to live out the rest of my life as a criminal, and all the doors that once were open to me will close in my face!"

Annie struggled, not against Jeremy Covington, but against her own fear. She stared up at him and waited.

Without removing his hand from her mouth, Covington traced the outer perimeters of Annie's breasts with the point of his knife. Even through the thick fabric of her nightgown, she felt the deadly sharpness of it, and terror threatened to swamp her again.

Show me what to do, she prayed, in frantic silence. *I don't want to die!*

Covington pressed the blade to her throat again and shifted his weight, so that he straddled her. "I'm going to take my hand away from your mouth for a moment," he said, in a horribly reasonable tone. "But I warn you, Annie. If you scream, I'll drive this knife right through your lovely neck." He shook his head, making a *tsk-tsk* sound. "What a shock it will be to poor Rafael, when he finds his little American mistress awash in her own blood."

Annie held onto her courage with the last of her strength. *Rafael,* she called from deep within herself. *Help me!* But when Covington took his hand away, she didn't scream.

"Don't do this, Lieutenant," she said, in a voice so calm and detached that she wondered how it could have come from her mouth. Inside, Annie was shrieking. "It will only make things worse for you. You'll be a murderer. How many doors will be open to you then?"

Annie realized too late that she had made a grave error of judgment. Even in the gloom, she saw Covington's face contort, and she felt his terrible rage in the pressure of his thighs against her hips. Clasping the dagger's handle in both hands, he raised the weapon high and was poised for the downward thrust when suddenly he grunted and the point of a rapier came through his chest from behind.

Annie watched in horror as crimson spread around the small wound, and Covington stiffened in the shock of instantaneous death. The dagger dropped from his fingers, the handle striking the side of Annie's head.

She screamed at last, a shrill, piercing, catlike cry, and raised both hands to push the lieutenant off her. He fell heavily to the floor and there, at the side of the bed, staring blankly and clad in a plain brown robe with a hood, stood Felicia Covington. Her hands extended, fingers interlaced, as though she still held the rapier that was now lodged in her brother's body.

The door of Annie's chamber flew open and there were people all around. Annie saw Phaedra among them, and Chandler Haslett, and Lucian, and she didn't move or speak. But when Rafael strode over the threshold, his shirt untucked and his hair rumpled, the dam burst and she let out a loud wail, followed by a series of plaintive sobs.

The prince didn't bother with the steps; he vaulted onto the dais and gathered Annie's trembling body into his arms. She clung to him, unashamed of her need, and the contact calmed her as quickly and effectively as a shot of whiskey would have done.

Over Rafael's shoulder, Annie saw Lucian crouch beside Covington's corpse. "Good Christ," he rasped, before raising his gaze to poor, stricken Felicia, who had not, in all this time, moved a muscle. "She's killed him."

Annie heard grief in Rafael's voice when he responded, and she knew he was not mourning Jeremy Covington, but his murderess. "Barrett," he said gruffly, his embrace as tight and protective as before. "Take Miss Covington somewhere safe, and see that she's looked after."

Only then did Felicia lower her arms. She smiled angelically at Rafael, and went without protest when Mr. Barrett put his hands on her waist and lifted her down from the dais.

CHAPTER
17

"Miss Trevarren will be all right, then?" Barrett asked, in a quiet voice, when Rafael met him outside the study door, an hour after the incident in Annie's bedchamber.

Rafael nodded. He'd carried Annie to his own quarters, where the maid, Kathleen, had given her a strong sleeping draught. Only after Annie had tumbled into a shallow slumber had he left her side, and even then a part of him had remained behind.

"What have you learned?" he asked. "Did Felicia free Jeremy?"

Barrett sighed and leaned back against the stone wall of the passage, his arms folded. "Yes," he admitted. "She's been in the keep for several days as it happens, sleeping in one of the tower rooms and eating with the villagers."

Rafael shoved a hand through his hair, thinking of

the robed figure he'd glimpsed in the great hall, the day the jurors were selected. He'd believed, until that night, that Felicia was safe in France. Obviously, she'd made her way back. It was even possible, of course, that she never left Bavia in the first place, but had disguised herself as a peasant and entered the castle in the midst of the stream of refugees.

"How the devil did the woman manage to get by your guards?"

Barrett's tone was rueful. "Only too easily, I'm afraid. While they were sleeping, she must have walked right past them, taken the key from the wall and released Covington. He unlocked the other cells."

Rafael closed his eyes for a moment. "Have the other men been captured?"

"Most of them stayed right where they were—in fact, they kept Covington from killing the guards."

"Most of them stayed," Rafael prompted.

"Peter Maitland escaped. My men are looking for him now."

Rafael swore, then reached reluctantly for the latch on his study door. Felicia, he knew, was waiting inside. "Let's get this over with," he muttered.

She sat in a wing-backed chair, near the fire, her lovely face translucent with madness, holding a wine goblet in her hands. Seeing Rafael, she smiled.

"Hello, Your Highness."

Although Rafael wanted to weep for Felicia, he kept his emotions under strict control. In a way, he'd driven her to this himself by refusing to grant her beloved brother clemency, and while he didn't regret that decision itself, he did wish he'd found some way to shield her from it.

He approached her chair and she offered her hand, as though greeting a guest at a tea party. Rafael bent and brushed her knuckles with his lips. "Hello, Felicia," he replied. Then he crouched beside her chair, still holding her hand. "What happened tonight?" he asked gently.

She favored him with a bright, chillingly vacant smile. "I saved my brother from the gallows," she said. The smile faded. "But then, I had to kill him. I couldn't let him hurt Annie—that wasn't part of our agreement."

Rafael reached out and lightly touched the soft, fair hair. "Of course not. You never meant to hurt anyone, did you, sweet?"

Tears filled Felicia's brown eyes, made them luminous. "No. But it all went wrong, Rafael—such dreadful things have happened. I wish I'd never let Jeremy out of that cell, but he was so persuasive when I sneaked in to visit him. He said you wouldn't rest until he'd been hanged or even drawn and quartered."

Covington had not been sentenced to the noose, and torture of any sort had always been strictly out of the question, but Rafael did not point these things out. Felicia's state of mind was obviously an irrational one.

He patted her hand but said nothing for he was too overcome to speak.

"I'm so tired," Felicia said, and gave a delicate yawn. She was flushed and rumpled, more resembling a weary child than a woman who'd just run her beloved brother through with a rapier. "Do you suppose I could go to sleep now?"

"Yes," Rafael replied hoarsely, rising and then

helping Felicia to her feet as well. "I think that would be a very good idea."

She stood before him, gazing up into his eyes. "Will you put me in the dungeon, Rafael?" she asked simply, without rancor or guile. "Am I to be hanged for what I've done?"

Rafael looked away, struggling, once again, with a wellspring of emotion. "No," he said presently. "Whatever happens, you'll be kept safe. I promise you that." He flung an appealing glance at Barrett, who read it correctly and stepped forward to take Felicia's arm in a gentle hold.

"Come along, m'lady," the soldier said quietly. Over the fair head, Barrett met Rafael's gaze and, although neither man spoke again, much was communicated. Rafael knew Barrett would see Felicia installed in comfortable quarters with guards at the entrance and then report back to him.

Annie awakened early the next morning, shaken by an immediate flood of memories of her near-death the previous night and groggy from the sleeping medicine she'd been given. She wanted nothing so much as to cower in bed, but she'd long since decided that any desire to retreat from life was unhealthy, so she got up.

Kathleen, who had been sleeping in a chair next to the fireplace, woke with a start and launched straight into a protest. "Now, miss, you mustn't act as if this were an ordinary day. You've had a terrible shock, after all!"

Annie smiled, poured tepid water from a crockery pitcher into a basin, and scanned the surface of the washstand for soap and a cloth. "That's exactly why I must act as if this were an ordinary day," she replied. "It's just like taking a spill from a horse. One gets back into the saddle without delay."

A resigned expression came over Kathleen's face, though there was a zealous light in her eyes. "But you were almost killed," she reminded Annie stubbornly. "It's hardly the same thing as a topple off a mare's back, now is it?"

Annie had completed a hasty washing, and now stood with her hands on her hips, looking around the room to which she had been carried in the night. "It appears that I have no clothes to wear. Would you please be so kind, Kathleen, as to fetch me the brown dress and my sturdiest shoes?"

Kathleen hesitated only a moment. "That frock is being laundered, miss," she said. "There were plenty of nasty things on the skirt, in case you've forgotten."

She wrinkled her nose. Caring for the sick was messy business, and the dress had indeed been soiled. "Something else, then—my black gaberdine skirt and a shirtwaist with as few ruffles as possible."

Another hesitation. "Yes, miss," Kathleen agreed, with an unuttered sigh underlying the words. In a moment, she was gone.

Half an hour later, circumspectly clad, her hair wound into a single braid, Annie descended the stairs to the great hall as if nothing untoward had happened the night before. Because the trial had ended, the vast room was virtually empty and Annie proceeded through it at a brisk pace while Kathleen hurried to keep up.

They'd gained the courtyard and were moving toward the chapel when Lucian appeared, moving as casually as if he'd been out for a morning stroll. Annie felt a tingle of uneasiness in his presence, though he'd been behaving himself of late.

All geniality, Lucian stepped in front of Annie, forcing her to stop. "What's this?" he said, arching one eyebrow in a way that made him vaguely resemble Rafael. "The lady is out and about? After coming within a hair's breadth of being murdered?"

Annie folded her arms and tapped one foot. While she certainly didn't find her duties among the sick enjoyable, she wanted to do something that would serve a useful purpose and, at the same time, distract her from thoughts of Lieutenant Covington's attack. "Lucian, I am in no frame of mind for nonsense this morning. Either step aside or let us put you to work in the chapel or the village."

He sighed and, after a maddening delay, moved out of Annie's path. "I'm afraid I wouldn't be much help." Annie went briskly past him, Kathleen beside her, but Lucian kept pace and, at the door of the chapel, caught hold of her arm and held her at the threshold. His tone, affable before, was now earnest, and he spoke rapidly. "For God's sake, Annie, let me take you away from this place before we're overrun by barbarians! Don't you understand what's happening in this country—within the very walls of this keep? In a matter of days, maybe hours, the whole place will be awash in blood!"

He was probably right, Annie reflected, with a curious sense of calm. In any case, she had no intention of leaving St. James Keep without Rafael.

"You know my answer," she said, and then pulled free of his grasp and marched into the chapel, rolling up the sleeves of her shirtwaist as she went.

Throughout that morning, Annie listened with half an ear for more cannon fire, expecting another attack by the rebels. Incredibly, more wedding guests arrived instead.

Late in the afternoon, while she was sitting beside the courtyard fountain, Annie caught her first glimpse of Rafael. He stood on one of the battlements and, as usual, Mr. Barrett was at his side. As if he'd felt Annie's gaze on him, the prince turned and looked in her direction.

Mildly stung that he had not inquired about her, given his attentiveness the night before, Annie stared brazenly back at him, refusing to avert her eyes.

Rafael started down a steep set of stone steps, motioning to Barrett to stay behind, and strode toward her. As he drew nearer, Annie saw that the prince's manner was grim, and his lithe, powerful body was taut with tension.

In the hope of forestalling some of the things he might say, and because she truly was concerned, Annie blurted, "Is Felicia all right? Where is she?"

For a moment, Rafael looked even more solemn than before. He shoved a hand through his hair. "Don't worry," he replied irritably, "I haven't clapped the woman in irons. She's in a comfortable chamber, with a maid to take care of her. When the next ship drops anchor off the coast—and I admit to a wild hope that it will be one of the Trevarren vessels— Felicia will be brought aboard and escorted to a hospital in France."

Annie felt heat rise in her cheeks. "I didn't think for a moment that you had thrown the poor woman into the dungeon," she said, her voice trembling with the effort to speak calmly. She drew a breath and released it slowly. "Do you have reason to expect a visit from my father?"

"Beyond the fact that I've written him, on several occasions, begging him to come to Bavia and collect his daughter?" Rafael asked coldly. "No."

Annie was stunned. She should have known, she supposed, just how much Rafael wanted to be rid of her. It was difficult to believe that this was the same man who had taught her how to love with passion and with power, who had held her so tenderly after the tragic incident with Lieutenant Covington.

"Are we still under siege?" she asked evenly. Rafael, she realized, was trying to distance himself from her emotionally, and she knew he wouldn't retreat from this stance.

"No," he said, folding his arms—another barrier, Annie thought. "It might be days before anything else happens. How are you and the others faring against the fever?"

She sighed, feeling inexpressibly weary. "I think we've seen the worst of it," she answered, "though heaven knows I'm no expert. Several of our patients have recovered and gone back to the village, so the chapel isn't quite so crowded."

Rafael turned at the clatter of carriage wheels on the drawbridge and watched as yet another horde of guests arrived. "Oh, to have this damnable wedding over and done," he muttered, speaking more to himself, Annie suspected, than to her. "You'd think people would have the good sense to stay home, given the fact that the country is at war, but instead they risk their fat, foolish necks for free-flowing wine and sugar-cakes."

"Occasions for joy are rare in Bavia these days,"

Annie observed softly. "They can be forgiven for wanting to celebrate instead of mourn."

Rafael made no move to go and greet his guests, though he watched them alight from their dusty carriages for several moments before turning his attention back to Annie. "How ironic," he said, in the voice of a stranger, "that there is to be both a wedding and an execution within the week."

Annie stared at him. She'd known about Peter Maitland's sentence, of course, but she hadn't expected it to be carried out so soon. "But Mr. Maitland had escaped with Jeremy Covington. Kathleen told me—"

"He was recaptured," Rafael interrupted. "Now, if you'll excuse me, I must oversee the building of the gallows." He would have walked away from her then, but Annie caught hold of his arm as he passed, the color draining from her face.

"Rafael, you can't erect a scaffold now, of all times—you'll spoil the wedding. Think of how Phaedra will feel."

His smile was cool and belonged, like his voice, to someone Annie had never met before. "You've apparently forgotten," he said, "that I am still the ruler of this godforsaken country. I can do whatever I wish, Miss Trevarren. And I'm afraid my sister's tender sentiments are the least of my problems at this point."

With that, Rafael St. James, prince of Bavia, walked away, disappearing into the great hall.

Annie stood where she was for a few moments stewing and then went into the chapel. She was taken aback to find Phaedra there, with a flock of servants and half a dozen soldiers, spouting genteel orders.

"Please carry these people out," the princess said,

making a fluttering gesture with her handkerchief that took in all the patients who remained within those hallowed walls. "Every last one. Then I want the floors and pews scrubbed, and get as much air as possible flowing through this place."

Annie approached slowly. "Phaedra?"

The princess turned to her with a slightly frenzied smile. "Hello, Annie." She frowned and touched her friend's arm, lowering her voice to a near whisper. "Are you all right? Dear heaven, after what happened last night, anyone else but you would be crouched in a corner, blathering and biting their nails—"

"I'm fine, Phaedra," Annie broke in, a bit tart in her impatience. "Where are these people being taken?"

The smile was back, too bright and very brittle. Phaedra was not herself, though Annie supposed that was natural, given the upheaval and chaos all around them. "Away," she said reasonably. "Annie, the wedding is to be held in this very chapel in only five days. I can't have the place looking and smelling like a pesthouse."

Annie closed her eyes for a moment. "Of course you can't," she said, after a brief pause. "But where will you put them?"

Phaedra waved one of the soldiers over, her pretty face full of polite confusion. "Pardon me, but where exactly are we going to put these poor people?"

Annie bit her lower lip and waited, barely resisting the urge to tap her foot. The soldier flushed at the princess's inquiry, but answered with admirable restraint.

"We were expecting you to tell us that, Your Highness," he said.

"Oh, dear," said Phaedra, blotting her forehead

with the handkerchief. Then she turned bewildered eyes to Annie. "Where *shall* we put them? It must be a place where they won't be in the way." There was a queer, greenish cast to her skin.

Patience, Annie told herself. This is your dearest friend, and she is overwrought, and as exasperating as Phaedra St. James can be, you love her devotedly.

"There are unused rooms in the area behind the kitchen," Annie said, addressing the young soldier. "I believe the wounded rebels are being cared for there."

There was a look of wry gratitude in the man's eyes. He nodded and the process of transferring the patients progressed. Annie watched attentively as they were lifted onto makeshift stretchers, old doors and planks, and borne away to the interior of the castle.

The maids were already scrubbing industriously, and those few windows that could be opened were pried, squeaking, from their sills so that fresh air could enter. The front door was propped ajar as well, and Annie felt a touch of chagrin, along with her irritation, because she hadn't thought of doing those things herself.

Phaedra linked her arm with Annie's. "I need to talk to you," she announced. "In private."

"Heaven help me," Annie muttered.

The princess laughed, a little wildly. "Do you really find me so difficult, Annie, dear?"

"Yes," Annie answered forthrightly, but she let Phaedra take her hand and lead her to the back of the chapel, where they sat together on a pew, beneath a stained glass window. The light bathed them in dusty shades of blue and red and green and yellow.

"The dress is finished, you know," Phaedra said.

Annie felt another flash of annoyance, recalling the

fittings she'd endured for that blasted gown. She'd gone to great lengths to avoid Miss Rendennon and her minions for the past several days, lest she be made to stand still for more pinpricks and grumblings.

"I'm relieved to hear that," Annie replied, smoothing her skirt.

Phaedra scooted closer, and her voice was barely more than a breath. "There's something I must confide."

Alarm niggled in the pit of Annie's stomach. "What?" she demanded, almost angrily. Her own patience was greatly taxed.

The princess started, and her great gray eyes brimmed with royal tears. "I thought you of all people, Annie Trevarren, would be on my side!"

"I am on your side," Annie insisted furiously. "But that doesn't mean I never wish I could murder you!"

"I can't marry Chandler Haslett."

Annie's very bones seemed to melt; she slumped against the back of the pew, amazed. *"What?"*

A tear escaped and ran, shimmering, down Phaedra's cheek. The look of desperation in her eyes pulled at Annie's heart. "I love someone else. I'm going to leave with him."

"You can't do that," Annie cried, though in a low voice. "There are more wedding guests arriving every day, and the dress is finished, and Rafael will be furious—"

"There will be a wedding," Phaedra said. "I just won't be the bride, that's all."

Annie gaped for a moment, then recovered herself sufficiently to ask, "What the devil are you talking about?"

"Goose," Phaedra chimed good-naturedly. "Don't

you see? I never intended to go through with the ceremony in the first place. That's why I asked you to be fitted for the dress."

The implication of that loomed before Annie, and she wondered that she had missed it before. *"You want me to stand in for you at the wedding?* Well, I won't do it." She folded her arms and spoke firmly, even though she already felt her resolve slipping. "Do you hear me, Phaedra St. James? *I won't do it!"*

Phaedra seemed undaunted. "Of course you will," she said reasonably, "because you know we're talking about the rest of my life. Imagine it, Annie—my happiness, perhaps even my sanity, is in your hands!"

"Don't," Annie warned, but the word wavered. She had always protected Phaedra, and the habit was hard to break.

"Please," Phaedra pressed, clutching both Annie's hands in her own. "It's the only way."

Annie cast an uneasy glance toward the maids, but they were all busy, scouring and chattering among themselves. "Why can't you just go to Chandler and tell him the truth?"

"He *knows* how I feel," the princess said, "and he doesn't care. Even with Bavia falling apart the way it is, Mr. Haslett has much to gain by marrying me. And you know how Rafael is—he'll sacrifice me like a she-goat before he'll go back on his precious honor."

Annie closed her eyes. A month ago, she would have argued against Phaedra's logic, but now she knew her friend was right. To Chandler Haslett and to Rafael, marriage was not a matter of love, but of contracts and bargains and exchanges of property.

"Who is this mysterious man you claim to love?" she asked, after a brief interlude of silence.

Phaedra looked down at her delicate hands, which were clasped in her lap. "I can't tell you that just now," she said.

"Don't you trust me?"

"It isn't that," the princess insisted earnestly, tears spilling once again. "I know you wouldn't tell on pain of death. But I don't dare breathe his name—if someone were to overhear, word might get back to Rafael. And heaven only knows what would happen then."

Annie was insulted on Rafael's behalf. "You don't mean you actually believe your brother would do the man some injury?"

Phaedra brought out her handkerchief and dabbed away her tears. "You wouldn't question the possibility if you weren't besotted with Rafael," she accused, with a prim sniffle. "You don't see his faults."

That made Annie smile. She knew Rafael's failings well enough; it was just that she accepted them as part of the whole person. "His insufferable arrogance, you mean? His stubbornness? Or perhaps you're referring to the prince's terrible pride?"

Phaedra subsided slightly. "You will help me," she pleaded breathlessly, "won't you?"

"I don't know," Annie said. "I have to think about this."

"Since when do you *think* about things before you do them?"

Annie watched the maids at their work for several moments before answering. "A lot has happened to me since I came to Bavia," she said finally. "Perhaps I've grown up a little."

With that, Annie rose and walked out of the chapel, leaving the princess behind. She visited the dry and dusty rooms behind the castle kitchen where the sick had been taken. The three surviving rebel soldiers, wounded in the ill-fated attack on the castle, lay on cots next to the far wall. Two were asleep; one stared sullenly up at the ceiling.

Annie found a water pitcher and a clean cup and approached. "Hello," she said.

The soldier glared at her with dark, insolent eyes, but Annie didn't miss the slight, involuntary motion of his lips when he saw what she carried.

She poured, and he watched the progress of the water as it moved from pitcher to cup. "My name is Miss Trevarren," she informed him. "What's yours?"

"Why do you want to know?" he countered. "So you can have it carved on my tombstone?"

Annie smiled and held the cup to his lips, and he drank thirstily, almost desperately. "You won't be needing one for some time, I think," she said. "A tombstone, I mean. Are you hungry?"

He sank back onto his pillows, his brown hair as shaggy and matted as a wild pony's mane, his skin pale beneath a layer of dirt. "No," he said, even as his stomach rumbled.

"Your name?" Annie persisted, extorting the information by holding the cup near his mouth again, but just a little out of reach. "And don't lie to me. There is no point in it."

"Josiah," he said, grudgingly. "Josiah Vaughn."

Annie allowed him to drink his fill that time, though she urged him to sip slowly. When he'd finished, he was white with exhaustion. Blood was seeping through the dingy bandage someone had plastered to his right shoulder.

Josiah flinched as Annie lifted the cloth and looked

beneath. He had been struck by shrapnel from a cluster shell, and the inflamed wound went deep. Annie thought she might have spoken too soon where the necessity of a tombstone was concerned.

"I'll have to clean that for you," she said. "There's nothing to use but good Scots whiskey, and I'm afraid it's going to hurt."

Josiah was young, probably no older than seventeen, and Annie glimpsed abject fear in his eyes, though he quickly veiled it. He set his jaw for a moment. "His Highness the Prince will want his prisoners mended properlike, I suppose, before he chops us apart at the joints like rabbit carcasses."

Annie shuddered, but her expression was wry. "Good heavens. That kind of thing was outlawed generations ago. Which is not to say that you aren't in a great deal of trouble." She left him long enough to collect a bottle of whiskey and a stack of clean cloths. Someone, probably Kathleen or one of her practical colleagues, had torn old linens into strips for bandages.

"Treason is punishable by death," Josiah informed Annie, when she had dragged a stool over and sat down beside his cot with the liquor and cloth on her lap. "I could be shot for what I've done. Or hanged."

Annie removed his old bandage and prepared to douse the wound. She'd heard her grandmother Lydia say, more than once, that alcohol sometimes staved off infection. "If I were you," she said briskly, "I wouldn't trouble myself, for the moment, with anything so spectacularly melodramatic as being shot or hanged. You've got problems enough already, it seems to me." She sighed. "Now, brace yourself, Josiah, and be strong. As much as I regret the fact, this is going to hurt like the very devil."

Josiah set his teeth and closed his eyes.

Annie poured.

Josiah screamed and then swooned.

Before Annie had recovered from that, the man in the next cot bolted to his feet, swayed and bellowed, "What have you done to him? What have you done?"

Fortunately, some of Rafael's soldiers were still in the chamber, and the raving rebel was subdued before he could reach Annie.

"Don't hurt him!" she cried, as two men flung him down with such force that his cot nearly collapsed. "He was only trying to help his friend!"

Somewhat reluctantly, the soldiers stepped back, but Annie saw the desire to do violence coiled in their eyes and straining in their powerful young muscles, and she was afraid. When they'd moved away, she turned back to Josiah and noted with relief that he was already coming around. She stepped close to the other man's bed.

He was middle-aged, unlike Josiah, a squat, burly bear of a man with a wild red beard and bushy hair that was full of briars and straw. "The lad's young," he said, in a hoarse voice. He was breathing hard, and his chest was bandaged. "He didn't know what he was about, joining up with the likes of us."

Annie's heart twisted with pity but, since she knew Josiah's would-be rescuer wouldn't appreciate the emotion, she kept it hidden. "He's nothing to fear from me," she said quietly. "I'm only a guest in this keep—I have no power."

He closed his eyes for a moment and when he spoke

again, it was in tones as ragged as his clothes. "You were only trying to help," he said. "I heard him scream, and I thought—"

"You were disoriented and you thought I was hurting your friend. I won't harbor hard feelings if you won't."

"Tom?" Josiah spoke weakly from the next bed. "Don't let her pour that whiskey on you."

Tom made a visible effort to sound hale and hearty. "Well, if she does, you sure as hell won't hear me carrying on the way you just did."

Annie smiled to herself and went about tending Josiah's wound. Kathleen, in the meantime, came to look after Tom, and one of the village women tended the third soldier, who was just awakening.

It was a good morning's work, and when Annie left the castle, intending to sit next to the fountain and enjoy the sunshine for a while, she was humming softly to herself.

The sound died in her throat when she stepped out of the great hall, however. Peter Maitland's scaffold was already rising, a skeleton of timber, in plain sight.

CHAPTER
18

For three days, the sounds of hammers and saws pounded and clawed at the summer air, setting the meter for Annie's pulse, screeching across her nerve endings. She worked doggedly in the new infirmary behind the kitchen, bathing faces, spooning soup and water into mouths, changing bandages and dressings. Nothing distracted her from the ominous din for long.

"Is that for us?" Josiah asked, late in the afternoon of the third day. "That gallows they're building out there in the courtyard?" He was still gaunt, of course, but since Annie had cleaned his wound—Kathleen had later sutured it—he'd been on the mend.

Annie gave him the last spoonful of his chicken broth. "Of course not," she said. "It's for a man named Peter Maitland. He shot a student in Morovia, during a riot. He was tried and condemned and now he's going to hang."

Josiah narrowed his eyes. He and Annie were not friends, though a certain fragile bond had developed, and his attitude remained a grudging and wary one. "He's a rebel, this Maitland?"

"No," Annie said, returning the spoon to the wooden bowl with a slight clatter and reaching back to check the tie on her apron. "He was one of the prince's soldiers. It was the murdered student who was a rebel."

Josiah was plainly surprised, and still suspicious. "You're sure you've got the straight of that, miss?"

I should have, Annie thought. *I saw it happen and my testimony helped convict the man.*

"Yes," she said simply. "Stop worrying and try to rest."

"You might heed your own advice," commented Tom, he of the bushy beard, from the next cot. Like Josiah, Tom was recovering fast, though the third man seemed to be losing ground moment by moment. "If you don't mind my saying so, miss, you've got shadows under your eyes and you're pale."

"Who's the nurse here?" Annie demanded, forcing a cheerful note into her voice and smiling at Tom, whom she'd come to like very much, despite his gruff manner and wild appearance. "You or me?"

Tom chuckled, but his eyes were kind and solemn. "You're a regular Florence Nightingale, miss. If only you'd look after yourself the way you tend to us. You seem fit to drop and that's the truth of it. Someone needs to do something about you."

Annie cast a despondent glance around the large room. Most of the fever patients had recovered enough to be absorbed into the chaotic life of St.

James Keep, but four remained. Besides them, of course, there were the three wounded rebels.

"I'm fine," she lied. Her knees felt as though they might give out at any moment, and her stomach was so upset that she hadn't been able to swallow a bite of food all day. The clamor from the courtyard jarred her very bones.

"Are you really so sorry for him," Tom asked, with uncanny perception, "this soldier they're about to hang?"

Bile surged into Annie's throat and she swallowed. "Yes," she said. "But I feel pity for the man he killed, too." In her mind's eye, she saw the marketplace in Morovia again, saw the earnest young student tumble with ludicrous grace into the fountain, his blood curling through the water like scarlet ribbons.

"She's rich," Josiah put in obstinately, addressing Tom. "And she's one of them in the bargain. She probably wishes they'd take the poor bugger somewhere far away to do him in, so she wouldn't have to watch and listen."

Color flared in Annie's cheeks, on a tide of fury so dizzying that for a moment she thought she would faint. She started to protest but before she could speak Tom broke in.

"Have you forgotten," he demanded, eyes blazing in his sun-browned face, "that you're speaking to the woman who saved your life?"

Josiah flushed, but his expression remained defiant. He folded his arms and glared. "No," he replied. "And I haven't forgotten that she nearly killed me in the process, either."

Calmer now, because Tom's intercession had given

her a few moments to collect her dignity, Annie raised her chin and swept over to stand next to the third man's bed. He was wretchedly thin, with old scars crisscrossing his body like a web, and between the network of marks his skin was a grayish blue color. His wounds were relatively minor, but he hadn't rallied like his comrades.

The sudden hush that fell over the chamber distracted Annie and made her look toward the doorway.

Mr. Barrett entered and, without so much as a glance in Annie's direction, strode across the room to stand between Tom and Josiah's cots.

"It looks as though the two of you are well enough to answer for your act of treason," he said. He acknowledged the unconscious man in the other bed with a brief nod. "Your friend isn't so fortunate."

Annie's breath caught in her throat and she stood still, her fingers intertwined. "Mr. Barrett," she said, with as much force as she could muster.

The strain of recent weeks showed in Rafael's friend and advisor; he was thinner, and Annie saw tension in his jawline and in his eyes as he turned to her. "You may wish to leave us for a little while, Miss Trevarren," he said, showing nothing but quiet good manners.

Annie felt the sting of dismissal all the same. "These men are still quite ill," she said in a tremulous voice. "I want your assurances, sir, that no harm will come to them in the course of questioning."

Mr. Barrett raised one eyebrow, and his expression was grimly wry. "Very well, Miss Trevarren," he said, after a moment or two of deliberation, "I promise to show restraint, if not kindness."

Annie hesitated, glanced at Tom.

Remarkably, Tom gave her a twinkling smile and gestured toward the door.

With reluctance, looking back over her shoulder as she went, Annie left the infirmary. Two village women who had been helping with the remaining fever patients followed silently on her heels.

The hammering echoed in her ears and in the very marrow of her bones. While the sound repelled Annie, it also drew her, in some inexplicable way, and she followed it like a child enchanted by a piper. In the great hall, preparations for the wedding feast had already begun—long, rustic tables were being carried in, while servants bustled about with feather dusters and scrub brushes.

Annie's stomach clenched painfully.

Outside, the sunlight was dazzling, the air fresh and faintly salted with the scent of the sea. The gallows, an object Annie had avoided successfully until then, loomed against the shimmering blue sky, an ugly monument to all the graces humankind had yet to acquire.

She stood looking at it, one hand shading her eyes, her thoughts divided. On one level, she considered the execution that would take place the following morning, while another part of her lingered in the infirmary, where Mr. Barrett was interrogating Tom and Josiah. She felt like a mother hen, separated from her chicks.

"Terrible-looking thing, isn't it?"

Annie started, then turned her head and saw Lucian standing beside her. It gave her the chills, the way he could sneak up on a person. "Yes," was all she managed to say.

She shivered when her eyes adjusted and she saw

Rafael on the scaffold with another man, both of them framed in sunlight. They were crouching to inspect the trapdoor that would spring open beneath Peter Maitland's feet.

"It's ironic, don't you think?" Lucian asked smoothly. "Rafael ordering that monstrosity built, I mean. He's an intelligent man, my brother—surely he's aware that he himself might be forced to stand up there with a noose around his neck."

Annie put a hand over her mouth, for the image Lucian's words engendered was a vivid one, and burning nausea rushed up from her stomach to scald the back of her throat. She recovered quickly, but not before Lucian noted her reaction and smiled a bitter little smile.

"This is not a game, Annie, or a fairy tale. Sooner or later, you must stop playing nurse and pretending that everything is going to be all right. It isn't. Bavia is doomed, and so is Rafael." He gestured, taking in the castle itself and the walls that surrounded it. "And all of this is an illusion. Escape, Annie, before it crumbles into rubble around you."

Tears stung Annie's eyes. "I can't," she said.

"Then you're a fool."

She sniffled and squared her shoulders. "Perhaps."

"Do you love my brother so much? More than your own precious life? More than the children who will never be born because you insist on sacrificing yourself on Rafael's altar?"

Annie didn't want to die, and for a moment she felt the loss of the children Lucian mentioned as keenly as if they already existed, flesh and blood testaments to her love for Rafael. "I don't have to explain to you," she said bluntly. "And I won't."

"Convenient," Lucian said with a sigh, "since you probably can't even explain it to yourself."

Annie kept her gaze fixed on Rafael and felt the familiar stir of excitement, deep in her middle, when he sensed her regard and raised his head to look at her. In that moment, Annie understood her commitment to this man completely, but it was still too great a thing, too marvelous and elemental, to be confined to words. Her only answer to Lucian was a shrug.

Rafael made no move to descend the scaffold stairs but instead returned to his conversation with his companion.

"Perhaps I should kidnap you, since you won't listen to reason," Lucian said.

The remark struck Annie with the impact of a stone hurled from a slingshot, all but knocking the breath out of her. "What did you say?"

"You heard me," Lucian replied succinctly. He stood like a soldier, his hands clasped behind his back. "If you refuse to save yourself, I might be forced to do it for you."

A wild, nervous rage surged within Annie, heating her blood and making her head feel light. "I will warn you once and only once, Lucian," she said, when she could speak. "Don't attempt such a thing, don't even *think* about it, because if you try anything remotely like that, I will tear out your liver and roast it on a spit. I am not nearly so helpless as I look!"

Lucian laughed, but no note of humor rang in the sound. "You? Helpless? I'm a man of many delusions, Annie, but I never indulged in that particular one." His gaze moved back to Rafael, who remained occupied on the scaffold, rimmed in an aureole of sunlight.

"Still, even the strongest among us have their weaknesses."

The observation gave Annie another chill. "Is that a threat?" she demanded.

Lucian shrugged. "More of a premonition," he said. "Watch out for kidnappers."

"Watch out for your liver," Annie retorted, as Lucian walked away.

She stared up at Rafael for a while, wishing they were both far from that place, then turned and went back into the castle. Mr. Barrett had already left the infirmary by the time she reached it, and both Tom and Josiah were alive and unmarked.

"He hanged us by our heels and beat us bloody," teased Tom, when he read the relief in Annie's face. "We told him all our secrets."

Josiah, lying back against his pillows, was flushed and sullen. "It might be a joke to you, Tom Wallcreek, but I don't look forward to spending the next twenty years rotting in the dungeons of St. James Keep."

"You won't," Tom said, with utter confidence.

Annie offered no comment. If Tom and Josiah were freed in a rebel raid, as Tom probably expected, she would be glad for them. At one and the same time, Annie dreaded the prospect with the whole of her being, for it would mean almost certain death for Rafael.

She stayed in the infirmary for another hour or so, puttering about. When Kathleen came to relieve her, with a stern warning to eat something and lie down for a while, she made her way into the busy kitchen.

Here, as in the great hall, preparations for the wedding were well underway. With no attempt to enter into the conversations swirling around her or to draw attention to herself—in her plain clothes, with her hair tied back, she often went unnoticed—Annie walked to the washstand and scrubbed her hands with warm water and strong soap. Then she slipped into the larder, helping herself to a heel of brown bread and a small wedge of cheese.

There was stout tea brewing in a brown pot in the center of the crowded table, so Annie took a cup to wash down her food.

"They carted poor Miss Covington away this morning, you know," one of the maids told another.

Annie didn't react or even glance in the speaker's direction but she was listening all the same. She crumbled the strong golden cheese into tiny pieces and began eating them one by one.

"Crazy as a bedbug," commented a painfully plain girl, holding a tray full of small cakes sparkling under a coating of white sugar.

The sight reminded Annie of snowy mornings on Puget Sound, when the world was so still and beautiful that it nearly stopped a person's heart. The yearning to be there, safe and warm under one of her grandmother's colorful quilts, was so intense that it made her stomach hurt.

A ship had put in off the shore just as Rafael had predicted, and Miss Covington had been taken aboard. The vessel hadn't been her father's, obviously, for Patrick Trevarren would never have left Bavia without Annie herself. Even if the captain had been willing to leave her, Rafael never would have allowed it—he wanted to be rid of her.

"Do you know what ship it was?" Annie heard herself ask. She hadn't meant to speak at all and was impatient with herself.

"Just some boat from England, bringing wedding guests and supplies," answered the cook's helper, who was used to seeing Annie in the kitchen fetching broth and filling pitchers with fresh water. "They're probably waiting out there to take the fancy people away again, when all the excitement's over."

Annie nodded and went back to eating her cheese. It still surprised her that the St. Jameses' friends and relatives were willing to risk their lives to attend a wedding, even if it *was* a royal one. That thought, in its turn, served to remind her that Phaedra wasn't planning to go through with the ceremony in the first place—the princess had maneuvered Annie into posing as the bride.

She groaned aloud and covered her face with both hands.

Someone touched her shoulder. "Are you all right, miss?" asked a gentle voice. Perhaps because of her work with the fever victims, Annie was well-liked within the keep.

Annie raised her eyes and recognized Ellen, one of Kathleen's friends. She answered with a fitful nod. She must look a sight, she concluded. Everyone seemed to think she was sprawled across death's threshold, half in this world and half in the next.

"All she needs is a sweet," said Cook, setting one of the glittering little cakes down in front of Annie. It smelled wonderful, warm and sweet and rich enough to tempt a saint in a horsehair shirt. "Here you are, miss. Swallow that down, and I'll give you another. Nothing like a treat to restore a body's hope."

Annie had her doubts about the medicinal value of sugar cakes, but she wanted mothering so she ate the morsel and found it delicious. Before Cook could induce her to eat another, however, Annie's fretful stomach rebelled. She clasped a hand over her mouth, bolted from the kitchen and threw up in a patch of morning glories growing beside the step.

Cook, the same matronly soul who had overseen the palace kitchen in Morovia, appeared at her side like a corpulent genie, holding a cup of cool water in one hand and a soft cloth in the other. The older woman touched Annie's forehead and sighed.

"It isn't the fever, then," she said, shaking her head.

Annie rinsed her mouth and wiped her face with the cloth. Her skin felt clammy, and her knees were unsteady. Her eyes widened as a possibility struck her, and she sat down hard on the step.

"When did you last have your woman-time?" Cook asked, in a sympathetic whisper.

Annie couldn't remember the date—she wasn't regular anyway—but it didn't matter. She knew instantly that she was carrying Rafael's child, and both jubilation and despair rode the crest of that realization.

Still seated on the step, she bent until her forehead touched her knees.

"Miss Trevarren?" Cook queried, worried. "Shall I send someone for His Highness?"

Of course everyone probably knew Annie and the prince were intimate. She didn't take the trouble to work out her feelings about that. "No," she answered, without raising her head. "And please don't speak of this to anyone else."

"You can be sure I won't," Cook insisted, somewhat huffily. "Never let it be said that Elnora Hayes is a gossip."

Annie didn't know whether she could trust the

woman or not. Her thoughts and emotions were caught up in a staggering, reeling tangle, impossible to separate one from another. "Leave me," she said. "Please. I'll be all right."

Exuding reluctance, Cook retreated into the kitchen, and Annie sat with her head down until her heart stopped pounding and her breath settled down to a reasonable rate. She didn't want to speak to anyone, but neither could she bear to go to her room, so Annie rose, crossed the yard and began following the keep's outer wall.

As she walked, she thought of nothing. It was business enough, for the time being, just to exist.

Presently, Annie came to the place where she'd found the hidden passage. It was still invisible, behind its shield of climbing vines and bushes. She waded through them, uncovered the gate and opened it.

As before, it took several moments for her eyes to adjust. When they did, Annie got another shock. Someone had been staying in the cavelike chamber; the stub of a tallow candle was stuck to an upended crate, and there was a pallet in the corner, rumpled and recently slept upon.

Annie panicked, then calmed herself with a series of deep breaths. She had neglected, with so much going on, to tell Rafael about this place. She didn't intend to make the same mistake twice; she would go straight to the prince and correct the oversight.

In the meantime, though, she had to see if the outer gate would open. She broke the tallow free of the box, lit the wick with one of several matches found nearby and moved deeper into the cave.

The other gate sprang ajar with ease, opening into a dense thicket of blackberry bushes. Annie could see that someone had been hacking their way through the thick, spiky vines, but the task had not been completed. A hand scythe lay abandoned on the ground.

She blew out the candle and peered through the foliage, seeing bits of green land and sparkling sea beyond. At a small sound behind her, Annie whirled and found herself face-to-face with Phaedra.

"You found our hiding place," she said, with such brave resignation that Annie felt a stab of pity for her. "I should have known you would."

Annie suppressed a need to confide her own momentous news. It must remain a secret until she found the right time to tell Rafael. "Is this where you've been meeting your secret lover?" she asked, without judgment or derision. Annie was in no position to throw stones.

"Yes," Phaedra answered, folding her arms in a sign of stubbornness that presaged another refusal to divulge the man's identity. "And don't ask me his name, because I'm not about to tell you."

"I should think it would be safe enough to speak of him—there's no one else to hear besides the mice." Annie made this observation without any real hope of persuading her friend. She and the princess were cut from the same cloth in many ways, and obstinance was a trait they shared.

"You'll know soon enough," Phaedra said, with a small smile and a twinkle in her gray eyes. "Everyone will. I almost wish I could be there to see Rafael's expression—not to mention Chandler's—when my clever deception is uncovered."

"Don't be overconfident," Annie warned. "We're about the same size, it's true, and there's no doubt that your wedding gown will fit me perfectly. But what

327

about the difference in our coloring? My hair is much lighter than yours."

"The veil is made up of layers and layers of net. As for the color of your hair, that can be fixed easily. We'll simply dye it."

For a brief moment, Annie forgot her pregnancy, the imminence of war, and tomorrow's hanging. "Dye my—now just a minute, Phaedra. I didn't agree—"

"Relax," the princess interrupted. "It's only temporary—a rinse I read about in some musty old volume I found in the library. It's made from herbs. I've already gathered the ingredients."

Annie rolled her eyes. "Thank heaven I'm no taller than you are—you'd probably want to cut me off at the knees so I'd better suit your bloody plan!"

Phaedra shook a finger. "A lady never stoops to profanity," she scolded, in a perfect imitation of Sister Rose at St. Aspasia's.

"Not unless she's had the poor judgment to get herself mixed up with you, Phaedra St. James!" Annie gathered her skirts and swept past the princess, into the shadowy interior of the cave. They were on the other side of the wall, within the keep's grounds, before she spoke again. "Has it occurred to you, in the midst of all this scheming and sneaking about, that Rafael will be furious *with me* when he finds out you've eloped and I've helped you to do it?"

Phaedra was unruffled. "Rafael adores you. He'll go into a rage, of course, but it won't last."

Annie sighed and started back toward the castle. "I don't like this."

"Really? I think it's exciting."

"You would."

As they neared the heart of St. James Keep, Annie

realized that, blessedly, the hammering and sawing had ceased. Tears of frustration, fear and weariness stung her eyes, but she held them back by sheer force of will.

"The hanging is tomorrow," she said.

Phaedra slipped a comforting arm around Annie's waist and squeezed. "Yes. But you needn't see it. I plan to stay inside until it's over and the poor wretch has been taken away for burial."

Annie thought of Josiah's remark in the infirmary that morning. *She probably wishes they'd take the poor bugger somewhere far away to do him in, so she wouldn't have to watch and listen.*

"Rafael will be there, won't he?" she asked.

"Oh, yes," replied the princess confidently. "I daresay it will turn his stomach, but Rafael is determined to allow the Bavian people their chosen justice. Besides, his honor alone demands that he see the thing through to its end."

Annie felt like lying down in the sweet summer grass and weeping. She, too, would attend Peter Maitland's hanging, and watch steadfastly until it was over, for Phaedra was right. Rafael would not wash his hands of the prisoner's blood, like a modern-day Pontius Pilate. Annie could do no less, for she was, in her heart, his mate, and must stand by him in whatever way she could. Besides, she, too, had had her part in the drama. Now she must remain onstage until the final curtain fell or bear forever the memory of her cowardice.

"You look ghastly," Phaedra remarked airily, when they reached the edge of one of the rear gardens, a place of tangled vines and crumbling statues scarred with moss. "Are you all right?"

"No," Annie replied. "I am not all right. But that simply doesn't matter at the moment, so don't concern yourself."

Phaedra stepped in front of Annie and clasped both her hands. The princess' face glowed with earnestness. "You *are* doing the right thing by helping me escape St. James Keep, Annie, I swear it!" she whispered.

"If I didn't think so," Annie said coolly, "you may be sure that I would not have agreed to participate in the first place."

Phaedra smiled, gave Annie's hands another squeeze, kissed her lightly on the forehead and turned to hurry away. She vanished into the overgrown garden like a wood sprite, leaving Annie to wonder, for one fey moment, if she'd imagined the whole encounter.

Annie had dinner in her room that night, with Kathleen for company. The keep was fairly bursting with wedding guests, and Annie was in no frame of mind to socialize. In fact, she felt as if *she* were the condemned, Anne Boleyn or Catherine Howard, on their eve of doom.

"There's a babe growing inside you, I think," Kathleen said gently, when Annie had choked down all she could of a meager supper and pushed her plate away.

There had been too many shocks that day for Kathleen's words to startle Annie overmuch. "Yes," she said. "Did Cook tell you?"

"Oh, no," Kathleen said quickly. "I worked it out myself, by the look of you. And I knew, I confess, that the prince came to your room at the palace, the night of the princess's engagement ball."

Annie was too weary to be embarrassed. "I suppose that's common knowledge," she said ruefully.

Kathleen brightened. "Certainly not, miss. It's just . . ." The glow in the maid's skin took on shades of deep pink. "It's only that I changed the sheets myself."

Elbows on the edge of the table, Annie lowered her face to her hands. "What am I going to do?" she murmured, asking herself, Kathleen and whatever benevolent angels that might be tarrying nearby.

"Tell the prince, first of all," Kathleen said. "This might be just the news he needs to turn him from the terrible course he's set for himself."

Annie lowered her hands and stared at the young woman she regarded as her unquestioned equal. Perhaps even her superior. "It won't work," she said despairingly. "Lucian told me today that Rafael will hang from that very same scaffold when the rebels finally take the keep. And he's probably right, damn him."

Kathleen was still of good cheer. "His Highness wants a baby more than anything in the world. His wife, the Princess Georgiana, was with child when she died. They say it compounded his grief a hundredfold, knowing he'd lost an heir as well as the woman he loved."

Annie's sorrows deepened, for somewhere along the line Rafael's losses had become hers as well. Even this one, though it was personal and part of a past she had not shared with him.

"This news might be nothing more to Rafael than another burden," Annie said. "You are not to tell him there's a child, Kathleen. Or anyone else."

"But—"

"I mean it," Annie insisted. "For now, this is our secret."

Kathleen was clearly opposed to Annie's decision, but she bit her lip and nodded her unwilling compliance.

CHAPTER
19

Even before the first pinkish gold fingers of dawn crept into the courtyard of St. James Keep, a crowd had gathered. Sickened, clasping a borrowed shawl close around her shoulders, Annie scanned the gathering for Rafael and finally found him on the study terrace. Mr. Barrett stood, in full military regalia, at his side.

Annie was not Rafael's princess and thus could not stand next to him at any formal occasion. Still, she loved him as much as any wife had ever loved a husband, and his child was already taking shape inside her. She hurried back across the courtyard, into the great hall, up a rear staircase and along the hall to the study doors. Guards were posted, and when Annie tried to pass between them, they barred her way with crossed rifles and glares.

She fell back on bravado. "Let me in, this instant!" she commanded.

The guards looked at each other, then at Annie.

"Sorry, miss," one of them said. "Orders from Mr. Barrett himself. No one goes in."

Annie started to argue, but before she got more than a few words out, one of the study doors opened and Rafael appeared. He looked as though he'd lost weight, just during the night, and he was pale as the ghost of Hamlet's father.

His gray eyes lit on Annie, narrowed, and then he smiled slightly. "Let her pass," he said, with resignation rather than welcome, and Barrett's men complied.

Once they were both inside, Rafael closed the door again.

"How did you know I was out there?" Annie asked.

Rafael cocked an eyebrow and sighed. "I saw you in the courtyard and guessed that you were on your way." He paused to run splayed fingers through his still-unbarbered hair. If someone didn't take the shears to him right away, he'd soon be every bit as bushy as Tom Wallcreek, the rebel. "Go back to your room, Annie. A hanging is not a pleasant thing to witness."

Color pulsed in Annie's cheeks. "Do you think I *want* to watch, like some of those ghouls down in the courtyard?" she hissed, moving past the prince toward the entrance to the terrace. "You, of all people, ought to understand that it's a matter of honor—if my testimony brought this on, I can do no less than see it through to the wretched finish." She did not mention her other motive in attending the execution, the need to share Rafael's sorrows as well as his joys.

Rafael caught her arm before she'd gained the terrace. Outside, in the cool stillness of that new morning, the crowd erupted with a raucous hurrah.

The prince closed his eyes for a moment, then looked deep into Annie's very soul and said, "I release you from that responsibility. Go—please."

Annie shook her head. "I'm sorry, Rafael, but even you haven't the authority to override the dictates of my conscience."

"I don't have time to argue," he said, as another jubilant cry rose on a swell of quiet.

Annie wondered if the spectators would enjoy the wedding as much as the hanging. They were bound to, she decided, for the holy sacrament of marriage was to be turned into a circus before their eyes. She felt a stab of guilt for the part she meant to take in the deception.

"Nor do I," Annie replied. "Let me stand with you, Rafael. If you refuse, I shall simply take myself to another balcony."

The prince clasped her hand, muttered something better unheard and dragged her off toward the terrace. She stood a little behind Rafael, and to the side, her fingers still tightly intertwined with his.

Peter Maitland had already been led up the stairs to the scaffold. He stood rigid in the soft, chilly light, a strangely romantic figure with his hands bound behind him. Annie watched, not even allowing herself to blink, as a hood was fitted over his head. Beside him, a priest spoke words Annie couldn't hear and made the sign of the cross.

The noose was put into place, and Annie locked her knees. She stole a glance at Rafael and saw that he was standing as stiff and straight as the prisoner, and his face, in profile, was bloodless.

The hangman, who wore a hooded robe and mask for anonymity, turned to look up at Rafael, his eyes invisible behind two narrow slits in the cloth covering his face.

Rafael's fingers tightened painfully on Annie's hand, but she did not flinch. Out of the corner of her eye, she saw the prince raise his other arm in response to the hangman's unspoken question.

The executioner nodded, checked the noose and finally took hold of a wooden lever with both hands. There was a shriek of wood grinding against wood, and then the trapdoor gave way under Peter Maitland's feet. He fell through the opening, and could be seen dangling beneath the scaffold at the end of the taut rope.

It might not have been so terrible if he hadn't kicked and struggled and spun, if Annie had not seen the wet stain on the front of his trousers. She forced herself to watch, barely able to keep her head above the level of consciousness, until the swinging body went still.

The instant Maitland's corpse had been cut down, however, Annie sank to the floor of the terrace in a dead faint.

Only moments had passed, she supposed, when she awakened to find herself in Rafael's arms. He carried her to the couch in the study and laid her down, and Mr. Barrett soon appeared with a brandy snifter.

"Drink this," Rafael commanded in grim tones, taking the glass from his friend's hand and pressing the rim gently to Annie's mouth. "You'll feel better in a few minutes."

Annie refused the brandy, mindful of her baby and

knowing the liquor wouldn't stay down anyway. "I'm
. . . I'm sorry," she said. "I tried so hard to be strong."

A look passed between Rafael and Mr. Barrett and,
at the prince's nod, the faithful soldier left the room.

"And you succeeded," Rafael replied, with a sort of
tender ruefulness. "God in heaven, Annie Trevarren,
what a woman you are, and how I wish I were going to
live to make you my princess."

The unexpected words revitalized Annie, sent a
surge of glorious strength and courage flowing through
her. She hardly dared ask, but the question that
sprang to her lips was of such grave importance that
she couldn't stop it. "Are you . . . are you saying that
you love me?"

He kissed her forehead. "Devotedly. And with a
passion that is positively unholy. But it isn't to be, and
you know that as well as I do."

Tears blurred Annie's vision, and she battled them
valiantly, for she would not have used weakness or
wiles to hold Rafael. For that same reason, she did not
tell him about the child they'd conceived together.

"Then I will stay here, and die beside you," she said
rashly. Even as she uttered the words, however, Annie
knew she could not sacrifice her innocent child. Not
even for its father's sake.

"You must know I won't permit that," Rafael told
her. Then he kissed her again, this time on the mouth,
and with such tenderness that pieces of her heart
broke away and tumbled into the fathomless reaches
of her soul. "There's a ship waiting off the coast.
Saturday, after the wedding, you'll be taken aboard
with the bride and groom." When Annie started to
protest, he touched her lips with an index finger and

added, "Whether you want to go or not. Pack your things, Annie—you're going to France."

"I wish I'd never come here," Annie lamented, reckless with pain.

"So do I," Rafael replied, rising slowly to his feet and gazing down at her with tormented eyes. "Believe me, so do I."

With that, he went out, leaving Annie to a very somber and uncertain future. Presently, she got off the couch, sniffling, and took herself back to her room, where she splashed cold water on her face and willed the starch back into her knees.

That done, she marched down to the infirmary, head held high, and found Kathleen already there. The maid was sitting by Tom Wallcreek's bed, combing his great mass of bushy hair, and she blushed when she saw Annie.

Love, it seemed, was everywhere. Perhaps, God willing, this pair would have more success.

"Oh, miss—just look at your pale face!" Kathleen cried, bolting off her stool when she'd gotten a second look at her friend. "Don't tell me you watched the hanging!"

"All right," Annie said. "I won't."

Kathleen clapped a hand over her mouth, plainly horrified, but Annie shifted her gaze to Josiah, who had the good grace to look abashed.

Tom sat up straighter in his cot. "It's almost a pity, this being the end of the St. James family," he said. "You would have made a fine mistress for such a house as this one, Annie Trevarren."

Even here, Annie marveled, people knew about her and Rafael. She said nothing.

Josiah made a scoffing sound. "A pity, is it?" he

snapped, gesturing toward the near-dead man in the cot on the other side of Tom's. "Tell that to poor Harry, over there, with all his marks and mended bones. He'd not mourn the end of such a family."

Annie frowned. "What do you mean?"

"I mean," Josiah said, raising his voice a little to override Tom's furious protest, "he bears the mark of a St. James whip on near every part of him. And do you know why? Because the last prince got a bastard off his only daughter, and drowned the babe in a brook when it was over, like a motherless kitten. Harry's crime was that he tried to save the little one, and got His Highness's fine clothes drenched in the attempt."

Annie felt her knees go weak again and stiffened them. "The last prince must have been a horrible man," she allowed. "But Rafael is decent and fair. He'd never do such a thing."

Josiah shrugged, his expression as obdurate as ever, and quoted, " 'The sins of the fathers—' "

Instinctively, Annie laid a hand to her flat abdomen. If the fruits of sin could be passed down from one generation to another, perhaps a just reward could, too. Rafael would leave a heritage of honor and strength, courage and intelligence for his son or daughter.

Realization sparked in Tom's eyes when he looked from Annie's face to her hand and back again, followed by the most abject sorrow.

Annie turned away, unable to bear his pity, and fled the infirmary. For the first time since she'd appointed herself to the position of nurse, she shirked her duties.

The courtyard was empty, when she stepped outside, but the scaffold loomed, sturdy and ominous.

Annie could cheerfully have set fire to the thing, but she knew someone would only put out the blaze before it had done any real harm.

She passed by it, through the village, which seemed unusually quiet that day, and up the hill to the graveyard. Rafael's late wife, the Princess Georgiana, was buried there, along with generations of St. Jameses. Annie did not pause to pay her respects, but went over the knoll to the other side, where lesser personages were laid to rest.

There, six soldiers were in the process of burying their rebellious comrade, Peter Maitland. Their faces were set and grim, and Annie wondered if any of them bore a grudge on the dead man's behalf. Nearby, earth mounded raw upon it, was the resting place of Jeremy Covington.

Annie felt a little shudder go through her. So much death, and it was probably only the beginning.

One of the soldiers looked up. "You wanted something, miss?" he asked, with a sort of annoyed deference.

His tone took Annie aback for a moment, but then she realized that she didn't belong in this place. She was intruding.

She shook her head and turned away.

By Saturday morning, the hated scaffold had been partially dismantled and dragged around to the back of the castle, out of sight of the wedding guests. Not, Rafael reflected ruefully, standing at one of the study windows, that the structure had ever seemed to trouble them much.

"Rafael?"

He turned at the sound of the small, feminine voice

behind him and smiled to see Phaedra standing there. She looked too young, suddenly, to be a bride. He remembered her with pigtails and skinned knees, though his encounters with her had been rare and brief, because he had spent most of his life in England.

Rafael held out his arms to his sister and she scurried into his embrace, clutching him tightly. Almost desperately. He kissed the top of her dark head, and she looked up into his eyes.

"You'll be married today," he said, unnecessarily. The whole keep was in an uproar of preparation and almost frenzied festivity.

She hesitated for a fraction of a second, then replied with a shaky smile, "Yes."

He smoothed her lovely hair. "I know you've had your doubts about this marriage," he said tenderly, "but Chandler is a good man and he will look after you."

Phaedra nodded, her eyes feverishly bright and her cheeks flushed. "I'll be safe and happy," she said, looking away for a moment and then turning her gaze back to Rafael's face, as if by an act of will. "I wanted to tell you that I love you, for all that we've never truly known each other very well, and I shall hate leaving you behind."

Rafael smiled. "Don't worry about me, sweetheart, especially not today of all days. There are worse things, you know, than living out one's destiny."

Phaedra's pretty face tightened into an expression of ladylike fury. "Damn your destiny," she spat. "If I were strong enough, I'd knock you senseless and carry you out of this coffin of a castle myself!"

"But you're not," Rafael reminded her.

She seemed to sag a little, to become smaller. "No,"

she agreed. "I'm not. Will you promise me, at least, that you'll do whatever you must to survive?"

"No," he answered honestly. "But I will vow to take no foolish chances. Is that good enough for you?"

She echoed his response to her earlier question. "No," she said, "but I suppose that's the best I'm going to get and I shall have to settle." She rose on tiptoe and kissed his cheek. "Remember, Rafael, I am and shall always be your loyal subject. And so will my handsome bridegroom."

Rafael frowned. He had never questioned his sister's loyalty, or that of her future husband. Why, then, should she make so solemn an avowal on such a joyous occasion? Ah, but he did not need to ask, he thought, smiling again. Phaedra was a woman, and women were mysterious creatures, full of schemes and secrets.

The herbal rinse Phaedra put on Annie's hair that morning in the royal bedchamber smelled like pig swill, but it did the job. Annie's red-gold tresses dried to a rich brown. Beneath the multilayered wedding veil, she would look enough like the princess to fool everyone in the keep.

She hoped.

"The way this stuff stinks," Annie protested, turning on the vanity bench to look directly into Phaedra's dancing eyes, "we'll be lucky if Mr. Haslett doesn't object to the marriage on principle."

Phaedra smiled. "He won't object," she said. "Chandler thinks he's getting my fortune. He'd go through with the ceremony even if I—if *you* smelled like a henhouse."

At midmorning, the splendid wedding dress was carried into Phaedra's chamber by Miss Rendennon herself and no less than six helpers. Watching from behind the changing screen as the gown was carefully laid out on the princess's bed, Annie felt a wicked thrill at the prospect of wearing it.

Her pleasure faded, along with the odor in her hair, as the day wore on. It wasn't to be a real wedding, after all. Rafael wasn't the groom, and she would be an imposter, not a real bride.

Annie yearned for the whole disastrous experience to be over, and yet she clung to each moment as it passed. Rafael had told her he loved her the day of the hanging but he'd also warned that he intended to send her away. She felt certain that he would carry out his promise, one way or another, even though Phaedra's elopement would certainly alter his plans.

At one in the afternoon—Annie had not been able to eat a bite of the lunch Phaedra had so generously shared—the bells in the chapel began to peal joyously. The sound made Annie jittery; she paced the room in her chemise, muttering to herself.

At half past one, Phaedra helped Annie into the dress, pinned up her hair and put the veil in place. As they had hoped, Annie's face was only a pale shadow beneath all that gossamer netting. Her hair, while not precisely the same shade as the princess's, was dark enough to fool the casual observer.

When the clock chimed a quarter of two, Rafael came to the door to collect his sister and escort her to the chapel. Phaedra ducked behind the changing screen while Annie admitted the prince.

He smiled and moved to raise the veil, in order to

kiss his sister's cheek, but Annie stepped back and shook her head.

Rafael shrugged good-naturedly and offered his arm.

As Annie descended the stairs and crossed the great hall with Rafael, she both regretted her deception and reveled in it. Even though he'd admitted that he cared for her, and she was certainly in love with him, this might be the closest Annie ever got to exchanging holy vows with Rafael. She would savor the memory all her life—however long or short said life might turn out to be.

The courtyard was crowded with villagers and servants, for the family chapel would not hold the whole assembly. Annie blushed with pleasure and chagrin as her "subjects" cheered boisterously and showered her with flowers.

At the door of the chapel, Rafael paused and patted her hand. Chandler stood at the front, by the altar, along with a priest and a bevy of Phaedra's female cousins, all clad in pink ruffles.

I would not have chosen pink, Annie thought righteously, but of course she said nothing, because to speak would be to betray herself.

The organ music began, and Rafael led her slowly down the aisle. From inside her cloud of netting, Annie scanned the jammed pews. Someone was missing, someone who should have been present, besides Phaedra, of course, but the identity of that person eluded her. It was all she could do, as it was, to hold back a hysterical giggle.

The notes of the wedding march reverberated in the dim chapel for several moments after Rafael had delivered Annie to the man who thought he would be Phaedra's husband, then gradually faded into a churning silence. When Rafael moved back, Annie barely kept herself from grabbing for his hand and clinging to him.

"Who giveth this woman to be married?" intoned the priest.

Annie couldn't remember if the man of God had said anything of importance before that and, for one horrible moment, thought she'd really and truly married Chandler Haslett.

"Her brothers," Rafael replied respectfully, from somewhere in the throbbing void behind Annie.

The ceremony began.

"Dearly beloved . . ."

Annie swayed, and Chandler took a subtle hold on her arm to lend support. Her self-recrimination redoubled at his kindness. At that very moment, the real princess was fleeing St. James Keep with her lover. Had they reached the secret gate yet? Was it safe for Annie to reveal her identity and put an end to this shameful duplicity?

The priest droned on, preaching an interminable sermon on the sanctity of marriage and the value of trust between a husband and wife, and Annie leaned heavily on Chandler's arm.

" 'Who can find a virtuous woman?' " the clergyman quoted sonorously, before lapsing into paraphrase. "Yea, verily, her price is far above rubies, and the heart of her husband does, indeed, safely trust in her."

Annie let out a small moan, but no one seemed to hear.

Let this be over, she prayed. Then, remembering that she would be sent away directly afterward, Annie added, *Let it go on forever.*

She wondered if any bride had ever been struck dead at the altar before.

"Chandler Haslett," the priest boomed, "do you take this woman to be your lawful wedded wife?"

Chandler squeezed her arm. "I do," he said.

Annie choked back a wail of shame and protest and waited for the ax to fall.

"Do you, Phaedra Elisabeth Madeline St. James, princess of Bavia, take this man to be your lawful wedded husband?"

Annie was silent.

"Your Highness?" the priest prompted kindly, in a low voice, when the silence had extended beyond an acceptable length.

Arms trembling, knees melting like spring snow, Annie slowly raised the veil and pushed it back from her face. "No," she said clearly. "I do not."

Chandler stared at her, the color draining from his face and then flooding back again. A thunderous hush fell over the pews.

"By God!" Chandler rasped. "What trickery is this?"

The wedding guests erupted into comment, all talking at once, and the priest looked downright flummoxed, as though he might crawl under the altar and hide himself.

Rafael strode forward, full of fury. Annie was not prepared for the extent of his anger. "What is this?" he demanded, in a hissing whisper, his teeth clenched. "Where is Phaedra?"

"Gone," Annie said. And then she went down in a

pool of silk and pearls and veiling, having reached the end of her endurance.

As he had done the day of the hanging, Rafael lifted her into his arms. He carried her down the aisle and out of the chapel, while the guests buzzed behind them and Chandler vowed loudly that he would have satisfaction for this insult.

Annie, still dizzy from her faint, rested her head against Rafael's shoulder.

"Where is Barrett?" the prince demanded of someone she couldn't see, as they crossed the courtyard. "I need his help."

"Isn't he inside, sir?" came the surprised response.

Rafael stopped, glaring at Annie, and she saw the truth dawn in his eyes even as she grasped it herself.

Phaedra and Mr. Barrett were lovers. Why hadn't she guessed it before?

Rafael swore colorfully. "I ought to fling you right into this fountain," he said, once he'd finished. "For what you've done to your hair alone."

"It would be a sin to ruin a dress like this," she said, with somewhat tremulous reason, "especially in these hard times."

The prince began striding toward the keep again. In the middle of the great hall, Kathleen appeared, her expression frantic. Plainly, she thought Annie was being carried off to the whipping post or the rack.

"Where are you taking my mistress, sir?" that loyal and intrepid maid demanded, stepping in front of the prince and blocking his path.

"I haven't decided," Rafael replied acidly. "In any case, young woman, it's none of your business."

"Kathleen—" Annie pleaded.

"Oh, but it is, sir, begging your pardon," Kathleen

insisted, flushed but apparently undaunted. "Miss Trevarren and I are fast friends, and I can't let you hurt her."

"Hurt her?" Rafael echoed, plainly insulted. "Good God, woman, what gives you the idea that I would do Miss Trevarren or anyone else any harm?"

Kathleen swallowed visibly, and Annie marveled at her courage. "Well, sir, we keep fearing that your father's blood will come out in you, you see. He was a mean one. Just have a look at that poor man in the infirmary, with all his scars, if you don't believe me."

Annie felt the impact of Kathleen's words strike Rafael, felt him brace himself against it. He still made no move to set her down.

"I believe you," he said, after a long and despondent sigh. "But I love this woman in my arms, God help me, and you may trust that I will subject her to nothing more than a blistering lecture."

With that, Kathleen stepped aside, eyes lowered, and Rafael progressed up the staircase and along the passageway, headed in the direction of Annie's room. Reaching that chamber, he climbed the steps to the dais and hurled her onto the bed, the dress billowing ridiculously around her.

Annie flailed her way to an upright position, watching as Rafael vaulted off the dais and strode toward the door adjoining Annie's room to Phaedra's. He stopped in the middle of the floor, clearly just remembering that his sister was gone from St. James Keep.

He turned. "I'll find her," he said. "If it's the last thing I ever do, I'll find them both and drag them back here to give an accounting!"

The look on Rafael's face frightened Annie. She clambered awkwardly off the bed, damning the unwieldy dress in her thoughts and nearly tumbling from the dais in a heap. "Don't you see," she pleaded, "that it's too late? Let them go with your blessing, Rafael."

He rammed a hand through his hair. "How could you be a part of something like this? Do you realize what you've done?"

"I think so," Annie said. "My best friend in all the world begged me to help her escape a marriage she didn't want, and I did." She raised her chin. "Furthermore, I'm not sorry, though I do regret the problems my deception caused you and poor Mr. Haslett."

Rafael closed his eyes for a moment, his jawline taut, and Annie knew he was struggling to contain his temper. She certainly wished him every success in the endeavor.

At last, he spoke. "Pack your things, Annie. You're leaving."

The words struck Annie like so many stones, but she held onto her dignity with the last shreds of her strength. Between her near murder at the hands of Lieutenant Covington, the hanging of Peter Maitland, the fact that she was unmarried and pregnant, and the fraudulent wedding, she had exhausted her reserves.

"Come with me," she said, forsaking her pride.

Rafael shook his head, gave her one last appraising look, and left the chamber, slamming the door behind him.

Annie got out of the accursed dress as quickly as she

could and pulled on her trousers and shirt. Then she dashed down the back steps to find out what was happening.

She had to go no farther than the kitchen, where the servants had gathered to gossip about the grand events of the day. Tucked into a doorway, Annie learned that Rafael had sent soldiers after the princess and her paramour, but no one really expected them to be found.

Annie closed her eyes and offered a prayer that Phaedra and Mr. Barrett would make good on their escape. After all, they loved each other, and belonged together.

"This makes Mr. Barrett a traitor," Cook pointed out importantly. "He's gone and left the prince in his hour of need. Even love isn't reason enough to do that."

An uncomfortable silence fell over the kitchen, then Kathleen spoke up, wide-eyed. If she'd seen Annie huddled in the doorway, she gave no sign of it.

"The prince is a reasonable man," Kathleen argued. "Once he's had time to cool his temper, he'll see that Mr. Barrett meant him no disservice."

Annie hoped that was true, but she wasn't as certain as Kathleen sounded, and her heart ached for Rafael. He was surrounded by trouble, his enemies were at the door, and now he'd lost his closest and most trusted friend.

"It's a dark day for the St. James family," said Cook, with a shake of her head.

"The end can't be far off," someone else agreed. "I suppose I'll be taking myself away before the fighting starts."

There was a murmur of agreement among the other servants.

Full of sorrow, Annie turned, went back up the stairs to her room. After an arduous shampooing, her hair was almost back to its original color and she brushed it dry on the terrace. That done, Annie got out her bags and began to pack.

CHAPTER
20

Chandler Haslett decamped before the sun had set on his would-be wedding day, with an entourage of guards and relatives. The thwarted bridegroom, though politely asked, had refused to let Annie Trevarren travel with the company.

Watching the departure from one of the parapets, Rafael sighed. He couldn't blame Haslett for being furious, for the man had been dealt a devastating blow and his pride was in tatters.

"Quite a day," Lucian commented.

Rafael did not look at his brother, nor was he taken by surprise. Disasters, he'd discovered, tended to happen in tandem. "Yes. You warned me about Phaedra and Barrett. I should have listened."

Lucian stood beside him, one foot braced against the crenel in the wall. "That's something, I suppose," he replied evenly. "At least she's out of Bavia, or soon will be. Phaedra is safe with Barrett, after all."

Rafael emitted a humorless chuckle. "Yes," he agreed. "But is Barrett safe with our sister?"

Lucian smiled wanly at the question. "What will you do without him?"

For a moment, Rafael could not answer. He felt as though his right arm had been severed with Barrett's leaving and yet, now that he'd had time to think, he was more charitably inclined. Barrett had tried to tell him that he loved Phaedra and he, Rafael, had not taken his friend's declaration seriously. He'd been so certain that Barrett would see, as he'd seen, the impossibility of a union between a princess and a soldier.

"Perhaps it's better that he's gone," the prince replied, at considerable length. "Why should Barrett hang beside me? Bavia isn't his country, it's mine."

"Why indeed?" Lucian agreed. "What do you plan to do with Annie Trevarren, if you don't mind my asking?"

Rafael met his half brother's gaze. "I do mind," he said. "But I'll answer: I don't know. Haslett's ruffled dignity precluded Annie's traveling with his party. There is a ship off the coast, but I wouldn't trust anyone other than Edmund Barrett or her own father to get her safely aboard, and I can't leave the keep long enough to do it myself."

"Quite a conundrum," Lucian remarked. "I don't suppose you've considered me as an escort for the lovely Miss Trevarren?"

"I'd sooner consider the head of the rebel army," Rafael answered pleasantly. "Which is not to say that you shouldn't leave on your own. Your dislike for me won't save you from them, Lucien."

"Is it too late to prove myself a loyal and repentant sibling?" There was a familiar, wheedling note in Lucian's voice that struck a painful chord in Rafael, reminding him of the little boy Lucian had once been. Rafael had been fond of that child, though, like Phaedra, he had not known him well.

"Yes," Rafael said. "It is."

Lucian was silent for a few moments, watching the sunlight dance and play on the sea. "So be it," he said finally. Then he turned and walked away, leaving Rafael to his vigil.

Annie waited in her chambers for a summons, trunks and bags packed, but none came. Finally, at eight that evening, Kathleen appeared, bringing a supper tray. The maid's eyes were downcast as she brought the food to the small table situated near the fireplace and set it down.

"I suppose you're angry with me, too," Annie said, feeling uncommonly lonesome.

Kathleen looked up. "Angry? Oh, no, miss. But I'm afraid for you, right enough. The rebels won't wait long now, and they're not such poor soldiers as you might think from what happened the first time they attacked the keep. They're inside the walls already, in numbers that would surprise you."

Annie glanced at the food Kathleen had brought without appetite. She dreaded eating, but knew she must, for the sake of her child. No doubt in coming days, she would be called upon to do other things she did not want to do as well, in order to protect the baby.

She sat down at the table and gestured for Kathleen to join her.

"Were they waiting for the wedding to be over?" she asked.

Kathleen took the second chair. "Some of them were invited guests, miss," she said sadly. "People who call the prince friend, or cousin." She paused. "Or brother."

Annie had been pouring tea for herself, but she set the small china pot down with a thump. "Do you mean Lucian is . . . ?"

Kathleen reached out a firm hand and stopped Annie from bolting to her feet. "No need to hurry off to the prince with the news," she said. "His Highness has known the truth for a long time."

"Damn Lucian," Annie whispered, feeling the sting of his betrayal even though it had never been directed at her.

"He's a rotten apple, all right," Kathleen conceded, "but you can't judge the rest of the rebels by him. They're ordinary folk, for the most part, like Tom Wallcreek." At the mere mention of that man's name, the maid flushed bright pink.

Annie's heart did a skidding lurch, then righted itself. She'd been right, then—the maid was enamored with Tom. Was there more to it than that?

"Kathleen, are you one of them?"

"No," was the earnest answer, and Annie believed it. "But they're going to win, miss, and their leader's put a price on the prince's head. He'll hang, they say, before the month is out."

In her mind's eye, Annie saw Peter Maitland's slender figure standing on the scaffold, watched him fall through the trapdoor. It was only too easy to imagine Rafael meeting the same fate.

She pushed her chair back a little way, unable to touch her food, and put her hands to her face. "Dear God, Kathleen, what am I going to do?"

Kathleen answered with conviction. "You must tell the prince about his child," she said. "I know you wanted to do it in a certain way, miss, but the fact is, the right moment may never come."

Annie rose slowly to her feet and nodded. "Yes," she murmured. "I'll tell him. Now."

"God go with you," Kathleen said gently.

After some searching inside the castle, Annie ventured out into the courtyard and saw Rafael on the parapet. Still wearing her trousers and shirt, she climbed nimbly up the stone stairway and walked along the battlement until she reached his side.

"Has my ship sailed?" she asked.

He engaged in a somewhat bitter smile. "Yes. But I still haven't abandoned hope that your pirate of a father will arrive and take you away from here."

"You might have more to fear from Patrick Trevarren than the rebels," Annie said, her voice shaking a little. "He'll want you to do right by his daughter."

Only then did Rafael turn his head to look at her. "There can be no denying that Patrick will be furious when he learns I've deflowered such a prize. Let us hope, for your sake, that he gets to me before my own countrymen do."

Annie bit her lower lip, then blurted out, "I've heard rumors that they're already within the keep's walls. The rebels, I mean."

Rafael nodded. "There can be no doubt of that."

"And Lucian—"

He held up a hand. "Yes, I know that my brother is a Judas. Please spare me another hearing of the fact."

Annie could no longer avoid what she'd come to say, and it nearly destroyed her, having to use otherwise wonderful news as a club. She held her breath for a moment, like a swimmer about to plunge into freezing water, then spilled the jumbled contents of her heart.

"I'm going to have a child."

For a moment, Rafael looked as he might have done if Annie had pushed him right off the parapet. He said nothing at all for the longest time, and for Annie the world stopped turning, the stars fizzled, and the sun and moon dissolved to dust.

"Surely you're mistaken," he finally muttered.

Annie shook her head.

"The fainting spells . . . ?"

Annie nodded. "And other things. It's true, Rafael. Now, what do you intend to do about the situation?"

Rafael's answer startled her completely. "Marry you," he said, taking her hand and dragging her toward the stairway. "Find that priest and send him to the chapel," he called to a soldier up ahead. Then he turned and looked down into Annie's eyes. "At least there's a proper dress for you to wear, and wine and wedding cake, too, if the locusts haven't consumed it all."

"Rafael—"

He was pulling her down the stairs. "I'll hear no maidenly protests," he said, over one shoulder. "My child will have a name, if not a father."

Annie stopped cold and dug in her heels. "What do you mean, 'if not a father'?"

Rafael wrenched her into motion again. "We'll discuss that later, Miss Trevarren. For now, let's just get ourselves married."

After that, everything happened in an even greater hurry. Annie was given no more opportunity to protest, for Rafael abandoned her in the center of the courtyard and disappeared into the chapel. Moments later, the bell in the tower was ringing, and the population of the keep rushed to investigate.

Some of them surely thought the prince had gone mad when he put his head out of the belfry window and shouted that there would, after all, be a royal wedding in St. James Keep, and within the hour.

Annie wanted the marriage above all things, but she had a hollow feeling in her heart as she went inside to don Phaedra's magnificent gown and veil. There *was* a kind of madness in Rafael's actions, and he was, after all, only taking her to wife because of the child.

He had not even promised to leave the keep with her and seek safety in France, or spoken of a shared future at all.

Half an hour later, resplendent in a bride's garb, Annie was escorted down the main staircase and across the great hall by Kathleen and two of Rafael's soldiers. The chapel and courtyard were packed, as they had been during her performance earlier in the day, and Annie had a weird sense of going backward in time.

It was all real enough, however. The organ music thundered, and Rafael stood at the front of the chapel, beside the same priest. Lucian caught her eye as she hesitated on the threshold, and she saw such malice in his face that a shiver trembled down her spine.

"Go to him," Kathleen said, giving her a little push from behind.

Annie took a stumbling step toward her bride-groom, full of trepidation and ecstasy, fearing the future and at the same time hoping for miracles. Rafael held out a hand to her, and it was that gesture that drew her the rest of the way.

Even when she'd reached Rafael's side, and could feel him standing next to her, strong and solid, Annie feared she was only dreaming. If she awakened to find herself alone in her room, she thought, she wouldn't be able to bear it.

She listened to every word the priest said, stealing an occasional glimpse of Rafael out of the corner of one eye. The assembly was asked if anyone could give just cause why these two should not be joined together in holy matrimony, and Annie held her breath. Though there was some shuffling in the pews at this point—enough to make Rafael turn and sweep the congregation up in one grand glower of warning—no one spoke up.

Annie responded when a response was requested of her, and tried not to think beyond the moment.

Finally, the priest pronounced them man and wife and said, "You may kiss the bride."

Rafael bent his head, his lips a breath away from hers, and whispered, "My Princess Annie." Then he kissed her, albeit with such chaste restraint that Annie opened her eyes and stared at him in surprise.

He chuckled and hooked her arm through his, saying in a low voice, "Don't worry, my love. Ours will be a wedding night to remember."

Foreboding brushed Annie's spirit like the wing of a

mourning dove. Rafael sounded as though he thought that was all they would have, that single night.

The prospect was unbearable for Annie. Losing Rafael would be infinitely harder, should the worst happen, now that he was her husband. The idea of being parted from him was too painful to entertain, so Annie permitted herself to pretend the world wasn't going to end at any moment.

After the ceremony, an impromptu reception was held in the great hall. Rafael was cheerful, even buoyant, drinking toast after toast and singing raucous songs with friends and soldiers. That his enemies numbered among both groups did not seem to trouble him.

Annie, for her part, wanted only to be alone with her new husband. To her, every moment was precious.

The drinking went on and so did the singing. Annie smiled and accepted congratulations from people who had probably been gossiping about her in the shadowy corners of the hall. She danced with Rafael, when a gypsy band struck up a tune on fiddles and mouth harps, the skirts of Phaedra's wedding gown making the rushes whisper on the stone floor.

It was after one in the morning when Rafael finally took Annie's hand and led her toward the staircase. A great cheer went up when he whisked her off her feet and carried her to the second floor, and Annie blushed. She had always been too forward for her own good—or so said the nuns at St. Aspasia's—but having everyone in the castle know she was about to be formally bedded was disconcerting.

Rafael did not take his bride to his chambers, however, or to hers. Instead, he strode along the passageways toward the back of the keep, and Annie realized with some surprise that he was not the slightest bit drunk. The singing and the toasts and the boisterous celebration had been some sort of act.

"Where are you taking me?" she asked, thinking it a reasonable question.

Rafael smiled. "Away from here," he replied, setting her on her feet with a teasing frown. "You've already been eating for two, I see."

Annie laughed. "Cad! No gentleman ever refers to a lady's weight."

He took her hand and set out again, at full stride, pulling her behind him. "I will refrain," he said, "from the obvious response to that remark."

Presently, they came to one of the castle's many rear-staircases and started down. They walked out into a garden, and Annie was pleased to feel a soft, misty rain touch her skin. After the heat of the crowded hall and the exertion of dancing, the sensation was a welcome one.

At the edge of the garden, a buggy waited, hitched to a single horse. The groom in attendance touched his hat in silent acknowledgment.

Rafael lifted Annie into the seat, then climbed up beside her and took the reins. "Remember," he said, flipping a coin to the stable hand, "you haven't seen a sign of us."

The groom smiled and touched his hat again.

Soon, the buggy was bumping and rolling through the orchards. Up ahead, Annie could make out the shapes of the forest, and catch an occasional sparkling glimpse of the lake. She had guessed by then that Rafael was taking her to the spare little cottage, where he had taught her the first lessons of pleasure.

She rested her head against his shoulder.

The cottage had been prepared; there were lamps burning, the sheets were fresh and the covers turned back, a fire flickered on the hearth.

Rafael had carried Annie over the threshold, as tradition demanded, and her heart brimmed as she looked around at their private hideaway.

"I wish we could stay here forever," she said, before she could stop herself.

Rafael, standing behind her, kissed her bare, mist-dampened shoulder. "Forever is too much to ask," he replied.

Annie flinched at the reminder and turned in his arms. "Why did you marry me?"

He bent and brushed her lips lightly, teasingly, with his own. "No questions, Princess. I love you, and if tonight is to be all we have of eternity, let's make the memory worth cherishing."

Annie could not speak, but her eyes filled with tears, and her heart brimmed with bittersweet emotions she had never felt before, let alone named. She trembled as Rafael turned her around and began working the tiny buttons at the back of the dress.

Completing the task, he pushed the gossamer fabric down over her shoulders, then her waist and hips. The splendid gown made a glittering cloud at her feet, and she turned slowly to face him before stepping out of it.

Rafael's gaze consumed her as the firelight danced over her camisole and petticoats. She saw a muscle pulse in his jawline and stood on tiptoe to still it with the softest of kisses.

He groaned when Annie boldly removed his jacket and tie, then unfastened his stiff collar and threw it aside. When she began opening his shirt, he stopped her by taking her hands in his and holding them against his chest.

"Annie—" he began hoarsely.

She shook her head. "Don't, Rafael. Don't say anything about tomorrow, or next week, or next year."

Rafael raised one of her hands to his mouth and kissed her palm, sending silver fire rushing through her veins. He didn't speak, but traced a shivery path along the underside of her wrist and the tender skin of her inner arm with his lips. By the time he'd reached the satiny flesh in the crook of her elbow, Annie was unable to hide her trembling.

She made a breathless plea of his name.

He denied her the quick, fierce conquering she craved and continued to find and kiss the most vulnerable hollows and pulse points on her body. When he laid her on the bed at last, it was only to nibble at the backs of her knees at his maddening leisure.

Rafael took away Annie's petticoat, and the drawers beneath, and finally, the camisole, opening it inch by inch. The ritual took so long that Annie felt feverish by the time it was over and could not make herself lie still.

The prince stripped away his own clothes, and in the dancing firelight he looked like a magnificent savage returning triumphantly from the hunt. Annie reached for him, and he fell to her, burying his face in her neck for a moment, as if to breathe in the scent of her, and memorize the substance. Then, with a low, primitive sound, born somewhere deep in his chest, he slid down to take her nipple.

Annie cried out in pleasure and welcome, arching her back in instinctive invitation, but Rafael was still in no apparent hurry to consummate their marriage. He stroked her side and hip and thigh with a slow, continuous motion of one hand and took his time at her breast.

She began to fling her head from side to side on the pillow, beyond verbal pleas now, but Rafael only moved to her other nipple, and took greedy suckle from it.

Annie was wild when he began trailing his lips down over her rib cage and stomach. She bucked like a wild thing set free when he took her completely with his mouth, plunging her fingers into his hair and trying to press him even closer.

He withdrew a moment before the universe would have realigned itself and watched her with an unreadable expression in his pewter eyes.

"Rafael," she gasped, amazed that she could still speak the same language, "I love you. And I need you so much."

Rafael moved up over her then, gracefully, giving her none of his weight. His mouth, as he kissed her, was musky with her own feminine scent. The contact, cautious at first, was soon a battle of wills and tongues, a fencing match with no clear winner.

He broke away, with a breathless groan, and gazed deep into her eyes. She felt his manhood, hard and vibrant with life, prodding her gently.

"Annie?" Rafael asked.

"Yes," Annie answered, flinging back her head and raising her hips to grant her husband an easy entrance to her body. "Oh, yes!"

Rafael lunged into her, his thrust deep and powerful, and Annie welcomed him with a cry, her fingers clasping the taut flesh of his buttocks and urging him on.

The consummation of the royal marriage was a glorious, blazing thing, as ferocious as the mating of two sleek young panthers in some unexplored jungle. Their bodies collided, gathered force, and collided again, and soon they were both drenched in perspiration. Finally, finally, they were one flesh, and their satisfaction was shattering.

They slept when it was over, arms and legs entwined, their exhaustion so complete that it took them beyond slumber, into a deeper darkness. They awakened and made love again, quickly, fiercely, as though they feared to be stolen one from the other, and then tumbled back into the same black void that had swallowed them before.

The rain stopped in the night, and began again at dawn. Rafael built up the fire and returned to bed, drawing Annie into his arms.

All that day, they loved and slept, pretending there was no world beyond the walls of that enchanted cottage. They talked and ate the food that had been brought for them, and told each other the deepest secrets of their hearts.

That dangerous, magical time was, to Annie, all she needed to know of heaven. They had fallen asleep, late the second night, drunk with the wine of their passion, when suddenly a fist thundered against the cottage door.

Annie bolted upright with a gasp, and Rafael reached beneath the bed and brought out a pistol. In the next instant, the wooden panel splintered around the knob and crashed against the inside wall.

Moonlight illuminated the outraged frame of Patrick Trevarren.

"So, by God," he bellowed, "it's true, then!"

Rafael laid the pistol down on the mattress and struck a match to the wick in the bedside lantern. "Hold your tongue, Trevarren, before you say something that will alienate you from your own child. Annie is my wife."

Annie could only nod, peering at her illustrious father over the edge of the sheet. He was a tall, powerfully built man, with ink blue eyes and strong white teeth. His dark hair, fanned with silver at the temples, was fairly long, drawn back at his nape and tied with a thin strip of leather.

"Your wife, is it?" Patrick demanded, closing the door against the other men in his party who, Annie supposed, would have crowded into the cottage with their eyes popping if he'd let them. "Is this true, Annie Trevarren? I want none of your nonsense."

"It's true, Papa," Annie said, with unaccustomed meekness. "Rafael and I were married the day before yesterday. You can ask the priest at the keep if you don't believe me."

"Ask the priest," Patrick scoffed. "Not likely I'd do that. They've got enough to think about in the castle, with the rebels about to take the place over."

Rafael hurled himself out of bed and began wrenching on his clothes, rasping, "What's happened?"

"They're on the march, that's all. Ought to be right on top of you by morning."

"Get her out of here, Patrick," Rafael said, as though Annie weren't there at all, jamming his shirt tails into his breeches as he spoke. "Now, tonight."

Patrick gave his daughter a stern look and turned his back to the bed. "Put some clothes on, Daughter. I want you on board the *Enchantress* before the sun rises."

Annie obeyed, moving awkwardly as she tried to pull on her garments and contain her panic at the same time.

"Why didn't someone come for me?" Rafael demanded, of himself, Patrick and Fate, as he snatched up the pistol he'd almost used to shoot his father-in-law.

Patrick looked distinctly uncomfortable. "You were with your new bride," he reminded the prince, with a gruff clearing of his throat and a faint rise of color on his neck. "Besides, they probably took their time getting over the wedding celebration."

Annie had gotten into her underthings and the simple cotton dress someone, probably Kathleen, had brought to the cottage for her with the food and clean linens. She stood absolutely still when Rafael came over to her, took her upper arms in his hands and kissed her hard on the mouth.

"I love you, Annie Trevarren St. James," he said. "Take care of my child."

With that, he turned and strode away, and Annie would have bolted after him if her father hadn't stopped her with tender force.

She struggled, sobbing, and Patrick held her tight against his chest. "There now, sweetheart. I know how you're feeling, but I can't let you dash headlong into the jaws of a lion."

Annie wailed and tried again to get free, but Patrick only hoisted her into his arms and carried her outside.

The buggy loomed in the yard, but the horse was gone and so was Rafael.

Among the trees, other horses waited, and silent men.

"Papa," Annie pleaded, when her father set her in the saddle and climbed up behind her, "you've got to stop Rafael—please—they'll kill him!"

"I'll come back and do what I can for him," Patrick said, urging the horse into a trot, "but my first priority is getting you out of this place, and the harder you fight me, the longer it's going to take."

Annie subsided against Patrick's impervious chest and wept.

The party had entered the keep through the cave Annie herself had found, and they left it by the same way, leading their horses single file between the two gates. Descending the hillside, with Patrick's men close behind them, they met a lone rider.

Patrick spun his horse around with a quick, fierce pull on the reins, to put himself between Annie and the stranger. "Who goes there?" he called, in a tone that would brook no delay. "State your name."

"Edmund Barrett," replied a familiar voice. "I serve the prince, and if you're enemies, you'd better kill me now, for I won't turn back."

Hope stirred in Annie, and she said quickly, "Mr. Barrett is Rafael's best friend, Papa. My husband needs him."

"Go on with you, then," Patrick agreed, "but have a care. There's trouble brewing in St. James Keep tonight."

"That is nothing new," Barrett replied, with wry resignation.

"Wait," Annie pleaded, when the captain of the guard would have ridden past them, into the keep. "What about the princess?" she said to him. "Is she safe and well?"

She thought she saw Mr. Barrett smile, though it was too dark to be sure.

"Safe, well and furious," replied Phaedra's husband. "My wife is in Paris, with friends of mine, learning the virtue of patience."

Annie nodded, amused, in spite of everything, by the images Mr. Barrett's words had brought to mind. "Good luck to you, sir, and thank you for coming back."

"There was never any doubt of it," Barrett replied, touching his brow in a graceful salute and then riding on.

Annie took comfort in the knowledge that Rafael was not completely friendless after all. Of course, Mr. Barrett was only one man, and the chances were good that he would die with the prince instead of saving him.

Patrick's strong arms tightened around his daughter as they rode down the hillside and along the coast road, in the opposite direction from Morovia. Just before sunrise, they came to a beach, where men waited with a small boat.

Annie, exhausted and distraught to the point of insensibility, didn't resist when she was lifted inside. After telling his men to wait for him and look after the horses as if they were the last they would ever own, Patrick pushed the dinghy off the sand, climbed deftly inside and took up the oars.

Annie Trevarren was being saved, but in those

wretched, despairing moments, salvation was the last thing she wanted.

"There's a babe," Patrick reminded her gently, but sternly, too, after they'd rowed some distance over the dark, star-splattered water. "Reason enough to hold onto your courage with hands, heart and back teeth, I think."

CHAPTER

21

Even in his darkest reflections, Rafael had not begun to imagine the true horror of the invasion. The attack came just after dawn, and the enemy seemed without number, legions of men scaling the walls here, blasting through them with cannon fire there, burrowing beneath like moles in still other places. They poured out of the cellars, a demon army, and even though the prince's men fought valiantly, defeat came with humiliating dispatch. After only a little over an hour, unwilling for even one more soldier to perish in the pursuit of a lost cause, Rafael gave the command to surrender.

Reluctantly, the troops laid down their swords and rifles and stepped back from their overheated cannon, hands clasped behind their backs, heads high, eyes insolent.

Rafael was proud of their dignity and stubborn loyalty, but he knew he would be given no chance to praise them. The rebel general, an imposing savage from a northern province of the country, rode over the drawbridge and beneath the portcullis, which had been raised by his own shouting, triumphant men.

He seemed to know Rafael, just as Rafael knew him, and rode directly to where the prince stood, beside the fountain in the main courtyard.

Rafael's clothes were torn and soaked with a mingling of his own blood and that of several assailants. Four rebel soldiers lay dead and dying at his feet, and he leaned upon his stained sword as though it were a walking stick, unconsciously protecting the deep slash wound in his side.

"Rafael St. James, prince of Bavia?" inquired the general. He was perhaps thirty-five, with a shock of golden brown hair and blue eyes that showed both intelligence and humor.

Rafael merely inclined his head in acknowledgment.

"Simon Carpenter," the rebel leader supplied, swinging deftly down from the back of his great gray stallion. He was roughly dressed, in loose breeches and a woolen shirt, and his scuffed boots had seen much service.

With a pleasant smile, Carpenter pulled off his leather riding gloves, secured them beneath his belt and held out one hand for the bloody sword. "Your soldiers will be treated fairly," he said. "After all, they are Bavians, and cannot be faulted for doing what they perceived as their duty."

Rafael said nothing; his throat was filled with bitter

gall. He had known this moment was coming, of course—even as a very small boy, in the days before his exile to England, he'd heard his nurse speak of the end of the St. Jameses, and seen her weep over the fate of her charge. It was and had always been his destiny to atone for the many and grievous sins of his forefathers. Still, having known Annie, and loving her as he had never loved another, even Georgiana, Rafael was painfully conscious of all he'd lost.

Castles and palaces, power and prestige, were the least of it.

"The sword, Your Highness," Carpenter urged, with cool civility, his hand still extended.

Rafael surrendered the weapon, hilt first, heedless of the razor-sharp blade slicing into his fingers.

Carpenter accepted the sword without drawing it through Rafael's hand, as many enemies might have done. The two mens' gazes were interlocked as Carpenter spoke again. "I regret that we'll have to hang you," he said. "You've shown uncommon courage."

"I am an uncommon man," Rafael replied, lightheaded from a copious loss of blood. He swayed on his feet and then steadied himself, one arm clutching his torn middle.

"Fetch the surgeon," Carpenter said, to one of his men, as Rafael's knees buckled and blackness swamped his senses.

When the prince regained consciousness, he was lying in fetid straw in one of the dungeons. His side had been crudely stitched and bandaged, and the pain was like a white-hot poker thrust beneath his ribs. He felt a fever brewing in his blood, as well, but his first coherent thought was one of soaring, joyous gratitude.

Annie was safe with Patrick. He could ask no more of the fates than that.

Rafael lay still for a long time, struggling to keep from toppling back into the black void. Finally, with an effort so agonizing that sweat came out on every part of his body, he clasped the bars of his cell and hauled himself to his feet. There was a high, narrow window behind him, rimmed in fading sunlight, and through it he heard the steady pounding of a hammer.

He sighed and rested his forehead against the bars. No doubt the rebels were reconstructing the scaffold from which Peter Maitland had hanged.

Annie, Rafael thought, grieving not for himself, but for his beautiful, spirited bride and for their child. How wretchedly unfair he had been, how selfish, yielding to his desires and siring an infant who would never see its father.

His strength ebbing away in a scant tide, Rafael slid to his knees, his fingers still locked around the iron bars, and prayed that Patrick's ship would carry Annie far from the shores of Bavia.

When Patrick Trevarren installed his daughter in his own quarters and ordered his things moved to another cabin, she was in a semistupor of shock and despair. He laid her gently on the bed, took off her shoes, and covered her with a blanket. After placing a light kiss on her forehead and murmuring that everything would be all right, he went out.

Annie curled into a tight ball when he was gone, so undone and so numb that she couldn't think or feel or weep. The rocking motion of the ship made her sleep, granting her a merciful release from reality.

After a while, however, terrible dreams drove her back to the surface of awareness, and she sat bolt upright on the bed, gasping, her skin moist with perspiration. The room was dark, and Annie leaped off the mattress and scrambled across to the door, groping frantically for the latch.

Annie held her breath for a moment and then tried the handle. The lock was not engaged.

Weak with relief, she sagged against the heavy door panel, trembling. When that interlude had passed, she felt her way back to the bed, found a lamp on the nighttable and struck a match to the wick. Dim light illuminated the small, tidy room, and Annie looked down at her dress with real despair. It would be impossible to climb, swim or crawl in such a garment, and her trousers and shirt were still at St. James Keep.

Her eyes fell on a rosewood trunk tucked into a corner, and hope surged through her, along with a burst of determined energy. Her mother, Charlotte, often traveled aboard the *Enchantress,* and shared her daughter's fondness for unconventional clothing.

Within moments, Annie was kneeling before the chest and raising the lid. Inside were gowns, scandalous nightdresses and, glory of glories, breeches and shirts. Annie helped herself to the latter, shed her dress like a snake's skin, and pulled on her mother's clothes.

It was a perfect fit.

Annie smiled grimly at her reflection in the looking glass affixed to the wall. Now, to find a cap to hide her hair . . .

Moments later, she took a quick peek into the passageway and saw that the door was unguarded.

Given his daughter's state of mind earlier that day, Patrick had probably concluded that sentries were unnecessary.

Annie smiled, in spite of herself, and sneaked down the short hall and up the steps to the main deck. The ship was still at anchor and, she soon discovered, very nearly unmanned. Her father had gone back to St. James Keep, as he had assured her he would, and taken most of his crew with him.

It was an easy matter, having spent much of her childhood onboard that ship, to lower one of the remaining lifeboats, already rigged, to the water and slide down to it by a dangling rope. Before an alarm could be sounded, Annie was rowing toward shore, the oars dripping black water and starlight as she lifted and then lowered them again.

Her skill notwithstanding, it took more than fifteen sweaty minutes to reach shallow water, and it was difficult to find the coast road in the dark. Several times, Annie heard horsemen approaching and hid in the ditch, lest she be captured by rebels or found by her father's people.

Dawn was breaking when Annie reached the once-secret gate in the wall of the keep and hurried through it. The keep towered against the sky, stark and broken. The royal flag, usually visible from that spot, had been taken down.

Fear threatened to swamp her. Rafael might already be dead, and her father too, for that matter. Even if they weren't, what could she do to save them?

Annie didn't have a single plan in her mind, but her heart wouldn't let her turn back without trying to effect a rescue. Rafael was her husband, the father of her child, and Patrick Trevarren had given her life. She wasn't about to abandon either of them.

Taking care not to be seen, Annie made her way toward the castle. The place seemed unnervingly quiet, almost deserted.

Crossing one of the overgrown gardens, Annie frowned, recalling the tunnels Lucian had shown her that day when they'd gone exploring together. She would find one of those, she decided, crawl through it, arm herself somehow and find Rafael.

She stopped and looked around, spotting a small stone building on the other side of a thicket of blackberry vines. Thorns tore at the legs of her breeches as she hurried toward it.

The door was heavy, and when Annie pulled it open, the hinges creaked loudly. She ducked inside, heart pounding, breath rasping in and out of her chest, only to feel two steely arms close around her from behind. A hand covered her mouth and, though she struggled fiercely, it was soon clear that she wouldn't escape.

Her captor closed the door and latched it before releasing her with a flinging motion of one arm. Before she'd righted herself, light flared in the tiny, filthy room, and she saw the grim face of Edmund Barrett looming in the glow of a kerosene lantern.

"You," he marveled, with heavy resignation. "I don't believe it."

Annie was half-sick with relief, and she saw no need to defend her reasons for returning to St. James Keep. She folded her arms. "Where is Rafael?"

"In the dungeon," Barrett answered. "They plan to hang him tomorrow morning."

Annie's stomach did a slow roll, and her knees threatened to give way again. Leaning against the wall, she fought to keep her composure. "Have you seen my father?"

"No," Barrett said, "but this is a big place. He could be anywhere."

"How do you know the rebels plan to hang Rafael?"

"They've set up the scaffold in the courtyard," he replied, averting his eyes. It seemed an eternity before he went on. "They've already executed Lucian."

Annie swallowed a scalding rush of horror. "My God. Why?" she whispered. "He was one of their own, wasn't he?"

"No one likes a traitor," Mr. Barrett said, and though he spoke without apparent emotion, Annie knew he regretted Lucian's tragedy.

It was then, in her need to look anywhere but at Barrett's face, that Annie saw the gaping hole in the center of the shed's long-rotted floor.

"A tunnel," she said moderately. In silence, she felt a certain grim pride that her guess had been right. "Does it go all the way into the cellars?"

Barrett uttered a heavy sigh and shoved a filthy hand through his hair. "I don't know," he confessed. "I tried to get through, but the passage is too narrow."

"For you," Annie clarified, stepping toward the pit, ready to lower herself into it, rats, spiders, moles and all, without the slightest hesitation.

Rafael's friend stopped her forcibly. "No, Annie. Rafael would never forgive me if I let anything happen to you."

Annie wrenched free, and her desperation caused her to speak in a fierce whisper. "Rafael won't *survive* to forgive you if we don't do something!"

Barrett swallowed visibly and murmured an expletive. "Just be careful," he added, on the next breath.

Eagerly, Annie dropped into the hole and got down on her hands and knees. She couldn't see anything, it was so dark, but the smells of dirt and rodents and roots filled her nostrils.

"I mean it, Annie," Barrett's voice echoed after her. "Don't take any foolish chances!"

Annie was already moving toward the castle as fast as she dared move, and she didn't trouble herself to answer. As she crawled, trying not to think of the things she heard skittering and cheeping in the gloom, she wept for Lucian St. James. He might have been so much more than he was, so much better, if it hadn't been for his jealous and cunning nature. He died so young, and had he lived, he might possibly have come to see the error of his ways.

She had traveled a considerable distance when she came to a section of the tunnel that had partially collapsed. Breathing was difficult and it was hot, and Annie figured her chances of success were slight. For lack of a better idea, she cleared the passage as best she could and squirmed onward.

In places, the ancient dirt walls were so close to each other that she feared being stuck. With her vivid imagination, it was only too easy to picture her bones being unearthed and exclaimed over in a century or so.

The thought of her mother, crawling through a similar tunnel beneath a sultan's palace in Riz gave Annie the courage to go on. Charlotte Trevarren had survived and prevailed, and so would she.

It was, after all, something of a family tradition.

A long time had passed when Annie struck something solid with the top of her head. After a few moments of mild profanity, she raised both hands and pushed, praying she wouldn't find a pack of rebels on the other side.

Something enormous crashed to the stone floor, and so much dust billowed into the tunnel that Annie was momentarily blinded. She crawled, coughing, into the light pouring in from a high window, and found herself in an empty cellar. The heavy cabinet she'd overturned lay shattered before her.

She waited, half expecting an enemy guard to burst in and arrest her, but no one came. Annie went to the door and pressed her ear against it, listening for voices or footsteps but, again, there was nothing. She couldn't be sure exactly what part of the keep she was in, since the underground passage had taken so many twists and turns, but she hoped she was near the dungeon.

It was evident, when Annie tried to push the outer door open, that no one had used that particular chamber in years. Finally, when she thought she had no strength left, the hinges screamed and she gained the hallway.

The passage was dark, since there were no windows, and Annie wished for a candle or even a match. She felt her way along the wall, flinching when a spider's web fell across her shoulders like a gossamer cloak. Finally, she found the light again, and recognized her surroundings. She and Lucian had passed this way while they were exploring, she was certain, and the dungeon was nearby.

Biting her lip, Annie proceeded, boldly but with prudent caution. By that time, she'd lost her cap, and her hair fell down her back in a dusty tangle. She couldn't remember a time when she'd been in greater need of a bath, even during her illustrious career as a tomboy.

The sound of voices made her stop and hold her breath. She would have held her heartbeat, too, if that had been possible.

"Why go to the trouble of hanging him?" a man asked. "He wouldn't know what was happening anyway, with this fever."

Annie swallowed a cry of panic and stayed in the shadows.

"It's a matter of principle," answered another voice, also male. "Someone has to pay for the crimes of the St. James family."

"Well," came the reply, "we'll see if he survives long enough to mount the scaffold, won't we?"

Annie flattened her back against the wall, hands outspread, and waited. The men continued to talk, and the length of the shadows changed, and still the vigil went on.

She did not know how much time had passed when the guards finally ambled away to have something to eat. As soon as they were gone, she hurried out of her hiding place and tried Rafael's cell door. It was soundly locked, and she saw no sign of a key.

The prince was nothing but a shadow, flung carelessly into a corner.

"Rafael," Annie whispered desperately, "where is the key?"

He didn't move or answer.

"Rafael!"

The prince groaned, and Annie wanted so badly to touch and comfort him that she extended one arm through the bars and strained to reach him. In her terrible fear, she took several seconds to realize the effort was impossible.

Wildly, she searched the guards' table for the key, but it wasn't to be found. When she heard the voices of approaching men, she was forced to hurry back into the unused passage and hide herself in the shadows.

Another set of guards had arrived to replace the others. They settled at the crude table, ignoring Rafael, and began to play cards.

Annie waited for a long time, but she didn't have another chance to get close to Rafael. In the end, she was forced to go back to the tunnel and crawl back to the shed, where Mr. Barrett was waiting. Perhaps she would be able to find her father, and ask him to help.

Before she'd even reached the shed, however, Annie had discarded that idea. If Patrick Trevarren learned that his daughter was inside St. James Keep, he would drop whatever plan he'd formulated to help Rafael and take her back to the *Enchantress*. In the meantime, the rebels might well drag Rafael to the scaffold, put a noose around his neck, and hang him.

"Did you get inside?" Mr. Barrett asked, the instant Annie stuck her head out of the pit.

She fought back tears of frustration and fear. "Yes," she said. "You were right—Rafael is in the dungeon." Mr. Barrett lifted her easily from the hole, listening in silence when she went on. "He's hurt or sick—I called his name, and he hardly stirred."

"I'm going in," Barrett said, moving toward the hole in the floor.

Annie prevented it. "You'll never squeeze through," she said. "I barely managed myself."

Barrett was utterly still for a long moment. "I'll find another way in, then, as soon as it gets dark. Stay here, out of sight, and I'll bring you some food and water as soon as I can."

Annie didn't protest, for there was nothing to do but wait. She sat down on the floor, figuring she couldn't get much dirtier than she already was, folded her arms across her knees, and rested her head on them.

Barrett cleared his throat. "I don't suppose it means much, under the circumstances, but I've got to say it, Annie. You're the boldest, most hardheaded female I have ever run across."

She smiled, though she was near tears, and did not raise her head. "Life belongs to the bold," she replied, in a muffled voice.

Mr. Barrett went out, without replying, and closed the shed door softly behind him.

Exhausted by stress and the tunnel exploit, Annie dropped off into a troubled sleep, and when she awakened Mr. Barrett was back. There was a candle burning on an upended crate, and he'd set a crude table with two dented metal plates and one cup.

Annie didn't ask where he'd gotten the dried meat and bread he produced from a canvas bag. He had wine from a dusty bottle, while she drank well water from the single cup.

"I saw your father," he said, after a long time.

"Where?" Annie demanded sharply. "Was he all right?"

"One question at a time," Barrett scolded, with a weary smile in his voice. "He looked like a fine savage to me, though of course we didn't speak. He's pretending to be one of the poorer villagers."

Annie was amused, in spite of everything. "Are you sure it was Patrick Trevarren you saw? He's a notorious dandy, you know. His shirts are specially made in Paris, and he wears only the finest Italian boots."

Barrett laughed. "His friends wouldn't recognize him, then. I guess I noticed him because I know all the villagers."

"I wonder what he's up to," Annie speculated.

Mr. Barrett's mirthful expression turned solemn, and he took a long draught from the wine bottle. "Whatever your father's plan is, Miss Trevarren, I hope to God it's brilliant. Rafael's life may depend on it."

Annie's throat thickened with tears, but she did not give way to them. "Yes," she said, offering a silent prayer, in addition, that Rafael would not die of his fever before they could save him.

When they'd eaten, Mr. Barrett went out again, probably seeking a way into the castle. Annie was reluctant to leave the shed, not because she feared the rebels—which, of course, she did—but because she couldn't risk encountering her father.

She waited several hours, growing more and more restless, and finally had to venture out to relieve herself in the bushes. She started back through the tunnel, wanting to be as close to Rafael as she could, even if she couldn't reach him, but she hadn't traveled more than halfway before the passage began to cave in in front of her.

She froze, terrified of discovery, while only a few feet away someone cursed and said, "These damnable tunnels. The whole place ought to be razed."

Barbarian, Annie thought, not even daring to breathe.

When dirt began to filter down on top of her,

however, and she imagined being buried alive, Annie forced herself to move back along the passage. In the shed, she slept again, and when she awakened, it was with a horrible, wrenching sense of urgency.

It was almost morning, and Rafael was scheduled to be hanged first thing.

Perhaps, Rafael reflected feverishly, as he was hauled to his feet and half-dragged, half-carried from his cell, it would not be such a bad thing to die. He was very nearly dead already, as far as he could tell, and while he felt tremendous regret at leaving Annie, there was no fear in him.

Annie. He smiled, a little drunkenly perhaps, and did not resist when his hands were wrenched behind his back and bound at the wrists. Once or twice, he'd thought he heard her calling his name. It had been a dream, of course, for she was far away by now—God be thanked.

They got through the passageways, somehow, and up a staircase, and then they were in the courtyard. Torches burned, to guide the dawn's light over the horizon, and there were surprisingly few spectators about. He wondered whether he should be flattered or insulted by that.

Now that the keep had been taken, he supposed, most of the rebel troops were occupied elsewhere.

A girl he recognized as Annie's maid, Kathleen, approached, white-faced, with a cup of water. She lifted the rim gently to his mouth, and he sipped from it.

"God be with you, Your Highness," she whispered, before his guards thrust him onto the first step.

The gallows loomed overhead, and Rafael put one foot in front of the other. He recalled snatches of a ditty he'd learned from his nurse as a child, something about climbing Jacob's ladder.

At the top of the gallows, a priest waited, but he wasn't the same man who had married Rafael and Annie. Indeed, Rafael didn't recall seeing this burly fellow before. He frowned and started to ask his name, but was silenced by a warning look.

Rafael shrugged and began to hum. *We are climbing . . . Jacob's ladder . . .*

A clatter on the wooden steps behind him distracted his attention. Rafael turned, along with the hangman and the priest, to see Annie hurtling toward him, covered in dirt from her head to her feet.

He told himself it was a hallucination, but she flung herself into his arms, sobbing, and then he knew she was real. Believing Annie to be safe had been his only consolation, and now even that was gone.

Rafael heard a shot and sank instantly to his knees, thinking he'd been hit. Before he could scream at Annie to run, however, he realized the rope had been severed. There was a scuffle of some sort, and the new wood of the scaffold whined as more bullets struck it.

He screamed Annie's name and then pitched forward onto his face, knocked insensible by a blow to the back of his head.

"Run, you little idiot!" the priest bellowed, bending to hoist Rafael's inert frame over one beefy shoulder.

Recognizing her father's first mate, at long last, Annie obeyed and dashed down the steps of the scaffold. At the bottom, she encountered Josiah

Vaughn. He stepped into her path, jaw set, sword in hand.

Chaos was everywhere, for some of Rafael's defeated soldiers had taken up arms to aid in the rescue, and Annie was well aware that they had only minutes to escape.

"Go ahead, Josiah," she said, "run me through."

He glared at her for a long, tense moment, while the priest stood behind her, powerless to help because of his burden. Finally, reluctantly, Josiah stepped aside.

Suddenly, there were horses all around, and Annie was pulled roughly onto an animal's back. She was too dazed to see much, but she noticed Mr. Barrett nearby, and she heard her father's voice rasp past her ear.

"You'll give an accounting for this, Annie Trevarren."

She didn't care. "Rafael!" she screamed, struggling to look for him.

Patrick's arm tightened around her, and the horse bolted toward the main gate, where the portcullis had been raised. "He's behind us, love," he said, and then the wind was rushing into her face and the hooves of the horses made a deafening clatter on the drawbridge. There were more shots, too, but the loudest noise of all was the thudding of Annie's own heart.

Six small boats awaited them near the shore. Patrick rode straight into the surf and lowered Annie into one of the vessels before dismounting and scrambling in himself. She saw Rafael flung, dead or unconscious, into a nearby craft, where Mr. Barrett sat, clasping the oar handles, and she tried in vain to go to her husband. The experienced crew of the *Enchantress* pushed off in speedy unison, and the bullets of the pursuing rebels splashed in their wake.

Only when they'd reached the waiting ship, and rope ladders were being flung over the side, did Annie tear her gaze from Rafael to look up at St. James Keep.

It rose against the sky like a majestic tombstone, a fitting marker for the old ways, and Annie cried tears of mourning and of relief.

"Time to go now," Patrick said gently, lifting her onto the first rung of one of the ladders.

Annie looked for Rafael, saw that he was safe, and began to climb.

Southern France, Six Weeks Later . . .

Rafael stood, mostly mended now but still a bit gaunt from his ordeal in Bavia, watching the sunset splash the vineyard with a spectacle of color. Annie was at his side, her arm linked with his, and behind them loomed the huge brick farmhouse that would be their home from then on. The place had belonged to Rafael for years, although he had never actually visited it before bringing his bride there a month before.

"Will you be happy," Annie asked, knowing the answer, "as a wine-maker?"

He smiled down at her, pressing her arm close against his side, closing his fingers over hers. "Will you be happy as a wine-maker's wife?"

"Yes," Annie answered. "All I need is the wine-maker."

Rafael laughed and kissed her forehead, but some sorrow still lingered in his eyes. Beyond the vineyards and the low stone winery, where the great vats and presses, long-abandoned, were being prepared for production, beyond the horizon, lay Bavia, bruised and bleeding. It would be a long time before the wounds were healed—generations, perhaps—and Rafael grieved for all that his people had suffered, and must suffer still. He was thinking of his lost country at that moment, Annie sensed, and she brought his hand to her lips and kissed the knuckles.

"Perhaps someday we'll be able to go back, Rafael," she said, hoping to comfort him.

He shook his head, and when his gaze met hers again, his eyes were clear. "No, love. We can only go forward—you know that. The Bavia I loved is gone, if it ever existed at all."

They turned, making their way over the rough, newly cultivated ground together, through a twilight streaked with crimson and purple and gold. Annie looked forward to the night, which would bring lovemaking, and the morning, and the great tapestry of tomorrows to be woven by their love.

"I had my palm read in the village today," Annie said, as they neared the house. "By the gypsy woman, Rifka. The butcher claims she's three hundred years old."

Rafael pretended fascination. "What did she say?"

Annie sighed in a long-suffering fashion and fondly patted her flat stomach. "That this child—our daughter—is only the first of six healthy children."

They had reached the threshold of the kitchen door, and Rafael paused there to lean forward and touch

Annie's mouth with his own. "That's a prediction I can well believe," he said. "How shall our fairy tale end, Princess Annie?"

She laughed. "It doesn't take a gypsy to answer that question," she replied. "We'll live happily ever after."

Pocket Books
Proudly Announces

PIRATES

LINDA LAEL MILLER

Coming from
Pocket Books Hardcover
mid-June 1995

The following is a preview of
Pirates . . .

When the dog deserted her and moved in with Jeffrey and his new bride, it was, for Phoebe Turlow, the proverbial last straw.

She had weathered the divorce well enough, considering how many of her dreams had come crashing down in the process. She'd even been philosophical about losing her job as a research assistant to Professor Benning, knowing that finding a comparable position would be virtually impossible given recent government budget cuts. The professor had been writing and lecturing at Seattle College for forty-five fruitful and illustrious years; he was ready, by his own admission, to spend his days reading, fishing and playing chess.

Phoebe had held herself together through it all. And now, even her dog, Murphy, whom she'd rescued from the pound as a mangy, slat-ribbed mongrel, and carefully nursed back to health, had turned on her.

She lowered the telephone receiver slowly back to its cradle, gazing through narrowed blue eyes at the dismal Seattle rain sheeting the window of her rented house. Heather, the light of Jeffrey's life, hadn't been able—she probably hadn't even tried—to suppress the smug note in her voice when she called to tell Phoebe that Murphy was "safe and sound" in their kitchen. To hear Heather tell it, that furry ingrate had crossed a continent, fording icy rivers and surmounting insurmountable obstacles, enduring desperate privations of all sorts. Phoebe could almost hear the theme music of a new movie, rated G, of course.

Murphy, Come Home.

Muttering, she crossed the worn linoleum floor, picked up the dog's red plastic bowl and dumped it into the trash, kibbles and all. She emptied the water dish and tossed that away as well. Then, running her hands down the worn legs of her blue jeans and feeling more alone than she had since her grandmother's death, Phoebe wandered into her small, uncarpeted living room and stared despondently out the front window.

Mel, the postman, was just pulling up to her mailbox in his blue and white jeep. He tooted the horn and waved. Phoebe waved back with a dispirited smile. Her unemployment check was due, but the prospect didn't cheer her up. If it hadn't been for her savings and the small amount of money Gran had left when she passed away, Phoebe figured she would have been sitting on a rain-slickened sidewalk, down by the Pike Place Market, with a cigar box in front of her to catch coins.

Okay, she thought, so that was a bit of an exaggeration. She could last for about six months, if she didn't get a new job soon, and *then* she would join the ranks of Seattle's panhandlers.

Snatching her blue hooded rain slicker from the peg beside the door and tossing it over her shoulders, Phoebe dashed out into the chilly drizzle to fetch her mail. She'd sent out over fifty resumes since losing her job with Professor Benning—maybe there would be a positive response, or one of the rare, brightly colored postcards her half brother, Eliott, sometimes sent from Europe or South America or Africa, or wherever he happened to be. Or a letter from a friend . . .

Except that all their friends were really Jeffrey's, not hers.

And Eliott didn't give a damn about her, and never had.

Phoebe brought herself up short; she was feeling sorry for herself, and that was against her personal code. Resolutely, she wrenched open the door of her rural mailbox, which was affixed to a rusted metal post by the front gate, and reached inside. There was nothing but a sales circular, and although she was tempted to crumple it up and toss it into the nearest mud puddle, she couldn't bring herself to litter.

She walked slowly back up the cracked walk to her sagging porch and the open door beyond it. The bright yellow envelope, now sodden and limp from the rain, was addressed to "Occupant," and the street numbers were off by two blocks. Damn, she thought, with a wry grimace. Even her junk mail belonged to somebody else.

The letter was about to join Murphy's kibbles and tooth-marked food and water bowls when an impulse—maybe it was desperation, maybe it was some kind of weird premonition—made Phoebe stop. She carried the envelope to her kitchen table and sat down, wondering all the while why she hadn't just chucked the thing. Instead, she opened it and smoothed the single page inside with as much care as if it were an ancient scroll, unearthed only moments before.

SUNSHINE! screamed the cheaply printed block letters at the top of the paper, which had been designed to resemble a telegram. SPARKLING, CRYSTAL-BLUE SEAS! VISIT PARADISE ISLAND ABSOLUTELY FREE! WALK IN THE FABLED FOOTSTEPS OF DUNCAN ROURKE, THE PIRATE PATRIOT!

Phoebe was twenty-eight years old and intelligent. She'd put herself through college, worked at a responsible job from the day she graduated until two months ago and voted in every major election. She was by no means stupid—even if she had married Jeffrey Brewster with her eyes wide open—and she knew a tacky advertising scheme when she saw one.

All the same, the prospects of "sunshine" and "crystal-blue seas" prodded at something slumbering deep in her heart behind a bruise and a stack of dusty, broken hopes.

She frowned. That name—Duncan Rourke. She'd seen it

somewhere before—probably while doing research for Professor Benning.

Phoebe rose from the table, leaving the sales flier spread out on its shiny surface, and took herself to the stove to brew a cup of herbal tea. Knowing that the promise of a free trip to Paradise Island—wherever that might be—was a scam of some kind did nothing to lessen the odd, excited sense of impending adventure tingling in the pit of her stomach.

The kettle gave a shrill whistle, and Phoebe poured boiling water over a tea bag and carried her cup back to the table. She read the flier again, this time very slowly and carefully, one eyebrow raised in skepticism, the fingers of her right hand buried in her short, chestnut-brown hair.

To take advantage of the "vacation all her friends would envy," Phoebe had only to inspect a "glamorous beach-front condominium guaranteed to increase in value" and listen to a sales pitch. In return, her generous benefactors would fly her to the small Caribbean island "justly named Paradise," put her up in the "distinctive Eden Hotel for two fun-filled days and nights," and provide one "gala affair, followed by a truly festive dinner."

The whole thing was one big rip-off, Phoebe insisted to herself, and yet she was intrigued, and perhaps just a little frantic. So what if she had to look at a condo made of ticky-tacky, watch a few promotional slides and listen to a spiel from a schmaltzy, fast-talking salesman or two? She needed to get away, if only for a weekend, and here was her chance to soak up some tropical sunshine without doing damage to her rapidly dwindling bank account.

Phoebe's conscience, always overactive, pricked a little. Okay, suppose she *did* call the toll-free number and book herself on the next flight to Paradise. She'd be making the trip under false pretenses, since she had no intention of buying a condominium. Her credit was fine, but she was divorced, female and unemployed, and there was no way she'd ever get a mortgage.

Still, there was nothing in the flier specifying that buyers had to be qualified. It was an invitation, pure and simple.

Phoebe closed her eyes and imagined the warmth of the

sun on her face, in her hair, settling deep into her muscles and veins and organs, nourishing her spirit. The yearning she felt was almost mystical, and wholly irresistible.

She told herself that she who hesitates is lost, and that it couldn't hurt to call. So, she went to the wall phone next to the sink and punched in the number.

Four hectic days later, Phoebe found herself on a small chartered airplane, aimed in the general direction of the Caribbean, with her one bag tucked neatly under the seat. The man across the aisle wore plaid polyester pants and a sweater emblazoned with tiny golf clubs, and the woman sitting behind her sported white pedal pushers, copious varicose veins, a T-shirt showing two silhouettes engaged in either mortal combat or coitus, and a baseball cap adorned with tiny Christmas tree lights—all flashing. The seven other passengers were equally eccentric.

Phoebe settled against the back of her seat with a sigh and closed her eyes, feeling like a freak in her brown loafers, jeans and blue cashmere turtleneck, all purchased with a credit card and a great deal of optimism. She might have been on a cut-rate night flight to Reno, she thought, with rueful humor, judging by the costumes of her fellow travelers.

The plane lifted off at seven o'clock in the morning, rising into the foggy skies over Seattle, and presently a flight attendant appeared. Since the aisle was too narrow for a cart, the slender young man carried a yellow plastic basket in one hand, dispensing peanuts and cola and other refreshments as he moved through the cabin.

The woman in the battery-powered hat ordered a Bloody Mary, and received a look of disapproval from the steward and a generic beer for her trouble.

Phoebe, who had planned to ask for mineral water, merely shook her head and smiled. She was making the trip under false pretenses, after all, and the less she accepted from these people in the way of amenities, the better she would feel about it afterward.

She tried to sleep and failed, even though she'd lain awake worrying the night before. So, she pulled a thin volume, borrowed from Professor Benning's extensive personal library, from her bag. The book, published by an obscure press, was entitled, "Duncan Rourke—Traitor or Patriot?"

Phoebe opened it to the first page, frowning a little, and began to read.

Mr. Rourke, according to the biographer, had been born in Charlotte, in the colony of North Carolina, to gentle and aristocratic parents. His education was impeccable—he spoke French, Italian and Spanish fluently, and was well versed in the work of the poets, those of his own time, and those of antiquity. He was also known to be proficient with the harpsichord and the mandolin, as well as the sword and musket, and he'd been no slouch in the boudoir, either, the writer hinted.

Phoebe yawned. Duncan Rourke, it seemed, qualified as a true Renaissance man. She read on.

Until the very day of his death, no one had known for certain whether Rourke had been a cutthroat or a hero. Speculation abounded, of course.

For her part, Phoebe wondered why he couldn't have been both rascal and paragon? No one, after all, was entirely good or bad—a human being, particularly a complex one, as Rourke must have been, could hardly be reduced to one dimension.

Presently, Phoebe closed her eyes—and the musty pages of the old book—and a faint smile trembled on her lips. Pondering Mr. Rourke's morality, or lack of same, she slept at long last.

1780
Paradise Island, the Caribbean

The precious letter, penned by Duncan's sister, Phillippa, and sent to him by devious and complex means, lay slightly crumpled on the desk before him.

Come home . . . the diabolical angel had written, in her ornate and flowing script.

Please, Duncan, I implore you to act for our sakes, Mama's and Papa's and Lucas's and mine, if not for your own. You must return to Charlotte, and the bosom of your family. Surely nothing more would be required to prove your loyalty to His Majesty than this. Papa might then cease his endless pacing—he traverses the length of his study, over and over again, night after night, from moonrise until the sun's awakening—if only he knew you could be counted among the king's men, like himself and our esteemed elder brother, Lucas . . . Papa fears, dear Duncan, as we all do, that your escapes in those southerly seas you so love will be misunderstood, that you will be arrested or even hanged. . . .

Duncan sighed and reached for the glass of port a serving girl had set within his reach only moments before.

"Troublesome news?" inquired his friend and first mate, Alex Maxwell, from his post before the terrace doors. A cool, faintly salty breeze ruffled the gauzy curtains and eased the otherwise relentless heat of a summer afternoon in the Caribbean.

"Only the usual rhetoric and prattle," Duncan replied, after taking a sip of his wine. "My sister pleads with me to return to the fold and take up my place among His Majesty's devoted adherents. Her implication is that, should I fail to heed this warning, our sorrowing and much-tormented sire shall wear out either the soles of his boots or my mother's rugs, in his eternal and evidently ambulatory ruminations."

Alex grimaced. "Good God, man," he said, with some impatience, turning at last from his vigil at the window overlooking the sultry blue and gold waters of a sun-splashed, temperamental sea. "Would it do you injury to speak in simple English for once in your bloody life?"

Duncan arched one dark eyebrow. Language was, to him, a toy as well as a tool. He loved to explore its every nuance and corner, to exercise various words and combinations of words, to savor them upon his tongue as he would a fine brandy or an exquisite wine. Although he liked and even admired Maxwell—indeed, Duncan had entrusted Alex with his very life on more than one occasion—he would not have foresworn linguistic indulgence even for him. "Tell me, my friend—are you liverish today, or simply obstreperous in the extreme?"

Alex shoved the fingers of both hands into his butternut hair in a dramatic show of frustration. Like Duncan, Alex was thirty years old; they had been tutored together from the time they could toddle out of their separate nurseries. Both loved fast horses, witty women with sinful inclinations and good bourbon, and their political views were, in the opinion of the Crown, at least, equally subversive. Physically and emotionally, however, the two men were quite different— Alex being small and delicately built, with the ingenuous brown eyes of a fawn and all the subtlety, when vexed, of a bear batting at a swarm of wasps with both paws. Duncan's temperament was cool and somewhat detached, and he stood tall enough, as his father said, to be hanged from a high branch without a scaffold. He prided himself on his self-control, and his enemies, no less than his friends, credited him with the tenacity and cunning of a winter-starved wolf. His hair was dark as jet, and he wore it tied back at his nape with a narrow ribbon, and his eyes a deep and, so he'd been told by grand ladies and whores alike, patently disturbing blue. His features, aristocratic from birth, had been hardened by the injustices he had both witnessed and suffered.

"I'm sorry," Alex said, with a weariness that troubled Duncan greatly, turning at last to face his friend. "I don't deny that I've been in a foul temper in recent days."

"I trust there is a reason," Duncan ventured, in a quiet voice, folding Phillippa's letter and placing it, with more tenderness than he would have confessed to, in the top drawer of his desk. "Or are your moods, like those of the delicate gender, governed by the waxing and waning of the moon?"

"Oh, Christ," Alex moaned. "Sometimes you drive me mad."

"Be that as it may," Duncan replied moderately, "I

should still like to know what troubles you. We are yet friends, are we not? Besides, a distracted man makes a poor leader, prone to grave errors of judgment." He paused to utter a philosophical sigh. "If some comely wench has addled your wits, the only prudent course of action, in my view, would be to relieve you of your duties straightaway, before someone in your command suffers the consequences of your preoccupation."

Alex's fine-boned face seemed strained and shadowed as he met Duncan's searching gaze, and his eyes reflected annoyance and something very like despair. "How long?" he asked, in a rasping whisper. "How long must we endure this interminable war?"

Duncan stood, but did not round the desk to approach Alex. There were times, he knew too well, when an ill-chosen word, intended to comfort, could be a man's undoing instead. "Until it has been won," he said tautly.

The vast, sprawling house, dating back to the middle of the seventeenth century, seemed to breathe like a living creature, drawing in the first cool breezes since dawn and then expelling them in soft sighs. A goddess of white stone, with the sapphire sea writhing in unceasing worship at her feet, the palatial structure was a haven to Duncan, like the welcoming embrace of a tenderhearted woman. And it gave him solace, that place, as well as shelter.

Alas, he was wedded to his ship, the *Francesca,* a swift and agile vessel brazenly named for his first lover, the disenchanted wife of a British infantry officer named Sheffield. While the lady had been spurned and sent back to England, years ago, where she languished yet, according to the gossips, in a state of seedy disgrace, her husband remained in the Colonies, waiting, taking each opportunity for revenge as it presented itself.

Duncan tightened his jaw, remembering even though he had schooled himself, through the years, to forget. He rotated his shoulders once, twice, as the tangle of old scars came alive on the flesh of his back, a searing tracery mapping another man's hatred. He'd been fifteen when

Sheffield had ordered him bound to a post in a public square and whipped into unconsciousness.

"Sometimes I wonder," Alex said, startling Duncan out of his bitter reverie, "whether it's Mother England you're at war with, or the lovely Francesca's jealous husband."

It was by no means new, Alex's propensity for mind reading, and neither was Duncan's reaction. "If you will be so kind," he said curtly, "as to keep your fatuous and sentimental attempts at mystical wisdom to yourself, I shall be most appreciative."

Alex rolled his eyes. "I have it," he said, in the next instant, feigning a rapture of revelation. "We'll capture Major Sheffield, truss him up like a Christmas goose so he can't cover his ears, and force him to endure the full range of your vocabulary! He'll be screaming for mercy inside half an hour."

Despite the memories that had overtaken him, Duncan clasped his friend's slightly stooped shoulder and laughed. "Suppose I recited the whole of Dante's *Divine Comedy*," he said.

"In Italian, of course," Alex agreed. "With footnotes."

Duncan withdrew his hand, and he knew his expression was as solemn as his voice. "If you want to beat your sword into a plowshare and spend the rest of your life tilling the earth," he said, "I'll understand, and not think less of you for it."

"I know," Alex said. "And I am weary to my soul from this blasted war. I long to settle down, take a wife, father a houseful of children. But if I don't fight, the sons and daughters I hope to sire will stand mute before Parliament, as we do now." He stopped and thrust his fingers through his hair, which was, as always, hopelessly mussed. "No, my friend, to paraphrase Mr. Franklin, if we don't hang together, we shall surely hang separately. I will see the conflict through to its end or mine, as God wills."

Duncan smiled, just as the supper bell chimed, muffled and far off. "You are right, and so is Mr. Franklin. But I must take exception with one of your remarks—we rebels can hardly be accused of 'standing mute before Parliament.' Our musket balls and cannon have been eloquent, I think."

Alex nodded and smiled.

A bell chimed in the distance, a signal that dinner was about to be served.

Without speaking, the two men moved through the great house together, mindful now of their empty stomachs. They sat at the long table in the dining room, with its ten arched windows overlooking the sea, watching as the sun spilled over the dancing waters, melting in a dazzling spectacle of liquid light. A premonition touched Duncan's spirit in that moment of terrible beauty, a warning or a promise, or perhaps both.

For good or ill, he thought, with resignation, something of significance was about to happen.

"Geez," complained the woman with the flashing hat and the dreadful T-shirt, when the small party of potential investors left the plane, at last, to stand on the grass-buckled tarmac of Paradise Island's one and only airport. "The place don't look like much in the dark, does it?"

Phoebe, blinking in a stupor of exhaustion, offered no reply. She could hear the tide whispering elemental vows in the distance, though, and the breeze was gentle and cool. A minibus, yellow with pink splotches painted on for a pintolike effect, chugged out of the gloom, horn tooting.

"Welcome to Paradise!" cried the driver, a plump, middle-aged man with a crewcut and a Jack Nicholson smile, scrambling out of the van to greet each of the tired travelers with an exuberant handshake. "Don't make any snap judgments, now," he boomed, before anyone could express a misgiving. "After all, it's late and you've had a long trip. Tomorrow, you'll get a good look at the place and, trust me, you'll be impressed."

Phoebe didn't want to think about tomorrow, didn't want to do anything but take a quick shower and fall into bed. This guy was certainly right about one thing: It *had* been a long trip. After leaving Seattle, the plane had landed in Los Angeles, Houston, Kansas City and Miami to pick up a dozen other weird characters, before proceeding on to Condo Heaven.

The motley crew boarded the bus, yawning and murmuring, and despite her decision not to think, Phoebe found herself studying each passenger out of the corner of her eye. She'd eat every postcard in the hotel gift shop if a single one of them could get a mortgage to buy a fancy island hideaway, let alone scrape up the cash to buy one outright.

The young couple who'd boarded the plane in Kansas City were newlyweds, Phoebe figured, because they'd been necking and staring into each other's eyes for most of the flight. Some honeymoon. The man in the plaid pants and golf club sweater had come along strictly for the free liquor, from the look and smell of him, and the Human Beacon, whose batteries had finally run down, appeared to be the sort who'd try anything as long as it was free.

So what's your excuse? Phoebe asked the sleepy and rumpled reflection gazing back at her from the darkened window of the minibus.

The hotel appeared suddenly out of the night, looming like smoke from some underground volcano, or an enormous genie rising out of a lamp. Phoebe's breath caught on a small, sharp gasp, and she sat bolt upright on the bus seat. A strange progression of emotions unfolded in her heart.

Recognition, for one. And that was impossible, because she'd never even been to the Carribean before, let alone this particular building. Nostalgia. And a strange, sweet joy, as if she were coming home after a long and difficult journey. Underlying these emotions, however, was a poignant and wrenching loss, threaded through with sorrow.

Tears sprang to Phoebe's eyes.

"Here's the Eden Hotel now, folks," the bus driver announced, with relentless good will. "It's a grand old place. Belonged to a pirate once, name of Rourke, and before that, to a Dutch planter who raised indigo." The minivan's brakes squealed as it came to a sprightly stop under an ugly pink and green neon palm tree affixed to the wall. Two of the fronds were burned out. "Near as we could find out, the house was built in 1675, or thereabouts."

Phoebe sniffled, dried her eyes with the back of one grubby hand and got off the bus, staring at the shoddy hotel in mute grief. She'd read a brief description of the place in Professor Benning's book about Duncan Rourke; that explained her complicated and overwrought reactions. The odd sensations lingered, though—Phoebe had known every nook and corner of this house once, had loved it when it was grand and elegant, and taken refuge within its walls when storms swept in from the sea. She had come home, to a place she had never seen before, and she was too late.

Look for

Pirates

Wherever Hardcover Books
Are Sold
mid-June 1995